Facelift

Leanna Ellis

PUBLISHING GROUP

Nashville, Tennessee

Copyright © 2010 by Leanna Ellis
All rights reserved.
Printed in the United States of America

978-0-8054-4989-1

Published by B&H Publishing Group,
Nashville, Tennessee

Dewey Decimal Classification: F
Subject Heading: DOMESTIC RELATIONS—FICTION \
FAMILY LIFE—FICTION \ CHRISTIAN LIFE—FICTION

Scripture quotations are from the Holy Bible, New
International Version, copyright © 1973, 1978, 1984 by
International Bible Society.

1 2 3 4 5 6 7 8 • 14 13 12 11 10

To all the women who feel like they don't measure up to the "Proverbs 31 Woman"

⤜❧ Acknowledgments ❧⤛

We all have beauty secrets, and I have a few writing secrets—a terrific team of God-loving folks around me who encourage and help me get a book ready for publication.

My B&H Publishing family is top-notch! Thank you, Karen, Julie, Kim, Pat, Diana, and all the sales team. You guys are the best! I have to pinch myself so I know it's not a dream and that I really am blessed to work with y'all.

My ultra-talented agent: Natasha, I love working with you. You're the best!

So many friends pray for me and encourage me. I am truly blessed!

My incredible critique partner: Julie Whitby. I love our lunches on Fridays . . . even when we get around to working.

My wonderful family: Mom, thanks for always saying, "Yes," when I need a babysitter (even for the Hilo Monster). Laurel, what would I do without you? Thanks for babysitting and for technical help on dealing with newfangled computers.

My fantabulous children: Graham and Caroline, you make me a better person and a better writer. Thank you for loving me even when I'm under deadline!

My secret ingredient: Gary, I couldn't do what I do without your love and support. You are the greatest blessing.

"Charm is deceptive, and beauty is fleeting;
but a woman who fears the LORD is to be praised."

PROVERBS 31:30

&

"Some day when you are old and wrinkled and ugly,
when thought has seared your forehead with its lines,
and passion branded your lips with its hideous fires, you
will feel it, you will feel it terribly."

LORD HENRY IN *THE PICTURE OF DORIAN GRAY*
—OSCAR WILDE

⊰ Chapter One ⊱

Once upon a time implies a fairy tale is about to unfold, something lush and grand and mythical, something with a happy ending. But the brothers Grimm had a twisted sense of humor and, as it turns out, "once upon a time" is actually literary gobbledygook for "impending doom."

They weren't called Grimm for nothing.

In tale after tale, "once upon a time" invariably precedes certain disaster. Just ask Snow White, Cinderella, or Sleeping Beauty. They'll back me up on this. Those innocuous few words are the harbinger of cursing fairies, parental fatalities, and death marches into dark forests for the near perfect princesses. Not that I consider myself a fairy princess by any stretch of the warped imagination, or even remotely close to perfect, but like those fair, aforementioned ladies, my own story begins with "once upon a time."

If I'd only been given a five-minute warning.

Doom comes to call for me on a warm autumn day, when the grass is still green and a slight breeze ruffles the yet-to-turn-brown leaves. No letter from the IRS arrives. No mammogram shows an area of concern. God doesn't send a lightning bolt to strike my house. The announcement comes in the form of Darth Vader's theme song amplified in the confines of my Volvo. The ominous tune marches out of my cell phone with determination and self-importance, the perfect reflection of the one calling, and prickles the hairs at the base of my neck.

"Don't answer that, Mom."

I glance past my teenage daughter to the backseat where my purse sits. "It could be important."

The clock on the dash glows eerily in the darkness. Who calls at 5:45 in the morning? But we both know that answer without stating the obvious.

Isabel picked the Darth Vader ringtone herself. For her grandmother. Of course, most fairy tales have the evil stepmother. My nemesis is my ex-mother-in-law.

I hesitate as the dirge repeats once more, working its way to the base of my spine and giving me a solid nudge. But my daughter's grim look holds me back. "I'll check my voice mail later and call *her* back then." Already I dread dialing the number. Though the woman is only five foot two and petite as a cherry tomato, she could just as well be wearing a dark mask and cape of black macabre.

Isabel slumps back into the front passenger seat. At seventeen she seems content to be dependent on me forever as she hasn't shown one iota of interest in obtaining her driver's license. Kids today are different than when I was a teen bursting with the need to stretch my wings and fall out of the nest. At least her reluctance saves me the cost of insurance.

"What do you think *she* wants?" Izzie closes her eyes and tilts her head back against the headrest.

"Probably about her house finally selling." I click the blinker light and make a right turn at the corner of our street, which winds through our neighborhood, where all the houses remain dark as everyone with sense is still snoozing. Or at least hitting their snooze button. "My advice worked, didn't it? She's probably calling to thank me."

"Yeah, right." Izzie's voice sounds groggy still. "Can't she wait till the sun wakes up?"

"You know Marla."

We long ago gave up the notion of Izzie calling her father's mother any of the usual terms of endearment—grandmother, Nana, or granny. "No, thank you," Marla said curtly, her bow-like mouth scrunched into a firm line. "I am not about to be called that at my age! Isabel can call me by my first name." Who was I to argue? I was barely nineteen, just a silly girl who'd jumped into a situation I was never prepared to handle.

"Yeah." Izzie's tone is flat and unbending. "I do."

"Did your dad call last night?" I manage to keep my voice level and not let it spike like a crazed, bitter ex-wife, but my hands automatically clench the steering wheel. *Your dad* is my newly acquired way of referring to my ex since I've had to drop "honey" and "husband" and all other usual references while I avoid using the words I've told Isabel are unacceptable. Even though the papers were signed a year and a half ago, dissolving our marriage like a grass stain under attack from *Shout*, my teeth still clench when I say his name. I glance over at my daughter who hasn't yet responded. She's staring out the side window, her head bobbing, long white cords trailing down her chest to the iPod in her hand. "Izzie?"

She gives me a surly look. It often surprises me how a near perfect face—smooth complexion, startling blue eyes, and naturally pouty lips—can turn into a visage reminiscent of Medusa. Did I mention she looks like her grandmother, the one who won't be called such? Except Isabel's at least a head taller. My grandfather's words (at which I rolled my eyes when I was the same too-smart-for-my-own-good age of seventeen) come back to me. *Pretty is as pretty does, Kaye.* It's one of those sayings easily dismissed when *you're* the pretty monster, but a truth worth clinging to wholeheartedly when you've hit midlife and clear skin and cellulite-free thighs are a distant memory.

Delusions start simply—where I convince myself I look good in a pair of new jeans until a friend takes a picture and captures my backside. It's usually an accident, this picture. I'm not the primary focus, just bending over, mostly out of frame, when it's snapped. But I innately recognize the jeans when I'm tagged on Facebook or it's stuck in some computerized photo album for all eternity. That's when I see my own bulges in pixilated Technicolor. It's the same horrifying feeling of self-conscious exposure Dorian Gray experienced when he recognized his own unsightliness in his portrait.

So, why, today, do I buy into this tiny pretense—which is not based on anything but Disney reality—when I self-talk and promise myself everything is all right? Maybe it's simply a wellspring of hope erupting from a crater of despair. What if it isn't going to be all right? What if I'm only seeing things from the angle of my choosing, not with the eye of a dispassionate camera? What if it's about to get a lot worse?

If I'd accepted that bit of gray reality a few years ago, then maybe the dark truth wouldn't have hit me so hard when my world fell apart. The truth didn't set me free at all. It shattered my rose-colored glasses and gouged my eyes out.

Still, I continue to stumble foolishly forward, hands out, feeling my way in the dark, like the vision-challenged person refusing to admit she can't see a blasted thing. Yet, I cling to that lie as if it's a magical cane and believe. All is well. All is well. All is well.

My latest ill-fated belief is that I can do it all—bring home the proverbial bacon (turkey bacon, that is), fry it up in the pan (or microwave), and never ever let him forget he's a man . . .

Well, that absurd fantasy comes to a screeching halt and should be the big tip-off that I'm not being truthful to myself. Because the reality is that some other woman made *him* (my ex) feel more like a man (less like a husband). Or that's my interpretation. The woman I ultimately blame isn't Barbie (his mistress, now turned "legitimate" *girlfriend*). Still my perception is a bit off the norm for why my soufflé of a marriage collapsed, but I try not to dwell on the past and keep stirring up that same blinding optimism.

The reason for which is Isabel. I glance over at her slumped in the passenger seat, blonde hair mussed from sleep, totally clueless about what it takes to make her life run seamlessly. She looks like she rolled straight out of bed (after I poked and prodded and then threatened). I take casual note of the blue knit shorts that reveal her long tan legs and the skimpy tank top that exposes too much of . . . well, everything. It's hard to distinguish the difference between workout and nighttime wear, especially when the teen years hit. And boy did they hit hard.

"Are those your pjs?"

She ignores my question with a roll of the eyes and a sullen sigh.

Sometimes I ache to see her back in those frilly, baby-doll nightgowns that went from the base of her neck to the tip of her toes and covered everything in between with tiny pink rosebuds. Sweet. Simple. Safe. Those were the days. When our family was whole. Before Ken (actually Cliff) went and moved into the Dream House with Barbie.

I note the green numbers glowing on the dash. "We're a couple of minutes early." I've learned the caffeinated key to opening a teen's heart as we approach the high school. "Do you want to stop by Starbucks?"

She shakes her head.

"Your dad, did you hear from him?" Cliff's promise is locked firmly in my brain. I want to make sure he holds to it.

"Oh, yeah, right, Mom. Right after *The Bachelor* chose me." She looks away, her head jerks harder in rhythm to something presumably musical, but which sounds like tiny insect chirps emanating from her earbuds.

Guilt acts like peanut butter for a mother. It can be spread on thin or glopped on thick. I prefer the crunchy variety myself, with a bit of a bite. To make it go down smoother, just sweeten it with grape jelly platitudes. "He probably was delayed in a meeting, Iz."

"Quit making excuses for him, Mom." Her anger, palpable as a throbbing bass, bombards me, and I fear she will never forgive Cliff. That ol' looking glass glares back at me.

A deep breath cannot loosen the tightening in my chest. I brake the Volvo near the double glass doors and shove the gear into Park. "I'll pick you up after school."

She grabs my arm. "There he is!"

"Who?" My heart lurches. Cliff? I manage to duck and shift in my seat, wishing I'd dressed up to take Izzie to swim practice instead of wearing these sweats, which have stretched along with my skin to accommodate my latest size. They're no longer workout clothes but what I curl up in most nights to fall asleep while watching late, late night TV. I crane my neck and peer out the rearview mirror. All I can see are mostly empty parking spaces. But a pair of headlights bobs in the distance as a car turns into the parking lot.

"Don't look!"

"Where?" I slouch down in my seat, my fingers combing my hair in a last desperate attempt to salvage my already shredded dignity.

"Coming this way!" She's squealing. My daughter is squealing like one of the Jonas brothers just arrived. She points toward the bricked high school building next to the natatorium.

I squint toward a tall, lanky blond boy walking in a loose-limbed amble. He keys the door and swings it open. His warm-ups don't make his frame look fuzzy and frumpy like mine but somehow accentuate his muscle tone. Not that I'm noticing. I release a pent-up sigh. At least it isn't Cliff. I wouldn't want him to see me dressed in old sweats with my hair just pulled in a quick ponytail and sans makeup. Great. Now I'm starting to sound like Marla. "Who is it?"

"The new coach. Cute, huh?"

That last bit makes my forehead fold into a frown. Her reaction to his appearance rivals what I imagine would happen if Michael Phelps were to show up for practice. Izzie's breathing shallows. Her eyes dilate even more. My motherly concern ratchets up a notch, but I manage a fake, unconcerned shrug. Still, I can't hold back a warning. "You know, he's way too old for you. And if you're—"

She huffs out a breath, making her bangs poof outward, then rolls those eyes, transforming her features from Anne Hathaway to Britney Spears. "That's perverted, Mom. Not for me." She grabs my arm. "For you!"

"Me?" I squeak back and pull my arm away from her. "No no no no no no."

Her mouth twists. In one smooth motion, she grabs her goggles, bag of clothes, and another tote with kickboard and flippers then practically leaps from the car. "I'll catch a ride this afternoon."

The car door slams shut before I can respond. My throat tightens, making it difficult to swallow. Her fantasy collides with my own. It's not the first time I've disappointed my daughter by not looking longingly at a "hot" guy. Her idealistic dreams of Prince Charming and happily ever after should have shattered the day her father walked out on us. Maybe, in a warped way, it's good to have those silly images destroyed early in life. Before they wreak havoc on your future.

It's why I never hid arguments Cliff and I had from Izzie. I wanted her to know relationships weren't perfect. They required work. Or maybe I should have pretended more.

Grasping at shards of hope that someone else will come along—preferably a rich Daniel Craig type—is simply as unrealistic as Jiminy Cricket transforming a puppet into a real boy. Believing in the impossible could slice through our hearts all over again. I appreciate she thinks I could get (and keep) a man like that, but suspect she's delusional. She doesn't need some hunky guy to be her father. She needs her own. She needs the stability, security, and strength of a family.

I glance down and realize my right hand has found my left. Specifically, the blank space between my knuckles on my ring finger. I rub the spot, missing the gold ring that once occupied the place of honor. A sudden lump in my throat pushes upward and I blink back hot tears.

Shifting my gaze, I watch Izzie walk to the doorway, her long limbs loose, her stride displaying more confidence than I've ever felt, and her flip-flops snapping at her heels the way she often snaps at me these days. Ah, the joys of raising a teenager. Alone. If every potential parent experienced this thrill prior to getting pregnant, there would be no need for birth control.

A car pulls up behind me to deposit another swimmer. A glance at the dash's clock tells me I have time to go home, shower, change, then stop for café mocha and maybe a slice of pumpkin loaf from Starbucks before my early morning appointment. The growth of Altered Images over the past few months is a mixed bag. Needed income, I suppose, outweighs the negatives. As a suddenly single mom, I had to find a job, but after fifteen years of staying at home, making arts and crafts, painting and decorating rooms in a succession of houses as my ex moved up the corporate ladder and we moved into more exclusive neighborhoods, I wasn't qualified for anything other than working retail and making minimum wage. Or was I? Once Cliff left, a friend suggested I start a house staging company since I had so much experience and success selling our houses in the past—Altered Images became the phoenix from the ashes of my marriage.

Before I can shift into Drive, a flash of blue draws my attention back to the double glass doors. Izzie's walking toward me with that same determined stride I'm quite certain she inherited from Cliff's mother and beside her is the boy . . . *man* she called coach.

"No, no, no," I whisper to no one but myself. Swallowing back the urge to step on the gas and make a fast getaway, I plaster on a fake, Dallas smile that comes too easily and hit the button to roll down the window.

"Mom"— she leans in the opening—"I wanted you to meet Coach Derrick. Coach, my mom."

He bends down to peer in the open window. His smile is friendly. Too friendly. He sticks out a hand, which I shake quickly, then pull away.

"Nice to meet you." I settle my hand on the gear shift.

"Isabel's one of my top swimmers."

"That's nice to hear."

"She has potential."

Does that translate *scholarship*? "Oh, uh . . . good."

My phone sounds off, this time with "If I Loved You," a song from the Oscar and Hammerstein musical *Carousel*. It was a stupidly sentimental late-night download I made over a year ago. Since Cliff never calls, I haven't had to admit to the weak moment or regret it even once. In fact, I'd actually forgotten about it.

Until this moment, when the song soars through my car like an anthem.

For a millisecond, I am frozen in place, unable to move. Cliff is calling? This early? Something must be wrong. Does he suddenly have regrets? I can't miss this rare call.

Izzie's eyes widen. Coach Derrick asks, "That your phone?"

I lunge over the backseat for my purse, but my phone isn't in its usual pocket. With my backside skyward, probably showing Coach Derrick that Izzie didn't inherit her athleticism from me, I gopher-dig down to the depths of my purse, trying to make the song stop sooner. Finally I find the phone and flip it open. "Hello? Are you there?"

"Kaye? What took you so long?"

"Hi!" I swivel and turn, righting myself in my seat, ignoring Izzie's scowl and Coach Derrick's raised eyebrows. I press a hand against my heart as if I can still its sudden riotous cadence.

"Thought you were—" His voice is tight. Either he cuts out or he restrains himself. "I'm here at the hospital."

A spike of fear wedges between my diaphragm and heart. "Hospital? Which one?"

"All Saints. Can you come?"

Jolted by the fact that Cliff needs me—*me*, not Barbie—I clench the phone. "Yes, yes. Of course. I'll be right there."

He hangs up first, and I toss my phone on the seat next to me. "Get in the car, Iz. Your dad is in the hospital."

The coach opens the door for Izzie but she steps back. "I've got practice, Mom."

Maybe it's for the best. Putting her and Cliff in a room together is like pouring kerosene on fire. I'll call her, take her out of school, if this proves life-threatening. But maybe the fact that Cliff called proves he'll be all right. Still . . .

"I've got to go."

The coach slams the door closed as I shove the gear in Drive.

"I'll call you later." I step on the gas. The Volvo lurches forward. I'm three blocks away before I realize the window is still open. *Breathe, Kaye, breathe.*

-⟨ Chapter Two ⟩-

*P*lease, God, let Cliff live. Let him live. Let him live long enough *for him to say he's sorry . . . he needs me . . . he regrets leaving, wants to come back.*

It's the moment after I speed-stop by my house to change out of sweats and put on two swipes of mascara, and as I'm driving toward the hospital that I realize I never asked Cliff on the phone what happened, why he's in the hospital. A car wreck? Chest pains? A four-hour side effect from some medication? I give myself a mental shake and settle on Cliff having chest pains. *Severe* chest pains.

Fear and panic collide in my cluttered thoughts. With my hands at ten and two, I grip the steering wheel. All my self-centered worries fall behind me. I whip into the hospital parking lot, squeezing my sedan into a compact car space near the Emergency Room entrance. At my approach the automatic doors slide sideways, opening a floodgate of overwhelming fear.

What if I'm too late? What if Barbie is here in all her toned and surgically enhanced glory? What if Cliff is delusional from pain medication?

I walk straight to the nurse's station where a busy middle-aged woman shuffles paperwork. Prominent signs forbid cell phones.

11

"Excuse me?" My voice crackles. Dread surges up within me. *What if I'm too late? What if Cliff is having that coronary I always told him was coming if he didn't quit eating trans fats?* "My husband was brought in this morning."

She ignores me, writes in a folder.

It occurs to me I omitted *ex* from my statement, but it feels perfectly normal and makes it easier to say the second time. "Excuse me? My husband—"

She holds up one rigid finger. Finally, after what seems like a whole pass on the clock's dozen numbers, she gives a huff and brushes back her bangs with her forearm. "Name?"

"Kaye Redmond."

The nurse poises her fingers over a computer keyboard and begins typing.

"No. Sorry." I shake my head. *"His* name is Cliff . . . Clifford Peter Redmond."

A baby coughs in the waiting area. A siren wails outside. Each sound makes me flinch, look around, then back at the nurse.

With irritated punches at the backspace key, she backs over my name and inserts my ex's. "Not here."

"What? But he called. He said All Saints."

"What was the last name again?"

"Redmond."

She clicks in the name. "No Cliff or Clifford. But there is *a* Redmond."

"Could he have been released already?" I'm thinking aloud. Did I take too long changing from sweats to khakis? Maybe I should have skipped the mascara, blush, and lip gloss. "Maybe he moved to a room?" I lean on the counter, press my fingers against my throbbing temple, and imagine the worst. *What if I'm too late? What if he was sent to the morgue?* Irrational tears press, hot and urgent, against my eyes. *Please, God, no.*

Then reason, brief but clear, settles over me. "Did you . . . say there's another, as in a different, Redmond?"

The nurse nods and studies the computer screen. "It's a woman."

"A woman?" My brain clicks through possibilities and I remember the call before Cliff's. Darth Vader's march. No, it couldn't be . . . or could it? "Marla?"

"Yes. You know her?"

Boy, do I! "She's my mother-in-law."

It takes much more effort to leave out the *ex* in that statement as that was the only part of my divorce worth celebrating. A mixture of wariness and relief filters through me. At least Cliff isn't knocking on death's door. But my first (admittedly unChristian) instinct is to thank the nurse and return to my car. Then I imagine my coddled and spoiled ex-husband wrought with grief over the possibility of losing his mother. He needs someone strong comforting him. He needs me. *Me!* God wants to use this moment, I'm sure of it. After all, He turns everything into good, even hospital visits. "Can you give me her room number?"

"Room 525."

Is that the psych ward? But I refrain from asking that particular question. I glance around. "And where . . . ?"

"Around the corner to the elevators. Take one to five."

"Thanks." I walk through the maze of hospital corridors passing gurneys, medical personnel, and wheelchairs. My footsteps are slow, almost dragging. I should have taken longer with my makeup, maybe even showered. In the steel, industrial-sized elevators, I see a blurry reflection of myself—face elongated, eyes narrowed with determination. Not exactly what "Mirror, mirror" had in mind.

⚜

I step out of the elevator and try to get my bearings. Locating the sign that points me in the right direction, I follow it down one hall, bypassing breakfast carts and doctors making their rounds.

When I spot the room number, I verify the name beside the door: *Redmond, M.* I gather my courage as if piling laundry into my arms, but I sense my composure slipping out on the floor like wayward socks and worn-out bras.

The door is cracked open, and I inch it forward, peer inside. A nurse stands beside the first bed. A patient (which I can tell by the bleached blonde hair is not my ex-mother-in-law) sniffles, and the nurse pats her arm. "It's going to be all right."

"Excuse me?"

Both nurse and patient look over and stare at me as if I've barged in during an exam. The patient, her face mottled red, looks about Isabel's age. She wears a tight bandage around her chest. "I'm sorry. I'm looking for Marla Redmond."

"Next bed." The nurse tilts her head in the direction of a mauve curtain.

"Sorry." I move past the first bed, edging around the moveable table with an untouched breakfast tray. A giant step over an open suitcase brings me to the curtain, which reminds me of a circus tent where I'm not sure what oddity I'll find on the other side. What should I do? Knock? Scratch? Whisper, "Cliff?"

I breathe in a deep, cleansing breath, fortifying me with the strength I never had during our marriage, and release it slow and steady. Straightening my blouse and praying Cliff is on the other side, I pull the thick material to the left.

A woman swathed in bandages groans. Tubes spring forth from her like antennae on an alien. She looks like a mummy waking up. My hand clutches the curtain. "Marla?" A glance to either side tells me Cliff must have gone for coffee. I hope he brings two cups. "Marla?" I take a hesitant step into the inner chamber, hoping it isn't her. Marla Redmond has never been my favorite person, but I wouldn't wish something like this on her. Unfortunately I recognize her auburn hair sticking upward in places and matted down in others and her blue eyes—well, *one* eye—staring straight at me. "It's me, Kaye." She attempts to drink from a straw, but her mouth pulls to the side, and water dribbles down her chin. It somehow galvanizes me into action. A tissue box sits beside her breakfast tray, and I yank out a square and dab at her chin.

"Careful." Her consonants slur, making it sound like, "car full."

I can't imagine what happened to her . . . a fall? A car wreck?

"What happened?" I reach out to touch her but stop short at the sight of the IV taped to the back of her hand. The skin covering her petite bones is pale, almost iridescent, but that's normal for her.

The nurse comes around the edge of the curtain. "How are you doing there, Mrs. Redmond? Getting a sip of water? That's good. It'll help wash the anesthetics out of you."

The nurse doesn't seem to be interested in any answers to her questions and simply checks the machine next to the bed, which I realize is hooked up to Marla's heart. At one time I imagined nothing occupied that space. But from the steady green blip on the monitor, I see I was wrong. My own heartbeat accelerates. Then with a "See you later," the nurse leaves the curtained-off portion of Marla's room.

"What happened?" I repeat. But Marla doesn't seem capable of answering. Or maybe she's simply ignoring me as she did when Cliff and I were married.

Reluctantly I sit in the chair next to the bed and stare at the tubes and wires hooked up to my *ex*-mother-in-law. Guilt settles into a cozy nook in my heart, as if I somehow willed this to happen. Usually so formidable, Marla looks fragile. Around the edges of the bandages, her skin looks dark, bluish, bruised.

Glancing toward the doorway, which is obscured by the curtain, I wish Cliff would hurry back. Where is he? Maybe talking to the doctor in the hallway? Or buying flowers down in the gift shop? I don't have time to babysit Marla all morning. I'd like to see Cliff, see if I can bring him something, and be on my way.

After all, I do have appointments today. Guilt once again pinches my conscience. Wasn't there a sermon at church recently about God's time, not our own? Cliff used to say, "I'm not tithing to hear that!" when the pastor would preach on a prickly subject. Which is probably why he wasn't paying attention the weeks the topic was infidelity. Gritting my teeth, I lean forward, touch Marla's hand. "Did you have a car wreck?"

"Surgery." Her words are loose like she can't quite handle them in her mouth. "Heart."

I glance at her chest, then to the heart monitor blinking at me. "You had heart surgery?"

"Heart arrythm."

"Arrhythmia?" My own heart skips a beat. "But why surgery?"

"Cosm," she mumbles.

Did she mean *because*? I state my question slowly, clearly, and loudly. "Because why?"

She gives a tiny shake of her head, then grimaces. "Plastic."

"Plastic what?" Memories of the nauseous feelings I suffered after my C-section have me searching around for a plastic container. "Are you going to throw up?"

"No," she croaks. "Face"—she draws the end sound out like the hissing of a snake—"lift."

My knees suddenly feel like the threads holding them together have come undone. "All of this"—I indicate the tubes and bandages—"for plastic surgery?" I stare at the heart monitor and watch the blips and numbers. *Heart arrhythmia*. What does that mean? That her heart is off rhythm? Someone should have consulted me. I could have told them that years ago.

I grimace at my sarcasm. Bad habits are hard to break.

Marla's one visible eye shutters closed. She looks tragic. She went through all this to look younger? I'm not surprised at the lengths Marla would go to find the fountain of youth at her over-ripe age. What is she sixty? Sixty-five? Even though she took meticulous care of her skin, having weekly facials and staying out of the sun, I suppose age catches up to all of us. Would I do this? Go to all this trouble, and face possible death just to hold onto Cliff? How desperate am I?

A knock at the door breaks the awkward silence. I jump up, readjust my clothes and poke my head out of the curtain's slit. Instead of Cliff, an older gentleman stands in the doorway. I notice the woman in the next bed has fallen asleep.

"Yes?" I answer for both women.

He glances down at the flowers he holds, which appear to be a literal garden variety and not the hothouse kind. "I'm looking for Sylvia—"

"Sylvia?" I prompt when he seems to have forgotten the last name.

"Plath."

"Oh, well, um . . ." I try to remember the other name beside Marla's on the outside of the door but can't. "I'm not sure of her name. But this is—"

Marla gives an alarmed cry. She holds her hands up, waving her arms like windshield wipers gone amok.

"Sorry, wrong room." The man backs away.

"You might check at the nurse's station." I move toward Marla.

"What's wrong?" Her heart monitor blinks rapidly. "Should I call somebody?"

Marla gives a stiff shake of her head, making a drainage tube bob, and reaches for the Styrofoam cup of water. I place the straw between her lips, which are pinched and dry. "I thought that might be Cliff. I wonder when he'll be back."

"Wok," she says but did she mean "work."

"What?" I pinch the straw and water spurts out of the end, dotting Marla's hospital gown. "Oh, sorry." I dab gently at her chin. "Did you say Cliff's at work?"

She nods.

Terrific. Now I'm fully entrenched in my nightmare. "Well, how do you like that?" Figures that's where he'd hide out. His relationship with Marla can be characterized as cat and mouse.

"Kaye," Marla's mouth barely moves as her fingers curl around mine and squeeze tight. "Don't go."

With anger tightening its grip on my throat, I manage to pry loose its tentacles and draw a steadying breath. "He could have at least told me."

"Kaye," she says again, her voice slightly clearer, more forceful. "What am I going to do?"

"What do you mean?"

She sighs through her partially open mouth. "I'm fifty-five. Old."

That can't be right. I'd have thought she was at least over sixty. My gaze follows the IV. Maybe the drugs are making her hallucinate. I cup my hand over hers and try to reassure her. "You're not old, Marla."

"Don't know what it's like." Her face crumples like a rumpled tissue. She moans. "Now this!"

"What do you mean?"

"Such mess. My face . . ."

Stunned, unable to believe my stoic mother-in-law (ex-mother-in-law) is admitting anything other than, "I'm fine," I hope she's also had a change of heart. Or maybe the drugs she's been given are making her babble. Or the anesthesiologist could have used truth serum.

She squeezes the stiff hospital sheet, her knuckles white. Her eye wells with tears.

"Don't cry, Marla. You'll make your bandages soggy." I reach for another tissue. "It takes a while to heal from surgery. You'll be better in no time."

She sniffs, tries to regain her composure. I've never seen her lose control, not even when her husband died suddenly five years ago. "Dr. Scar—" her tongue overworks the 'r'—"didn't finish."

"Who?"

"Surr . . ." She garbles the word.

"What?"

"Doctor," she says carefully, barely moving her mouth.

"What do you mean?"

"Could not finish lift." She taps her heart. Her mouth twists. "One side, one eye."

I draw a quick breath and plop back into the chair. Over the years, I've joked with friends that my mother-in-law was Frankenstein.

Now, she truly is.

⋅⟨ Chapter Three ⟩⋅

Living in the most affluent area of the Dallas and Fort Worth metroplex has its plusses (and a few items in the negative column). Though I'm unable to keep up with the Joneses, the Joneses are able to hire me to help sell their mini-mansions, which in turn helps me keep the lights on at my own humble abode.

Southlake teems with all the best stores from Ann Taylor to Williams-Sonoma, along with every bistro and boutique imaginable. Nip and tucked between them are plastic surgeons and day spas for the relaxing and pampering of the already pampered, places I once frequented but which I now avoid. Even though the economy has been hard hit in the past year, the parking lots full of Mercedes, Beamers, and gas-guzzling Escalades seem to indicate otherwise. Either credit cards are smoking from overuse and credit agencies are hounding the rich and careless, or money really does grow on trees. If so, I need to find that variety at my local Calloway's Nursery and plant an orchard.

After returning home from the hospital to don a suit and the dreaded panty hose, which make me look ultraprofessional, I stop in at the local coffee shop for fortification before my meeting with a potential new client. As I wait in line, I notice my advertisement is still stuck to the community board. I've received several calls off of it.

"Kaye!"

I turn and find a group of moms I recognize from PTA meetings. "Elise!" I stuff my receipt in my bulging wallet—more full of receipts and bills than actual money. "How are you?" I move toward the women while I wait for my order. They're all wearing workout shorts and tank tops, revealing tanned and toned arms and new polish on their sculpted fingertips. "I haven't seen you in forever."

Elise, a petite blonde who looks like she could put on a cheerleader outfit and go out for the high school squad even though I know for a fact she's several months over forty, pivots around, exaggerating the swing of her backside. "What do you think?"

She's wearing a formfitting warm-up and looks like she's lost a good twenty pounds, which I undoubtedly found. "You look great. What's your secret?"

The other women, who I vaguely recognize but don't actually know, resume their conversation while Elise moves closer to me. "Want the number?"

My stomach drops, as has everything else—or so it seems. "For what? Weight Watchers or Marie Osmond?"

"My surgeon! I had breast implants and a tummy tuck. Next year"—she wiggles her fanny and a couple of businessmen at the next table pause in their conversation—"when my checking account has recovered, I'm having a butt lift."

"Really?"

"Oh, yeah." She winks.

"Well, I . . . uh . . ." I'm not sure what to say.

She leans forward. "You should try it. Maybe it's the ticket you need."

"Oh, well, thanks." My mind wanders down that slippery slope as I imagine myself slimmer, lifted, wrinkle free, my cups set high and overflowing. Would that bring Cliff back? Is that what drove him away? And am I just a few procedures shy of bringing joy back to my family? The big roadblock to me, besides my depleted checking account, is Marla and the very solid memory of what could happen. Not to mention the doubt that would settle firmly between Cliff and me. What kind of a marriage is based on smooth skin and flat abs?

Elise puts a hand on my arm. "You won't believe who I saw last night."

Her half-lidded squint and the catch in my chest tells me it was Cliff. "Where?"

"Doesn't matter."

"Was he with—"

"Oooh"— she draws out her answer—"yeah."

My untucked tummy flips over. I don't want to hear anymore.

"You could do so much better, Kaye. Really! I know someone—"

"No, really. I'm not—"

"Café mocha," the barrister calls out. "Venti, no whip."

Saved by the mighty coffee bean. "That's me." I give Elise a quick hug. "I've got an appointment."

"Call me!"

Ten minutes later, still sipping my coffee, I turn my Volvo in to an exclusive neighborhood and leave my name with the round-the-clock guard, who acts like he's guarding Buckingham Palace rather than a tiny nine-by-nine-foot, bricked, child-sized fort, which sits outside the gates of a community of massive estates, each with its own security system. A kid Izzie once babysat lives in this neighborhood. Lily probably has a nanny now, so the parents no longer need an undependable teenager for their date nights.

Following my spiral-bound map, which sits in the passenger seat, (my GPS system is on the fritz and I don't have extra cash lying around to repair it), I locate the jaw-dropping estate. Giant oaks and elms dominate the yard and offer a shady respite from the Texas heat. The money trees must be in the backyard, probably offering provisions to the pool boy. The curve of the circular drive angles toward the stone entrance replete with oversized urns filled with flowering rose bushes. Red, my favorite. I hope the lady of the manor won't take offense to any of my suggestions. Not that I have any at the moment. But it's my job (or so I hope) to find something to suggest.

My arms laden with materials, I approach the expansive porch. The arched double door with an old-world charm leaves me speechless and aware that Lancelot astride his war horse could gallop through any ol' time. Wish my Prince Charming would come galloping along. But I've given up on such nonsense—I simply want my husband back.

A miniature window doorway of beveled glass and wrought iron bars is a classy touch. My services may not be required here. From my peripheral vision, something hot pink grabs my attention—a battery-powered Hot Wheels Barbie Jeep lurks at the corner of the house. *That needs to go.* I take a mental note.

The beveled glass distorts my reflection, making my shoulder-length brown hair appear like a football helmet and enlarging my short stature to the proportions of a linebacker. Or maybe it's the pumpkin loaves. Arms tucked around the photo album and decorator sample books, I scowl at my image and elbow the doorbell. The bell echoes through what sounds like cavernous square footage, and I peer through the tiny diamond-shaped windows.

Marble flooring and a heavy brass chandelier sparkle in the morning sunlight. The caramel painted walls give way to a wrought iron and wood banister that curls upward to the second floor. This job looks easy. Or maybe there won't be a need for any consulting. Which won't help my checking account. So far, no clown pictures or menagerie of baby photos clutter the walls. Simple, elegant furnishings should result in a quick, painless sale for the homeowner, which always makes for a happy client and often brings referrals.

Through the door I hear someone bounding down the stairs and watch socked feet slide across the slick floor. The lock clicks and the door opens with a whoosh. A young man with peach fuzz along his jaw says, "Yeah?"

"Hi, I'm Kaye with Altered Images. I have an appointment with—"

The teenager turns to holler behind him. His blond hair is pulled back in a short ponytail. "Jack! Someone at the door for you." He opens it wider and moves backward. His khaki slacks and collared knit shirt set off a deep tan, as if he spent the summer next to a pool. "I'm late," he tells me, then louder, "I'm outta here!"

I blink, but he's disappeared into the house, leaving me standing alone in the grand foyer. With a moment to glance around unnoticed and unobserved, it's easy to see the house is neatly maintained. No dust on the furniture or cobwebs in the corners. But the expansive entryway is empty and hints nothing of its impressive possibilities. I dig for a pen in my bag and scribble a note: *Needs table. Rug. Grandfather clock?*

Peering around the corner, I almost drop my load of books. Doubt about being needed fades and a new one springs up: What will I do with *this*? Inside what appears to be the main living area, a Star Wars X-wing Fighter arcade game sits idle. Nearby is an intricately carved pool table, but even its magnificence is crowded out by an air hockey table squaring off with foosball and shielding an old-fashioned popcorn machine. A juke box decorated in reds, oranges, and purples pulls me toward it like a three-headed snake at a carnival. I step into the room, bend down, and examine the impressive list of CDs available in the juke box—everything from the Bangles to the Beatles, Miley Cyrus to Beyonce, and Coldplay to Taylor Swift. Lingering in the air is a sickly-sweet cotton candy odor mixed with the greasy scent of corn dogs.

No wonder the owner needs staging. This house wouldn't sell if a hundred grand were knocked off the asking price.

Obviously, from the looks of the house so far, there's no lady of the manor. At least, not anymore. Did she take all the furniture? There seem to be children in the fallout. So the sale must be due to an impending divorce. I can so relate, and I know to tread carefully.

From some far corner of the house, I hear a door close, then a scrabbling scratching sound.

"It!" a deep voice hollers.

I turn toward the sound, just as the blur of a giant black furball zooms around the corner. A scream lodges in my throat. Before I can even throw up my hands to protect myself, it hits me full throttle, knocking me back a step, sending my books and sunglasses, notepad and pen flying. Baseball glove-sized paws hook onto my shoulders and a pink, slobbery tongue slurps the side of my face.

"Come." The voice from somewhere behind this assault weapon gives me hope.

Smothered by the giant, wiggling carpet, I try to ward off the squirming, wagging, panting beast. Then suddenly it's gone, yanked backward by a collar.

"Sorry about that." A flash of a smile unsettles me more. "She got away from me."

Out of breath and flustered, I wipe my face with my hand, readjust my clothing. "What is it?"

"Cousin It. Or that's what we call her. She's still a puppy."

"A puppy?" My gaze settles back on the black furry mass.

"But she's learning."

"What? How to attack?"

The man, wearing an untucked khaki shirt, faded jeans, and tan work boots, laughs, and the robust sound echoes through the room and irritates me. He looks as shaggy as the dog. "She's just overly friendly. Sit." He makes a hand motion. The dog sits, but her furry round backside pops right up off the scraped hardwoods within half a second. "Sit," the man says more patiently than I'd manage. "Good girl."

A shadow of a beard darkens his jaw. His dark hair curls over his shirt collar, but the rest is hidden beneath the brim of a New York Yankees baseball cap. Shaded hazel eyes watch me along with the dog's brown ones.

"She'll settle down once she greets you."

"Oh? I thought we just met."

"If you don't mind." He waves me over, and I take a cautious step toward him. Once upon a time I liked dogs. But I haven't been around any pets in a long while, and I've become used to not having any shedding or panting or messes of any kind in my house.

"Put your hand out," he advises. "So she can get a good sniff."

"What if she's hungry?"

He chuckles. "She's really sweet. I promise."

The thing is, one does not want to offend a client. Even though I suspect this man just works in this giant-sized house, maybe as the dog trainer, insulting the help or a beloved pet equals insulting the owner. So I inch closer. Cousin It sniffs my hand, placing her cold, black nose against my knuckles. The man steps closer.

"Don't worry." His voice is low and calming. And yet, not. A part of me feels rattled by his nearness. "It's okay."

I'm not sure if he's talking to me or the dog.

"Dogs can tell a lot by scent."

"Uh-huh." Women can too. This man doesn't smell of sweat or dirt as I anticipated, but something alluring that draws me toward him. Something light and purely male. Back in college, I knew all the colognes by name: freshmen wore Polo, frat boys Obsession, and law students Drakkar Noir. But now, at the ripe old age of thirty-six, I no longer know what men (other than my husband . . . okay *ex*-husband) wear. Admittedly my knowledge of

Cliff's choice of fragrance may be outdated now that Barbie has her manicured claws into him. Sure, I've been alone more than a year now, but I must be getting desperate if this man is appealing to me.

"Now," he encourages, "give her a little loving and she'll be your friend for life."

I stare into his eyes and something deep inside me quivers. I feel more in that moment than a woman should for a stranger. I clear my throat, step toward the dog, pat It's head, and then move away. The man rubs his hands over the dog's body and murmurs approval. Feeling the itch of discomfort deep inside my bones, I look around at all my materials, strewn across the floor.

"Sorry about that." He lets go of the dog's red collar and holds a hand up toward the dog. "Stay." The sweeping tail twitches. The man scoops up one of my decorator books. Some of the pages ended up dog-eared in the melee and he carefully unbends them. "Let me help you with all of this."

"That's okay." I step toward my purse—its contents falling out of the opening. I shove wallet, checkbook, makeup bag, cell phone back inside. "I can get it. Is the owner here?"

He reaches for my appointment book. "Sure is."

But I bend to retrieve it, bumping his arm with my hand. "I got it." But two more books crash to the floor.

The gardener's self-assured smile widens, his white teeth flashing. With as much dignity as I can muster, I haul my load of books over to the pool table. "Mind?"

"Go ahead."

I set my books on the green felt surface, and he steps beside me, placing more on the stack. "Thanks."

Finally I stick out my hand. "I'm Kaye. Kaye Redmond. I'm here to see Mr. Franklin."

He shakes my hand. There's much to digest in a simple handshake—the grip, the duration, the texture of skin. His hand is warm, the skin not as smooth as my ex's, the grip firm and strong. Working man's hands, strong and sure. "Jack Franklin, at your service."

"Oh, you're—" My new client. Why didn't I figure that out? Was my first impression clouding my judgment? Maybe I expected a suit—or at the very least, manicured hands.

"Sit, It." His tone is forceful but a smile crinkles those intriguing eyes that never waver off me.

I glance at the panting, black mop-of-a-dog. Her bottom automatically touches the floor again. Hoping she'll stay put, I look back at Jack Franklin. What must he think of me snooping around his house? "Your . . . uh, son let me in. But he had to go and I thought . . . well, I didn't know. . . ."

He blinks slowly as if digesting my remarks. "My Realtor thought I could use your services to get the house to move faster."

"Of course." I glance around the room, past It to the assortment of arcade games, imagining that Jack's wife must have moved out and taken all the furniture. Maybe she hated the dog. Or maybe he lost his job and has sold much of the furniture to make ends meet. The first thing I'll suggest is that he find another home for Cousin It. "I have a few ideas." I lean on the edge of the pool table. "You like games, huh?"

"As much as anybody." He walks toward another doorway and It follows. "There are a few more in here." An arched opening leads to a sitting area with built-ins and fireplace, a cozy nook now crammed with more arcade games and pinball machines.

Does he think anyone else would fill their house with this many toys? "What do you do for a living, Mr. Franklin?"

"Jack." His tone is even softer than when he addressed Cousin It. "I have a travel agency."

"Do you travel much, then?" My gaze shifts back toward It, who has settled on the floor, taking up a wide swath of space like a bear rug. She lays her chin on her giant paws and watches us.

"Not as much anymore. I've had some . . . well, I've needed to stay in town more and more. The agency focuses on high-end clientele who want exotic locations and specialized hunting expeditions. I used to conduct private tours or safaris but now . . ."

Since he doesn't look like the museum type, I ask, "Hunting?"

"Anything from deep-sea fishing for marlin to wild boar."

Daring to look at what else I have to contend with, hoping it won't be a room full of Bambis mounted on the wall, I follow him through the house, taking note of the empty spaces and blank walls, mismatched towels, and diverse furniture. Cousin It wanders off during the tour. Right now it wouldn't surprise me if Chuck E. Cheese waddled around a corner. Hopefully the giant rat won't attack like the dog.

Instead, Darth Vader storms the house.

"Your phone?" Jack asks as we return to the den.

I contemplate answering it, but I only left Marla an hour and a half ago and promised to be back after my meeting. If it's an emergency, she has a whole staff of doctors and nurses to care for her. Then the ringtone stops. "It's okay. I'll call her back."

"Her? Not your regular ringtone, then?"

"My *ex* mother-in-law." I suppress the bitterness trying to creep into my voice. "My daughter downloaded that ringtone for her."

"Interesting song for Grandma." He crosses his arms over his chest and looks around at the menagerie of games. "So, what do you think?"

I search for pride in his features, but I'm not sure how he feels about the bombarding colors and jumbled chaos around us. Eager to avoid a conversation about Marla, I glance past the rump of Cousin It as she chews on a bone, crunching it between those powerful jaws, and around the wood-paneled room up to the cathedral ceiling bisected by long cedar beams. I focus first on the positive. "You have a beautiful home. I'm sure Altered Images can help you get it sold quickly."

A glance at his worn work boots makes me consider the possibility that his ex took him for every penny. Or has the economic downturn affected his business? Or maybe he's the token nonpretentious person in the whole city of Southlake. "The idea of staging is completely opposite of how you or I might decorate a house in which we want to live. It's like a . . . facelift." Gee, where'd that idea come from? "It shows off the best features. You want someone to walk in and imagine how great their furniture will look here."

"So it's better to have completely empty rooms?"

"Not at all. Most people don't have that good of an imagination. They need a little help. You see, all these wonderful games might distract buyers from actually seeing the features of the house." I silently congratulate myself on my tact. "They might want to play the games rather than buy. So what I see happening here is putting—"

"If I Loved You" begins. Even though I suspect Marla called Cliff when she couldn't reach me, I lunge past Jack for my purse. But when I reach the pool table, I realize the ringtone is coming from the corner of the room. From the dog.

"Not your ex-mother-in-law this time, huh?"

"The dog has my phone!"

Cousin It must sense she's caught, because she scrambles to her feet. A flash of gray metal hangs out of her mouth.

"It!" Jack's tone is forceful but much calmer than my own. "Leave it."

She drops down, planting her paws on the floor, and her backside arcs upward, tail dusting the air.

"I have to get that call!"

"Okay. Stay right there." Jack points in my direction as the ringtone suddenly stops. "Don't let her run past you."

"What am I supposed to do?"

"Tackle her if you have to."

"Do what?"

But Jack moves stealth-like toward the dog. "It." His tone is commanding. "Leave it." The romantic song soars through the room again like an anthem, my marriage calling to me. And Cousin It couldn't care less. Jack fakes right, the dog leaps sideways, but Jack is quicker. His arms fold around the scruffy body. He pries open her jaws and pulls out my cell phone. Wiping the slobber off on his jeans, he then hands it to me.

I stare at it, noting a tooth mark in the flat panel. "You've got to get rid of that dog."

He opens the phone for me and holds it out to me.

I can hear Cliff's voice. "Kaye? Are you there? Kaye?"

Taking the phone between forefinger and thumb and trying not to touch any more of the phone before it's been disinfected, I say, "I'm here, Cliff."

"Where are you?" The accusation in his voice chafes against me. "I've been trying—"

"I'm in a meeting."

"Mother called."

"And?"

"She needs someone there with her."

"Be my guest." My gaze darts toward Jack who turns his back discreetly on me. He has a hand firmly around Cousin It's collar and is walking her toward the back door. "She's *your* mother."

"I'm working, Kaye." Irritation tightens Cliff's voice. "I have responsibilities."

Like alimony, but I keep that to myself, as well as his little two-week trip to the Caribbean with Barbie. "So do I."

"I can't just drop everything."

"Of course not." I grit my teeth. He believes I can. Probably because I always have.

"Let me know what the doctor says then." He skips over or doesn't recognize my sarcasm. His assumption that I'm going to race back to care for his mother nettles me like a sticker burr against my ankle.

"Where's Barbie? Can't she help?'

"Her name is Barbara." He mutters something under his breath. "It doesn't matter anyway."

"What? What do you mean?"

"We've separated."

"You have?" I cringe at the hope springing in my voice. "When?"

"You don't have to sound so smug and happy."

I bite down another sarcastic remark and pray for guidance as I tread over this icy patch. *Cliff is available!* God, help me say the right thing. Maybe his midlife crisis has skidded into a blockade and he's come to his senses. Finally! Or will soon enough. Of course God has placed me right smack dab in Cliff's path. Which tells me once again, God's will is for us to get back together. He's all about restoration. But I can't be selfish and think only about me and my excitement at this moment. Cliff must be devastated. Temporarily.

"I'm sorry, Cliff. I know how painful a breakup can be." Now that his bed is empty and his town home vacated, I guide the conversation to a more pressing issue. "So"—I turn my shoulder away from Jack—"what's going to happen when your mother goes home?"

"How should I know? Ask the doctor."

I roll my eyes. *Men.* They never think ahead and make plans. Or at least Cliff never has. "Fine, I will ask the doctor what he recommends. I'll call you later." Before he can hang up, I have another thought. "Cliff?"

"Yeah?" There's a note of intimacy in his voice, one that stirs memories of us lying in bed together, limbs entwined, sleep settling over us. I learned over our fifteen years of marriage that this tone meant it was the perfect moment to make a request—

a swimming pool, trip to Bermuda, girls' night out—but those days are long behind us.

"Could you call Isabel?" I refrain from reminding him he was supposed to call her last night. He'd consider it nagging and it wouldn't put him in the right frame of mind. I realize I may be pushing my luck at the moment. "Let her know what's happening. Tell her I'll be late getting home tonight."

A heavy sigh from his end of the phone provides an image of his face scrunched in irritation. "Yeah, all right."

I smile to myself. Of course I've already talked to our daughter but Cliff won't dare forget to call her now. *Because he wants me at the hospital with his mother.* Inside my head the thought replays as *he wants me, he needs me. Me, not Barbie.* My heart rate accelerates.

Then with a click he's gone. I snap my cell phone closed and dance a little jig as if I've just won *Are You Smarter Than a 5th Grader?*, but which leaves a lingering prickly question of whether I am or not. I'm not one to raise my hands and jump around at church, but if ever there was a moment to rejoice it's this one. All the prayers I've said in the past months are finally coming to fruition. *Thank You, God! Thank You, thank You, thank You!*

"Good news?" The sound of Jack's voice laced with humor makes me freeze.

Slowly I lower my arms, still my backside in its imitation of Chita Rivera. "Oh, well . . . sort of. Yes." I give a firm jerk on the hem of my jacket to make it lie flat. "More like answered prayer."

He grins, and the effect is disarming. "I'm all for prayer. Sorry about your phone. But I'm glad it's still working."

I turn it over in my hand, notice several teeth marks mar the once smooth surface.

"Is it too personal to share?" Jack asks.

I swallow back any hesitations. "My husband"—I tilt my head, admitting the truth—"*ex*-husband's girlfriend is now out of the picture." I don't usually discuss such things, especially with a stranger, but it seems appropriate as if I'm reaffirming in my head that no matter what hot man comes along—either Izzie's coach or this potential new client—I have a goal.

"Ah, I think I see."

Does he? Can he understand the way my heart feels suddenly stronger in its steady, unwavering beat? "You do?"

"Vengeance, right?"

"No, no. Not at all." And a smile breaks across my face. "Opportunity."

ᐊ Chapter Four ᐅ

Barbie is gone!

B I knew it couldn't last. What would a twenty-something find interesting in a man pushing forty? Almost from the moment I found out he was seeing another woman, which was precisely ten seconds after he told me he was leaving, I began praying for the restoration of our family. Of course, this came after I had a few days of extreme anger where I made more than a few suggestions to God about how He could have Cliff run over by a bus. It didn't take me long to realize though that I simply wanted him back. After all, God certainly doesn't want a marriage to end. That's not His will. Right? Now, maybe the fact that Barbie is out of the picture is a sign. Maybe Cliff calling me to help with his mother is a step in the right direction. An opportunity.

A door opening.

I imagine taking dinner over to Cliff's, serving him and his mother the lasagna that he always loved. I'll take magazines for Marla to peruse during her recovery process, along with DVDs (ones with happy families) for entertainment. Flowers, too. Tulips were always her favorite. And herbal tea. What kind does she like? Lemon ginger, isn't it? Marla might offer a rare compliment or show gratitude for my thoughtfulness. Cliff will walk me to the door, touch my elbow, pull me back toward him. "I've been a fool," he'll say, his arms sliding around my ever-widening middle. But with his new perspective he won't notice or care. "I never should have left," he'll say. "Do you think you can ever forgive me?"

I, of course, will resist the impulse to throw myself into his arms. Instead, I'll place a steady, uncompromising hand against his chest, contemplate his pseudoapology, then with a sly glance upward at him I'll suggest, "Let's take it slow and see what develops."

It shouldn't take more than a couple of dinners. I might have to escort Marla to a follow-up doctor's visit, but eventually Cliff will realize just how much he has lost. Only God can heal a heart, but I can disinfect the surgical area and sharpen the scalpel.

Back at the hospital, waiting next to Marla's bed, I try to sit still when there is so much to do. Her mouth makes puttering snores. Ice packs cover most of her face, just the tip of her nose poking through. When my marriage is once again restored, Marla will be delighted to have me as a daughter-in-law rather than Barbie.

The squeak of the hospital door interrupts my fantasies of rec-onciliation. I readjust my blouse and straighten my spine against the plastic cushion in the spare chair, ankles crossed, hands clasped. I'm ready for Cliff to make his grand entrance. I prepare to stand slowly, hesitate as he reaches for me, then after a quick embrace break contact before he does first.

The curtain parts. A man in a white doctor's coat over blue scrubs offers a blindingly white smile. It's Dr. McDreamy from TV, or so it seems, but of course a closer look tells me it's not the actor but a real doctor with his hair mussed in an offhanded way. His gaze shifts from Marla to me. "Good evening, ladies."

"Kaye Redmond." I stand, straighten my posture, which I hope makes me look less like a candidate for a tummy tuck, and stick out my hand. "I'm Marla's daughter-in-law."

Or will be again.

"Mark Scarr." He takes my hand in a delicate grip, barely touching flesh to flesh as if I might be carrying H1N1. "I know"— his grin broadens, if possible—"ironic name for a plastic surgeon, huh? But my patients never forget it."

Marla stirs. One ice pack slides off her face onto her pillow. She lifts her hand with the IV stuck in the back of it.

The doctor edges around me to the side of the bed, touches her arm, and cups her hand between his. Dr. Scarr checks her vitals on the monitor then peruses her chart he carried tucked under his arm. "Do you remember us talking yesterday evening? After the surgery?"

Marla nods, a drainage tube sticking out of her head bobs.

"You couldn't finish?" I probe.

He scribbles a note on her chart. "Happens occasionally. We take precautions of course. Your mother . . . ?"

"In-law," I fill in the blanks for him.

He pockets his pen then checks his cell phone. "She's never had any heart problems before this."

No visible ones.

"She was a good candidate for surgery," he continues as he sends a text message. "But you never know how someone will react to anesthesia."

"Death would be better," Marla mumbles.

"Oh, Marla!" I reach for her other hand. "Don't say that."

"Marla—" He closes the chart, lays it on the side of the bed, and touches Marla's shoulder "—it's not as bad as you think."

"Not your face."

His smile never wavers. "The majority of the surgery was complete. It was only the excision of the fat pockets under the eyes that we couldn't complete." He neatly sidesteps that quagmire. How would this guy ever understand what it was like to have saddlebags or need fat excised around his eyes? "In six months you won't notice a difference at all."

"Six months." She speaks without moving her lips. "I have to hide for six months?"

"Not at all. It's going to take some time though. We talked about that before the surgery. Remember?"

"You did a full consultation before the surgery?" I cross my arms over my chest, feeling defensive of my mother-in-law. A first.

Dr. Scarr's smile congeals at my implication. "Of course. I saw Mrs. Redmond in my office where we talked about what she wanted done, what was realistic, what *wasn't*. We looked at a lot of before and after pictures to give her a better idea of what to expect."

I imagine him grinning and winking and joking until Marla simply batted her wilting lashes and agreed to anything . . . at any price. "And did you discuss the possibility of something like this happening?"

"There are always dangers during any kind of surgical procedure. She signed the consent forms."

I wish Cliff were here to ask these difficult questions, but I'm not sure he would. When Izzie was born, he simply handed out cigars to strangers and clapped the doctor on the back. What would he hand out today? Cover-up? "How long will Marla be in the hospital?"

"A couple of days for observation." He slips the chart beneath his arm and moves toward the slit in the curtain. "To be cautious, I think we'll go ahead and keep the monitors on overnight. If she continues to do as well, then she should be able to go home—"

"No!" Fear spikes Marla's voice.

The doctor halts midstride.

I lean toward her, pat her hand. "Don't you want to go home?"

She shakes her head, making the tube coming out the top of her head sway precariously.

"Easy, Mrs. Redmond." Dr. Scarr slants his magnetic gaze toward me. I have an urge to raise my hand to ward off being lured into a trap. "Sometimes patients after a lift need seclusion, where they won't be bothered by friends. They're self-conscious about the bruising and swelling."

"She lives in a retirement village. I'm sure she won't be the first to have had a facelift."

"I'll be the first disaster. Everyone"—Marla's voice sounds scratchy "—will stare."

"Maybe . . ." Dr. Scarr suggests, still staring at me as if he's found an ally. That, or he's paying me back for my pointed questions. "She could stay with you."

"What?"

"Or another family member," he tacks on as an afterthought.

Marla fixes me with her one fatty eye.

"You could stay with Cliff." I'm beginning to see my plan coming to fruition. "That's her beloved son," I explain to Dr. Scarr.

"They *were* married." Marla's voice is decisively clearer than it's been. Her use of the past tense glares like a neon sign.

"Were?" He pins me with his gaze.

Something inside me compresses, but I lift my chin a notch and meet the doctor eye-to-eye. "Yes, he's my *ex*. Okay? Marla is my *ex*-mother-in-law. But they called *me*. Of course I came to help."

McDreamy's eyebrows arch. He slides a hand in his pocket and pulls out his cell phone again.

Focusing on Marla, I smooth the sheet across her flat stomach. "Of course I'll come check on you. Every day if you need it."

She shakes her head. "Cliff works."

So do I, but I keep that surly thought to myself.

"And *that* woman is there." Now I know Marla's true feelings for Barbie, which gives me delicious reassurance. Suddenly my compassion for Marla multiplies exponentially.

The weight of Dr. Scarr's gaze makes my face swell like I'm trying to lift three hundred pound dumbbells.

"No, Barbie"—I shake my head. *"Barbara* left him. So there's plenty of room at Cliff's."

"But he's gone *all* the time." Her words are amazingly clearer, her voice stronger.

"She shouldn't be totally alone." McDreamy gives me a slow blink. I'm positive now he's getting back at me. "Are there other siblings who could bear the—" He stops abruptly and checks the Caller ID on his cell phone, then steps toward the curtain opening. "I need to take this."

I turn to Marla. Surely she'd rather be with one of her three sons. "Want me to call Chandler or Chris?"

She shakes her head, making the drainage tubes bob and weave.

Fear, guilt, and panic collide. I swallow hard. With three boys . . . men, you'd think there would be someone who could take care of Marla besides me. But Chandler moved to California with his wife. Chris went in the opposite direction with his significant other, who had even more money than his father. Their wives must be more assertive than I ever was in my marriage. But if caring for Marla means I'll see Cliff more often, then maybe it'll be worth the ordeal of having her move in with us. *Temporarily.* It is the Christian thing to do, right?

"Are we good here?" Dr. Scarr, still holding his phone, walks back toward Marla's bed.

"I can stay with her." Marla points at me.

The doctor's gaze follows her trajectory. It feels as if I'm splayed out on a slide and shoved under a microscope, all my motivations and reservations being scrutinized and catalogued. But I've also been searching for a sign from God, waiting . . . not always so patiently . . . for Him to reveal His will, His plan. Could this be it?

"Well, of course. If that's what she needs. If that's what you want, Marla, then . . ." I have to clear my throat to utter my acceptance, ". . . sure." My throat tightens and I force myself to say the rest. "You can stay with us."

Maybe this is God's answer to my prayers. Just maybe Marla living with us will bring Cliff and me back together.

⚘

Izzie turns on her heel and retreats to her bedroom, slamming the door behind her. The sound echoes through our small three bed-room house. After the divorce I had to downsize, but I insisted on finding a house with a pool so Izzie would enjoy inviting friends over. All of her friends have media rooms that rival any cinema in the area. Some have weekend homes on nearby lakes. I can't compete.

With a defeated sigh, I follow after her down the narrow hallway, scuffing my bare feet on the worn carpet. My back aches from sitting at the hospital all day. With only a cursory knock on the door, I turn the knob.

"She's not coming here, Mom! No."

"She's your grandmother."

"I don't care." Izzie shrugs a shoulder. She's lying on her bed, feet propped on the white wicker headboard.

Knowing I'm facing a brick wall, I take a detour. "Who drove you home after school?"

"Some guy."

Alarm bells go off in my head. "Does *this guy* have a name?"

"Yeah. But you don't know him. He's new."

I pick up dirty laundry off the floor, gathering it in my arms like the courage I'm going to need to once again broach the sub-ject of Marla coming here. But I'm not ready to change the subject again. "We have rules about this sort of thing."

"You were busy, remember? At the hospital. With *her.*"

I look forward to the day when we can return to communicating in complete sentences. "I'm sorry about that. I was trying to be helpful." I scoop up one of Izzie's bras off the floor. "If you told me his name, then I'd sort of be getting to know him."

"Gabe. All right?" The huffiness in her tone warns me the detour is getting rocky.

"Nice name. Is he cute?"

She shrugs one shoulder.

"Oh, come on. I *know* you notice if a guy is cute or not."

"Do you?"

I smile and try not to think back to her coach, my new client, and Marla's doctor. It's definitely been a surprising day. "Yeah."

"Okay. In a bad boy kind of way, he is."

That gets my attention. "And is he a bad boy?"

She gives me a noncommittal shrug. "I'm telling you, Mom, Marla is a nutcase. And she'll only cause trouble. You *know* how she is."

"If you'd seen her—"

"Don't *you* remember—"

"—at the hospital, then you'd feel sorry for her too."

"—what it was like?"

"Yes, Izzie, I remember." I smooth back a lock of her long blonde hair off her forehead and toy with the silky threads. "But it's the right thing to do."

Her blue eyes blaze. She glares at me from an upside-down angle then swings her legs around and sits upright. "You want him back!" It's an accusation, not a question. "Admit it."

Beneath the heat of her indignation, I can only nod. I blink back the tears threatening. "If it's the Lord's will."

She utters a word that isn't allowed in our house and definitely not in the Lord's house.

My eyebrow arches. Gritting my teeth and clenching my hands, I make an abrupt turn on my bare heel.

"Why, Mom? Don't grovel."

At the door I pause and look back, somewhat composed, but my heart still jackhammers inside my chest. "Because I made a vow. Because marriages aren't supposed to end as if they don't matter."

"I know. I know. Till death do you part. So call Annie. She'll tell you."

Annie. My best friend since fourth grade. She lives half a state away in San Antonio. I know exactly what she'd say about my plan, which is why I'm not calling. "Your father and Barbara"— I force out her real name instead of the nickname I've called her over the last year in my effort to be the grown-up here—"they broke up."

She rolls her eyes. "And Dad will go crawling back, begging, giving away more of my college tuition. And ta-da, they'll be back together. Doin' the—"

"Isabel!" My hand tightens on the doorknob.

"I'm not stupid, Mom."

I slump against the door jamb. Defeat settles over me like an iron chain around my neck. "You're right. So here's the deal. Your grandmother is coming here for a short visit and that's final. And you will be polite and helpful and make her feel welcome. Understand?"

She glares right back at me. "If you do this, I'll—"

"What?"

"Nothing," she mumbles, backing down. Relief gives me a smidgen of strength. The conversation is over but far from being resolved. She flops back on the bed, plugs in the iPod earbuds to completely tune me out, and begins texting on her cell phone.

⤙ Chapter Five ⤚

What appears to be a white gardener's truck sits in Jack Franklin's circular drive, but no logo identifies the company. Over the last year I've learned advertising is vital to business. I park my Volvo behind the truck. Rake and shovel handles stick over the edge of the tailgate. Several refrigerator-sized cardboard boxes are piled into the bed. Around the side of the house, where the battery-powered pink Barbie Jeep still remains, Jack and his son amble toward me. The giant dog lopes alongside, its black hair waving with each springy step.

I roll my window down and wave from the safety of my car. "Hi!"

Jack coils a yellow nylon rope, looping it hand to elbow. "Hello there. How'd your emergency work out?"

His son grabs the oversized puppy by the collar and lowers the truck's tailgate. The dog jumps into the bed in a seemingly effortless move.

"It's going to work out just perfectly." I smile, feeling the possibilities deep in my bones as I climb out of the car. "I'm sorry again that I had to leave so abruptly."

"No problem. Those things happen."

He gestures toward the teenage boy who swings himself into the truck's bed with an ease and agility that accentuates his age. "This is Gabe."

I realize this is Jack's truck, not the gardener's. "Hi, Gabe. We met briefly the other morning. You a Southlake Dragon?"

He rubs his temple with his thumb. "Yes, ma'am."

"What year?"

"Senior."

"My daughter's a junior."

Gabe nods but doesn't say anything else. He steps onto the lowered tailgate and pushes the oversized boxes together in the middle.

"You guys doing yard work today?" Why isn't Gabe in class? If I were Marla, I'd probably blurt out my question. But it's not my business.

"An Eagle Scout project actually." Jack loops one end of the rope through a hole in the side of the truck and hands the rest to Gabe.

"That's terrific." I eye the boxes curiously, hoping they might be filled with the pinball machines I saw the other day inside Jack's house.

"We're taking any and all volunteers." Gabe wraps the rope around the clumped boxes. "So if you're interested just show up at Kirkland's Park the next two Saturdays."

Jack forms a knot in one end of the rope, and I try to avoid watching the muscles along his arm bunch and twitch with the effort. Then he walks around the truck to the other side where Gabe hands him the other end of the rope.

"So what exactly is the project?" My gaze shifts from man to dog. The beast seems content in the truck, so I hook around the front of my own car to retrieve my books, measuring tape, and notes out of the passenger seat.

Jack pulls down hard on the rope, tightening it around the boxes to hold them firmly in the truck bed. "Tell her, Gabe. It's your project."

"We're making a park accessible to kids with special needs."

Surprised, my mouth opens briefly until I can pull my faculties together. I watch Gabe for a moment, deeply impressed. He's obviously not an ordinary teen. "What a wonderful idea."

The teen's ears turn red. He adjusts the ropes even though they don't seem to need it.

"Sounds like quite an undertaking."

Finishing the last knot in the rope, Jack turns to me. "I've got to take this over to the park and get Gabe to school. Did you want to talk about the house?"

"I'd love to when you have a chance."

"Go on in the house and look around. I won't be long. The door's unlocked."

"Sure, I'll work up some preliminary figures of what we could do and the cost. I could just leave it, and you could call me when you've had a chance to look it over."

With a warm smile, Jack jumps over the truck's side, his work boots hitting the gravel drive with a crunch. "Will do."

⁂

"Are you sick?" Izzie's voice startles me.

I turn, pushing away from the bathroom counter, toothbrush in hand. "You're up late. Or is it early?"

Izzie leans against the doorjamb. She squints against the glaring light "It's late."

"I'm sorry. Did I wake you?"

"No."

"You weren't talking on your cell phone, were you?"

"What are *you* doing, Mom?" She's wearing boxers and a skimpy T-shirt. And she didn't answer my question.

"Cleaning." I squirt more Windex on the faucet and take the toothbrush (not mine) to the grime around the edges.

"It's two in the morning!" She scratches her flat stomach, lifting the tail of her shirt enough for me to catch sight of her pierced belly button—something she did without my consent after her dad walked out. "I cleaned the bathroom yesterday, Mom. Is this about Marla?"

My hand pauses for only a beat before I rinse the brush and start in on the tile. This time, I'm the one ignoring an uncomfortable question.

"Her face is a wreck, Mom. She won't be able to give it the white-glove treatment. At least not for a few days."

I just scrub. Maybe this is a test—a motherly approval test. If I pass, maybe I can get my husband back. Maybe Marla will take my side. Cliff always does what his mother wants. I'm not saying it's a logical assessment, but it makes my arm push harder against any perceived grime around the faucet. "It's been a while since you've seen her."

"So when does Medusa arrive?"

I huff out a breath and brush my bangs off my sweaty forehead. "Tomorrow. That's why I'm—"

"She won't like the house or *you* any better. Even if you Clorox everything including the fireplace."

"I'm not trying to make her like me." It's a total lie, and we both know it.

"Uh-huh." Izzie turns on her bare heels and goes back to bed or to her cell phone. I hear the springs creak in confirmation.

I slide down the cabinet to the cold, tile floor. I feel nothing. Nothing. Just a dull *thump, thump-thump* of my pulse. Memories of when Marla came to stay with us after Izzie was born haunt me still. My own mother couldn't come for another couple of weeks as she had a full-time job and made it clear my mistake was not her problem, so Cliff's mother was waiting at our apartment like a spider on its web when I came home from the hospital, carrying a six-pound bundle in my arms.

"That's not the way to change a diaper," Marla said right off the bat.

I was a clueless nineteen-year-old. And when I say clueless, I mean in more ways than one. "They showed me at the hospital—"

"Where's the baby powder? She'll get diaper rash."

"No one uses baby powder anymore, Mrs. Redmond." That's what I called her then, when I was just a baby myself. As the years passed and my respect for her faded, I didn't refer to her in any particular way. I avoided any reference to her name if I could, sticking with *your mother* when appropriate.

She rounded on me. "Why not? Baby powder was good enough for Cliff and his brothers."

"Experts say it's dangerous for their lungs."

"Experts?" Marla scoffed. "*Mothers* are the experts. Besides, baby powder doesn't go anywhere near their lungs."

Blocking out the memory, I push back to my feet, gather my cleaning materials. It will be better this time. Time has thickened my skin and hopefully made me marginally wiser. Her words and insinuations have made her feelings plain. But now faced with the possibility of Barbie as a daughter-in-law, Marla's sure to like me better.

Or so I hope.

※

"Not that suitcase." Marla grits the words through clenched teeth, which has become her new way of speaking.

After her release from the hospital and into my custody (so to speak), we drove to her apartment. It was a solemn experience.

A pressure bandage around the rim of her face remains but might serve all of us better if it tightened her lips and prevented her from speaking. Bruises have sprouted over most of the rest in an impressive garden of colors. She moves as if in slow motion, like she finally realizes she's fragile. Of course, if she wasn't walking around in high heels, then she might be more steady.

I replace the small carry-on bag I found in her coat closet. Marla's new apartment consists of two tandem bedrooms, a compact den, and lipstick-size kitchen. It's small. Quaint, as she describes it. She recently moved into this retirement village because of the elaborate and varied activities offered with other active seniors. Where did she put all of her belongings, her antique furniture, expensive vases and dishes, oil paintings that she once had in her seven-thousand-square-foot house? It took over a year for her estate to sell, or so I heard. I recommended to Cliff she should call me to help her stage it. She did, of course, after several months. She argued every suggestion I made, but she ultimately must have incorporated a few—the house sold not long after I visited. Not that I'm taking any credit. Especially since she never paid me. Not that I wanted compensation.

"We're family!" she crowed before I could produce a bill and I didn't want to quibble over the facts.

Above the small fireplace mantel sits the gargantuan portrait of Marla she had commissioned in her thirties. She was a striking woman with aristocratic features and vibrant red hair that made her easy to spot in any crowd. And Marla always wants to stand out in a crowd. She wants to be memorable. If she wasn't before, she sure is now.

There's a scene in *The Picture of Dorian Gray*, which I read my freshman year in college, when Dorian sees himself immortalized on canvas and is so taken with how beautiful he is. Is that how Marla feels when she looks at her own portrait? Or does she only see perceived flaws? A heavy sorrow expands my heart for this woman who is obviously desperate for something of worth.

She walks up beside me, follows my gaze to her portrait, and snorts. "At least I looked good once."

"You will again." But is that another lie? Are my words hollow or filled with promise? Marla's down-turned mouth indicates she's not buying my Pollyanna routine.

"This way." She moves back toward her bedroom. "My suitcase is in there." She waves toward her closet and sits gingerly on the edge of her queen-size bed, which overpowers the room with its bold mahogany headboard and four posters.

Her clothes are lined up neatly in her walk-in closet, sectioned off by season and designer. A shrink would have a field day with her. I spot a Louis Vuitton bag on the top shelf and jump to tip it with my fingers then catch it in my arms. I set the oversized bag on her bed. "This good?"

"May not be big enough. If we need more space, I have a trunk in the attic."

"Terrific." I dare not ask how long she plans to visit, but I should probably get something in writing that she'll only stay for a week. What flack Izzie will give me when she sees me haul in this suitcase! I unzip the suitcase and begin to pack the clothes she's laid out, but something catches my eye. On the bedside table sits something I haven't seen in years—Bradford's pipe.

"It's a rusticated bent Dublin," he explained to me when I showed interest back in the early days of Cliff's and my marriage.

I reach for it, run a finger along the roughened wooden bowl. The smell bothered me back then, making me sneeze or simply stuffing up my sinuses. He'd puff away in his leather armchair, and Marla would come into his home office, jerk up the windows, and wave her arms about like a magpie. But as I grew to know Bradford, or "Dad" as I happily called him when he gave me that privilege after Izzie was born, I didn't mind his pipe smoking. In fact, it became endearing. It was the one vice Marla allowed him.

He showed me how he cleaned the pipe, scooped up the Scottish blend of tobacco, and tapped it down with his thumb before lighting it. "Would you like a puff?" I pulled back and he smiled. "Won't hurt you."

So I agreed and quickly regretted it as my throat burned, eyes watered, and lungs contracted.

His merry blue eyes twinkled as he laughed, then he fetched me a glass of cold water. "Don't worry"—he patted my back—"it won't last long. You'll be asking for a pipe in your stocking next year."

Gulping the water, I met his amused gaze. So he knew I'd bought him an expensive pipe and slipped it into his Christmas stocking without anyone knowing. The glower on Marla's face had been worth the price, but Bradford's rumbling laugh gave me the greatest pleasure.

With all the complaining Marla did about his smoking, and then harping about how his bad habit had caused his heart problems, I'm surprised she's kept it all these years after his death.

Bradford and I became partners in crime after my foray into pipe smoking. Because I loved him as the father I wanted and needed, I never questioned his elaborate pranks. He wouldn't necessarily tell me where X marked the spot, but he'd give me the chore of planting traps along the way or hiding the ticking time bomb. I learned not to laugh out loud when a bucket of water spilled on one of his boys or when toilet seats were covered in Saran Wrap. Instead I perfected a shocked, open-mouth expression, stretching my cheeks downward so they wouldn't break into a grin. Bradford carefully targeted everyone but Marla. She often laughed louder than anyone, enjoying everyone's discomfort and humiliation. Instinctively, or maybe through experience, Bradford knew not to cross that line.

But one time a joke backfired. Bradford told everyone at Marla's annual New Year's Eve bash that he had made a chili cheese dip all by himself. Everyone of course sampled the concoction and dutifully raved about it. They came back for seconds and thirds, bragging what a wonderful chef Bradford had become. But then guests began to leave early, long before midnight, rushing out the door, as Bradford's secret ingredient—bran—kicked in. Marla was not amused.

But Bradford's most endearing quality, for me at least, was that he often stepped verbally between Marla and me when she aimed her criticism in my direction. "Oh, Marla, let the kids alone. They're fine. They have their own lives now."

When he passed away five years ago from a massive heart attack, the restraining belt snapped and Marla began her full-fledged assault on our marriage.

A carefully demure cough grabs my full attention. "I'd like to get settled at your house sooner rather than later."

"Of course."

Marla leans back against her headboard, readjusting a pillow at her back and indicating the chest of drawers. "My unmention-ables are in the third drawer. Probably should take it all, just in case."

In case of what? My washer breaks? She decides to move in permanently? I pull open the drawer. The rainbow of silks and satins look more like Izzie's than my ex-mother-in-law's and appear to have come straight from Victoria's Secret. Beneath the intimate apparel are several slinky negligees made of sheer mate-rial and lace trimmed satin, peek-a-boo baby-doll styles and fly-aways, bustiers, and corsets. What kind of activities do they have in this retirement village anyway? If she wears any of these, then she'd definitely have some recovering to do. The material slides and slips through my fingers like mercury and into the luggage bag. Where are her sensible pjs? My pinky snags on a garter and I hold it up. It dances in the air like a stripper.

"Is there a problem?" Marla asks from behind me.

"Uh, no. I was . . . uh, just wondering if you were sure you'd need these."

"You can never be sure what you'll need."

Oh, really?

"Of course, I need something to wear to bed."

Okay then. Grabbing a handful, I stuff the rest of the lingerie into the suitcase, not wanting to think about it or know anymore about Marla's private life. I'd rather just keep it under lock and key.

From there I move to her closet, holding out first one outfit for her approval, then another. All seem overkill for recovering as a couch potato while watching Oprah. She discards more outfits than she approves, but finally the suitcase is full to the brim. I pray she doesn't make me climb into the attic for the trunk.

"Ready?" She props a hand on her narrow hip, tapping a bare fingernail against the seam of her A-line skirt.

"I think so." I zip her bag, tugging hard as the contents threaten to burst the seams. "You have a lot here for just a few days."

"If I need more," she says in that gritty way, "you can come back for it."

How long does she intend to stay? I match her squinty gaze, but her one remaining drainage tube bobs, tapping into my guilt. She looks like she's gone fifteen rounds with Rocky Balboa.

Who knows what she'll look like after she heals. I still don't understand why she did it. Was she so unhappy with herself, so desperate to feel beautiful? Is the competition in the retirement village *that* brutal?

I wander back into the kitchen, carrying the designer bag, which is heavier than a brick of gold out of Fort Knox. "I think we're about ready. You must be getting tired."

She waves away my comment as if it's inconsequential.

A knock at the door makes Marla gasp. Automatically I take a step toward the door.

"Don't get that."

The fear in her voice, the panic, stops me midstride. "What? Why? What's wrong?"

"Pretend we're not here."

"But—"

"Do as I say." Marla stands beside the door wide eyed (well, one eye wide, the other still squinting from the swelling), her hands splayed, forming a diminutive human barricade. Her look is more formidable than her stance. A clock in the apartment tick-tocks away the seconds, minutes.

Finally she steps sideways. "Check the door." As I peer through the peephole, she checks the front window, barely moving the drapes. "Do you see anyone?"

"Just an older man—"

She elbows me out of the way, raises up on tiptoe, and peers with her good eye through the peephole.

"I think he's probably gone now."

"We should be going. You load the car and I'll wait here until you're ready."

It feels like we're about to make a mad getaway. Actually, I'm mad for following her orders and inviting her to stay. Indefinitely!

I'm beginning to see the wisdom of my teenage daughter.

⊰ Chapter Six ⊱

Marla's stuffed-to-the-gills bag weighs as much as a Texas-sized catfish. I back through the front door, dragging the heavy bag. A deep-throated bark signals something is wrong. Either I've entered the wrong house or a burglar brought his own dog.

From the corner of my eye, I spot a furry black blur. As I fully turn, what looks like the creature from the black lagoon launches at me. I recognize the dog as the force of its paws hits me right in my middle. "What are *you* doing here?"

I wrestle my way through the door, slamming it behind me in a pathetic effort to protect Marla and her face.

"Izzie!" I elbow the beast out of my way, placing Marla's suit-case between me and those platter-sized paws. The crazy dog jumps and barks in a circle around me. "Sit!"

Surprisingly, It does. But there must be springs on its backside as it pops right back up. Four fat, furry paws prance around me. Keeping my focus on the dog, I glance around to see if Jack is nearby. But my client isn't here. Just his dog.

Izzie comes around the corner into the foyer. She sports an innocent look but registers no surprise at me being cornered. "Need help?"

"Where did this"—I push the dog off me again—"thing come from?"

"Cousin It." She grabs the collar. "That's its name. Cute, huh?"

"We've met before but—"

"You have? Where?"

I wave my hand to brush aside that unimportant topic. "Question is—how did you?" Distracted from the real problem, I glare down at the menace. My blood pressure surges. "Why is It here?"

"A friend needed a place for his dog. It's just temporary."

"Yeah, it is. Get it out of my house now."

"Dad never let me have a dog." It's the parent-versus-parent sand trap. "Come on, Mom."

"No."

"Just for a couple of weeks."

"Your grandmother is going to be here. She's outside right now. We don't have room for that . . . that . . . thing."

"If you can invite someone here without my agreeing, then why can't I?"

I square off with my daughter. This time I'm taller than she is, because she's bent at the waist holding the dog's collar. "Because I own this house. You don't."

She jerks on It's collar and drags the furry mass to a giant crate occupying half of my den. "Fine. I'll call an animal shelter."

"Izzie . . ." I regret my words. I've tried to maintain a better relationship with my daughter than the one I had with my parents and their ever-present, "Because I said so." Convenient as that might have been a few times in my daughter's life, it doesn't necessarily promote happy relations or diplomatic understanding. "Look, how do you know Cousin It anyway?"

"A guy I know."

"Gabe." I supply his name and enjoy watching Izzie's eyes widen momentarily.

"They're trying to sell their house." Her voice slows. "And he needs a place for Cousin It to stay. Temporarily."

"My new client."

"Of course. Well, good, then it helps you too."

Scowling, because I have no rebuttal for that, I stare at the beast in the crate. His—or is it a her (I can't remember)—whatever, *It's* tongue lolls out of its mouth, a pink ribbon of cuteness. I admit only to myself that the dog is kind of sweet. Frankly I have an inkling it's because I do like outdoing Cliff in this regard. But I know for a fact looks can be deceiving.

I go back to the garage. Marla stands at the side of the car looking disoriented. She props a hand on her hip. "What took you so long?"

"I'm sorry. You must be tired. Come on." I take her arm. "Let's get you settled."

She wobbles on her heels. Why didn't she just wear tennis shoes or house slippers? But that's not Marla's style. She's not about to show any weakness.

"What is that?"

Cousin It stares out from her crate, pink tongue still lolling.

"Another house guest."

"You're not going to put *me* in a crate, are you?"

Good idea. "Of course not."

When I start to pull out the sofa bed, I catch the shock in her one good eye, the fatty one. I'm being selfish. Nettled by my own good conscience, I pick up her Big Louie bag and carry it to my bedroom. Of course, I change the sheets, fluff the pillows, and invite her to "make yourself at home." This time with *my* teeth gritted.

Marla crawls into my bed fully clothed.

"Want some help?"

She sticks out a foot like I'm her newly acquired servant girl, and I tug off her three-inch heels and pray she won't use them to stab me in the back.

"Where is *she?*" Izzie whispers after she's cleaned the pool and taken Cousin It for a long walk.

"Sleeping," I pause, cutting carrots for homemade chicken noodle soup. "At least for now." I can hear Cousin It's gruff barks from the crate. She's discovered our neighbor's poodle and they like to share the local neighborhood gossip through the slatted fence.

Izzie peeks into the den then back into the kitchen. "Better not be *my* room."

"No, Iz." I present a tight smile. "Mine."

"Where are *you* gonna sleep?"

"With Cousin It. I'll take the sofa." My voice lifts in my attempt to make light of the situation. "She can have the crate."

"You're taking this well."

My automatic smile feels stiff, like I need some lubrication in the corners.

Izzie shrugs one unconcerned shoulder. "I've got a paper to write."

"Let the dog out, will you?" I call, thinking the beast needs a reprieve.

With the chicken boiling in an oversized stockpot, I set the table, taking care to make everything just right, even placing fresh flowers in a vase for a centerpiece. No tulips were available as it's the wrong season. I certainly hope I'm not.

When the phone rings, I jump toward it, not wanting Marla disturbed. Before I answer, I check caller Caller ID, hoping its Cliff. No such luck. *Unlisted.* I ignore the disappointment, which feels like Cousin It jumping on me for attention as irritation follows on its heels. Grabbing the receiver before it can ring again, I say in hushed tones, "Hello?"

"Isabel?" The rusty voice puts my motherly instinct on alert.

"No, it's her mom. Can I tell her who's calling?"

"Gabe."

"Oh, hi, Gabe. We met this morning. You and Jack . . . Mr. Franklin, were loading up the truck."

"Yeah. Course. Hi, Mrs. Redmond."

"Okay, hold on."

The oven's buzzer sounds. I silence the timer, take the chicken off the hot burner, and walk to Izzie's room. Two light taps on the door is enough of a warning. Inside her room she's lounging across her bed, earbuds in place, toes tapping against the headboard. "Iz?" I repeat it louder. "Iz? Phone's for you."

She tugs on one of the cords that attaches her to the iPod. "What?"

"Phone."

She glances at her cell phone charging on the table beside her bed.

"The regular phone." I waggle it at her.

Her brow creases. "Oh, okay." She rolls over and off the bed, landing like a cat on her feet. "Dinner ready?"

"In about thirty minutes."

Much as I'd like to eavesdrop on her phone conversation, I move to my bedroom and there I hesitate. Should I check on Marla? It's not yet time for more medicine. Closing my hand over the door knob, I question what exactly my obligations are here. Before the surgery I never would have bothered her behind a closed door. But now is different. She might be in pain, unable to call for help. Which gives me an idea.

I knock a couple of times, then open the door. Marla lies on the bed as if she's in a casket, hands clasped over her chest, eyes closed. "Marla?"

She opens one eye then closes it.

"Can I get you anything?"

"No." Her voice is weak and raspy.

My closet is a quick escape. I refuse to feel guilty since it's my own space with my own clothes and shoes. In a box toward the back, I find a little brass bell I used once for a play Izzie was in at school. "I thought this might be useful." I place the bell on the bedside table. "In case you need something . . . anything."

"Fine." She doesn't open her eye. I've been dismissed.

Still I hesitate. "Dinner will be ready soon. Are you hungry?"

"No."

"It's homemade chicken noodle soup."

No answer.

"Well . . . let me know if you need anything. Water. Your pills. An ice pack. Okay?"

Still no answer. Definitely dismissed. I slip out of the room and close the door as quietly as I can. When I reach the den, I glance out the back window and realize something is wrong. Dirt splotches the pool decking like it has just rained soil. The roots of a plant are upturned, the leaves shredded and scattered about like confetti. Mixed among them are the pink and yellow petals of my roses. Next to it all is the panting, eager face of Cousin It. Which makes me growl low and menacing at the back of my throat.

꿎

The bell was obviously a mistake on my part. I should don a uniform of some kind to complete my new role of servant. Maybe I should answer, "You rang?" in the same ghastly voice of Lurch.

"Mom!" Izzie appears in the den. I'm curled upon my new bed, exhausted from the day of being Marla's beck-and-call girl. "Did you get me cotton balls at the store today?"

"I didn't go to the store." I feel as if I didn't accomplish much today but drop the balls I've been juggling, scamper around to pick them up, rush around to help Marla, and chase after Cousin It. "Did you ask for some?"

"Yeah." The disgusted look on Izzie's face reminds me of my full-blown reaction when Cousin It dug up my roses. I took a long time-out, walking around the block to cool off my temper. I took another this morning with Cousin It in my effort to tame her. But I'm not sure who walked whom.

"I'll pick you up some cotton balls tomorrow. There may be some in my bathroom if you want to check."

"I'm not going in *there*." *There* now means where *she* is. But *she* also means Cousin It. As in, *she* has a pen. Or *she's* eating toilet paper. Or *she's* counter surfing again.

Before this week I would have considered it a toss-up as to which would be in the lead for worst house guest—Marla or Cousin It. But the dog seems to be winning. Maybe God planned it this way to give me more patience and appreciation for Marla. After all, if Cliff and I are to get back together, then I'll have to get along with his mother. At least she doesn't drink out of the toilet.

"I'll sneak in later and find some for you. Okay?"

"We have to sneak around in our own home," Izzie grumbles.

"Yes, and we also have to keep the toilet seat down and food away from the counter's edge. You can't blame your grandmother for that!"

She gives me a look—the teen kind that means I've stepped in it. She turns on her heel and heads back to her room. I follow. At least Izzie is less intimidating than Marla. And that's saying something as my daughter's temper could be considered a perfect storm at times. "I'm just trying to be considerate. Marla needs her rest."

"She always needs something."

Carefully I close the door. A crunching noise alerts me. I glare at the dog. "What's she chewing on?"

"A bone. Gabe gave me a supply at school."

"Look, Izzie, I know you're not happy about this, but we have to make the best of the situation. Can we at least try to get along? Marla hasn't done anything to hurt you."

"Lately." She crosses her arms over her chest. "Did she eat that soup you went to so much trouble to make?"

"No, but you didn't either. And she didn't eat my roses either." Ignoring her scowl, I walk toward my daughter's closet. "Can I borrow your tennis shoes?"

"Why?"

"Because I want to go for a run." It's not my usual. In fact, it's unusual. But I feel an urgent need to get out of the house. And a run or fast walk might get me back in shape before I see Cliff again. Desperate times call for desperate measures.

"A run?" Izzie stares at me as if I've just spoken Aramaic.

"Do you mind?"

"No, sure. But they're too big for you."

"I'll be okay this time. I'm not running far."

She drops her chin and stares at me. "You're running? Really running?"

I lift mine a notch. "Yeah." But under the weight of her stare I give. "Okay, walking."

Her mouth curves in a satisfied smile. "Do you want to borrow some shorts?"

"I'd probably be arrested for indecent exposure." I pull socks out of her drawer and shoes out of the closet, which, ironically, I put away earlier in the day before Cousin It helped herself to a leathery snack.

"You know, Mom, it's kind of late to be going for a walk."

"I'll be fine." It actually feels good to have my daughter worrying about my safety rather than the other way around.

"It's dark."

"So?"

"You always tell me not to go out at night alone."

The words slither around my brain, strike me as odd. Now she's biting back at me with my own words. "I'll take Cousin It. Okay?"

"Whatever."

The irony that Cousin It is the reason I need to get out is not lost on me as I grab the leash. She bounds around me, a seventy-or-more-pound bouncing ball. Her barks echo off the entryway ceiling.

"Shh." I try to shush her before she wakes Marla. Before I lose my chance to escape for even a few minutes. It finally sits near my feet, her tail brushing the tile and thumping against the wall.

I push open the front door and step into the darkness. The warm night envelopes me with scents of gardenias and damp grass. Sniffing freedom, Cousin It bolts. The leash jerks my arm, and I follow, my feet *thump, thump, thumping* along the sidewalk as I trip and stumble along in the oversized shoes. Prancing and dancing around me, It manages to tie me up like a hostage. Oh sure, this is safe. Anyone who wants to assault me can find me already hog-tied. I wiggle and turn, unwrapping myself from the leash. It barks. The sound rebounds off the rooftops. In the distance, other dogs answer her.

With the warmth of the fall day still heavy in the air, I begin running. It yanks me forward. Two houses later, my legs burning, my lungs exploding, I stumble to a halt, grab my pinched side. My workouts stopped about the time Cliff left. I never could find the energy or time to lift weights or take a jog around the block. My membership to a workout facility, of course, had to be dropped as my financial situation changed. Now, I suck in oxygen like it's on sale.

But Coach It hasn't finished with my workout. She tugs on the leash and I stumble forward. We walk and walk and walk. She darts right then left, sniffing at each mailbox as if she might be tracking the postman or expecting a letter. When my pulse slows close to normal, I attempt jogging again. Two houses more,

I stop, gulp air, then walk again. I repeat this around the block three times until both of our tongues hang out, though thankfully mine doesn't drip slobber, and we find ourselves back at our starting point.

I stare at the outline of our house presented by the moon. It has a low-lying roof, square windows, red bricks. *Southern Living* would never stop here to take a photo. The house is over thirty years old. It's small, but it's all mine. Everything Cliff and I bought together over the years was with *his* money, whatever he earned or borrowed from his parents. Now I am earning a living on my own. I was thrilled to find a house with a yard large enough for a pool for Izzie.

I contemplate going to see my friend, Terry, whom I haven't seen in months. Or has it been longer? She lives in the same exclusive neighborhood as Jack Franklin, in her Tara-esque mansion. It wouldn't be but a ten-minute walk. I'm sure Cousin It is up for it. But I'm not sure I am. Besides my hair is matted with sweat. What would I say anyway? Maybe, "Do you ever feel like running away?" But I know her answer. Why would she run from her perfect life, husband, daughter, and house? She'd also tell me I brought my *ex*-mother-in-law on myself. So would my best friend, Annie, which causes me to nurse my misery in private.

For a long while I study this place I now call home. All I see are things that need fixing, kind of like staring into a mirror and seeing only the threadlike wrinkles appearing between my eyebrows and at the corners of my eyes, sun blotches, freckles, a gray hair sneaking into my brown. My house needs a fresh coat of paint and some of the bushes replaced. I need moisturizer, hair dye, and tweezers.

Let's face it, we both need a facelift.

The irony strikes me as funny, but I'm too tired to laugh.

The sound of laughter leaps out from down the darkened street and grabs me. Cousin It jumps to her feet, barks and lunges toward the noise. My skin contracts.

"Kaye? Is that you?" A familiar voice reaches out to me from across the street. I feel guilty for my instinct to duck and run. But it's too late.

"Terry!" I yank back on the leash as It lunges and barks. "What a coincidence, I was just thinking about you." I jerk the leash hard. "Sit." She doesn't.

"Did you get a dog?" Terry slows, her hand clasped in her husband's, and stands across the street from me. Miles shifts from one foot to the other as if anxious to move on.

"Oh, it's a temporary situation. How are you?"

Terry glances at her husband. "We're okay. Just enjoying a few minutes together."

"It's good to see you." Suddenly, I feel like a third wheel . . . with a furry sidekick.

"Call me!" She and Miles move past. Over her shoulder she adds, "We need to catch up."

I nod and watch them move into the darkness. Cousin It's barking rings out into the night. I sit down on the curb, the over-sized tennis shoes in the street, and Cousin It butts up against my hip. I place an arm around her narrow but furry shoulders. "Well, at least I have you. Temporarily."

⚜

The flash of headlights alerts me to a car coming down the street. I wrap Cousin It's leash tighter around my hand. Already she's on her feet, her furry body quivering with the feral urge to give chase. Surprisingly the headlights slow, blinding me for a moment. I scramble to my feet as the truck pulls in front of my house. Cousin It carries on as if I'm going to be dragged off. Her eagerness to defend me would be semisweet, that is, if her raucous bark and jerking on the leash wasn't so annoying. If only Cliff had defended our marriage so nobly.

The driver's door opens and out steps Jack. Instinctively I step behind the mailbox and wish it were larger instead of just a cantankerous pole that leans slightly toward the street. "Hi!"

"Sorry to bother you so late." He walks toward me, bending at the waist to greet Cousin It. "Hey, big girl, how are you?"

Behind them, the passenger door opens, and Gabe emerges. He waves at us but heads toward the front door.

"Gabe needed to borrow a book from your daughter. And I thought I'd bring this contract by."

"Oh! Sure. No problem. Isabel didn't tell me you were coming." Or I would have put my suit back on instead of leaving on jeans and Izzie's oversized tennis shoes. Thank the Lord good sense prevailed and I didn't take her up on her offer and wear *her* shorts around the neighborhood, which seems to have turned into Grand Central Station tonight. I jerk back on the leash as Cousin It strains forward.

But Jack leans over, producing a hand for the dog to sniff and then lick. He smiles and rubs the furry head. "Thanks for taking care of Cousin It for us."

"No problem. I didn't know Gabe and Izzie were friends."

Kneeling, Jack pats the dog. "I think they just met." He glances upward at me, studying me for a long moment that makes my insides crimp. "Isabel said it was okay for It to crash here—she did ask you, didn't she?"

"In her own way." I smile, this time my smile not quite so tight.

"She isn't being any trouble, is she?"

"Trouble?" My smile freezes in place as I recall my shredded roses. "Not at all." As if to prove I've forgiven her, I lean forward and brush the top of her moppy head with my fingers, accidentally grazing Jack's arm. "Nope. It's fine." I rub my fingers against my jeans. "Good."

He stands upright. "You don't strike me as the dog type."

"I used to have a dog a long time ago. When I was in college. Her name was Brontë. She was an English bulldog."

"Which sister?"

"Emily."

His mouth pulls to one side. "So, you have a dark side."

"Don't we all?"

He laughs and pulls a rolled set of papers from his hip pocket. After he carefully unfolds it, he hands me the contract.

I glance down at his bold, confident signature and notice he changed the amount—making the sum he owes larger. Beside the tacked-on excess fee he wrote—Cousin It Boarding. "You didn't have to do that."

He glances down at the dog. "Oh yeah. She's not a simple houseguest."

His thoughtfulness surprises me. What would Cliff have done in a similar business deal? Would he have added on a charge he'd have to pay? Or would he have assumed his good fortune? Probably the latter. Jack is definitely a different type of man. "Did you have any questions?"

"Seems straightforward. How soon can we get started?"

"You're in a hurry." It's more a confirmation to my suspicions than a question.

"I thought you would be."

In question, I tilt my head.

"To get rid of Cousin It."

I laugh but feel the reality of caring for the monster dog, as well as Marla, settle into my bones. "I'll get furniture ordered tomorrow morning."

"Fine." His gaze feels heavy.

Maybe it's only my imagination, this awkwardness that springs up between us, probably my paranoia and needs arcing through the dark landscape of my social life like a search light.

Last week I was in Barnes and Noble and the checkout guy asked for my license to verify my credit card.

"Nice picture." He studied my ten-year-old driver's license picture a moment too long. Then his bushy-browed gaze shifted toward me.

I snatched my license out of his hand. "It's old." About ten years and twenty pounds ago. I tucked my license back into my wallet and grabbed my bag. "Thanks."

"Mom!" Izzie nudged my shoulder as we turned away from the counter. "He was flirting with you."

"No, he wasn't."

"Yes, he was."

I stole a glance over my shoulder and sure enough the man with gray hair and thick glasses was watching me instead of paying attention to the next customer. Then I smacked my shoulder on the door Izzie had opened for me. "Ooh, Mom! You're putting out vibes. Good for you!"

A blush blooms inside of me now as I feel Jack's heady gaze upon me like a warm caress. I glance away from him. I'm not putting out vibes. I'm not interested in dating. I'm working on getting my husband back.

In that brief instant of self-indulgent introspection, Cousin It pounces forward, placing two big paws on Jack's chest, which doesn't knock him back a step or make him grimace.

His smile remains steady and real. "Miss you too, baby girl."

Cousin It jumps and licks, while Jack dodges that pink tongue.

I yank on the leash, irritated more at myself and my own foolhardiness than the beast.

Jack laughs and rubs the dog's sides and back, then he takes the leash from me, our hands brushing. "Let me. She can be a handful."

He takes her through several commands—sit, down, roll over, come—all of which she obeys quickly and eagerly.

"How come she doesn't do that for me?"

Jack plants a knee on the ground, a solid hand on Cousin It's back, and peers up at me. "You have to show her who's the boss. Be alpha dog."

My brow pinches together. "I've always been the roll-over-and-submit kinda gal."

His eyes twinkle as a smile spreads across his face. "Maybe she'll be good for you and teach you a few new tricks."

"Alpha dog, huh?" I laugh, enjoying the taste of the words and the powerful feelings they invoke.

"That"—Jack pulls something from his pocket—"and liver treats." He holds out the little block on his palm and Cousin It gulps it down. "She'll do anything for a liver treat. Just not too many."

"Or she'll get fat?"

He shakes his head and pats It. "Gas."

The sound of the front door slamming echoes through the neighborhood.

Jack winces. "Hope Gabe and Isabel didn't have a fight."

But neither Gabe nor Izzie emerge from the shadows. Instead, Marla steps onto the edge of the top step into the porch light. At her glare, I cringe.

"*What* is going on here?" Her fists are mounted on her narrow hips. A soft fall breeze ruffles her yellow negligee. "Is there some sort of disaster?"

I step even with Jack, noticing his eyes widen at the sight of her. "I'm sorry, Marla. We'll be quiet. I promise."

Jack dips his chin just slightly and his features compress as he stares at the formidable, alien-like creature on my porch.

"Well, I should hope so. I came here to get rest, not be the watchdog of the neighborhood."

"We're sorry, ma'am." Jack's smile fixes as if Botox has been administered and he can no longer move those muscles. "We didn't mean to disturb you."

Marla gives him a dismissive glance and focuses on me. "You'll just have to tell your boyfriend to come back later."

"Boyf—? Uh, no." I take a decisive step away from Jack. "You don't understand."

She gives a condescending wave as if she is returning to her throne. "Just keep the noise down."

Cousin It gives a resounding bark.

Marla turns back, narrows her gaze on the back-talking beast. She bares her teeth and a low growl emerges from her throat. It takes a step back and whimpers. A moment later the front door closes, the sound echoing through the neighborhood.

Jack slowly faces me. His features are blank as if he's been stunned. "What happened to her?"

"Facelift."

"Ouch." He rubs the back of his neck.

"They show before and after pictures, but not *during* for a reason."

A smile breaks through his shock. "She has the right attitude for what we were talking about."

"Alpha dog?"

"Was she Darth Vader?"

I tilt my chin downward to hide a smile. "Good guess."

"And she's living with you?" He holds a hand up. "Sorry. Not my business."

"I roll over, remember?" Or maybe I am doing what I want, taking action to get Cliff back. Maybe I need to be more aggressive in that regard. "It's temporary. Very temporary while she recovers from surgery."

"That's cool."

I stare at him. "Not cool at all. She's driving me crazy."

"I meant," he amends, "cool that she trusts you enough, thinks highly enough about you to depend on you. That says a lot about you as a person."

I rub my forehead where a headache is gathering like storm clouds. "I don't know about that. More likely it says I'm a sucker."

His gaze settles on me, his eyes narrowed, but it doesn't feel judgmental. In fact, it feels too much like how men used to look at me. That look of interest and discovery. A look that makes my insides flip over like a gooey pancake. "I don't buy that at all, Kaye." The rumbling of his voice rattles me. "It's okay to admit you're a nice person."

"To tell you the truth, I have personal motivations in taking Marla in." My confession will put a strong barrier between us and let Jack know exactly where I stand. "I'm hoping this will lead to reconciliation with my ex."

His gaze never wavers. There's not a flicker of disappointment or pity. But he steps toward me. "Now that's a noble cause."

The front door opens again, and Gabe jogs out toward the truck carrying a book under his arm.

"Time to go." Jack smiles. "You'll call me when the furniture is in?"

I nod, unable to say anything else, confused by an odd hybrid of disillusionment and empowerment.

⚜ Chapter Seven ⚜

My eyes ease open as a male voice penetrates my sleep-fogged brain. I blink and focus on an angry, frustrated discussion. Who could be angry this early unless they, too, were awakened? Then I catch something about the president, his staff, the White House.

Is Cliff here? He watches CNN and listens to talk radio, usually hurling insults at the talking heads. I throw back the covers and leap to my feet, trip over the blanket, which must have slipped off the side of the sofa bed. Prayer will have to be on the run today. I stumble forward to investigate the jarring voices and pans rattling in the kitchen.

Marla, dressed in a blue robe, actually more a negligee with flowing sleeves and lacy additions, fuzzy slippers with heels, an anomaly I can't quite grasp this early, along with her newly acquired head gear in place, rearranges a cabinet. I glance around the kitchen, which isn't big enough to hide a melon baller, and realize she's alone . . . except for me. No Cliff. From the radio on the counter come the angry male voices, which jangle my nerves as the talk show moves into a commercial and the volume escalates.

From the doorway I watch my ex-mother-in-law move cautiously from side to side, bending her knees, not stooping to reach things down low, not lifting her chin to reach up high, deftly keeping her drainage tube even and steady. Quite a balancing act. Maybe she could audition for Cirque du Soleil. Or a freak show since she resembles *My Favorite Martian*. Still, she makes me feel like a sloth with my mismatched faded red T-shirt and orange threadbare pajama bottoms.

"Marla?" I reach for the volume knob on the radio.

"Good morning!" Her voice sounds chipper despite her gritting her teeth. How does she manage to appear regal with a lopsided antenna bobbing above her swollen left eye? She places a juice glass in a cabinet that contained spices before her arrival. To deal with this, I should have taken an hour or longer for prayer. *Lord, help me!*

I finger my right temple, which has begun to throb. "What's going on?"

"Thought I'd get breakfast started." She pulls the silverware bin out of the dishwasher. "Isabel should eat heartily before her swim."

"You're supposed to be resting." I manage a calm tone, then add a command as if she's Cousin It. "Go. Rest. Please." Thankfully I hold back what I long to say: *Get out of my kitchen!* Instead I offer, "I'll fix breakfast if you're hungry." And she probably is since she didn't touch the homemade chicken noodle soup I made especially for her. I steer her toward the kitchen table where she sits, poised on the edge of a chair.

"I had my yogurt." She touches her flat stomach. "Don't want to need a tummy tuck too." She gives a slight glance in my direction and I do a quick intake to suck in the dome that has emerged across my once flat belly. Too many late-night snacks since Cliff left. Too many stress snacks—the refrigerator offering comfort when I had no solutions for money troubles, loneliness, and raising a teen all alone.

I close the dishwasher and the cabinet, lean heavily on the counter as I get my bearings. I feel as if I've been on one of those spinning rides at the Texas State Fair and the fried butter, fried pickles, and corn dogs are backing up on me. Picking up an egg from the carton, I fold my hand around its coolness. "Did you want an egg?"

Marla taps her fingers on the edges of her knees. "I was *about* to boil some."

A yawn takes over me for a full ten seconds. "Okay." I spot a pan on the stove, the water starting to boil, and plop three eggs into the roiling bubbles. "Did you sleep well?"

"Those pills work like a dream. Think I'll keep taking them after I've recovered. No more tossing and turning."

My eyebrow arcs automatically, but I refrain from stirring the pot. After all, Marla seems to be in a good mood. Instead, I focus on a foil-covered pan. "What's this?"

"I made a casserole for dinner." She indicates the dish on the table next to her. "We need to put it in the oven an hour before we want to eat."

"Marla, you're a guest. You don't have to–"

"I would have called takeout, but I couldn't find any menus. This, however"—her hands bracket the pan—"is Cliff's favorite."

My heart kicks up a notch. "Is he coming?"

"I haven't called him yet. But don't you think he should?"

Oh, yeah, I do. The sooner the better! Then I glance down at my pathetic pjs and revise that thought to: *After I shower and shop for a new outfit!* "I better wake Izzie. It's almost time to leave for swim practice."

"I already woke her." Marla rises. "She should be ready any minute."

I want to ask how she managed that feat, but refrain.

"You shouldn't let Isabel sleep with that nasty dog in her bed."

"Dog?" My brain begins to clear as I remember Cousin It. "She's always wanted a dog," I defend my acquiescence last night when Izzie begged to take It to her room instead of putting her in the crate.

"They're smelly and carry vermin."

"Vermin?"

"Fleas." Marla shivers. "You cannot keep a house clean with animals living with you. It's like living in a barn."

As if on cue, the jangle of a collar precedes Cousin It's arrival. She comes bounding around the corner and jumps at me, but I yell, "No!"

She plants all four feet back on the floor but noses my leg, her tail whipping back and forth.

Satisfied and pleased with my forthrightness, I pat her head. "Good, girl. She is cute though."

"Cliff hates dogs."

I frown. "Yes, I know. But she's a *temporary* guest." As is Marla. But Cliff will be permanent.

"I certainly hope so."

She's not the only one. Cousin It sniffs at the table, just beneath the casserole. Before I can utter a sound, she rears up and places her paws on either side of the foil pan.

"Stop that!' Marla shrieks. "You *beast.*" She swats at Cousin It's round, furry backside with a slotted spoon.

I reach forward, grab It's collar. "Come on, let's go *out.*"

"Do you think she ruined the casserole?" Marla frets over the crinkled foil.

"It was covered." I tug the dog toward the back door, but she puts on the brakes. Suddenly I'm embracing the dog's middle and hefting her forward. When she catches a sniff of the cool morning air, she breaks free and runs outside. I close and lock the door, feeling the need for a tanker to pull up beside me and dump a load of caffeine straight into my veins. I rub my back where the metal bar in the sofa bed attacked me all night and walk back into the kitchen. "Do you want some coffee, Marla?"

"I gave up coffee. It's not healthy. Causes wrinkles, you know."

"No, I, uh, didn't." But then without coffee, I can't see my wrinkles in the mirror.

"I should have brought some of my herbal teas. You'd probably sleep better without all that caffeine."

I'd probably sleep better in my own bed too. Feeling a bit rebellious, I fill the coffeepot with water, grab the coffee tin, and pour the aromatic grounds into the filter. Wrinkles are the least of my worries today.

"Two scoops is enough, dear," Marla advises from her managerial spot at the table.

I attempt a smile, which doesn't quite emerge. Is this what Cinderella had to put up with?

"At least that's how I used to make it for Bradford and Cliff. The other boys never drank coffee much." She rolls a wrist. "But Cliff thought I made the best coffee in the world. Never a complaint!"

But I'm about to.

"I better check on Izzie." As I leave the room, Marla mumbles about how I shouldn't call my beautiful daughter a name that sounds like a lizard.

But I'm not nearly as hotheaded over Marla's comments as Isabel who is cramming clothes in her bag. I sigh. Each morning dawns with the question: what mood inhabits my daughter this morning?

"What is it with *her*? She told me last night I should style my hair. What does she want? Hot rollers? Or one of those stinky perms?"

I tsk and settle on my daughter's soft bed, pull the covers up over me, and enjoy the comforting warmth for a moment. I'm tempted to stay right here all day. "I'm sorry."

"She went through my closet this morning and told me what to wear!"

"Really?"

"She wanted me to wear hose, Mom. Hose! And a dress I wouldn't wear unless it was Easter. Or a funeral. And only if you made me."

"It's okay, Iz. She has different standards. It's been a while since she was in high school or had high schoolers."

"Obviously. My friends would think I'm a freak."

"We wouldn't want that. Breakfast is almost ready. Marla thinks you should eat before you swim."

"I'll throw up."

"Aim in her direction."

That coaxes a smile from Izzie.

With a flick of my wrist, I toss back the covers. It doesn't take much effort to make the bed. Then I place an arm around her shoulders. "This is temporary."

⚜

After school I pick Izzie up and head home. It's been a long day of transporting Marla to a doctor's appointment, picking up more prescriptions, buying lunch for her at the restaurant, which sells her favorite chicken noodle soup. Because of course mine didn't compare. I stayed out of the house for a couple of hours, giving Marla privacy and me a little peace.

Cousin It greets me in the backyard with muddy paw prints on my silk blouse. After wrenching free and pushing through the back door before Cousin It can follow, I stare out the mud-smeared window.

Marla walks over and stands beside me. "She's been digging."

Izzie sniffs me. "And it smells like—"

"Well, keep her out! So she doesn't get it all over the house." I step away from window. "How long has she been outside?"

"Since you left."

"All day?" Iz complains.

"Not quite," I play referee. "But long enough obviously."

"I'm not a dog sitter," Marla snaps.

She wasn't much of a babysitter either. If Cliff asked her to watch the baby so we could go out one night, Marla would say, "You made your bed."

"Guess I'll go take a shower." I glance down at my muddy clothes and hands and get a whiff of my new fragrance.

But Marla beats me to my bathroom, so I settle for Izzie's. Maybe Marla needs to powder her nose. Good thing she didn't have rhinoplasty. It would make for a slow recovery as she likes to stick her snout in everyone's business.

Before I can indulge in a hot, steaming shower, the warm spray hitting the plastic curtain, the doorbell rings. Izzie is outside bathing the dog, hosing off the decking, and cleaning up the mess. I can hear Cousin It barking like a gang of robbers is about to storm the house. I wait, hoping Marla will get the door but the ringer sounds again.

"Who could that be?" I wrap a beach towel around my nakedness and hope it's only FedEx delivery. The deadbolt resists but I wrestle it open. It's not until the lock clicks that I contemplate my foolishness. It could be Cliff. And toweled up is not the impression I want with my ex. Or maybe it is. But it could be a client. Not professional. Thankfully the man is a stranger. I poke my head out the door opening, edging my body as far back as possible. "Hello?"

A stately gentleman in gray suit and sky-blue tie stands on my front porch. He has silvery, wavy hair and a decisive jaw. He carries a vase of perfect red roses. Even the roses are dressed for the occasion, each with a tiny satin bow tied around the bud. Baby's breath and greenery fill in gaps between two dozen or more stems.

"Good morning." His tone is cultured. "I apologize for the surprise visit."

My towel begins to slip and I secure it in place with one well-placed hand. Squinting against the bright sunlight, I decide he's not a delivery boy.

"My name is Anderson Sterling. I'm a friend of Marla's. This *is* the right house, isn't it?" He glances above my head to the brass numbers screwed into the door frame. "Marla Redmond is staying here, is she not?"

"Uh, yes."

"Is she available? I'd like to give her these roses."

"I'll tell her you're here." I close the door, but jerk it back open. "Just a minute. I'll be right back." Again, I close the door, readjust my towel, and digest this new information. A friend, huh? More like a *boy*friend. Odd feelings swirl through me—surprise, indignation, hope. I'm not sure which to latch onto. I decide on hope. Hope that Marla will be distracted by some man's attention rather than paying attention to my plans for her son.

"Who is it?" Izzie stands in the hallway in her bikini, wet from head to toe, and holding a hairy, muddy towel.

"Someone for your grandmother. A beau." I whisper the last part.

Izzie blinks and the corner of her lip curls. "Really? That's gross."

It isn't quite my reaction. I don't trust what impression Marla might make on my impressionable about-to-start-dating daughter. I grip my towel to my chest and knock on my bedroom door. "Marla?"

"Yes?"

I find her sitting at the dressing table. It sounds luxurious but in reality it's just a bit of counter space with a place for a stool. Marla's staring at the mirror with a forlorn look. But with her bandages, I'm not sure any other look is possible. She doesn't turn her head in my direction, but her gaze slides toward me, her one good eye widening slightly. "Is something wrong, Kaye?"

"No." But I feel the opposite. And I'm not exactly sure why.

She fingers the edge of a silver rimmed tray that holds a couple of bottles of perfume Cliff gave me along with makeup and moisturizer. I notice she's rearranged things.

"Do you want to shower?"

"There's someone at the door. To see you."

Marla's chin lifts in a tiny gesture of triumph, then she grimaces. She touches the opening of her negligee, gliding her fingers along her neckline. Then I watch her throat convulse. Her fingers probe the edge of the pressure bandage. "Oh! Oh, no. I'm not here."

Are we reverting to junior high school?

"I didn't invite him." Her uncanny sense of who is waiting on the porch makes me suspicious.

"Him?"

"Anderson." She swivels the stool away from me, but I catch a glimpse of her profile, down-turned and pathetic. A twinge of sympathy pinches me. She puffs out little breaths, her back rounding with each one.

I reach out to her, my hand midair. "Are you all right?"

Slowly, her shoulders straighten. "Yes, yes, of course." But her hand trembles. "Please tell Mr. Sterling that I'm indisposed."

"But, Marla—"

"Please." Is that desperation in her tone? She faces me again. Her lips compress into a firm line of resolve.

"Are you feeling ill?"

"He's waiting."

"Then, should I—"

"Tell him thank you, but I'm not ready to see visitors as of yet."

Or she's not ready for them to see her. "Are you sure?"

She gives a slight nod.

"All right." I turn but she stops me with a purposeful clearing of her throat. "Did you change your mind?"

Her gaze shifts along my oversized towel and bare feet. "You are going to put on a robe, right?"

"He's waiting outside."

"No telling what kind of a place he'll believe this is."

In an effort to find levity in this bizarre situation, I give her a mischievous smile and bounce my hip a couple of times. "Are you worried I'll be a distraction?"

Marla turns away from me. "Now you're beginning to sound like my other daughters-in-law. They have no shame."

"I was—" But I halt that apology mid-sentence. Her number-one manipulative technique has always been to pit me against Cliff's brother's wives. Not this time. God has been teaching me so much since Cliff left, but I never knew I'd be tested with Marla once again. I square my shoulders, confidence growing. Knowing how to handle Marla will only help Cliff and me when we're once again married. So without another word, I turn and walk back to the front door. With a slight detour past Izzie's room, I grab a robe from her closet. It's silky and not my usual comfy fluffy oversized one, but it'll do.

"What now?" Izzie asks.

"Nothing. Just covering, so to speak, for your grandmother so she doesn't have to face her boyfriend yet."

When I open the front door again, I blink back my surprise. Not only is Mr. Sterling still waiting, but he has a male companion. I sense Izzie approaching from behind. But Cousin It sticks her nose under the back of my robe. My "hi" escalates as I bat her nose away.

My gaze shifts expectantly between the two men.

"Hello there." The shorter man standing next to Marla's first suitor grins. "I'm Harry Klum. Thought I'd give Marla a visit."

"Oh, I see." Is the retirement village she moved into the swinging singles of the AARP? Is the competition so fierce Marla believed she needed plastic surgery? Yet it appears she has the pick of the crop. Or at least an abundance of pickers.

Mr. Sterling stands tall, debonair with firm creases in his suit and shine in his polished shoes. But the other gentleman looks frumpy. Can a man be frumpy? This one is short, a bit shaggy around the edges, the seams of his clothes stretched to their limit.

I doubt his faded blue button-down shirt or stretch-waist, warm-up pants have ever been introduced to an iron. He looks familiar though. He holds a bunch of mismatched flowers still bundled in plastic, grocery-store wrapping.

"Well, Mr. Klum . . . Mr. Sterling, Marla isn't feeling well enough to see visitors just yet."

The skin between Mr. Sterling's brows pinches slightly, then smooths out. He offers the crystal vase of roses to me. "If you'd be so kind as to give her these."

"Yep"—Mr. Klum's forehead crinkles and remains so—"these too."

"Of course. And well, thank you, gentlemen. I'm sure Marla appreciates your thoughtfulness and concern."

The taller man turns and walks toward the black Escalade parked along the curb. When the huge SUV pulls away from the curb, it reveals another—a station wagon with fake wood siding, faded and worn, dating back to the seventies. It must be Mr. Klum's car.

"Uh, Miss . . ." Mr. Klum shuffles his scarred brown loafers on the concrete.

"Yes?"

"Is she, I mean, Miss Marla gonna be all right?"

"She's fine. It will take time for her to heal."

He scratches his mostly bald head, just a few strands of gray hair are combed over the top. "Tell her she's missed at the village."

"I will." When I close the door, juggling the vase and the bouquet of flowers, I find Izzie, Cousin It, and Marla waiting in the foyer.

Izzie stares at her grandmother. "You've got *two* boyfriends?"

"I wouldn't say that, dear. Oooh!" Marla reaches forward and takes the roses from me. "How utterly beautiful."

"Those are from Mr. Sterling."

She breathes in the sweet, tender scent that was making my nose itch and touches the little ribbons on each bud. "He has such exquisite taste." To Izzie, she says, "Always go for the money, dear. It can't buy you everything you want, but it sure doesn't hurt."

"Uh, Marla . . ." I distract her from dispensing any more sage advice by holding out the bunch of flowers, its plastic protection crinkling. "These are from Harry Klum."

Marla sighs and frowns at the water dripping from the wet paper towel wrapped around the cut stems. The doorbell rings again. A panicked expression widens Marla's good eye. She grimaces, then shifts her features back into neutral. "Who is that?"

"More boyfriends you'd like to tell me about?" I imagine a busload of suitors from the retirement village pulling up outside. My house, I decide, would make an interesting day trip for retirees.

Marla takes a step backward. "I'm not here."

That's usually Izzie's line. Maybe Marla will prove to my daughter how immature that response is. Or its validity.

"Yes, you are." I place my hand on the knob. "But don't worry. I'll cover for you." Again.

"What will you say?" She edges around the corner into the hallway and out of sight.

"That you're resting."

"Okay." She disappears.

"Or whacked out on medication."

Izzie grins at me.

Marla pokes her head around the corner again. "Kaye—"

"Kidding. I'll just tell him the truth."

She points a shaky finger at me. "Don't you dare."

No, no. We wouldn't want to speak the truth. At least I know I'm not the only one that lies to myself. Obviously God has more work to do with me.

But the comparison with my mother-in-law unsettles me.

⤦ Chapter Eight ⤧

The second I open the door, I scold myself for not checking through the peephole first. Standing in my daughter's bathrobe is not the way I want to greet a suitor of a younger generation. Or *any* generation, I suppose. Whereas I was amused with Marla's suitors and maybe a little irritated for the benefit of her dearly departed husband who I adored, *this* new visitor puts my mother-bear instincts on full alert.

Propping a hand on a hip in a motherly defensive move, I stare at Gabe. His gaze dips and instant sunburn scorches his face. I follow, glancing down at Izzie's robe, which has gaped open, revealing too much cleavage. I clutch the opening in a fist.

"Is Isabel home?"

"Are you and Izzie going for a run?"

"Yeah." She brushes past me and out the door. She's already changed into shorts and a tank top. "Bye, Mom."

"Wait!"

She turns around, walking backwards away from me, but doesn't slow her pace. "I'll be back later. Don't worry."

That usually translates into parental language as *WORRY*. Actually I was going to suggest she take Cousin It for protection and for the dog to expend some energy. Then all the questions I should ask before Izzie goes off with some boy, like to see

Gabe's driver's license and check police records, cause a pileup in my brain like a traffic jam. I step out of the doorway to wave them down, but they're already running down the street, their long legs matching each other stride for stride.

"It's good for Isabel to see boys." Marla stands behind me in the foyer. "She's certainly old enough."

I close the door, harder than I normally would.

"She's pretty enough to have them lined up around the block if she'd only take a little care with her appearance."

Slowly I turn and face my ex-mother-in-law and give a tolerant half smile. *Don't say anything, Kaye. Do not engage the enemy.* It's a debate I can't win. "I better go take a shower."

"Yes, you should. Before any more visitors arrive."

Like Cliff. My half-smile congeals. *Keep walking, Kaye. Just keep walking.*

"Are *you* seeing anyone, Kaye, besides that man who was here the other night?"

That stops me. "No, no I'm not." I regret my defensive tone. But I truly hate that question. I hear it all the time from old acquaintances, which implies I'm a loser if I haven't latched onto someone since Cliff left. "Besides I told you, Jack's a client."

"Really." The way she says that word is more like *of course.* "It's been two years."

"Fifteen months." What's the deal? Is there a time limit on letting go of a marriage vow? God doesn't have time limits, does He? Nothing is impossible with Him.

"That's plenty of time to get back in the game. Of course, you're probably still pining over Cliff. That's understandable. He's quite a catch. But honestly, he's interested in"—her gaze trails over my scantily clad and lumpier than usual form—"greener pastures."

My shoulders stiffen and my eyelids prickle with sudden tears. She hit the bull's-eye with that remark. I scramble to come up with a crushing reply, but I don't have one. Which only makes me feel even more inadequate.

"And, I hate to say this, Kaye, but that may be your problem."

"Oh really?" *Kaye! What are you doing? Be quiet. Disengage. Retreat! Retreat!* I cross my arms over my chest as if that can protect me and can't seem to stop myself from asking, "And what's that?"

"You have let yourself go in the past year. Why, I was actually stunned when you came to my house a few months ago. Stunned. Not that you were ever modelesque in appearance. But you presented yourself well enough before, or so . . ."

My hand automatically reaches up to touch my hair, which I haven't had cut in a while and my roots are showing at least three inches worth. I slap my hand down to my side. "Well, I should take a shower. So I'll be more presentable."

With as much dignity as I can manage, I sweep into Izzie's bathroom, step over the towel she left on the floor, shut the door, and turn the water in the shower on to block out any crying sounds I might make.

But I don't cry. Instead, I give myself a hard look in the mirror. This is not recommended at any time of day. With or without daylight.

Is that why Cliff left? Because of the way I look? Because of some inherent flaw? It doesn't matter now why it happened. What matters now is getting him back. And would he come back with me looking like this? Maybe Marla is right (for the first time ever). Maybe I should focus on me just a little bit more. In order to save my marriage.

And so I make a desperate, this-is-an-emergency call to my hair stylist. I'd call Marla's handsome surgeon but there isn't time before dinner. But I splurge and get a manicure and pedicure along with a new outfit.

Just in case Cliff does show up.

※✲※

"What happened to you?" Izzie asks when we all end up home together later in the evening. Cousin It leaps around me like she's eaten jumping beans.

"What do you mean?" But I know. I'm just being coy, actually embarrassed. I touch my new locks' length defensively then point at the dog. "Down!"

"Is that a new outfit?" She circles me. "And new hair?"

"Not exactly new. Trimmed."

"And highlighted." She nods. "Sweet."

I'm not sure if her scrutiny is more embarrassing than Marla's. She simply gave me a quick up-down glance and said, "I'm glad you decided to listen to my advice."

Which made me want to shave my head.

"You like?" Hope teeters on the brink, and I hate feeling as vulnerable as I do.

"Lookin' good, Mom." She winks. "Do you have a date or something?"

"A date?" I almost choke on the word. "No, no, no."

She leans close and I smell the faint scent of chlorine on her skin. "You want me to hook you up with my coach? I could drop a hint—"

"No." My tone is forceful, almost a bark. Definitely alpha-dog zone. I attempt to soften it. "Don't be ridiculous. I just felt the need for some updates." I stop short of telling her I'm hoping her father will come for dinner. I'm not up for her negative response. Besides, verbalizing my hopes too often ends up jinxing them. I'd rather keep my hopes and prayers between me and God.

She hugs me. "Well, you look good enough to go on a date."

"Speaking of dating"—I turn away, grab the casserole, and shove it into the preheated oven, hiding my hopes and dreams and closing the door on them—"you've been seeing that new boy . . . what's his name?" I feign ignorance.

She gives me a look that tells me my cover is blown. "We're just friends, Mom."

"Gabe is a nice guy."

"We're friends. That's it. He just lost his dad last year."

My eyebrow arcs. Is she as good at denial as I am? "But I thought Jack was—"

"His dad died from some disease or cancer or something. I can't remember. And he's living with his uncle."

"Uncle." I mouth the word, which disintegrates all my pre-conceived notions about Jack. So maybe he's not in the middle of a divorce. I shake loose the baggage I imagined Jack carrying. I'm the one with totes, carry-ons, and trunks of rejection and failure on my back. Have Izzie and Gabe connected because of their losses? "Well," I draw out my comment, not wanting to make her defensive and not wanting to push a relationship on her, "you can never have enough—"

Her cell phone buzzes, the beeps and blips forming some semblance of rhythm. She grabs it, reads the monitor, and begins texting a message back.

I watch the intensity tighten her features. "What's going on?"

"Can we have company for dinner?" Her thumbs move independently as they maneuver the tiny keypad of her cell phone.

I've always tried to accommodate Izzie, allowing her to invite friends over. Better here than going off somewhere I don't know about. And better than me being stuck alone. Still, I imagine Cliff coming for dinner and finding the table crowded with more than just his mother. I don't need any distractions. Especially cute young women at the table for competition. "Is that Amy?"

She continues texting.

"Tonight really isn't a good—"

"It's an emergency, Mom." She gives me a look that convicts me of selfishness.

"All right." God's in control, right? I just wish He'd zap Cliff with a sudden I-gotta-have-my-wife-back vision. You know, a Saul-on-the-road-to-Damascus type of moment. "Who's coming?"

She pushes the nosy dog away. "Cousin It's family."

"Gabe and . . . his uncle?" I swallow the sudden awkwardness. At least another couple of guys won't be a threat to my grabbing Cliff's attention. Definitely better than hip teen girls with firm thighs and cover-model bodies. When she sets down the phone, I ask, "So what's the emergency?"

"Oh, nothin'."

"I thought you said there was an emergency."

"Well, yeah, sorta. Movers are there. It's nuts."

"Movers?"

"Mom"—her tone dips into that why-are-you-making-my-life-so-hard range. She picks up her phone and holds it out to me. An offer or challenge? "If you want to know so bad, call him yourself."

⁂

Tossing together a quick salad, I glance over my shoulder at the sound of heels clicking against the linoleum. "Oh, good, you're dressed."

"What do you mean by that?" Marla places a hand on her hip even though her bloated, bruised features don't blink or flinch. She had a doctor's appointment earlier in the day when the drainage tube was removed. She looks slightly less like an insect.

"Oh, I'm sorry." I give myself a mental shake from the flustered feeling of having company dropping in suddenly. It's one thing to have teens over without preparation time. It's entirely another proposition to have adults—especially Cliff. I sent Izzie to pick up her bathroom, which will have to act as the guest bath. "We're going to have company for dinner."

"Did Cliff call?"

Her question jolts me. "No. Was he supposed to?"

She gives a tiny shrug of one narrow shoulder. "He said he would if he thought he could swing by."

The doorbell rings. Is that Cliff? Or Izzie's friend? With the back of my wrist, I push back a lock of hair and take a heaving breath. Am I ready to entertain? Am I ready to impress Cliff? Or will company only interfere? No, no . . . God can do all things.

"I'll be in my room then." Marla turns on her heel.

"But—"

She gives a defeated wave with her hand. "I'm not up for company."

"You look fine." I trail behind her, trying to appease her as I've so often done in our relationship. "Really. These folks won't care. They're just coming for a quick meal."

"Give them a gift card for Sonic."

That stops me in my tracks. I blink as she continues down the hallway toward her room . . . my room. Maybe it's for the best for her to be out of the way. Out from between Cliff and me. "I'll bring you a tray."

Izzie emerges from her bathroom. "They're here?"

"Apparently."

"What's up with Marla *now?*"

"She's feeling a bit self-conscious."

"That is *not* true!" Her voice barrels out of her room like a steaming freight train. Then she steps out into the hall. "I simply don't feel up to making idle chitchat with people I don't care to know." Her gaze flicks over Izzie. "Is that what you're wearing?"

With a huff and narrowing of her gaze, the evil look as I call it when it's aimed in my direction, Izzie turns on her bare heel.

A vein throbs in my temple.

As the doorbell rings again, I force my lips to lift upward in a variation of a smile. "Everybody ready?"

"I'll get it." Izzie brushes past me. "This'll be fun."

But when she opens the front door, she does a quick about-face and takes long, determined strides toward her room.

Surprised by her reaction, I move toward the front door as if I'm rubbernecking a wreck on the highway, unable to help myself. "Cliff!"

My ex stands on the front porch. He looks good, if I do say so myself. My hand flutters to my chest as I feel heat rising inside me.

"Kaye."

"Your mother said you might call."

"Didn't have time. Thought I better see how she's getting on here. If she's doing okay."

My smile falters, but I manage to press the corners in place and not let them compress into instant irritation. *Okay, God, I need a miracle here.* Because I feel my annoyance meter escalating in spite of my determination to smile and be gracious. No "Thanks for taking care of my mom." No "Gosh, it's nice of you to let my mom stay here." No "Wow! You're looking great, Kaye."

"If you don't think this is a suitable environment, then I can help her pack her bags and put them in your car." My words come out short and clipped and probably not from God. But I can't seem to stop them. "I'm sure she'd be perfectly happy at your place."

Cliff does that glance down his aquiline nose at me. He has an uncanny ability to flair his nostrils in a snort of superiority. "Have a bad day, Kaye?"

"Busy as usual."

Then his disconcerting look disappears under a bright smile, which is his usual business tactic for closing a sales deal. And he's good at it. But his teeth seem three times brighter than they used to be when we were married. Barbie probably took him off coffee and in to see the dentist. But she's gone now! *Out of the picture.*

He claps his hands, rubbing them together then steps into my house. "So what's for dinner, hon?"

I'm not ready for this. I should have bought flowers for the table, set out candles, turned on romantic music instead of feeling sweaty from running around trying to throw together the rest of dinner for a suddenly growing group of people who most probably won't get along.

Cliff turns around in the foyer, eyeing what I've done with the place. "Brings back memories."

Since he never lived here, I ask, "Of?"

He loops an arm around my waist and pulls me close. My heart flutters weakly in my chest. "When we first got married. Remember that horrible little house we had then?"

Horrible? My throat works up and down in an effort to swallow. I have fond memories of that time, of the early days of our marriage, of eating mac-and-cheese in bed. We were poor but happy. Or so I thought. But from Cliff's look, I can tell his memories of that time are skewed. We both gave up dreams—my college degree for a wedding ring and baby; his other girlfriends for a ball and chain.

Cliff releases me and walks into the den. He makes the room feel smaller, insignificant, as I suddenly see it through his eyes. Well aware of his particular tastes, I imagine the thoughts running through his mind about my secondhand furnishings. Which was all I could afford when we separated and divorced. But even though I wasn't happy with the circumstances, I tried to make the best of it. And I like my home. It's the first place I've ever been able to afford on my own.

In the time we've been apart, Cliff has never been here. When he's had Izzie for weekends—when he cared enough to force the issue and I could make her go—I've driven her to his posh townhome in Southlake Town Center, which he bought with money from a trust from his father. A trust that didn't transfer to spouses and was not part of community property. Money he never wanted to touch while we were married.

Which reminds me that Isabel originally answered the door, and I glance around for her. Nowhere in sight. I could really use her help while I gather myself together, escape to put on lipstick. "Izzie," I call out, desperate to gather our family together, "come say hello to your father! Izzie?"

"Hi, Dad," comes the unenthusiastic voice of our teen from down the hall.

"Iz." He sounds equally disenchanted. A soft whine carries through the house. "What was that?"

"Your mother," I joke.

He frowns. "Does Iz have a dog? You didn't—"

"I didn't." But I suddenly resent his insinuating I shouldn't have. What's it to him anyway? "It's just visiting, and she's apparently not happy in the crate."

"Best place for a dog."

His comment rankles me. Cousin It is goofy, destructive, and high-maintenance, but Cliff long ago lost the right to tell me what we should or shouldn't do.

Then he faces me. "So where's Mom?"

"In her room."

"Locked up like the dog?"

I roll my eyes like Izzie. "Resting. Hiding." I shrug. "You know her."

"She's had a trauma, Kaye. You could be a little sympathetic."

My jaw drops. "I've been *completely* sympathetic. I'm the one that opened my home to her, remember? I'm fixing her meals. I'm dispensing her meds. I'm taking her to the doctor. What, about all of that, implies a lack of sympathy?"

His forehead folds in on itself. "I know how you feel about her."

"Do you? Then why'd you let her come here?"

"Why did *you?*"

"It seemed the right thing to do. But after all these years you still don't want to see her the way she truly is."

"Cliff?" A weak voice floats down the hallway.

I release a huffy breath and manage to refrain from rolling my eyes again. Here it comes—manipulation in the extreme. Cinderella, I'm sure, didn't have to contend with this.

"Mom?" Cliff beelines it in the direction of my bedroom. "Yeah, it's me."

I take a slow, deep breath, feeling my flushed face dampen with sweat. Never when we were married would I have spoken to Cliff so forcefully. I'm not sure if I should have started earlier or if I'm ruining my chances now for reconciliation. I doubt Barbie ever raises her voice or Botoxed eyebrows.

Bracing myself for more dramatics, I follow him down the hallway and enter Marla's temporary sanctuary. The lights are off, but a candle I don't recognize on the bedside table is lit, giving the room an eerie, flickering glow. This could be a scene right out of *The Munsters*, with one bunch of limp flowers next to the stately roses overseeing the body splayed out on my bed like a corpse. Marla, dressed in a flowing negligee, is the monster pretending to be weak and lifeless. Her hand lifts limply.

Cliff cups his hands around Marla's and kisses the back of her knuckles. "How are you feeling, Mom?"

"I've been better, dear. How was work today?"

"Closed a deal."

She reaches up and pats his hands. "That's wonderful."

He glances over at a tray I brought Marla earlier with cheeses and fruits to snack on. Not one slice is missing. "Are you eating?"

"It's difficult to chew."

Cliff looks over his shoulder at me. "Don't you have something like . . . I don't know . . . applesauce?"

I cross my arms over my chest. "She didn't *want* any applesauce."

Marla pulls her arm back from Cliff, letting her hand flutter like a falling feather to her chest. "Don't worry about me. I'll be fine."

"Have you talked to the doctor?" Cliff plays the part of an armchair quarterback, which makes my spine snap into a straight line.

"We saw him this morning. He removed a drainage tube and said she's healing nicely."

"And you went with her?"

"She can't drive."

He doesn't glance in my direction. "What can I bring you, Mom? Something to read?"

"Her eyes hurt, Cliff."

"A movie? Something to eat or drink?"

"No, no, dear. I'm fine. I just need to rest, to be—"

"—pampered," he finishes for her. "Don't worry, Mom. We'll take care of you."

We? Who does he mean by "we"?

Or does he simply mean *me*?

"Come on." Cliff grabs my arm and moves me toward the door. "I'll be right back, Mom. Just want to talk to Kaye privately about your care."

Marla lifts her head off the pillow. She glances from Cliff to me, her gaze (one eye anyway) narrowing. Then she sits bolt upright in bed and stretches out a hand toward her son. "I think I need to sit up some . . . maybe walk around a bit."

Cliff hesitates, releases my arm, then goes back to help his mother. "Sure, Mom. Anything you want."

The ding of the doorbell sounds loud and clear.

"I'll get it!" Izzie hollers before I can.

"Who's that?" Cliff asks.

"Kaye's boyfriend probably," Marla states.

"Boyfriend?" Cliff focuses on me then. But is it disbelief or irritation? "*You* have a boyfriend?" Definitely the former.

Two reactions emerge at once inside me and fight for control. One wants to defend myself and bask in my ability to interest another male, crowing, "Yes, dadgumit, I have a boyfriend. Did you think this body could stay on the market forever?" And the other more pathetic response compels me to rush forward and make sure Cliff knows I wouldn't dream of seeing anyone but him.

Instead, to turn the tables, I confuse the situation with, "Could be one of Marla's."

Her head swivels in my direction. The moment freezes between us as if the devil's dwelling place gets a subzero blast.

"Mom!" Izzie yells down the hallway. "It's for you."

I manage a half smile. "If you'll excuse me . . ."

Cliff touches my arm. "You're seeing someone?"

"It's probably a client."

"Probably?"

Knowing I didn't answer his question, I walk down the hall, feeling his gaze on my backside. For the moment I'm glad I spent money on a new outfit and the Spanx beneath. His misconception could be useful. It's definitely garnered more interest from him than anything else I've done, including my new hairstyle.

⤖ Chapter Nine ⤖

T his is a bad time, isn't it?" Jack stands on the porch like
Sir Lancelot, tall, broad-shouldered, looking ready to save
this damsel in distress. Of course, his knightly stance is my
imagination. Still, his timing actually couldn't be more perfect.

"No, not at all." I hold open the door. Cousin It's maniacal
barks reverberate in my head.

"Gabe told me you'd invited us for dinner and to meet him
here. But I don't want to be an imposition." His gaze travels over
me, taking in my hair and outfit, as if he's noticing the changes.
A stirring inside makes me suspect he appreciates the alterations,
but that could be my imagination too. "It looks like you might be
on your way out."

I touch a lock of my hair, feeling the silky smoothness on the
newly trimmed ends. "Not at all. Come on in."

He takes a step toward me and stops. His clean scent drifts
over me, drawing me toward him. He seems even taller, his
shoulders wider. His yellow button-down acts as a second skin,
flowing over the contours of his well-muscled chest and flat abs.
Something Cliff hasn't had since college days. *Cliff.* The name
surfaces in my suddenly waterlogged brain, swimming in an
abundance of unexpected senses. Jack will be perfect for the part
I need him to play. If only he will cooperate.

"You look nice, by the way."

A flush warms me from the inside out. It's nice for someone to notice and yet quite frankly it's the wrong someone. Why didn't Cliff pay closer attention? On the tide of my awareness of Jack is an undertow of disappointment. But maybe Jack's interest will work for me . . . and Cliff, of course. "Thanks."

From behind his back, he produces a single white rose.

"What's this?"

"A white flag of surrender. An apology. Take your pick."

I laugh, hesitating to take the proffered bud. "I don't understand."

"I heard what the maniacal dog did to your roses."

"Oh, don't worry about that. I've been wanting to replace them anyway."

His questioning brow lifts.

"They were pink. I like red."

"Of course." He gives a slight, courtly bow and hands me the rose. Did Cinderella feel like this when she met Prince Charming? Except I'm no princess and my Prince Charming isn't exactly charming these days. "Still, Cousin It is very sorry."

"It's okay. Really." I hook my arm through his, kick the door shut behind us, and draw him toward the den. "Izzie said there was some kind of an emergency."

"Not that I know of. I burned the burgers on the grill. Probably constitutes an emergency to a starving teenage boy."

"Most definitely an emergency," I repeat like a blithering idiot as we move into the den. If confession is good for the soul, then hanging around Jack may cause the need for more confessions. His thickly corded muscles along his forearm and bicep are definite distractions.

"What kind of emergency?" Cliff's brusque tone intrudes, overriding Cousin It's staccatoed barks from Izzie's bedroom. His gaze settles on the white rose.

"Cliff"—I give him one of those old married looks we use to share but to which I think he lost the translation—"this is Jack Franklin. He's a client." I glance at Jack. "And this is my *ex*-husband, Cliff Redmond."

No hesitation flickers in Jack's hazel eyes as he reaches forward to shake hands. But I recognize the tiny creases at the corner of Cliff's.

I focus on my ex while still holding onto Jack's arm. "Will you be joining us for dinner, too?"

"Huh?" Cliff seems distracted himself, maybe by the incessant barking coming from Izzie's bedroom. My own ears have started to ring. "Yeah." He crosses his arms over his chest, which I have to admit, is not nearly as chiseled as Jack's. It's like comparing Gerard Butler's physique to Donald Trump. Totally unfair. "I wouldn't miss this for anything."

"Well, then, I better set an extra plate." I release Jack's arm.

Cousin It chooses that moment to bound around the corner, hair waving, ears flopping. She barrels through the den straight at us. It takes only half a second for her to cross the rug and she immediately leaps for Jack.

"Sit." He delivers the command in the tone of a powerful knight.

It stops mid-flight and sits, her body trembling like a small child unable to be still when the bathroom urge demands instant satisfaction.

"Good girl. Come." He pats his chest and she leaps up and taps her paws against him.

When she turns her snout toward Cliff, alarm tinges his features and he starts to turn away. "No!"

His command sounds more like a squeak.

Cousin It either doesn't hear him or doesn't obey. She pounces on him, knocking Cliff back a step or two. "Get her off!"

"It." Jack's command seems a second or two delayed. "Down."

When she obeys, Jack rewards her with a head rub. Her tail swishes across the floor, her grin wide, tongue pink and dangling—the face of pure contentment.

I glance toward the back door. "She might need to go out."

"Good idea." Jack leads and she readily follows. I stifle a laugh as my gaze shifts toward Cliff who is straightening his shirt and tie after It's assault.

"Thanks," I say as Jack rejoins us. "Gabe is still coming, isn't he?"

Cliff's eyes narrow. "Who's Gabe?"

"Think I just heard his truck." Jack heads toward the front door. "I'll let him in."

I move into the kitchen, followed on the heels by my ex, and find Marla sitting at the kitchen table. She's still dressed in her pale blue negligee. I find a bud vase, fill it with water and place Jack's rose as the centerpiece on the kitchen table.

"So who is this guy?" Cliff wastes no time in questioning me.

"A client."

"So she says."

For the first time I appreciate one of Marla's snide comments.

Cliff glances from her to me then presses, "Is that *all*?"

"So far." Hiding a grin, I open the fridge, blocking his question with the door.

He pokes his head around into the chilly air, which cools the heated flush on my skin. "What does that mean?"

I load up his arms with a wide assortment of salad dressings.

"Do you usually have clients over for dinner? And do they always bring roses?"

"Singular, not plural. And no, not usually." Pleasure tugs one side of my mouth into a smug smile.

His frown deepens. "What about this . . . Gabe. Who's that?"

"Jack's nephew."

"He has the hots for your daughter," Marla offers.

I pull fresh green beans from the hydrating drawer. "They're just friends."

"I wouldn't be too sure of that if I were you." The tone in Marla's voice unsettles me. She should know what it's like to have a kid involved with someone unsuitable. That person was me. But Gabe isn't exactly unsuitable. They're just too young.

"She's old enough to start dating." I ignore the helpless feeling that makes my knees wobbly at the thought of my daughter riding hither and yon in the car of some hormone-ravaged kid. When I held my baby girl in my arms, sat through tea parties with her baby dolls, and played Skipper to her Barbie in the Dream House, I never saw this hurdle looming along the horizon. But I'm slamming into it now.

Cliff leans against the cabinet, arms crossed as he assesses me with his heavy-lidded gaze. "What about *you*?"

"Me?" Amazing, this sudden buoyant sensation that floods me. "Well, yes, I *am* ready to start dating." I open the oven door and three-hundred-fifty degree heat rolls outward.

He mutters something under his breath.

The casserole bubbles around the edges and I turn off the oven and shut the door. "What?"

"So are you seeing this Jack?"

"His name is Jack. Not *this* Jack."

"That why you're all dressed up?" He stares down at my freshly coral-polished toenails peeking out of my new sandals.

Jealousy made him finally notice. This is where I should probably tell him that I spent too much money today just for him. The truth shall set you free, right? But I can't seem to go there. His ego doesn't need any more fuel. And jealousy seems to be working for us at the moment. Why kill it? "Izzie"—I toss the blame momentarily on our daughter—"invited them. Gabe and Iz are friends. That all right with you?"

There are words I wish I could take back in my life. "Yes" when Cliff pressured me in college and I ended up pregnant being one. And "Get out!" when I learned he was seeing someone else. That one especially because getting him back is proving to be the most difficult task of my life. But sarcasm at this delicate point is not how I should respond.

And yet, that's exactly what I dish out. *Help me, God!*

"Do *clients* show up here in the middle of the night?"

I'm not sure if Marla's question helps or hurts. Can fanning the flame of jealousy stir up the coals of desire?

Cliff's eyebrow peaks.

I start to form a rebuttal but silence seems the best answer. I just hope I haven't pushed Cliff too far. But for now, I'll let his thoughts smolder. He can think what he wants. Covering my hands with thick quilted mitts, I pull the casserole out of the oven. "Dinner's ready."

⁂

Are we having fun yet?

We're sitting around the too-small kitchen table. I added the extension in the middle, so now the table is too big for the kitchen nook and yet still too small for six people. Or should I say two enormous egos. Cousin It lies beneath the table, sniffing the aromas with her big, black nose. Izzie glares at her grandmother over another hair comment. "If you pulled it back off your face—" Marla's words set off fireworks. All of which I tried to snuff out with perky chitchat. Cliff stares suspiciously at Gabe as if the young man might be guilty of *thinking* all the things Cliff was guilty of *doing* in his youth.

Now Marla sticks her slightly disjointed nose into Jack's business. "How many clients do you have?"

"I've never counted." Jack concentrates on forking his salad.

"*Really.*" The way she says it implies incompetence. "Are most repeat customers?"

"I'd say so." He stuffs a fork full of lettuce into his mouth as if to keep from saying anything else. Definitely a wise man.

"And how many trips do you put together in a year?"

He takes his time chewing then swallows. "A few."

Undeterred Marla presses harder. "And do you take all of those trips with your clients?"

"No, ma'am. Not anymore."

"So you handle more than you have time to actually guide?"

"Yes, ma'am." His politeness highlights how irritated I usually get over her twenty questions. I wish I had his calm reserve.

Cliff leans back, crossing his arms over his chest, a smirk of approval on his face. Obviously he's enjoying himself while his mother continues her questioning. Is this good cop/bad cop?

"And do you only handle individual trips?"

"We handle company retreats as well."

"Ah, well." She dabs her mouth. "That's probably where the big bucks are." Carefully, she places her napkin back in her lap. "Has the economic downturn affected your business?"

"Not particularly."

"Interesting."

"Pass the casserole, Jack." Gabe has gobbled down his first helping. I'm not sure if it's because he likes it or is nervous at the tension in the air. From his quick glance at Marla, I ascertain he's trying to divert her attention. But that was a mistake. Her one good eye and other puffy one skewers the innocent teen.

"You don't call your uncle 'uncle'?" Marla appears to have adopted Lady Catherine de Burgh's dominance at *my* dining table.

Gabe downs half his glass of milk. "He's not my real uncle."

Marla's one good eye, the fatty one, widens at that choice tidbit. "Oh?"

A leading question if I ever heard one.

Izzie glares at her grandmother. "Gabe, you don't have to answer any of *her* questions."

Since she's straight across the table from me, I stretch my leg out to tap Iz's shin. But Jack coughs, making a strangled sound. Izzie shoots me a disgruntled look. Did I miss and reach him instead? Great. Now he probably thinks I'm playing footsies with him under the table. The peas I microwaved slip off my fork and loll around my plate and I focus on stabbing each one.

Marla leans forward. "So you're living with a man who you're not even related to? This *is* unusual."

Only Marla can make an innocent situation sound abnormal or wrong. At least I hope it's innocent, because I realize I like Jack—in a friendship sort of way.

"Marla," I interrupt, "would you pass the rolls?"

She lifts the basket, holding it while she continues staring at Gabe. Cousin It jumps to her feet at the sight of food dangling within reach. She noses Marla's hand. Marla fixes the beast with that one-eyed glare. "Don't think about it."

Cousin It retreats beneath the table. Marla is definitely alpha dog here.

Gabe takes another roll. "Jack was my dad's best friend."

"Was?" Marla pushes.

I clear my throat. "Would anyone else like more casserole?" Everyone stares at me for a minute but from a quick glance I see everyone's plate is full. "Don't be shy. Eat up because we have a lot."

Without glancing up, Gabe slaps a slab of butter on the roll. "My dad died last year."

Everyone at the table freezes. The only sound is the tiny intake of air, as if a glass was spilled. Then Marla's jaw falls slack.

"Oh, Gabe." I reach forward as if to touch his hand but he's too far away. "I'm so sorry."

He meets my gaze then looks back at his plate. A red hue creeps up his neckline and floods his face.

"What did he die from?" Apparently Marla has recovered from her surprise.

"Marla." I pass her the salad dressing, trying to give her a drop-it look, but she never even gives me a second glance.

"I don't need any of that." She waves away any hint.

"Would you like more casserole then?"

"No, I'm fine."

"Salad? Rolls?"

"*No.*" She nips the end of the word between her clenched teeth.

Suddenly Izzie pushes back from the table. "Come on, Gabe."

"Where do you think you're going, young lady?" Cliff demands, finally engaging in the conversation.

"Swimming."

Her father looks at me to see if that's permissible.

I smile. "That's a good idea. Gabe, you can use my bathroom to change if you'd like." To Cliff I say, "They're both on the swim team."

"They're teens." He gives a slight snort. And I know exactly what he means because we utilized his parents' pool.

After they walk out of the room, Cousin It tagging along behind, Marla leans forward breaking what used to be a cardinal rule and placing her elbow on the table. "Someone should supervise them. After all, we know what happened when you two were left alone."

"Mom," Cliff grumbles, "we were in college."

"I know what you two did in my own house." She clucks and shakes her head.

Heat ignites in my face. I can feel each capillary expanding and burning. Mortified that my sins are being branded on my chest like a big scarlet A, except the A isn't exactly accurate—maybe just a simple S—I glance toward Jack. Unfortunately there was never anything simple about it.

Jack reaches for a roll but does not meet my gaze.

"Marla," I manage through the rock-hard lump in my throat, "please."

"You better watch Gabe." She points a thin finger at Jack. "Girls were always after my boys. All three of them."

I stare at the beans lying limp and cold on my plate. I've lost my appetite.

The rest of the meal drags on as the conversation lags. Cliff's jaw pops as he chews, a sure sign of his irritation. While I poke at my food with my fork, I desperately search for something pleasant to discuss—politics maybe, or religion—anything but these laser questions from Marla and her divulgence of personal things. The minutes lollygag along and still my brain seems to have quit functioning in its hostess role. Wouldn't Cinderella find something nice to say? Maybe I could pass out like Snow White.

Cliff finally clears his throat. "So where is the kid"—he waves his fork—"Gabe from?"

Jack swallows a bite. "Oklahoma."

"So he'll be going back there soon. Good."

"Actually"—the corner of Jack's mouth twitches in what I imagine is the beginning of a smile—"his mom and siblings moved here this past summer to be closer to her parents, now that she's a widow."

"The kid in some kind of trouble?" Cliff jabs his roll with his knife. "Is that why he came to live with you?"

"He's working on his Eagle Scout project. It was easier for me to help him if we lived in the same location."

"Eagle Scout, huh?" Cliff's mouth thins as he pushes his chair back. "Maybe I'll go chaperone."

What's the problem? Has he heard some scandal about Eagle Scouts? I suspect he's being territorial in a Tarzan beating-his-chest kind of manner. In my mind Gabe's goal elevates him out of the ordinary teen realm. After the back door closes, silence settles in around the table. I dab my mouth with a linen napkin, avoid eye contact with Marla.

"Dinner was great." Jack jiggles the ice in his glass and takes a last gulp of tea. "Thanks for having us."

"You're welcome. Can I get you something else to drink? Eat?"

"No, thanks. I'm full. I should probably head on home and—"

The back door slams shut, and the sound reverberates through the house. Marla and Jack look to me as if for explanation.

"I think that must be my daughter." An unvoiced apology lingers on my tongue. Now what?

The back door opens again and Cliff's voice explodes through the house. "What were you *thinking?*"

"Leave me alone!" Izzie's voice hits a higher decibel.

"Have you gone insane? Come back here!"

I follow the chaos into the den, and sense I'm being followed by Marla and Jack. But then I come to a dead stop. My ex-husband and daughter stand toe-to-toe, hands fisted, bodies rigid. They look more alike than they ever have. The shiny tops of their heads gleam in the iridescent light. My ex has a receding hairline.

My daughter, on the other hand, is completely bald.

⁘⟨ Chapter Ten ⟩⁘

I zzie glares at her father.

Marla bumps into the back of me.

And I sense Jack standing beside me. But I can't take my eyes off my bald daughter. An uncontrollable trembling starts way down inside of me. Only Gabe and Cousin It are missing at the moment. Maybe they're smarter than the rest of us.

"Isabel." Marla is the first to speak. "What have you done *now?*"

Izzie huffs, turns on her bare heel, but Cliff stops her with a hand on her arm. "What were you thinking?" His demanding tone is not the type that is often tolerated by a teen. "Have you lost it?"

"Cliff." I step forward, my focus now on the red mark he's making on Izzie's arm.

She jerks away from him. "Leave me alone!"

She bolts out of the room. The slam of her door reverberates through the house with a decidedly angry note. My skin contracts. Cousin It noses the pane window on the back door. Gabe wisely sinks back down into the pool and stays put.

"You have some serious problems with that one." Marla's tone is that of a woman who has never dealt with a hormonal teenage girl.

"What on earth happened?" I manage, though my voice is shaky. One minute we're having dinner, the next there's an outburst and the breakout of a Telly Savalas convention in my den. I stare at my ex. "When did—"

"Don't blame me." He holds up his hands. "I went out to the pool and there she was. Bald as the day she was born."

"Well, she didn't shave her head out there." I can't seem to get beyond the fact that my daughter is bald. Or how it happened.

"I don't know the specifics, Kaye. I would imagine she did it in the bathroom. But, I tell you, she needs help."

"Psychological help," Marla adds.

"My daughter is perfectly normal." My denial whines in the room like the air surging out of a whoopee cushion. It's the rest of her family who don't measure up to normal.

"It's not normal to shave your head."

"It's also not normal to have your father run off with a woman half his age." I cringe and could bite off my tongue for going there.

"So you're going to blame *this* on me?"

"I meant, it's not normal to have your parents divorce. It's taken its toll."

"Look around, Kaye. Divorce happens all the time."

"It doesn't make it normal."

"Are you talking about Izzie or you?" His jab aims for the middle of my chest.

But I ignore the pain, let it glance off me. "It's also not normal for . . ." I manage to stop myself as my gaze shifts toward Marla's stack of magazines on the table—*Vogue*, *Cosmopolitan*, *People*, and *O*.

"Don't you dare blame me." Marla has her alpha dog voice on.

With my heart pounding as if I am cornered and have overstepped my bounds, I peer over at Jack who stands with his hands clasped behind his back and his head slightly bowed. I'm not looking for help (not from him anyway but I definitely need divine intervention), just wishing he wasn't here. He has witnessed way too much about my personal life for one evening. He's probably trying to think of a polite excuse to escape.

Marla rests a hand over her heart. "I need to lie down."

"Are you okay, Mom?" Cliff's angry expression softens.

But she waves him away and takes to her bed with what she calls heart palpitations.

"Should we call the doctor?" Cliff waffles on whether to go to his mother's side or stand here and continue our discussion.

"She's fine." I recognize Marla's symptoms as simply hysterics, because my own heart is creating a jackhammer effect in my chest and the concussion is rattling through my bones.

"But your daughter isn't."

"*My* daughter? What happened to *our* daughter?"

Cliff gives me a slow-burning glare and opens the front door to leave. "You're not handling all of this very well."

All of what? Being a single mother to my hurting teenage daughter? Caring for my husband's narcissistic mother? To dealing with him? No, I'm not.

"Probably all the wonderful help I'm receiving," I fire back, following him to the door. It's definitely an alpha dog statement. But it only gets me a glimpse of my ex's back as he walks toward his car. I slam the door in return. Immediately I regret my burst of anger. Leaning my head against the wooden door, I feel the hollowness of the wood and yearn for a solid strength in my life. A weak pathetic prayer lifts out of me as I draw in great gulps of air until my own heart rate returns to a more normal tempo.

"Can I help?"

At Jack's low voice behind me, I find myself fighting sudden helpless, angry tears. I face him. "I'm sorry about this. My mother-in-law . . . *ex*, I should say . . . my daughter . . . and her father . . . What can I say? They're not a good mix. I can't believe you had to see all of this. Please believe me this doesn't happen every—"

"You don't have to say anything."

A knock at the door gives me a start. I lean toward the peep-hole. "My ex."

Jack nods and steps back into the den, presumably to give us privacy.

I take a deep breath and open the door. "Forget dessert?"

He chuckles then ducks his head, looking down at the welcome mat. "That was uncalled for. I didn't mean it."

Not exactly a firm apology but close enough. "It's okay."

He tips his head back and releases a pent-up breath. Looks up at the stars for a moment, then back at me. Tipping his head to one side, he motions for me to step onto the porch. When I do, letting the door close behind me, his hands encircle my waist. "You're looking good, Kaye."

"You noticed?" A stupid response that flashes my insecurity. His abrupt change startles me, kicks my heart into gear. Why couldn't I have just said, 'thanks,' and left it at that?

"Of course. I always notice." He leans toward me, pressing his body against mine and my back bumps the brick wall. "I don't want to fight with you."

"Me either." Disappointment twists my insides. He's never uttered "I'm sorry," not even for his adventure with Barbie. The feel of his hands cupping my waist distracts me. I squirm, irritated at myself now more than Cliff.

"What's wrong?"

"Nothing."

He leans closer, draws a deep breath, and I feel his chest expand against mine. "What were we saying?"

"She can be . . ." I lose track of my thoughts as I breathe in his scent. It's different from the cologne he used when we were married. But this is nice. More than nice. "What?"

He dips his head and nibbles along my neck. Tingly sensations shoot along my nerves, and I'm not sure if it's a distress call or an "all-hands-on-deck" signal. "You're not serious about that yahoo, are you?"

My brain fogs over. "Yahoo?"

"That guy . . . Jake . . ."

"Jack."

"Is he more than a client?"

"Oh, uh . . ." My thoughts drift to what his hands are doing along my back. I revel in the sensations, snuggle closer, my arms embracing his shoulders. "Hmm . . ." What was the question? "Yes."

He pauses an inch below my earlobe. "So you are serious about him?"

My heart begins a staccato beat, working its way up to my throat. I scramble. My brain rewinds, replays. Cliff. Jack. Trouble. "He's a client. That's all."

"Good." He nuzzles my neck and I relax into his arms, my hands working their way along his shoulders and toward his hairline. "Thanks for watching out for Mom. She can be a handful."

Words fracture apart as the sensations I've needed, longed for, stampede through my body. A vibration zings my hip. He pulls back, yanks out his cell phone, and checks the Caller ID. "I have to go."

"Work?" I tug on his shoulders in an effort to pull him back.

He pockets the phone and hooks his arms around my waist. I lift my lips to his and kiss him, but he pulls back first. "I have to go."

This is not how it's supposed to go. Cinderella left Prince Charming holding a glass slipper. Desire building. Passion deferred. Which made Prince Charming chase after her. But Cliff is leaving, backing away, leaving me holding the bag . . . er, his mother. I attempt to camouflage my disappointment beneath a smile. "Okay. Come for dinner again if you want."

"I will." He squeezes my waist and moves away. "Maybe I'll stay for dessert next time."

Longing swells inside me.

He's halfway to his car before he turns back. "I'll be out of town for a few days. Business. I'll call to check on Mom."

Mom. Not Izzie. Not even me. Holding back a frown of frustration, I watch him jog down the walkway and slide into his BMW convertible. He revs the engine before peeling off down the street like he's a teenager. I give myself a minute to recompose myself, readjust my blouse, and fluff my hair back into place. For a moment I'm unsure what just happened. Was the evening a success or failure? I glance up at the stars as if searching for God's answer and decide the dinner was a step in the right direction.

❧❦

I find Jack leafing through a decorating magazine in my den. A splash of water from the pool tells me where Gabe is. Maybe even Cousin It.

"Sorry about that." I gesture toward the front door. "Cliff, uh . . . forgot something." His wife. His family. His responsibilities.

"No problem." He closes the magazine and sets it back in its rightful place alongside other magazines on the coffee table. "Figured Mom and Dad needed a few minutes to confer."

"Did Izzie . . . Isabel make another appearance?"

He shakes his head.

"Probably for the best."

"She'll be okay."

Empty words. How does he know? I should be relieved she *only* shaved her head. She could cut herself. Or jump in the car and go driving. Without a license. But how does Jack know those events aren't right around the corner?

Unsure if I should check on Izzie or leave her alone, I stand in the middle of the room. Jack pats the cushion next to him.

Reluctantly I take the seat. It's easier than dealing with another emotional scene at the moment. "I'm not so sure it was a good idea for me to invite Marla to stay with us. Izzie isn't fond of Cliff's mom."

"I admire you for taking in your ex-mother-in-law when she needed help. I'm sure it can't be easy, but maybe it will show Isabel about real love."

Guilt tightens its grip on my stomach. "My motives weren't totally altruistic."

He studies me for a long, slow minute and I feel stripped of all pretenses. It's exhilarating and terrifying at the same time. "You're hoping to get your ex back."

My foot turns inward and I cross my arms over my stomach. "That obvious, huh?"

He shrugs, stretches his arm out along the back of the sofa. "I'm not too smart, but I can connect the dots."

I rub my hands over my elbows and glance up at the ceiling. A tiny cobweb has started in the corner, a string dangling from one wall to the next as precarious as my hopes. "I'm trying to do God's will."

"And you believe getting your ex back is God's will?"

"Why wouldn't it be?"

He nods. "Admirable. Maybe I can help."

I blink. "How? Send him a note? Waylay him in the alley?"

He chuckles then shrugs one shoulder. "I'm a man."

So I noticed. I train my gaze to remain on his.

"I know how men think, what they like."

My arms tighten. "Twenty-somethings? Blonde? Blue eyes? Big—"

"Not all men are like that."

"You're saying you wouldn't want a twenty-something who looks like Barbie?"

"Are you asking for a confession?" He leans toward me. "Okay, for maybe five minutes. But once you get past the big—"

"Fake," I add.

"—ness." He grins. It's a mischievous smile that is disarming and contagious. "Then yeah, I'd be bored."

"You'd be an anomaly."

His gaze roams over me. "You look great. Maybe you don't need my help."

"Then why do I feel like I'm doing everything wrong?"

He shakes his head. "Some men are threatened by a strong woman. Have you thought of that?"

I flex my bicep. "And you're not?"

"Honestly? I can't stand it when a woman isn't strong enough to challenge me, to stand toe-to-toe. Not physically, but mentally."

"I'll keep that in mind." And I'm a bit relieved he doesn't want to arm wrestle.

His gaze seems to penetrate, as if he's trying to read my thoughts. "What were you like when you were married?"

I shrug. "Not alpha."

He raises a dubious brow. "I don't see you as the roll-over-and-take-it type that you claim to be."

"Oh, really?" My forearms press into my belly.

He scooches over a few inches, intruding on my space—and my peace of mind. Not that I had much of that to begin with. "I think you are more than capable of getting exactly what you want."

"That's not a compliment. You think I'm manipulative."

"Are you?" His mouth pulls sideways. "That is definitely one universal turnoff for men." He leans forward, bracing his elbows on his knees. "But men are split on the other extremes. Some only want simpering twenty-somethings who cater to their every need. And others"—he turns his head and looks at me over his rounded shoulder—"like a challenge."

Is he telling me something? My pulse skitters, and I don't know how to respond, what to say. Maybe it's simply his frank analysis that unnerves me. Or again it's my imagination at work. "You seem more insightful than most men I know."

Jack claps his hands together between his knees. "I was a psych major in college. Old habit. So, you're trying to do God's will. But is Cliff?"

"He's a good man. Really. He cares about his mother. That's a good thing, right?" I finger-comb back my new do, a tangle snags on the edge of a nail. "This hasn't been a great impression I'm making here on you, as a client, that is."

"You've already got my business, Kaye. You were gracious enough to open your house to us this evening. Not to mention Cousin It. Not every business—or woman—would do that. I'd say our relationship has moved past work-related to friends."

Friends. Okay. That's all right. I can handle friendship. Maybe I misread his statements earlier. He wouldn't be interested in me. Especially after he's learned about the boatload of baggage I carry, from my sex life to my angry daughter, not to mention my ex-husband and ex-mother-in-law. But I remind myself, Cinderella came with baggage too. And Snow White came with seven sleepy, dopey, grumpy dwarfs.

I crane my neck toward the back door and watch Gabe swimming laps in the pool. Being tall and lanky, it takes him approximately four whole strokes to reach the other end of our small pool. "Gabe seems like a good kid."

"He hasn't shaved his head, but then swim season is approaching."

"Ha-ha." My fingers touch the ends of my newly trimmed locks, self-consciously or worriedly. "Not sure what's going to happen with that. Do I buy Iz a hat? A wig? A therapist?"

"She'll let you know what she needs."

I lean forward, resting my elbows on my bent knees and study my fingernails. My shoulder is barely an inch from Jack's. "Parenting isn't for wimps. When I signed up for this gig, I had no idea how tough it would be."

"I can only imagine. I'm only a part-time uncle, not even close to being a parent, but it certainly gives the nerves a workout."

"How's Gabe's mom doing after losing her husband?"

"As well as anyone can. She's overwhelmed. Scared. Okay one day. Not the next."

No words or insights come to me, so I remain quiet.

"Pam's grateful I can help Gabe with his project. She has her hands full with the other kids. There's three more, all younger than Gabe." He reaches over and brushes the back of his fingers against my hand. His touch has an electrical current attached and causes my nerves to hum. *Get a grip, Kaye. He's trying to reassure you, not turn you on.* "Isabel is a good kid too. She's been kind to Gabe, made him feel welcome."

Slowly I lean back, breaking contact with him. "Izzie is a good kid. Just going through a hard time with her dad. I did the same thing when I was about her age."

"You shaved your head?"

I laugh. "No. I, well, uh . . . the trouble I got into had more lasting consequences."

He watches me, his gaze full of quiet sincerity and open curiosity.

"My parents divorced the fall I went off to college."

"Hard thing for a kid to deal with."

"I never saw it coming. They never fought. They were always polite to each other. Maybe too polite. Too unreal. But I suppose they were simply waiting for me to grow up and move off on my own. It was a quick, painless divorce. At least that's what they said. Maybe it was for them."

"But not for you."

"I felt abandoned. They were both busy getting on with their lives." I study the palm of my hand, rubbing my thumb along a crease. "I came to the conclusion, right or wrong, they'd simply lost the passion in their marriage. So very passionate men attracted me."

"Cliff." Jack's voice stuns me as if I'd forgotten for the moment he was even there.

Roughened, raw emotions stick in my throat. "What about you? Did your parents divorce?"

"They've been married almost forty years now. Maybe that's why I haven't made it down that long aisle yet."

I tilt my head in a silent question.

"Their marriage has always seemed so perfect that I've never felt the same type of connection with a woman. Plus, I know what it takes to make a forever kind of commitment. And I won't settle for less."

Since he opened that particular door, I don't hesitate to challenge him as he did me. Maybe he is more like Cliff than he wants to admit. "So, you're waiting for Ms. Perfect."

He rubs his jaw, but his gaze remains steadily focused on me. "Nah, the woman I have in mind isn't perfect."

A tiny pinch of disappointment surprises me. So he has someone he's interested in. Lucky girl. "What's she like?"

"She's trying to do what's right."

"And does she manage?"

"Not always."

"Okay, so not perfect." What kind of a woman does he find attractive? Tall? Blonde? Petite? Never been married? No crazed teenage daughter? "So do *you* need help? Maybe I could give you some pointers in getting her attention."

He grins. "I'll take all the help I can get. What does a woman want?"

I shrug and shake my head. "I don't know. That's probably the secret. None of us knows."

"Thanks. That's helpful." He grins.

"Okay." I laugh. "Let me think." I pull up all my complaints about Cliff and state the opposite. "Attention. Flowers, and not only on Valentine's or an anniversary. And not sent by a secretary either." Then I remember the single rose he brought me this evening. White is friendship, right? But I feel a rosy hue budding on my cheeks.

He watches me solemnly, as if taking mental notes. With us so close together, I can see gold sparkles in his hazel eyes. His lashes are long, longer than a man should have, and as dark as his hair. "What else?"

"Oh, you know . . . the usual." That gaze of his is absolutely mesmerizing. "Holding hands, kissing . . . you know, without expectations that it's always going to lead to—" I stop myself. Fiery embarrassment burns along my skin.

"Good tips." He slides his palms down the length of his thighs, his elbow brushing my arm. "So what are you going to do about Isabel? She doesn't want you and your husband to get back together."

I release a tense breath. "I honestly don't know. But what teenager knows what's best? She still blames him."

"But you love him." It's not a question, just a simple statement.

My response wells up in my throat and I can't speak for a moment. A moment that lasts too long. There isn't an easy answer to complex emotions. Love. Isn't it more than just a feeling? Those feelings haven't been around lately because of Barbie. But love requires more than an automatic response. How many times have I read First Corinthians? Love is a decision. It's action. It's more than a lovey-dovey, heart palpitating feeling that comes and goes. Over the past fifteen months I've struggled to maintain the faith, hope, and love the Bible talks about. Each has waned periodically and I've prayed and prayed and prayed for restoration. I made a decision to love Cliff for better or worse. And I'm clinging to that now.

Even if I feel like I'm dangling over the side of the cliff by the tips of my fingers.

Jack's gaze weighs heavily on me and forces my too-simple response. "Yes." I tilt my head, look away from him but I think he saw right through me in that instant and I can't seem to hide my doubts and questions from him. "We had problems. And . . . we need counseling. But it could still work." I fist my left hand and rub the spot my ring used to occupy. "It has to."

His silence feels like a gavel proclaiming me crazy.

"Our marriage," I babble on, "wasn't perfect, but I've always prayed we'd get back together."

"Then I hope it works out for you, Kaye." Sincerity weights his tone and makes me doubt the tantalizing impressions I sense around him.

"Maybe you were smart not to ever marry."

"Came close a time or two, but it wasn't meant to be. Maybe someday."

I study him but his aspirations seem hidden as much as mine seem plastered on a billboard sign. "I thought you were getting divorced when we first met . . . that you were downsizing because of the divorce settlement."

"That isn't my reason for selling the house."

I wait, hoping he'll answer my silent question.

Instead he plants his palms against his thighs and stands. "It's late. Gabe and I should go. Thanks for dinner."

More like dinner *theater.* "Anytime."

⁙⁙

"No, Marla's not able to come to the phone right now."

I've got the phone cradled against my ear. When it rang, she motioned she didn't want to take a call and made a quick escape back to her room.

Just what I always wanted. A job as her social secretary.

"Hello, this is Harry Klum. I believe we met the other day. How is Miss Marla?"

"She's doing better. It's a slow recovery." Slower than I ever imagined possible.

"Would there be a good time for me to see her?"

"I don't really know when she'll feel up to visitors." I peek around the corner at Marla, who apparently never made it to her room but is now standing in Izzie's doorway instructing her on proper etiquette. Or so I'm guessing. Or maybe she's giving her tips on styling nonexistent hair. I better hurry before Izzie retaliates with something worse than a shaved head.

I notice the phone is suddenly silent, a long pause waiting for an answer from me. But what was the question? "Uh, yes, she's stronger."

Marla places the back of her wrist against her hip. "If you're going to do something, you might as well do it right."

How many times have I heard that line? Her *helpful* comments like that when I was first married to Cliff always made me want to cry. I knew she was implying I was inept. Instead of tears flowing, I feel my hackles rise like a mother wolf defending my pup.

"Well, thank you for your concern," I say into the phone, feeling the need to chase Marla away from Izzie's doorway, and begin walking in that direction. "I'll tell Marla you called."

She looks toward me, her good eye opening wide.

I click the phone off and say, "That was Mr. Klum."

Her mouth tilts downward with disappointment then she grimaces. Occasionally another man calls, but when I tell him she's not taking calls yet he never asks how she's doing, just hangs up the phone without telling me his name. But I suspect it is Mr. Sterling. Marla seems pleased when these calls occur. She dotes on his roses, tending them daily like a horticulturist.

I glance in Izzie's room but stay outside in the hallway. A safe distance. My daughter lies on her bed, her bald head propped on a hand. She doesn't look upset. No red eyes or nose. No pile of tissues on the pillow. She acts like it's any normal evening at our house. So I take up the pretense and continue my conversation with Marla. "Mr. Klum seems nice. Personable."

"When will that stubborn man get the message?" Irritation darkens her face, making the bruises even deeper. She turns on her spiky heel toward her sanctuary.

"I like Harry Klum. He's kind." Offering a conspiratorial smile to Izzie, I wince as the door to Marla's bedroom bangs shut. I take a cautious step toward my daughter, taking in every detail that might give me a clue as to her current mood. "Everything okay?"

"Yeah." She looks as innocent as a buff-headed baby, except she has a couple of red nicks from the razor she used, along with a swath of fuzz where she didn't shave close enough.

"I like Gabe too. He's a nice kid."

"Mom." Her tone dips into that warning zone.

"I don't mean anything by that. I'm not suggesting you elope or anything. I'm just saying you two seem to have made quite a connection."

"We're just friends."

"That's fine. Good even. Do you have a lot in common?"

"Yeah. Neither of us has a dad anymore."

Leaning against the doorjamb, I sigh. "Izzie, you have a dad. He was here tonight. Trying—"

"Mom." She rolls over as if dismissing me. "Let it go."

I debate internally for half a second if I should hit the main subject head-on or not. "You sure everything is all right?"

"Yeah."

"Want to talk about what happened?"

"What do ya mean?"

I glance toward the trash can, which now has tresses of her long blonde hair draped over the edge. "Your hair."

"It's no big deal, Mom." Like she shaves her head every day. Headlines surface in my mind and fill me with dread . . . about some starlet who did a similar thing and then dove overboard for a few months.

"Really?" Could she be telling the truth? She doesn't look upset. Only slightly bristly in her normal teenage way.

"Yeah." She uses the same tone for when she utters, *Duh!*

Stupid me for thinking it's a big deal to be bald and in high school. What was I thinking? I guess things have changed since I was a teen. "All right then."

I head to the sofa for a night of restless sleep. Will this latest fabrication Izzie weaves that all is well (and fashionable) hit the light of day any time soon?

Chapter Eleven

Before the sun yawns, I take Izzie to swim practice (without a fuss or groan or even a complaint about her hair or lack thereof). It's a cool, clear morning. No clouds hover with the threat of rain, and I suspect it's a miracle all around. Izzie's coach gives me a hearty wave. I smile, scrunching down in my seat, and move out of the parking lot before he can come over for a chat.

Home again, I make a quick breakfast for Marla—scrambled eggs, which are the easiest for her to chew. Her bruises have begun to recede, if you know where to look. But if you're seeing her for the first time, she's still rather startling. Emotionally she seems more fragile than her exterior.

"What do you think?" She stares out the breakfast window. "Will I ever look normal again?" It's then I realize she's not looking out at the side yard but at her own reflection in the pane. Her vulnerability softens my heart.

"Of course. You look . . . fine." I hesitate only slightly to find a nonoffensive word to describe her. Is that considered a lie? What am I supposed to say—"You look like you were hit by a bus?" I can just imagine the hysterics that would cause.

But Marla sighs heavily and stares into the Windexed glass as if it holds all the answers to life.

Not eager for any more difficult questions, I gather my work materials, as I need to stop by Jack's and assess what needs to be done before his furniture arrives, but the doorbell rings. The sound is normal, hopeful, but its effect on Marla is the complete opposite.

She retreats down the hallway with the agility of a teen and calls over her shoulder, "I'm not here!"

The doorbell rings again. "I'll get it," I say to no one, as Marla has already barricaded herself in my bedroom. "You know," I glance back at Cousin It who barks from the other side of the back door and continue talking to myself on the way to the front door, "it could actually be for me."

When I open the door, I'm once again wrong. Harry Klum holds a grocery bag to his chest.

"Mr. Klum!"

"Ma'am. How's your mother today?"

Mother? Heaven help me if that were true. Not that I have a close relationship with my mother, but at least she isn't intrusive. More like absentee. I'm not sure I ever fully overcame what felt like betrayal when she and Dad split up. Besides, she's busy with her husband, just as Dad is busy with his wife, and neither has much time for Izzie and me. "Mother-*in-law*. And she's doing better, I think." But it's hard to tell.

"That's a relief." He motions for me to step outside.

Even though I know Marla is entrenched in her bedroom, I glance over my shoulder then pull the door closed behind me. "I'm afraid she's still not ready for visitors."

Which unfortunately translates that she's not ready to go home. If she's waiting for her face to return to normal . . . well, I might be waiting for icicles to form in the flaming furnaces.

"Of course, I understand, ma'am."

"What can I do for you?"

"Oh, no, ma'am." The thin gray hair combed over a balding spot on the top of his head lifts in a gently waving breeze. "Can't do nothing for me. What I'd like to know is what I can do for Marla. I mean, um, I brought her some candy." He lifts another grocery bag at his side, jostles the two against each other, then pulls a cellophane covered box from one.

"How sweet." I can just imagine Marla's reaction: I don't eat candy. Not this cheap brand anyway.

"This other bag was also on the porch. Some kind of delivery maybe." He hands me another brown bag folded at the top.

I pull it open, fish out a red box with the silhouette of a man and woman. "What's this?" I read part of the label across the top. Chocolate flavored. A lacy red flimsy piece of material is also in the bag. A panicked feeling makes me jittery and I cram it all back in the sack. Anderson Sterling must have left his own brand of calling card for Marla. My face smolders around the jaw-line, and I avoid looking directly at Mr. Klum. How can Harry's grocery-store-brand candy compete? "Okay, well, thank you." I crumple the top of the bag down and fist it tight. "I'll give them to Marla."

I start to back my way into the house when Harry stops me with, "Mrs. . . . ?"

"Oh, please call me Kaye."

"Kaye's a nice, friendly name. I thought maybe I could bring your mother . . . in-law some of her favorite magazines. Or a book. Just something she could do during her recovery."

"That's very kind of you."

He shrugs, looking awkward and gentle. "I don't know about that."

This man is a gentleman. And I retreat into the house with the two packages, weighing one against the other. From the quick glance I caught, I'm not sure the presents Mr. Sterling brought are as chivalrous.

⟡⟡⟡

As I place the packages on the kitchen table, Marla emerges from her room, curiosity overwhelming her need to hide. "What's all this?"

"Presents for you, it seems." Why do I see Marla so differently than everyone else? Is my impression off base? She has suitors coming out of the woodwork, and I can't get my ex to give me one glance, much less a phone call.

"Presents!"

My cell phone sounds off, and I recognize the rap ringtone as Izzie. "For you." I hand her the paper bags and grab my cell phone. "Hi!"

"Mom?" Izzie's voice sounds strained. "Can you come get me?"

"What's wrong?"

"What's wrong!?!" She repeats on a strangled note. "Are you kidding? I'm *bald!*"

"I'm on my way." Spurred by the urgency in my daughter's panicked voice, I'm out the door and down the block before I realize I never said good-bye to Marla. My guilt is outweighed by concern for Iz. While I'm sitting at a stoplight, I dial Jack's number and explain I'll be late for our meeting because Isabel has finally decided she doesn't want to stand out in the crowd as the only bald girl at the high school.

"That means she's normal." Jack's tone reassures me.

Normal is good. Normal is what *I* crave. And I believe Izzie has a realistic desire in craving normalcy. A home. Family. Hair. It's not until that exact moment that I realize how worried I was by her lack of pride or vanity. "Thank God."

He chuckles, his voice warm in my ear. "Gabe and I would like to take you both to dinner tonight if you're able."

"Oh, uh . . ." His invitation startles me out of my relief. "Why?" pops out of my mouth before I consider a polite response.

"As a thank-you for helping us out last night."

"Oh, that's sweet of you. But not necessary."

"If your ex is coming over, I'll understand why you can't."

He's given me the perfect out. But of course Cliff isn't coming. And for some reason I don't want an excuse. The light turns green and I urge the car forward. "No, Cliff's out of town. So, I guess we're free."

"Good."

Even though I shouldn't read anything into his response, my imagination takes flight. What if Jack is interested in something more than a working relationship, something more than a friendship? The memory of his steady gaze when he was telling me about his ideal woman stirs up a mixture of emotions that I can't quite sort through. His ideal woman seemed fairly normal. Maybe someone like me. Would that be such a bad thing? Not exactly. But it just seems too unlikely.

"Let's make it seven. And if your mother-in-law wants to come, she's welcome."

And then reality comes crashing in on me. It's not a date. Not even close. Jack isn't my suitor. I'm just too normal for anyone to be interested. "All right. Seven." I start to click off, then hesitate. "Jack?"

"Yeah?"

What if it's about Gabe and Isabel? *Gabe and I would like* . . . Gabe. Of course, it's Gabe and Isabel! Is this the first step to a first date? So Marla has a botched facelift and gets two suitors. Izzie shaves her head and has an Eagle Scout (well, almost) after her. And I'm just . . . boring. Maybe I should do something radical—a tummy tuck, a belly button piercing—to get someone's . . . anyone's attention.

"Do you think," I hesitate, "Gabe and Isabel are . . . you know?"

"Interested in each other?"

"They're friends, right?" My voice wavers.

"Sure." He, on the other hand, is self-assured. Maybe it's the assurance and peace of mind easily won by not being the actual parent. "They've both had a rough time. They get each other."

I nod to myself. It makes sense. I'm not sure if I latch onto his excuse for my security or insecurity. "Okay. Thanks."

"Call me when you've dealt with the hair issue."

"I will." I disconnect the call. Whose idea was dinner? Gabe's? Or Jack's? I decide I'm much more comfortable thinking Gabe's the instigator. The other is too complicated to consider. And too much of an impossibility. Besides, my focus must be on Cliff.

As I wait in the school office for Isabel to emerge from class, I call my hair stylist and ask for suggestions. I anticipate her telling me to get a hat or scarf, but she suggests, "Wigs and Pigs."

"Pigs?"

"You know, pigtails."

I sign Izzie out of school, usher her into the car, and then swing back by the house for a baseball cap. She's quiet. Is that normal or abnormal for this situation? Her arms remain crossed over her chest as she scrunches down in the front seat.

"So, what happened?"

"What do you mean?"

"Did the kids make fun of you?" My hands tighten on the steering wheel in a defensive, Mama-Bear way.

"I don't want to talk about it."

Sighing, I wish I had a parental guide, like *What to Expect When You Have a Teen: The Unexpected*, where I could look up this particular problem and the proper response. Step One: take a deep breath. Step Two: count to ten. But I skip both. "What did you expect, Iz?"

"I don't know!" Her voice is like an explosion inside the car, the repercussions reverberating in my head. "Okay? Can we just drop it?"

I maintain the tense silence until we reach the wig shop.

⁂

A fairy godmother swooshes in and with the flick of her magic wand makes a shabby dress sparkle, turns a pumpkin into a carriage, and softens a curse into something magical. Today I'm Izzie's fairy godmother, minus the magic wand. All I have are prayers, and I'm tossing them toward heaven as fast as I can. I hope producing luxurious hair on top of my bald daughter's head will be as simple as waving a wand or snapping my fingers. However, I suspect my motivations aren't as altruistic as they should be. Frankly, relief flooded me when she called from school. It's normal for her to be embarrassed by appearing in public bald, and I'm all about normal. I need normal to function. It's not fun stripping away this façade of mine or flattering to confess, but at least for once it's honest.

Wigs and Pigs is a sunny, bright store and reminds me of an ice cream parlor. Wigs line the walls like thirty-one flavors topping ice cream cones instead of white Styrofoam heads. The variety of shades range from gray to blonde, auburn to brunette, finally ending with black. Within each shade are different lengths and styles. Scattered throughout the room are tiny, pink tables accompanied by white wrought iron chairs next to them. Shiny, upright mirrors adorn the rounded tabletops. It's all so clean, so pretty, unlike the reason we're here. Because quite frankly, the bald head, even a teen one, just isn't that attractive.

Izzie stops at the open door. "I don't know about this, Mom."

"What are you going to do? Wear a hat for six months? Paint your head?" I grab her hand and pull her inside. "Come on. It'll be fine."

With a wary glance, she looks around at the walls of hair then slumps into a chair, leans forward, resting her head on her arms, the ball cap shades her face. For a moment we're alone together but without anything to say to each other. What is there to say?

A green and white striped curtain parts, then a young woman in her twenties emerges and greets us with a warm smile. She has shoulder length hair that is as thick and luxurious as a mink coat. Not a good sign. Izzie will hate her right off. "Hi. I'm Bettany. How can I help you?"

"We want to look at some wigs for my daughter, Isabel." I place a hand on Izzie's back. In spite of her relaxed position, I can feel the heat of nervousness rolling off her in waves. She pushes up from the table and moves away from us.

"Of course. Do you have a doctor's note?"

"Excuse me?"

"A doctor's letter of reference can qualify you for a donation by the foundation. We have connections with all of the oncologists in the area."

"Oncologist? Oh, no. I'm sorry. Uh . . . well, I'm not exactly sorry. But Isabel doesn't have cancer or anything." And that is a blessing. In spite of the trouble we seem to be swimming through these days, at least we don't have a serious illness pulling us deeper. "She . . . uh . . . shaved her head."

Bettany's large brown eyes widen. "Oh." She leans toward me, her gaze slipping toward Izzie who is fingering sample wigs. "Does she have a note from her psychiatrist?"

My earlier apology congeals. "N-no," I splutter. "She doesn't need—"

"I should warn you that our wigs can be quite expensive."

"It's okay." I glance toward the back of Izzie's baseball cap. "There's nothing else we can do. And she can't wear a hat to school. Against their policies. And, well, I'm at a loss as to what else to do."

"Then let's take a look at her face and see what might fit her shape and features best." Her tone is perky and confident and somehow points out my own insecurities.

"Isabel?"

She looks over her shoulder and glares at Bettany.

"I know this feels weird." Bettany moves toward a round table. "But honestly I know how you feel."

"Whatever." She does move toward us and plops down in the chair next to me.

"What's your natural hair color?" Bettany studies Izzie's head as if trying to peer under the ball cap. "Blonde?"

"How'd you know?"

"Your eyebrows and lashes."

"Oh. Yeah. Blonde."

"Well, that's a great color to have. We have all sorts of shades from white blonde to a dirty blonde to even strawberry blonde. If you want, we can even try on a different shade, something fun. You might like it."

Isabel doesn't respond.

Bettany pulls a bald mannequin's head out from behind the counter and sits it on the opposite side of the table from Izzie. "Are you in high school?"

"Yeah. A junior."

"Great. Now are you going to want your hair attached or do you want to remove it at night?"

"I'm a swimmer." Her voice wavers.

"Then you'll want to be able to remove it. Okay." Bettany smiles at her and suddenly removes her own hair. She places it carefully on the mannequin's head. But Bettany's scalp isn't smooth. It's scarred and crinkled in painful-looking pink patches. Tiny bits of dark hair poke through in places. "I was in an accident as a kid, Isabel. And now most of my hair won't grow. So I wear a wig too. I think you'll find out that it's not so bad. You might even like it."

Isabel stares at the young woman across from her, not even bothering to hide the horror and shock. "What happened?"

"Some acid hit me. I was really lucky that it didn't get on my face or in my eyes."

"Lucky?" Izzie's always lived a fairly sheltered life and to have someone feel fortunate that an accident of this magnitude isn't so bad is as foreign to her as the idea that some girls in the world aren't permitted to attend school. Reality has now pierced her protective bubble.

"Absolutely!" Bettany grins. "Most people never know I've got this." She runs a hand over her scalp. "And most people won't know you have a wig on either. I promise. I'll help you find the right one for you."

Tears well up in Isabel's eyes, and I smooth a hand over my daughter's back, aching to keep her innocent of the trials of this world, and yet knowing that's doing her a disservice.

❧

With the wig chosen and placed carefully on Izzie's head, I pull out my credit card.

"It's *how* much?" Izzie's voice rises, as does my blood pressure at the sight of the invoice.

"It's okay." I cup her arm to reassure her, but maybe it's simply to steady me from the staggering amount.

"No, Mom. I can't let you do this. All just because . . . no!"

I imagine my daughter, the only bald girl in school, and push my credit card toward Bettany. But Izzie snatches it away.

"My hair will grow." She tugs on my arm. "Let's go, Mom."

I look to Bettany for help, not sure what I'm asking. To be allowed to pay for it? Or for her to forgive us taking up so much of her time? "We're getting the wig, Izzie."

"No, we're not."

"Your dad will contribute." Or so I hope. "After all, it was his mother who instigated—"

"—escalated." A hint of a smile peeks through her dark scowl.

Behind us, the door opens, and Izzie ducks behind me. As if I can hide her when she's a good six inches taller. To help protect her from more ridicule or embarrassment, I suggest, "Why don't you wait in the car? It won't take but a few more minutes here."

"If you get the wig"—she takes my keys—"I won't wear it."

Grinding my teeth, I know her words are true. With an I'm-so-sorry glance at Bettany, I hope she doesn't work on commission, I slide my credit card back into my wallet.

"Isabel?"

I turn. "Terry!" I move forward to hug my friend who I haven't seen . . . since that night in my neighborhood. Didn't I promise to call her? A traffic jam of excuses piles up in my mind. "How are you?"

She hugs me back. "Good to see you, too."

Beside her is her daughter, Lily, several years younger than Izzie, who used to babysit the little girl. Lily's pale face and purple scarf covering her head makes my heart start to pound. Terry glances at Isabel, alarm showing in her face. "Is everything okay with *you*? With Isabel?"

I realize the unspoken question. "Oh, sure. We're fine. Isabel just had a close encounter with a razor."

Terry's eyes widen even more.

"Nothing bad. No nicks or cuts even." My joke falls flat. "Really, she's fine." I touch Izzie's bare nape. How can I stand here with my bald daughter and proclaim such a blessing when obviously it's not the case with Lily? "What about—?"

"Hi, Lily!" Bettany interrupts us. "Come with me. I've got something special for you."

Together they go into the back through the green and white curtain. I'm left standing beside Terry with more questions and fears crowding in on me. She meets my gaze solidly as if she's practiced this in the mirror. "Lily has cancer."

There is no punch line with a statement like that. It hits me squarely in the stomach. "What? When did this happen?"

"A year and a half ago. She's been through three rounds of chemo and radiation." Terry doesn't even attempt a smile or to sugarcoat the situation. Her honesty is breathtaking and heart-breaking. "She missed the end of third grade and all of fourth. But she's finally feeling better so we thought we'd get her a wig."

"I'm so sorry, Terry." My hand folds over her forearm, and I give a slight squeeze as if willing something . . . hope, help, I-don't-know-what into her. "I had no idea. What can I do to help?"

"Just pray. We need a miracle."

My throat works up and down, and I'm unable to respond except with a nod.

"We're hopeful things are going to work out."

I keep nodding and manage to stop myself when the curtain parts again. A smiling Lily emerges. She has a new do. Short wispy brown curls frame her tiny face. "What do you think, Momma?" Her Minnie Mouse voice cracks open my heart to expose every mother's worst nightmare. "Do you like it?"

Terry bends down and hugs her daughter fiercely yet tenderly. "I've never seen anything more beautiful."

"Come look at this, Lily!" Izzie calls from across the room. She's trying on a Cleopatra look.

While Izzie entertains Lily, Terry and I catch up. She didn't know about my divorce from Cliff any more than I knew about the hospital traumas her family has experienced. Izzie, Lily, and Bettany try on wigs together, pretending to be Miley Cyrus with long tresses then Cloris Leachman with a gray wig. They dance around like they're on *Dancing with the Stars*. Terry watches her daughter, the corners of her eyes pinched and her mouth pulling in a wistful smile.

Eventually we say good-bye, promising this time to keep in touch. Izzie and I climb back in our car, our own smiles and laughter dying quickly. Izzie's blue eyes brim with tears. "Is Lily going to be all right, Mom?"

Reassurances clog my throat. It's always been my job as her mom to put a positive spin on disappointments and difficult questions, waving my magic wand and making problems—disease and heartbreak—disappear. Is that what my parents did so many years ago? Did they hide the difficulty in their marriage under the delusion they were saving me heartache only to pull the rug out from under me with a quickie, no-pain divorce? Have I done the same thing to Izzie? Will this be the big hurdle to trip up Izzie, lay her out flat, the way my parents' divorce knocked me out cold?

When Cliff and I argued during our marriage, I reassured Izzie with, "All parents argue. It's okay. Daddy and Mommy love each other. We just don't always agree." I reassured myself that I was different from my folks. I was giving Izzie a realistic picture of married life. Arguments happen. But unfortunately so does divorce.

Maybe I was fooling myself then as much as Izzie. Because, obviously, Cliff did leave. I told Izzie at the time, "He'll come back when he realizes what he really lost." But who was I trying to convince? Maybe I was just sticking my head in the proverbial sand. So far, not facing the truth hasn't worked out so well for either of us. So, now, eyeball-to-eyeball with an even more devastating situation, one that could definitely end in heartbreak, I don't have an answer except for, "I don't know."

"I want to do something to help her!"

"I'm not sure there is anything we can do, Iz, except pray." But my prayers feel pretty impotent these days.

"There's got to be something."

"You can't save her, Iz." Anymore than I can protect Izzie from life.

She stares out the window and is silent all the way home.

⚜ Chapter Twelve ⚜

"You've got a date?" Marla's question lies somewhere between annoyance and skepticism when I tell her what's for dinner.

"It's not a date." I readjust the long, velveteen vest I found in my closet. "Just a . . . uh . . . thank-you. Sort of."

She pulls the phone book out of the cabinet. "A note says thank you. Flowers too. But dinner out? That's something else."

An uneasiness tightens my stomach. Flowers are usually impersonal, or so I learned with Cliff. The flowers he sent (or ordered his secretary to send) were usually out of guilt. My gaze slips toward the single white rosebud still on the kitchen table. The petals have opened. I'm not sure I'm open to any other reason for this dinner.

Marla waves a hand. "There's nothing wrong with you dating, Kaye. In fact, it's probably a good idea."

"Why do you say that?"

"You're not still waiting for Cliff to come back to you, are you?" She purses her lips and gives me a once-over, a bold assessment that declares the impossibility of my dream. While I'm scrambling for a comeback, Marla shakes her head. My silence is answer enough. "Cliff has moved on, dear. And so should you. You married too early. If you hadn't gotten yourself pregnant, the relationship never would have lasted more than two weeks."

If Marla had launched herself at me, teeth bared and claws protracted, I couldn't have been more shocked. Even Cousin It's attacks weren't vicious. As her words sink into me, shred my dignity, my hope, I blink copiously like a tragic butterfly trying to take flight in a gale. I sputter a useless sound, then my gaze shifts to Isabel, who has her arms crossed over her chest and is waiting, her flip-flop tapping out her impatience on the kitchen tile.

None of Marla's words are news to my daughter. After all, there comes a time when every kid can do the math and realizes her parents' wedding anniversary doesn't have a nine-month gap before her birth. But as I splutter to the surface of my thoughts, taking little tiny puffs of air, the audacity of Marla's bullying unplugs the dam of pent-up emotions stored over the years. "Are you saying I got pregnant all by myself?" I draw a quick breath of confidence, not allowing enough time for Marla to respond. "My recollection is that Cliff was more than eager to participate!"

"Mom!" Izzie's disgust couldn't be more clear if she'd slapped her palms over her ears and run out of the room.

Marla waves her hands like a baby bird flapping its weak wings and attempting to take flight and stay above my attempt to attack right back with my own claws. "Well, dear"—she flips through pages in the phone book, not looking down at the categories she's filing past—"there's no use crossing old bridges, now is there?"

She made that leap first. If we're crossing into uncharted waters, I'm not going alone. "None of that matters anyway." My gaze narrows as I gain control over my tossed and strewn emotions. "He made a vow. And—"

"And you're going to hold him to it." She laughs. *Laughs.* My emotions fray into raw strands of indignation, fury, and pain. "Good luck, dear." Then Marla glances down at the restaurant listings on the bright yellow pages as if I'm a humorous comic strip and not a tragic figure. "Divorce attorney and psychiatric offices are full of women who meant to hold onto their men and the vows they made."

"Mom"—Izzie interjects a lifeline into my nightmare—"we're going to be late."

I release a breath and look to my mother-in-law, who I'd like to boot out of my house at the moment. She still looks like a smaller, red-haired version of Rocky. I give what sounds like a polite clearing of the throat but which truthfully is clearing the way for me to offer a UN solution. I pray she won't take me up on the offer as I hook my purse over my shoulder. "You're invited to come with us for dinner."

Marla looks at me with that lopsided gaze as if she's trying to size up my intentions. "Thank you, but I'm not ready to go out in prime time yet. I'll just order something."

"But I made another casserole for you. It's in the oven."

"It'll keep. Don't worry about me. I'll be fine here. All alone."

I weigh her tone to see if that's a ploy for sympathy or simply desire. Reading between her not too subtle lines is not for a novice. It's her usual ploy laced with guilt, but I'm not swallowing it this time. She's perfectly capable of being alone for a couple of hours. "Suit yourself."

Izzie's forehead smooths out and she claps a bright pink baseball cap on her head.

"When will your wig be ready?" Marla's question halts us at the door.

"Never. I'm fine without it." And she whisks her cap off her head and tosses it onto the kitchen table, a gauntlet thrown in her grandmother's direction.

"What will you tell your friends, dear?" The added *dear* is a fabrication of deigned concern.

"Why do I have to tell them anything?"

Marla shrugs a narrow, indifferent shoulder. "They're not blind. They'll ask. And worst of all, they'll talk behind your back."

"Let 'em. I don't care." Izzie's bravado is admirable, but I'm afraid it might wane under the force of peer scrutiny. "I told them it's for swimming. I'm focused on setting a record this season."

"And impressing that new coach?" Marla throws back, making my maternal nerves quake.

"Yeah. He was impressed with Mom the other day." Izzie turns and walks out the back door, leaving it open for me to follow. Her bending of the truth disturbs me, especially when I realize that, just maybe, I'm equally guilty of distortions I've told in the past.

When we reach the car, Izzie places a comforting hand on my arm. "Ignore her, Mom. You *should* date."

"So you're in agreement with your grandmother?"

"Not for the same reasons."

I jerk the gear shift into Drive. "Close enough."

✁✁

Still rattled after the short drive to the crowded Asian restaurant, I greet Jack and Gabe, my face feeling stretched into a pained smile. After we order platters of Orange Beef, Thai Mango Chicken, tofu lo mei, and an assortment of pot stickers and spring rolls, Gabe and Isabel find a table for two, leaving Jack and me on our own. Which unnerves me. Should I insist we all sit together? Keep an eye on Gabe and Izzie? Play it cool? Pretend it's a date, even if it isn't?

"This okay?"

"Sure." I slide into the booth opposite Jack. The table is too small; the booth too intimate. He's wearing a pale yellow button-down shirt and jeans. His dark hair has that carefree, mussed look that makes me want to run my fingers through the slight waves. I fuss with my purse, stashing it beside me in the booth.

He holds out a straw for me. "You okay?"

"Of course." I plunk it into my iced tea then unfold a napkin and lay it across my lap. "How are things going at your place?"

He grabs both ends of the straw and pulls outward, popping the paper covering. "A bit on the crazy side. It's crunch time for Gabe's Eagle Scout project. You and Isabel should come out this weekend and see what he's doing."

I don't know anything about Boy Scouts . . . or Girl Scouts for that matter. "So remind me what exactly this project is."

"Gabe conceived it. He's altering a park to accommodate disabled kids. I only helped with the funding but he met with all the sponsors and convinced them to invest in his project." A waiter brings our food and Jack tells them which dishes belong with Gabe and Izzie across the room. Jack ladles out rice for both of us, scooping generous portions onto our plates. He offers me the platters of food first and I take a helping of Thai Chicken while he spoons Orange Beef onto his plate.

"What inspired Gabe?"

"His little sister is disabled. Amy's never been able to play on regular playgrounds. Neither can any kid with a wheelchair or walker. So Gabe petitioned the city council and got permission. Then he met with some of my wealthier clients and asked for donations. He raised almost fifty thousand dollars. With those donations, we've bought equipment plus some was donated to update the park. We've already done the grading and repaving. This weekend we're putting the rest of it together. Gabe's rallied a bunch of kids from school to help out, along with local troops."

"He's some kid."

Jack grins. It's a devastatingly charming smile that shines right through to my soul. "I couldn't be more proud of him if he was my own."

His comment strikes a nerve in me that resonates outward. If only Cliff would be half as involved in Izzie's life, but he hasn't made it to one swim meet since he left. He always has to work.

Or he's out of town. There's always some excuse. I glance over at Gabe and Isabel. Their heads are inclined toward each other and they're engaged in what appears to be a deep discussion. What are they talking about?

"So how are things at your place?" Jack interrupts my thoughts.

It's a delicate subject, which I approach cautiously. "She's improving."

"How long will she be with you?"

I blow out a breath as if it were candles on a birthday cake. "I wish I knew."

"That good, huh?"

Shrugging, I focus on the Thai Chicken, which has a bit of a kick to it. "She means well." If only I were as convinced as I sound.

"There's a wide road between meaning well and doing good."

I laugh. "You must have a Marla in your own life."

"I've known a couple."

"Is that the reason you're not married?" The intimate question takes even me by surprise. Jack is a curiosity to me. That's all.

His mouth twists as he ponders the question. "I'm cautious."

"Have you ever been in love?"

He hesitates almost too long. So does that mean it's a fresh wound or too painful to discuss? "I was. She wasn't." He lifts a shoulder awkwardly. "We were supposed to get married. And then didn't. It's one of the many reasons I'm selling the house. I kept it for a while, telling myself it was a good investment. But it's become an albatross. It definitely needs a woman's touch. And well . . ."

His hesitation makes me even more curious. Is he still aching over that love? Or has he chalked it up to experience? "The decorating is my job. The furniture should be delivered tomorrow, by the way." Back on a safe topic, I relax.

"Good." The tension in his face eases. It's easy to see why women chase after him.

"How long have you owned the house?"

"Five years."

I study him for a minute, seeing the way his hand grips the edge of the table. "She must have really broken your heart."

"Oh, I'm over her. Tiffany. That was . . . *is* her name." He shakes his head as if having a discussion with himself. "I've learned that once you get to a certain level of income, there's a reason to be cautious."

"So women are after your money?" And other things, I surmise, taking in his casual, no-fuss good looks.

"Let's just say I've learned that beauty is often *only* skin deep."

"And you're looking for more?"

He leans forward, meeting my gaze squarely. "Absolutely. Looks only last so long."

"Then it's the nip-and-tuck stage." Inwardly, I wince. Cliff nipped me out of his life and tucked his family out of sight. Maybe I should have visited a surgeon like Marla did. Was she just trying to hang onto what she had? Or grasp something more? Maybe I should have tried harder.

Jack grabs an egg roll, bites off the end, chews, and swallows. "I don't get plastic surgery at all. I understand it's needed for car accidents and to repair birth defects. But . . ."

"Could it be avoidance?" I voice my own fears and reasons for not pursuing such a course.

"Exactly. We're all headed in the same direction. You can't evade death. And seems to me, folks don't want to think about what could happen, what will eventually happen."

Nodding, I plunge my fork into fluffy white rice. "They don't want to have to make a decision about God."

"You're right. Interesting that God's Word says we'll grow more beautiful with age in heaven, and yet here on earth the opposite happens. Or we see it that way." For a moment he focuses on eating the egg roll and I scoop up rice. "When Gabe's father passed away, I knew I couldn't avoid the issue anymore either." He leans back, his mouth drawing to the side as if he's reluctant to share something. "We were best friends since fourth grade and went off to college together. Luke and I once made a bet on who would become a millionaire first."

His statement surprises me. It sounds so much like something Cliff would say or do. Maybe the two men are more alike than I originally thought. But I suspect something along their paths made them veer onto different trails.

"We came from nothing. Our families had no money. We both made it to college on scholarships." Having started out at opposite ends of the spectrum from Cliff, maybe Jack was destined for a different outcome. "I'm embarrassed to say I won our bet. I don't think Luke ever pursued it as seriously as I did though. He found his purpose in life—he was a great husband and father." Jack remains silent for a long moment, concentrating on his dinner then he glances toward Gabe. "He shouldn't have died."

"We all do though some day. We can't circumvent it."

"At least he died doing what he knew he was supposed to do." He stares down at his food, not eating, not pretending to. The weight of his loss rounds his shoulders. "Seems to me, there are better things to spend your money and time on than sucking out fat and lifting . . . well, you know."

"And what do you spend your money on? Not just those pin-ball machines."

"Oh, that." He laughs. "I bought those for Gabe and his siblings, while their dad was sick and in the aftermath of their dad. They came here on weekends to give their mom a break." He rubs his chin. "I got carried away. I wanted to distract them. Spoil them. Make up somehow for what they'd lost. Kind of foolish to think anything could take the place of their father."

His desperation to fix an unfixable situation pierces me. I offer him a tender smile. "It's sweet of you to try."

He shrugs and looks toward Gabe and Izzie. "I'm just a glorified uncle, but I think of Pam and Luke's kids as my own. I want to help them all I can. I promised Luke I would."

Does he worry the way a parent does? Does he toss and turn at night while contemplating all the things that can go wrong, from some crazy student at school bringing a gun to maneuvering through traffic to bad grades and stupid mistakes? Does he send up prayers of desperation, knowing there is nothing he can do to protect his child from all the dangers of this world?

"I donated the arcade games to local orphanages and church youth groups. That's why the movers were there last night."

His generosity admonishes me. What would I have done? Sold them on eBay? Cliff would have. "That's great." Maybe Gabe's unselfish act of establishing a park for challenged kids might not be such an anomaly. "So the house is clear?"

"Ready for the furniture."

My gaze shifts toward the newest threat to my peace of mind. "You think they're okay together? Iz and Gabe. I mean—" Heat works its way up from my chest, and I'm unsure if it's from the spicy Thai Mango or from embarrassment. "I know the trouble teens can get into. And I wouldn't want them to . . . well, you know."

Do what I did. But I keep that to myself. Will Jack's thoughts go down the same slippery slope?

"Nothing is going to happen in this restaurant."

A nervous laugh skips out of me. "I didn't mean here. I just meant—"

"I know what you meant." His gaze is solemn as if he's reading my very thoughts, my glaring mistakes. But there is no condemnation in that steady gaze. Simply understanding. "They're good kids. We'll keep an eye out for them, but I'm not too worried. I know Gabe."

"And I know Izzie."

"Then we should be okay." His gaze bores into me. "So how is it going on the get-your-husband-back front?"

A flush resurfaces. I tug on my vest and stare down at my napkin. I wish I could report success, even progress. "He's out of town."

"That's not very helpful."

I twirl my fork in the rice, no longer hungry. "My mother-in-law wants me to date."

"Her son?"

"Other men."

"Ouch. But that might be a way for you to regain his interest." Jack leans forward, resting his forearms on the edge of the table. "If Cliff thinks others are interested . . . well, that's how the game works, right? It's a lot like what you do for a living."

"Staging?"

"Yeah. Dating is another variation of staging. You know, take someone out, walk them through your life, see how they fit in."

Why doesn't that make me feel any better?

"If you need any help in that area"—his voice dips so low I'm not sure I'm hearing him correctly—"let me know."

"Uh, okay, I'll let you know."

Is he offering to be my pretend end table, a prop to help Cliff see himself stationed back in my life? Or is he thinking more of an arm decoration, as in taking my arm, walking through life with me?

❧

When I return home, Gabe and Izzie sit on the front steps still talking intently and Marla watches *The Bachelor* on television, so I put on my running shoes and grab the dog's leash. Jack's words create hurdles in my mind that I can't quite get over. What is my purpose? Jack seems so comfortable, and yet so determined.

So is the dog. Determined, that is. Cousin It drags me along behind as she noses the grass and every mailbox, jerking the leash each time she changes trajectory. Why do I always feel insecure and wishy-washy?

Keeping up a steady pace though, I manage to block out thoughts of Marla, Cliff, Jack, Izzie, and Gabe. I jog past pumpkins and a couple of ghouls dangling from trees, pumping my legs faster and faster until my lungs feel like they might burst, then slow to a walk, my tennis shoes feeling like steel boots; Cousin It still *boing-boing-boings* with energy. My breathing requires all of my attention and distracts me from unanswerable questions.

After a mile, more or less, I return to my house. A splash of water from the backyard tells me Izzie is swimming. Cousin It lunges and barks at the shadows, nearly pulling the leash out of my hand. Then I see a solid figure on the front porch. Could it be Cliff? Jack? My heart kicks into high gear.

As the dog pulls me along behind and we draw closer, I recognize Harry Klum. He stands on the front porch. He bends and holds out a hand for It to sniff. Behind his back, he holds a bouquet of what looks to be self-picked flowers. He's dressed in his usual mismatched style, wearing a button-down shirt that looks as if it came right out of the package, crease folds still in place. It's tucked into the elastic waistband (which is stretched to its breaking point) of his crinkly warm-up pants. "How's Miss Marla? I rang the doorbell several times but no one came."

"I think my daughter is in the pool. And Marla may have gone to bed." It's an easier explanation than *she hides like a teen with bad acne.* I unlock the door with the key I tucked in my sock and push open the door. From down the hallway, I hear water running. "Or maybe she's taking a bath."

I don't know what to tell this kind, thoughtful man. I probably should break the news that he doesn't stand a chance with Marla. Facing the inevitable is the right thing to do. She's the most particular woman I've ever known. Harry seems her direct opposite. I don't want to be the one to hurt him, so I dilute the truth. "She's still not ready for visitors."

"I understand." His words are simple but heartfelt. He doesn't seem to have any expectations.

"Thanks for the flowers, Harry. I'll tell Marla you came—"

"Kaye?" Marla's panicked voice startles me.

I peek inside the entryway but don't see her.

"I'm back, Marla!" Should I warn her she has company?

"Is that the plumber?" she calls from down the hall.

"Plumber?" Did I miss something? I start to close the door and stop at the sight of Harry. "I'm sorry, Harry. I better go." I have to figure out what Marla is talking about. Maybe she took too many of her pain meds and is hallucinating.

But Harry doesn't back away. He steps forward. "What's wrong?"

"I'm not sure." I turn my back on him. "Marla? Where are you? What's going on?"

"The water won't turn off—" Her voice carries around the corner just before she appears, wrapped in a bath towel. "I wasn't sure . . ." Her eyes widen, and her voice trails off.

"Miss Marla," Harry says in a courtly tone.

"Oh! Oh, no! Oh, my!" Marla's shocked look quickly vanishes as if erased by a sudden Botox injection. She raises her hands as if trying to hide behind them "Mr. Klum." Then she ducks and turns.

"I brought you these." He gestures toward the flowers I'm holding.

She stops, straightens her spine. I hand the bunch of flowers to her.

She blinks, one eyelid slightly slower than the other, then abruptly turns toward me. "I called 9-1-1 and they were supposed to call a plumber."

"You called the police because the water wouldn't turn off." I brace my hand against the door.

"What else was I supposed to do?"

Unplug the drain. Turn off the water to the house. Look up a plumber in the Yellow Pages and dial the number yourself! But my mental list of acceptable behaviors in this type of emergency are drowned out by a siren screaming up the street.

Harry steps toward me. "Maybe I could have a look."

"Do you know anything about plumbing?"

"Mr. Klum used to be a plumber." Disdain saturates Marla's tone. "He's retired now."

Her contempt pokes at me and I grab Harry's arm in defense. "Oh! You're a hero then. Would you mind taking a look?"

He steps into my house. The siren grows louder as a fire truck stops in front. The red light flashes in a side window, turning the carpet pink momentarily. Marla places her hands over her ears and yells, "This way!"

I turn to face the firefighter racing for my house. "It's okay. Everything is all right! There's no emergency."

Not yet anyway. Other than my mother-in-law is driving me crazy.

~{ Chapter Thirteen }~

Harry wipes his black greasy fingers on the side of his pants. He seems to know his way around a drain. "Looks like whoever installed this faucet, put it in backwards."

"Can it be fixed, Mr. Klum?" Exhaustion weights my words. After sending the fire department off and listening to Marla complain that she didn't know what to do or who to call over and over again because I didn't leave the plumber's number for her, I'm ready to crawl into my sofa bed, cover my head with the pillow, and try to block out this evening.

"Call me Harry."

"Harry," I test out his name.

He nods in a gentlemanly fashion, which strikes me as odd while we sit in my bathroom, he on the side of the tub and me on the toilet lid, as we watch the water slowly swirl down the bathtub drain like a miniature tornado. The water had just started to overflow when Harry came to the rescue. A pile of damp towels sits at my feet.

"I can fix this. No problem."

"I don't want to impose. I can call a plumber."

"You've already got one here. I don't mind helping." He looks at me with kind blue eyes, the corners crinkled with lines. "Makes me feel useful again." He focuses on wrenching off a bolt.

"Retirement isn't all it's cracked up to be. Besides I wouldn't want Miss Marla to forgo her bath."

I glance toward the door that leads to my bedroom, where Marla has barricaded herself. "Why *did* you retire? If you don't mind me asking."

"I had some things I needed to do around the house. And now, I piddle around here and there. Gives me more time for volunteer work at the church. There's always a stopped-up toilet. And we have a ministry to single moms, so I help with that."

"Your church sounds very ministry based."

He nods, focusing on replacing the handles for the faucet. "Aren't they all?"

I purse my lips. My church has prayed along with me that Cliff would return to his marriage and family. I've heard sermons on receiving blessings, doing good, tithing. There are mission trips to faraway places like Latvia and Africa. But there isn't a ministry to help single mothers. Or even single fathers. There are plenty of activities for singles. And seniors. Vacation Bible School. Family bowling or swim nights. The imaginary finger I'm pointing is aimed straight at me. But I focus on Harry's hands, with calluses and knobby knuckles as they move slowly but deliberately. "What do you do for single moms?"

"Well . . . we have a day where they drive their cars through and we check oil and tires and fix car seats. Then there's plumbing and other handyman type of work. Even yard work. Keeps me busy enough."

"I'd say." He's a plain man, but there's nothing plain or ordinary about his heart. It sparkles like gold. He makes me question if my church is deficient in not offering such a ministry or if I'm simply being selfish because I'd like someone to check the oil in my car, mow my yard, and fix my plumbing.

Harry pats me on the shoulder. "Don't worry. It's not so bad . . . your plumbing problem. It won't take long to fix it." He grins. "And you'll love my rates."

"I can pay you." At his dubious look, I add, "Really. Even though I'm a single mom, I can pay."

"Just consider: what goes around, comes around."

I tilt my head. Am I going to help with someone's plumbing? I glance at the tubes and tools. I wouldn't have a clue where to begin.

"You took in Miss Marla. Taxied her to the doctor. Fixed her meals. Made sure she took her medicine."

"Oh, well . . ."

"No, really." He taps my leg lightly with a wrench. "Sure, she could have hired someone to care for her. No problem. But what you did was generous. Generosity of the heart."

Harry's own generosity makes me question if I've been focused on what's right and wrong. Especially in my marriage. Of course Cliff was wrong. To prove it, he should come back. But has my focus been too self-serving? My heart feels skewered. "Have you ever done something really stupid, Harry?"

"Yeah." He begins placing his tools back in his neat and tidy toolbox. "But it usually has to do with love. Not drains."

I laugh. His answer surprises me, but then all the flowers he's brought to Marla come to mind. Does he feel foolish for courting her?

He twists the wrench around in his hands then lays it in his tool box. "When Marla was in the hospital, I took her some flowers."

The only flowers in her hospital room was the bunch of daisies, which I bought at the grocery store one morning on the way to see her. "You did?"

"Well, I would have, but I saw she had company." He glances away. "I panicked."

I snap my fingers. "I remember you now. You should have come in. It would have been okay."

"Not with Marla," he shrugs. "Chalk the whole thing up to my stupidity."

I chuckle along with him and pat him on the shoulder. "I guess we all do silly things. I certainly have lately. What kind of dumb things have you done for love, Harry?"

"Doesn't bear repeating." He frowns and reaches again for the wrench, using it again to tighten the faucet once more. "Love makes a person do strange, goofy things sometimes. And sometimes courageous things. Guess there's a fine line between bravery and foolishness. Only in retrospect can we know the difference. Sometimes it works out, sometimes not."

When he finishes hooking back up the faucet, the tub has almost completely drained. "You've got a clog."

I watch the water slipping down the drain and feel as if I'm that little Dutch boy holding my finger in the hole of my marriage. All alone. Unable to dam up the leaks by myself. "I guess so."

"Don't have my rotor rooter today. I can bring it tomorrow."

"Can't I pour something down the drain to dissolve it?"

He looks at me like I've spoken heresy. "I'll bring the right equipment tomorrow."

"Okay."

He ducks his head then looks at me again. "How"—his tone is hushed—"is Marla really doing?"

"Better, I think."

"Is she still seeing Andy?"

"Who?"

"Anderson Sterling."

Oh! The tuxedoed rose man. "I don't really know." I don't want to tell Harry how she dotes on his hothouse flowers and how he left her sexy items in a brown paper bag on the front porch. "She hasn't seen anyone really since her surgery."

"Guess it doesn't matter. She's obviously not interested in me. She didn't stick around long when I came in to fix this. And well, we men usually have a hard time understanding women, but Miss Marla has made her feelings pretty clear."

I glance at the closed bedroom door and my heart aches for this kind man. "Well, I think it has more to do with *her* rather than you."

He gives me a questioning look.

I want to say she's caught up in the superficial, but I refrain. "She doesn't really know you, Harry. Plus, she's a bit self-conscious right now."

He nods. "Think she'd see me? Talk to me?"

"You can try. But no guarantees."

He stands, rubs his hands on the front of his pant legs, and releases a slow breath. Walking out into the hallway, he hesitates at her door. Then he knocks.

Silence answers him. I reach for the towels at my feet, gathering them to me.

He knocks again, this time louder. I ache for him. Have I set him up for failure? Is it a lie I've fed him? My own hope for restoration with Cliff transferred to him? Or is there really hope?

"What is it?" Marla's voice comes through the door, curt, irritated. "*Who* is it?"

"It's me, Miss Marla. Harry . . . Harry Klum."

"Thank you for your services." Her tone is dismissive.

"My pleasure, ma'am." He glances over his shoulder with a triumphant smile. After a couple of minutes, he taps quietly on the door again. "Are you doing all right?"

"I'm not up to having visitors."

"Yes, yes, ma'am, I know. Of course, I understand. I just wanted you to know"—he touches the door as if reaching out to touch Marla—"you're missed back at the village."

"Really?"

Her response surprises me and yet it shouldn't. He appealed to her vanity, and she grabbed the lure—hook, line, and sinker.

"Yes, ma'am. Folks ask about you all the time. When are you coming back? How are you doing?"

"Anyone specific?" Her tone lifts with a hopeful note and probing edge.

He names several women. "Can I bring you anything? Books, magazines?"

"No, thank you."

He leans forward as if to capture every word. "I hope the flowers brightened up your room."

A long pause precedes a curt, "Thank you."

"Well"—he rubs his hands over the back of his pants—"I better be going." He glances back over his shoulder at me, and I offer him an encouraging smile. I'm proud of him for trying. But at the same time, I feel cruel for encouraging him.

When Marla doesn't answer with a *good-bye* or *have a nice day*, he starts down the hall, carrying his toolbox. His shoulders slump forward. His footsteps remain heavy and slow. My heart hurts for him. At the same time, anger rises up in me like the water in the bathtub. I want to wrench open the door, drag Marla out of her sanctuary, and push her toward Harry. Doesn't she know what a nice man he is? What is *wrong* with her?

What's worse—am I being like Harry in trying to get Cliff back? Are my actions just as foolishly hopeless? Is that how others see me? Poor pathetic Kaye, still trying to get her husband back after all this time. Can't she see the writing on the wall? He wants someone younger, prettier, thinner, someone other than me.

Hot tears scald my eyes.

Then Marla's door opens. Only a smidgen, allowing for a tiny bit of hope to enter.

My heart pounds. I squeeze back the tears. Will she reconsider? Will she call out to Harry? I hold my breath.

One of her eyes zeroes in on me. "Is he gone?"

"He's leaving right now."

She glances down the hallway, pushes the door open wider. She's traded her towel in for a pink negligee. "Thank you." Her voice is faint. "Thank you for fixing the tub."

He pauses, his shoulders straightening, and he turns back.

Marla stays mostly hidden behind the door.

"You're welcome, Miss Marla," he calls back. "You're mighty welcome." He grins at me and winks. Maybe he's not so foolish after all.

Maybe he's just exhibiting true patience.

✦

I must have prayed for patience at some time, which is why, I surmise, I'm stuck sitting in a doctor's office waiting on Marla. The magazine across my lap is full of airbrushed beauties that set my teeth on edge. I've seen documentaries exposing photo shoots that create a fantasy where models' waists are whittled with the click of a computer, pimples are zapped, wrinkles erased and other body parts enlarged. Hair extensions give the illusion of glorious oversized hairdos. It's all a façade that makes real women feel inadequate.

With the agitated flick of my wrist, the page turns and a headline grabs me: "Miss Plastic of Hungary . . . not hungry." Apparently, now there's some beauty pageant for those women who *admit* to having facelifts, boob jobs, and tummy tucks. Honesty! That's a first. Maybe Marla could go overseas and compete. What's next? Miss Let-It-All-Hang-Out America?

Pretending to read, I give a cursory glance around the waiting room. There are three other women flipping through magazines or checking their iPhones. All the women look calm and comfortable. Are they pre- or post-op? Are they here for their next Botox injection or simply a consultation?

The door where Marla disappeared thirty minutes ago opens. "Ms. Redmond?"

I close my magazine. "Yes. That's me."

I feel the gazes of the other women looking at me. Do they think I'm pre-op? Or here for my first injection?

The nurse motions for me to follow her. "If you could come this way."

"Me?" Then I realize Marla probably needs something. "Sure."

We weave through a maze of hallways, past islands of activities where everyone is either on the phone or scanning charts. I'm shown to an examination room where Marla sits on a comfortable chair as she sips a chilled glass of water.

"Oh, good, Kaye. Have a seat, will you?"

I glance around, realizing the nurse has left us alone. The only option for my backside is the exam table or the doctor's stool. I decide to remain standing until I can return safely to the waiting area. "What do you need, Marla?"

She sips her water. "If you want some, the nurse will get it."

"I'm fine. What—"

"I thought while we're here, you could see Dr. Scarr, see what he can do for you."

My heart rate skyrockets. "What?"

"Since you're so determined to get Cliff back, you should probably . . ." She hesitates, waving her hand around her face. "Freshen yourself up. Make the most of your assets."

Anger bursts inside me and my face grows hot. I cross my arms over my chest, well, propping up my droopy chest and covering my bulging middle. Words flounder around in my head like a fish flopping on the ground. I catch one solid word: "No." Then I turn on my heel and grab the door handle, but I face her again. "I'll be waiting in the car."

"Kaye, don't get so huffy. I only meant—"

"I know exactly what you meant. And . . . and . . . don't you understand? Being loved for . . . for *this* . . . for a lie is not really love. I want to be loved for me."

"Mom, get up."

I blink open my grainy eyes. "What is it? What's wrong?"

Isabel stands over me, dressed in a pink top and jean cutoffs. "Nothing. I need you to take me to the park to help Gabe."

I sit up, my back aching from the foldout sofa. "What time is it?"

"I don't know. Six."

"In the morning? It's Saturday." Our one day to sleep late. *Later.* Except when there's a swim meet. Already there's a soft glow coming through the window as the sun rises.

"I can take the car if you don't want to get up."

That wakes me up like a splash of cold water. "You don't have a license yet." Then I see the smile on her face. I swing my legs off the foldout sofa. "I'm coming."

"I can call Gabe."

I rub the sleep from my face. "No, no. It's okay. I'm up."

After a quick breakfast of oatmeal, which I figure Marla can swallow without chewing much but which she only stirs with her spoon, we promise to return in a little while.

"What should I tell Cliff?"

That stops me. "About what?"

She swirls her spoon through her uneaten oatmeal. Maybe she can use it for a facial mask later. "He said he'd be by sometime today . . . maybe."

Maybe is always the key word with him. But before I can respond, Izzie hooks her arm through mine and says, "Tell Dad he can come help us."

I settle into the driver's seat and glance at my reflection in the rearview mirror. I smooth a hand over my cheek, wishing I'd taken the time to put on more than mascara. "Do you think he will?"

"Are you kidding? Not a chance."

Unsure if I'm relieved that he won't see me dirty and grimy from working at the park or disappointed that I'll miss an opportunity with him, I jam the key into the ignition.

"So, what do you think about Jack?" Her tone is aloof, but I catch her pointed glance.

"Jack?" I back out of the driveway, keeping my eyes on the side mirror. "I don't think about Jack. He's a client."

Her mouth compresses. "But he's cute, don't you think?"

"I think he's way too old for you." I shove the gear shift into Drive.

"Mom." She draws it out dramatically. "Not for me."

"Oh, well, then okay, he's nice looking. Sure."

"According to Gabe, he is *very* successful."

"Whoa, Iz, I'm not interested in Jack. Nice as he is." Cute as he is, but I keep that piece of info to myself.

"I know. You want Dad." She says it as if she's four and I've set a bowl of broccoli in front of her. At that moment I want to smack Cliff for making his own daughter dislike him. If she were a client, her disinterest would bother him and he'd be determined to change her mind. "Whatever."

With that, the door of communication slams shut.

"Gabe is nice." I attempt to wedge that door open for a moment longer as I turn the car down the street toward the park. "He's cute too."

"He's too young for *you,"* she counters.

I smile. "And I thought I'd make a good Mrs. Robinson."

"Who?"

"Never mind." But I realize the door is still open, ever so slightly.

She stares out the side window but doesn't plug her iPod into her ears. Another good sign. We pass through a couple of stoplights. "Gabe and I are going to work on a project together. Is that okay? Cause if it's not, well, we're gonna do it anyway."

That kind of introduction draws a wary and irritated glance. "What kind of project?"

"We're going to raise money for Lily." She lifts her chin. "Gabe's dad was sick with cancer and so he knows insurance doesn't cover everything. Especially experimental stuff. It was *his* idea."

"That's great that you want to help." I hesitate, not sure what I should say, because I don't want Izzie disappointed if their efforts can't save Lily. Money so rarely can. "I don't know much about Lily's condition. Or what the doctors are saying," But Lily's mother said to pray for a miracle. My throat tightens. "So—"

"We *have* to do something, Mom."

"But there might not be anything you can do. Except pray, Izzie."

She pinches her lips closed.

I take several slow breaths, my hands tightening on the steering wheel. "I just don't want you hurt, Iz."

"I'm not the one with cancer, Mom. I want to do this. I *need* to do this!"

"Okay, then. What's the plan? Are you going door-to-door asking for donations?" My head reels. What kind of permit will they need for something like that?

"No, we're going to put on a swim-a-thon."

"A swim-a-what?"

"We'll get corporate sponsors. The swim team will volunteer. I know it."

"I've never heard of such a thing."

"Think of it like a luau, Mom. You and Dad used to throw lots of parties."

"A swim party?" I hate that I sound dubious . . . too much like Marla. She always loved playing Devil's advocate when Cliff and I would say we were buying a new house or putting in a pool or building a deck. Maybe that's simply the job of a mother. Or maybe I should simply shut up. But I can't seem to help myself.

I'm imagining a hundred teens swarming over our house. "So will it be at our pool?"

"Mom." She gives me one of those looks that tells me how dense I am. "We've already talked to the coach about a date for us to use the school's pool."

Safety issues arise in my mind like buoys popping up all over a harbor. "And will there be lifeguards?"

She sighs again. "We're all competitive swimmers."

"Yes, but—"

"There will be lots of us around who can save someone. Like you, if you start to drown."

"Me?" Does that mean I'm swimming? What I'm really asking is does that mean I have to don a swimsuit?

"Maybe *Jack* can rescue you."

I'm not sure if it's her tone or the slight smile that injects starch in my spine. "Why would you say that?"

"Why are you being so difficult about this?"

"About what? Jack? Or the swim-a-thon?"

"Why don't you want me to help Lily?"

Ah, Lily. An easier subject than . . . anything else. "It's not that I don't want you to help." It's that I don't want Izzie to know at this young age that sometimes your best efforts just aren't enough. "Or do something for Lily."

"We're being smart about this, Mom. We're doing it like foundations do marathons or walk-a-thons, where people sponsor a swimmer and pay a certain amount for each lap they swim. Jack's even taking care of the legal details."

"Are you going to limit it only to the swim team?"

"So you do want to swim laps."

I swallow hard not wanting to think about myself in a swimsuit. Lily. Concentrate on Lily. "I want to help too."

Then my daughter gives me a smile that makes my chest swell with love, crowding out all my fears and worries.

Temporarily.

꙳

It's been years since I've parked the car and walked into this park. Once upon a time, I brought Izzie here in her car seat and stroller. She'd toddle around wanting to swing and slide at the same time. "Swing!" she'd demand. And I'd push her until I thought my arms would fall off. Then she'd climb up the slide over and over while I watched and chatted with other mothers. It's how I met Elise and Terry.

Today though, teens rather than toddlers crowd the park as if free food is being provided. It's a fairly small park, but popular in the community. It has limited equipment but large trees surrounding it, which become vital in the summer months when the Texas heat intensifies.

Some teens lounge on swings and the teeter-totters, but most are actively engaged in carrying equipment and tools this way and that. They step over metal bars and large sheets of plastic lying on the ground. It looks like a giant pick-up-sticks game in action. Ramps and handrails are being added to the already existent play equipment.

Izzie immediately detaches herself from me and heads off to see friends. Gabe gives her the task of handing out water to those working on the project. It's a beautiful fall day with a bright blue sky with only a hint of a breeze. I walk around, remembering this park from when I brought Izzie here as a toddler. Those were tender days. I was young and naïve, blissfully unaware that other babies didn't have Izzie's good health, ignorant of the future of how my marriage would crash into a roadblock. The facelift the park is getting will be good for the community and for children of all shapes and sizes and abilities. My heart swells for what Gabe has envisioned.

I catch sight of Jack straddling two bars on the jungle gym, a battery-powered screwdriver in hand. He waves, and I smile, returning the wave, then trip over something hard and square.

Glancing down, I recognize a familiar toolbox. A quick look, right then left, before I find Harry stretched out under a slide. I nudge the toe of his boot, and he tilts his torso to look at me.

"Why, Miss Kaye, how are you?"

"I'm fine, Harry. And you?"

"Never better." He grins.

"Can I give you a hand?"

"I'm okay here, but you might check with Gabe."

I want to ask how he knows Izzie's friend, but he's already gone back to work. So I wander back over to the truck where Gabe is checking a notebook. I'm impressed that this young man has organized everything and that Jack hasn't done it all for him.

"Hi, Gabe."

"Mrs. Redmond! Thanks for coming. Izzie too."

I notice he's taken up her nickname. How is their relationship growing? "She insisted. Pushed *me* out of bed for a change."

Grinning, he lifts his baseball cap, revealing his newly shaved head, and wipes sweat off his brow before settling it back in place.

"Did Izzie start a trend?"

"Thought she wouldn't feel so self-conscious."

Smiling, I begin rolling up my sleeves. "What can I do to help?"

"Would you mind taking these over to Jack?" He hands me a sack of nails, screws and bolts.

"Not at all. And Gabe?"

"Yes, ma'am?"

"This is going to be an incredible place for kids to enjoy."

Even though his face is flushed from work, his color deepens even more. "I hope so."

"I *know* so."

The sun's rays slant down offering heavenly hope, but I step into the proffered shade of a giant oak where the jungle gym resides. Jack's lips pinch a nail as he hammers another into a ramp that will allow wheelchair access over the ground covered in wood chips.

I walk beneath him. "I've got something for you."

"Just what I've been waiting for." From his sly look, I'm not sure if he means the sack of nails or me.

I hand up the sack, careful not to brush Jack's hand. "Everything going well?"

"Except for a disgruntled mother's group who had to take their toddlers elsewhere for the day."

"They'll appreciate the changes later. So when will everything be set?"

"Tonight, I hope. Inspectors will be out to verify safety issues. And next weekend we'll have a grand opening."

"Is anybody invited?"

"You better be here. Because I think your daughter will be." His grin causes a prickling of awareness beneath my skin.

"I think you're right." I offer him a shy smile.

"Jack!" The long drawn out Scarlett O'Hara cry is one of those helpless female pleas that acts like bamboo shoved under my fingernails. I turn and see my friend, Elise, her newly nip-and-tucked body carefully clad in formfitting shorts and a tank, walking toward us. Her smile remains in place as her gaze slips toward me when my own falters. "Kaye?"

"Hello, Elise. How are you?"

"It's so good to see you." She gives me one of those appearance-only hugs, not too close, not too personal. "Is Izzie friends with Gabe?"

"They're on swim team together."

Elise leans close. "I saw her hair. Or lack thereof. Did you almost die when she shaved it?"

I shrug. "It'll grow."

But she's already turned her focus onto Jack. Her beaming smile is for him alone. "Jack, I am just so amazed at all you and Gabe are doing."

"Thanks, but it's all Gabe."

"You're just too modest. Do you think you could take a minute? I know what you're doing is important, but I could use some help unloading. It's way too heavy." She looks at me then. "I brought water and sodas for the workers."

Jack swings down and lands beside me.

"Come on." Elise slides her arm through Jack's. "I know everyone's just dying of thirst. Oh, and I brought donuts too."

"That was thoughtful."

Why didn't I think of that? I watch them walk together toward the parking lot and Elise's Suburban. She smiles up at him.

An about-face blocks the image but the tightening in my abdomen remains.

⤜ Chapter Fourteen ⤛

By late afternoon everyone is exhausted, sunburned pink, and sweaty. But smiles are passed around as we look over all the changes and improvements to the park.

"I need to get home, Iz. Marla has been alone all day."

"Well, that means trouble." But her gaze travels toward Gabe. "I'll catch a ride with someone. You go on."

"Are you sure?"

"Yeah."

"Okay. I'll see you later."

When I arrive home, a strange car sits in front of my house—a slick, red Mercedes convertible. Does Marla have another suitor visiting? Since no one is standing on the porch, I assume she let this one inside. Maybe it's Anderson Sterling. Maybe he has a different car for each day of the week. That would definitely interest Marla. As she'd like a different car to match each designer bag she owns. Or maybe one for each face.

After parking and greeting Cousin It who is stuck outside in the heat, I fill up the water bowl and pat her furry side. When she goes to bark at the dog next door, I open the back door and hear voices. Before I can close the door, Cousin It pushes past me, barreling inside.

Screeches and screams reach me before I can get to the den. Marla stands, a high-piercing squeal coming out of her clenched teeth. She teeters on heels and holds the sides of her face as if her stitches might come loose. I make a grab for Its collar, vaguely aware of a woman sitting on the sofa, legs crossed at the ankle. But It seeks her out like a homing beacon. The blonde holds a pillow between her and the chaos.

"It, sit!" I grab the dog's collar. "I'm sorry," I address the women then the dog, "Come!" I tug her toward the kitchen and the back door. "Out." With a final push against her furry behind, she's out the door.

"I'm so sorry." I reenter the den, pushing back bangs from my eyes. I'm sticky and gritty with dirt and sweat. A shower is in my near future. I glance from Marla to her friend who looks like a live airbrushed photo. She makes me feel like Ellie Mae Clampett with my jeans and untucked shirt. "Hi, I'm Kaye."

Marla settles back on the sofa. She's actually dressed in a yellow dress and heels. "Have you two not met?"

"I don't believe we have." The woman stands, unwinding those long legs. She has model height and slimness, perfectly polished nails, and exquisite taste in clothes. Her suit jacket reveals a voluptuous top that must be surgically enhanced. Not that I'm an expert on such things, but in my experience if someone is toothpick thin filling out a Cup D, *naturally* is unrealistic.

"Are you new to Southlake?"

"Not officially anyway."

Unsure if she's referring to our meeting or moving to Southlake, I give her a quizzical look.

"I'm Barbara." She says it as if her name should be in lights, like Rihanna or Donny and Marie. No last name needed. Then the name clicks in my brain, almost an audible sound.

"Barbara?" This time *I* squeak, but in my head there is a long, feral scream. I manage to keep my jaw from falling open and want to ask, "As in Cliff's personal Barbie?" But I refrain. "It's . . .

uh . . ." Do I have to be gracious to this woman? It's absolutely *not* nice to meet *her*. But what do I say? "Get out!"? Do I open the back door again and tell Cousin It, "Sic her"? That would be my preference but since I was raised to be a proper southern lady, I say in Marla's gritty way, "Welcome."

"Cliff has told me so much about you."

My brain fogs over with an image of Cliff wrapped in Barbie's satin sheets lamenting the fact that he's stuck married to a woman like me.

"It was all nice, of course," she says as if she's read my mind. "Cliff's the perfect gentleman." She reaches forward and touches my hand.

I pull away as if she were a snake striking. "That's not exactly the word I would use."

At Barbara's small intake of breath, as if she's shocked I would be miffed about all of this, I glance at Marla. What was she *thinking* letting this woman into my house? But then she probably approves of Barbie as a daughter-in-law. They shop at the same stores. They probably go to the same plastic surgeon. Maybe they can get a family discount—a buy-one-get-one-free deal.

"What on earth have you been doing?" Marla gives me a once-over. "Playing in the dirt?"

"As a matter of fact, I have." And I keep the details of the day to myself, refusing to cast my pearls before swine. I can't imagine Marla or Barbie hauling equipment and hanging out in a park all day with a bunch of teenagers. They're more the bring water, soda, and donuts type.

Marla shifts to one side and tucks her feet beneath her. "Wasn't it nice of Barbara to check in on me?"

I'm speechless. Dumbfounded. Or maybe just plain dumb to set myself up for something like this.

"She brought flowers and magazines, lotions and soaps. And a gift card to a day spa."

I manage to keep my smile aloft, but my cheeks start to quiver from the strain like an over-ambitious weight lifter, the barbells teetering, the legs trembling.

A moment of silence prevails, and I'm given the chance to catch my breath, but my brain feels as if it's chasing thoughts around like Cousin It after a fly.

"Where's Isabel?" Barbie asks.

"She's uh"—I wave a lethargic hand as I search for words—"helping a friend with a project."

Barbie glances at her watch. The diamonds glint in the afternoon sunlight pouring through the back windows. "I should be going. Cliff is flying in from New York."

And as quickly as I was forced to face the woman who stole my husband, Barbie leaves my house. I'm standing at the front door unsure how I even walked that far. Marla stands beside me.

"Nice of her to give you all that stuff." And I suppose it means she's back with Cliff.

"That was her way of telling me I need my hair washed and a manicure." She folds her nails against her palms.

"Well, you can't take a shower yet."

"Would you do it?"

"Wash your hair?" The grief in her eyes moves me out of my comfort zone. "Of course."

In a most surreal moment we watch Barbie climb into her fancy convertible, fluff her hair, don more lipstick and drive away.

Marla gives a heavy sigh of relief or exhaustion. "I can't stand that woman."

I stare at my ex-mother-in-law. For once we're in complete agreement.

After a long, hot shower to wash away the day's grime and irritations, I help Marla lie on the kitchen counter, her head over the sink, towels galore making her neck and back comfortable, and carefully without touching any incisions, I wash her hair, noticing her dark roots are starting to show. But, of course, I don't say anything.

"Be careful now."

"Are you comfortable?"

"Well, it's not a spa chair but it'll have to do." She stretches out her leg and bumps the coffee tin with her big toe.

With her eyes closed, her face mostly relaxed (although taut), I have a close-up look at the fine lines on her forehead and around her eyes. I hate to admit it, but she has beautiful structure and cheekbones. It makes me sad she can't appreciate what she has instead of focusing on what she's lost.

Right through my heart, I feel a jab. Maybe it's God nudging me with that sharp two-edged sword. Haven't I been doing the same thing? Focusing on what I've lost—Cliff—rather than what I have—Izzie. With all the pain my friend Terry is going through with Lily, I should pay attention and learn a lesson.

After I carefully blow-dry Marla's auburn hair, we move to the kitchen table where she picks out the color nail polish she wants me to apply.

"Let's jazz things up a bit." She reaches for the fiery bottle called *Racy Red-Hot*.

I file a ragged spot on Marla's thumbnail. "*She* wants him back."

"Apparently." Marla's lips press into a thin line. "Does that bother you?"

"Of course, it does. He's my—"

"Not anymore."

I grit my teeth and unscrew the bottle.

She studies me, tilting her head sideways as if sizing me up. "Why do you want him back?"

I hold out my hand for hers. "He's my husband. She stole him."

"Hmm." She places her hand daintily against mine. "But didn't you do the same thing?"

Her statement takes me aback. I stare at her smooth but bruised forehead. What is going on in that brain of hers? I press the end of the brush against the bottle until a big dollop of red polish falls off. "He wasn't even dating anyone when I met him."

"Ah, yes! But you seduced him just as much. He should have gone on to law school, but he had a family to support."

Suddenly the animosity I've felt from Marla our entire marriage is revealed in a new light. She believes I stole her little boy. Seduced him! When the opposite happened.

I went off to the University of Texas with wide-eyed hopes and dreams. I didn't know what I wanted to do with my life, but I was eager to find the right path. I'd had a happy childhood with what I thought were adoring parents. And when I returned home at Thanksgiving, I learned my parents had separated and were getting a divorce. They'd stayed married all those years. Why? For me? My happy childhood had been an illusion made of spun sugar.

They didn't even try to fight for their marriage, to make it work. They just quietly parted ways.

"It's amicable," my mother said.

"It's for the best," my father claimed.

But the solid world I thought my feet were planted on tilted, and I tumbled into a dark hole, questioning everything I'd ever known or believed.

I fell right into Cliff's arms. And ended up pregnant with Izzie.

Was our marriage only a figment of my imagination? Should we not have been together? Did that negate what we had created?

Or did our overheated decision in his apartment late one night change the course of our lives forever? Did that one moment of insanity change our destiny?

When Cliff left me for Barbie, all those questions bombarded me again. And I went to church, seeking answers.

"We'll pray your husband returns," many said.

"He's wrong. He made a mistake."

"It's God's will your husband sees the error of his ways and returns to his family."

But was giving myself to an immature, bad boy in college the real mistake? Was his decision to pursue Barbie inevitable, simply a course correction?

I didn't know then, and I still don't know. It doesn't seem important anymore what Marla thinks. I'm not going to change her mind after seventeen years. And if I did, I'm not sure it would matter anyway.

"Watch what you're doing!" Marla jerks her hand back.

Using the edge of my thumbnail, I scrape off a smudge of polish from Marla's cuticle. "Is that why you've always hated me?"

"I don't hate you, dear."

I switch to her other hand. "You haven't exactly embraced me."

"What if Izzie got pregnant by that boy she's seeing now. What's his name? Greg?"

"Gabe."

"Would you want her to ruin her life with the wrong boy?"

Polish splashes red on the palm of my hand. I meet Marla's inquiring gaze. Feeling a lump in my throat, I answer with a slight shake of my head and go back to the task of painting her nails.

"You have to see your marriage the way I viewed it. You got knocked up. You trapped my firstborn in a relationship that was totally inappropriate. It was simply a bad match. You two were from different worlds."

"Different classes, you mean."

"Well, yes. You were middle-class at best."

"And yet, you don't like Barbara either."

"She has *no* class."

"No morals for sure." I release her hand and at the same time realize how judgmental I sound. "I'll do another coat in a minute. Let that one dry." I screw the lid back on the bottle. "Not that I haven't made mistakes, but I'm thinking we might be blaming the wrong person."

I wait a moment, thinking she might make the connection. Finally a tiny wrinkle appears between Marla's high-arched brows as if she's finally considering Cliff might be responsible, but then it disappears as if she's liberally applied a heavy dose of wrinkle-free cream. Does she not see? Is she incapable of ever blaming her son?

⁂

Three days pass before I see Cliff again. He stops by the house on his way to work one morning. I'm crouched in the flower beds, pulling weeds and trying to help my poor bedraggled roses that Cousin It likes to dig up and gnaw on. Mud cakes my tennis shoes and dirt packs my nails.

"Lookin' good there, Kaye." He stands just inside the back gate. His gaze darts around.

"Don't worry, the dog is inside. Your mother is still asleep, unless you woke her, but you can go on in and check."

"That's all right." His gaze skims over me in a way it hasn't in more than a decade. Or at least that's my hopeful interpretation. "I came to see you."

"Me?" My pulse leaps. Slowly I stand. "What's up?"

He takes a step toward me, starts to reach out but hesitates.

I raise a hand to ward him off. "I'm dirty."

"Always were." His mouth curves in a sensuous smile, but despite what I thought I wanted, I can't manage a responding one. "I've been thinking about you while I was out of town."

"Me?" Not Barbie? Did he see her last night? Did she pick him up at the airport? Or did he tell her he didn't need a ride?

His eyebrows lift. "Thought you and I might have dinner tonight."

"Sure, you're welcome to come to dinner—"

"I meant—"

"—with Marla and Izzie—"

"—just *you* and *me*. You pick the place."

I feel a jolt down to my toes. "Oh! Uh, well, okay."

"Good. Tonight. Seven."

"All right."

He turns and heads back to his car but stops midway and calls out, "Mom doing okay?"

My thoughts tangle. Slowly I nod. "Yes, she's fine."

Although she might not like this turn of events. But I do. For the first time, it seems I've taken precedence over Marla. And Barbie.

꽃

I'm running late because I changed clothes five times before settling on a navy blue sheath dress and strappy sandals. I was pleasantly surprised to find this dress still fit. Or maybe it fits again. The last time I tried to wear it a few weeks ago, it showed every bump and bulge around my hips and backside. But maybe the running I've been doing has started to pay off. Which gives me a slight pause. Didn't I agree to swim at Izzie's and Gabe's swim-a-thon? A dress is unequal to a swimsuit in the humiliation factor.

Marla glances up from a magazine as I step into the den while juggling two purses. "Now that's how you should dress for appointments."

"I'll be home late." I take her comment as a backhanded compliment, which needs no response. "Can I bring you dinner?"

"I'll call in an order." She presses a hand against her belly as if gauging whether or not she's hungry. She has been given the A-OK to drive since she's no longer on heavy pain medicines, but she seems content to stay in *my* home.

She looks better with her hair washed and nails done, if I do say so myself. "You might want to get out and enjoy going to a restaurant."

Horror registers on her face . . . well, a slightly skewed shock since her face is now asymmetrical. "Maybe I'll skip dinner. I don't want to get fat and have to see Dr. Scarr for liposuction."

"Please, no." The words pop out before I consider them. How long is liposuction recovery?

"What?"

"I meant, no, you don't need liposuction. You're in great shape." I wave as I head out the door without a backward glance. Backing out of the garage, I notice Harry Klum getting out of his station wagon. "Mr. Klum!"

He turns in my direction and waves.

I smile and roll down my window. "How are you today?"

"Getting up my courage." He pulls his toolbox from the backseat of his car.

"Needing courage to face my drain again?"

He laughs and straightens. "To see Miss Marla."

"She's pretty formidable, isn't she?"

He nods. "You look pretty this evening."

"Thank you." Should I suggest he find someone else to love, someone more accessible, someone more deserving? After all, Harry is a nice guy. I don't want to see him hurt. But I don't want to be the one to hurt his feelings either. He is a grown man, able to make decisions for himself. "I have a business meeting, then dinner with my ex."

"Oh, I see."

"Harry, part of Marla's reluctance is her surgery. She's self-conscious. But . . ." I let the other reason for her reluctance dangle between us, unspoken but hopefully obvious.

"I don't care about that. I'm interested in her heart."

"Yes, but . . ." Does he really *know* Marla? Does anyone? Does she let anyone in that locked door? Maybe Harry could pry open her heart with his persistence.

"I understand what you're saying, Miss Kaye."

"Just Kaye."

He grins and winks.

"Mom!" Isabel barrels out of the house. She slings her backpack into the car. "Come on! We're going to be late."

꒰ꢇ꒱

I pull up to Jack's house one minute before our appointed time. After one ring of the doorbell, he opens the door. There's an odd look in his eyes. Gabe hollers for Izzie to meet him in the back office. They've been working out the details of their swim-a-thon. After she brushes past us and disappears into the house, I focus on Jack. His expression hasn't changed, like he's the only one that knows the punch line.

"Everything all right?"

"I'm not sure." He pushes the door wide.

Surprised by his response, I walk inside, waiting for an explanation. "Did the furniture arrive?"

"You might say that."

Peering through the arched foyer, I come to a sudden stop. Glaring at me from the middle of the den is a red velvet couch. *Red.* It looks like it belongs in Vegas or Graceland or even a red light district. "What's this?"

"A couch. The one you ordered."

"Trust me, I did *not* order . . . *that*. There must have been a mix-up." My gaze scans the room where more new furniture is clustered. I check the tables, lamps, and chairs that I did order for the room. Everything else is correct. Except the *love* seat.

"I'm not great at this decorating stuff," Jacks dusts a finger along the top of a table, "but I was beginning to wonder if you were trying to tell me something."

Unsure if he's making a joke or seriously concerned that I was making a move on him, I laugh more heartily than I'm feeling. "There's an old Doris Day movie my mom showed me when I was a kid. She was a decorator. Doris, that is. And Rock Hudson was this famous bachelor. To get back at him for something . . . I can't remember what now, she decorates his apartment. Hideously. The proverbial, contemptible bachelor pad."

He nods. "I've seen that movie."

"Not exactly a guy flick."

"My mom was a Doris Day and Rock Hudson fan."

"Well, I can assure you, Jack, that isn't what happened here."

"Good. Because I'm not exactly Rock Hudson."

"That's good news . . . considering." There's an awkward moment of awareness, me noticing him, his manly size and ways, and my skin tingles. For self-preservation, I laugh again then abruptly stop. "Don't worry. I'll call the company and get this straightened out, Jack. The company I ordered from, they're very reputable. They'll take care of it immediately."

He crosses his arms over his chest. "It does give a whole new meaning to perceptions, doesn't it? You'll want to tell them about the bed too."

I stare at him, trying to figure out if he's pulling my leg. But from his serious expression, I'm afraid to go down the hall to the master suite to verify.

"Check it out." He nods toward the hallway that leads to his bedroom.

Reluctantly I proceed without him. I walk down the long hallway, past his office. Through an arched passageway, I can see where Gabe and Isabel are staring intently at a computer screen. The elongated windows along the opposite wall reveal an inner courtyard housing flowering hibiscus and bougainvillea. When I reach the door leading to the owner's retreat, where there used to be a king-sized water bed with a beige comforter, I pause, glance over my shoulder, and am relieved I'm completely alone. I draw a breath for fortification and nudge open the door.

There in the middle of the room is a gigantic Valentine. It lies in the middle of the bedroom, taking up the majority of the space. My first thought is: how do you find heart-shaped sheets?

Defeated, I sit on one side of the bed, just to the left of the pointy end. How did this happen? This does not bode well for my newfound career—wrong furniture, wrong bed. But then obviously the marital bed didn't work out so well for me either. I feel my failures piling up on my shoulders, weighing me down. I flop back onto the pillow-top mattress. It is comfortable. Any discomfort is inside me.

What has happened to my life? As a little girl, I believed in fairy tales, where the princess avoids kissing the frog and gets the prince. *The right one.* I imagined living happily ever after, whatever that meant. But it was all an illusion stripped away. I should have realized the truth when my parents divorced. But no, I tried to make my own fairy tale come true. And I guess that was my mistake—taking the reins.

All I ever wanted was love. Was that too much to ask for? Was that an outrageous desire? Too lofty? Too pie-in-the-sky? I always thought God wanted to give me the desire of my heart. I always believed He was more than capable. But every family I've been a part of has fallen apart. If God couldn't save our family, if He couldn't bring my husband back, then what *could* He do?

Suddenly the bed starts to hum and spasm. My fillings rattle. I jerk to an upright position.

Jack grins at me. "Now what do you think?"

"I'm speechless."

"Yeah, I was too." He plops down beside me, on the other side of the pointy tip and lays back against the pillow-puff mattress. "You should have seen the looks I was getting from the delivery guys."

"Why didn't you stop them? Refuse the order?"

"I was in the office working." He pats the bed where I once lay. "Feels good with the motor running."

I imagine my friend Elise utilizing this situation to her advantage, maybe give a little bounce, a twittering laugh, a come-hither glance. But that's not me. "So you know Elise Whitfield?" I could kick myself for speaking her name at this inopportune time. "I mean, I saw her at the park the other day. I didn't know—"

"Yeah, before her divorce her husband was one of my clients. She's a nice lady. Has had a rough year."

Uh-oh. Do I hear sympathy? Protectiveness? "She's looking good now." *No, Kaye! Don't point out her attributes!* "I mean, um—"

"Yeah." His voice dips. "I'm glad."

I frown. I just bet he is!

"She needs it after her diagnosis."

My frown deepens. "Diagnosis?"

"Breast cancer. That's why she ended up with . . . well . . . reconstructive surgery." He stares at me. "You didn't know?"

I lay back on the bed, totally shocked. "No idea."

"I didn't know it was a big secret. I thought everyone knew."

Placing a firm hand against my jiggling belly, I allow guilt to squeeze through the sudden cracks in my jealousy. "I've been preoccupied the last year or so."

"Well, if you don't mind, don't say anything. In case I spoke out of turn."

"Sure." When the hum of the bed is the only communication between us, I offer, "I'm really sorry about this, Jack."

"About what? The bed?" He laughs. "Don't worry. I'm just glad you didn't see me in the role of Don Juan."

But do I? "Or Rock Hudson, right?"

His laugh deepens. "Definitely."

We lie there, side by side, with a wide space between us. I admit only to myself that he does look roguish lying sprawled across this bed with rumpled hair and those intoxicating eyes.

"Speaking of"—he rolls sideways, facing me fully, and props his hand under his head—"how is your Romeo?"

"If you mean Cliff, we're having dinner tonight."

"Terrific. That's why you're dressed up?" His gaze never veers off track. "You look great, by the way."

A blush surges up through my chest and expands outward. "Oh, thanks. I, uh . . ."

He rolls onto his back again. And the tension in my chest eases slightly.

"It's been a long time since I dated." My confession is easier without his direct gaze upon me.

"You worried? Nothing much has changed."

"Oh?" I tug at the bottom of my skirt, which with the vibration has risen slightly up my thighs.

"Everybody has their agenda."

"That's what my mother always said. Beware of those boys . . . they just want one thing. Is that true?"

"For boys, I suppose. But a man wants companionship that doesn't have to do with a sport or spitting."

I laugh. "Hopefully there will be no spitting tonight."

"Yeah, restaurants frown on that sort of thing."

His remark about agendas makes me wonder suddenly what Cliff wants out of tonight. To be cozy again? To talk about his mother? Daughter? Or could he want to get back together? How easily I jumped to the conclusion that it was the latter. But it could be something totally different.

"You okay?" Jack studies me, his gaze astute.

"Yeah, sure. Why?"

"You got this strange look. Sort of panicked like."

I shake my head as if I can shake off the fear as easily as the bed continues to shimmy and shake beneath me. "I was just thinking about tonight . . . and what Cliff wants." Tears flood my eyes, and Jack's image blurs. I sit upright, trying to blink the tears away and banish them to some hidden place within my heart. Where did they come from anyway? Maybe the bed jarred them loose. "It's okay. I'm okay."

Jack sits upright beside me and loops an arm around the back of my shoulders. "Did I say something? I'm sorry."

His words knock the tears aside, my vision clears. I shake my head, an attempt at an answer, and yet really it's just a way to sort out my thoughts and emotions into some semblance of order. But I'm amazed that Jack so easily could apologize for nothing. A line from an old movie comes back to me: "Love means never having to say you're sorry." Ironic that the name of the movie was *Love Story*. But I've learned all these years that love *is* saying you're sorry. It's how we find reconciliation.

It's frankly how we find redemption.

And the thing is, looking into Jack's intense gaze as he watches me like I might crumble within his embrace, I discover something that rattles me more than this crazy bed or when I learned Cliff was leaving me.

I could love this man.

"Can you forgive me?" His words are tender, even as his expression is fierce with what appears to be concern.

I'm taken aback by his intensity . . . insistence. "There's nothing to forgive. You just made me think realistically. That's all."

"Are you worried Cliff just wants one thing?"

"The direct opposite. I'm afraid he wants everything but." I lean into Jack's shoulder, feeling a raw need to be closer to him, as if I'm secure and safe in that place beside him. And I haven't felt safe since I was an innocent eighteen-year-old. I stare into those passionate eyes, then my gaze drifts down along the solid features of his face to his square and solid jaw, to his firm mouth.

He makes a tiny almost imperceptible move toward me. My stomach tilts. Or maybe it's the bed. As if I'm drawn toward him, I feel my body leaning, my chin lifting, and all I can think of is touching my mouth to his, tasting him, loving him.

"*Muh*-ther!"

My spine straightens. I spring off the bed as if an electrical spark hit my backside. Izzie stands in the doorway staring at us, her hands propped on her hips as if she's in the parental role now. "What are you doing?"

I blink at her as if trying to make sense of the situation. But sense seems to have flown the coop. "Nothing!"

Jack rises from the bed more leisurely, as if he's not aware of the implications. Or not aware of what might have just happened. And I'm not sure which is worse. The hum of the bed vibrates through the room and sounds as loud as a jackhammer. Gabe joins Izzie in the hallway. It seems to take forever before Jack turns off the vibrator. The silence only accentuates Izzie's shock and disapproval. I suppose it's one thing to try to set your mother up with men to date and quite another to find her sitting on a vibrating bed about to kiss some guy. Even though Jack is far from just "some guy."

But it's also in that moment that my decision is clear. I could kiss Jack. I could fall in love with him. I could probably even marry him. But that's not what Izzie needs. She needs her own father, her real family. Didn't I just learn I was focused on the wrong thing, the wrong reason? And so, no matter how much I am drawn to Jack, no matter how much I could fall in love with him, I must walk away from those possibilities, even if it might be what I've been looking for my whole life.

"I should go." I keep my gaze on Izzie, not daring to look at Jack. Would he look disappointed, relieved . . . or even indifferent? I gather up my purse. "I'll call the company and get them to pick this up and deliver . . . well, the right furniture."

"Sure." His voice is slow, sure. "No problem."

"Izzie, are you ready?"

"Not yet."

Gabe steps forward from the hallway. "I'll take her home, Mrs. Redmond."

"Okay, well," I check my watch, "I should go. Yes. That's right."

"You said that already, Mom."

"I did? Oh. Yeah. Okay then. I'll see you." I brush past my daughter. My heel wobbles and makes my footsteps faulty.

⤚⟨ Chapter Fifteen ⟩⤛

It's not a surprise that Cliff is late and that I'm early. Typical. So sitting at the table all alone gives me plenty of time to sit and think, fret and worry, anticipate and regret. My thoughts flit back to Izzie's horrified expression when she caught Jack and me about to kiss. If that's what was about to happen. Maybe it was good for me to see that kind of reaction from her. Deep down, she really does want her father and me to get back together.

My father was the first to date after my parents' divorce. Or the first to advertise it. Come to find out, he'd been seeing the "new" woman-in-his-life, who eventually became his wife, for years before my parents split.

Mom was slower to get her feet wet in the dating scene. But when she did, she took a dive off the deep end. It embarrassed me how she gushed about this strange man. Watching them kiss and hold hands in public made me uncomfortable. She'd never behaved that way with my father.

In many ways I divorced myself from my parents' antics while I immersed myself in my own dating dramatics during my college years . . . year. I wound up pregnant in my freshman year, which ended my career goals. Not that I really had any real goals at that point. I was just trying to discover myself. Instead of figuring out what I wanted to do, I discovered I was going to be a mother.

I didn't know I had it in me.

Now I don't regret Isabel. In spite of the challenges she's brought during her teen years, I've loved her, enjoyed having her in my life. But there *are* a few regrets. Should I have attempted parenthood alone? Was my marriage doomed from the beginning? My parents thought it was. They warned me, pleaded, and even suggested an abortion, which was never an option for me. Maybe that's another reason I've pulled away from them.

Today I'm glad my parents are happy and content in their new respective relationships. They've both remarried and have even remained friends. They kept their distance as if saying, "You're on your own," after I married. And I admittedly haven't tried very hard to bridge the gap. When I announced Cliff had left, even though they closed ranks and offered to help, I got the distinct impression they were whispering, "We told you so." The discomfort is all mine. And maybe it's simply that I don't trust in outward appearances anymore. Maybe I don't trust at all. Is that why I've grabbed hold of the reins and tried to force Cliff and myself back together instead of allowing God to move and work a miracle?

"Serious thoughts?" Cliff slides into his seat across the table from me.

I give myself a shake then smile. Maybe we can have a new beginning. A fresh start. A clean slate. Isn't that what God teaches? I give him a perky smile, the kind he always liked. "How was your day?"

Not dazzled by my pearly whites, he checks his cell phone. "Close to making a deal. That will be . . . well, it could make my year."

"That's great. I'm glad work is going well."

"So"—he leans back, stretching his arms wide across the back of the booth's seat—"how's your little business? You haven't gone belly-up yet, have you?"

That's not exactly a ringing endorsement. "It's growing. Surprisingly."

"No surprise there, Kaye. You were always good at shopping and stuff. I ought to ask for a commission on every deal you make and client you sign because I gave you all that practical experience."

My smile congeals. He did help me learn how to create an illusion. Now I create a fantasy of how perfect life could be. But Cliff doesn't like serious discussions. I glance around at the black and white décor. "I've never been to this restaurant." It's an Asian and Mediterranean mix. "Have you?"

"Oh, sure." The waitress brings him a drink, and he claps his hands as if ready to move on. "You ready to order?"

Wasabi salmon sounds intriguing to me, and he orders a Kobe steak and ginger potatoes. He has a penchant for fattening foods despite his mother's attempt to raise his taste buds out of the middle class. "A few starches on the side?"

"Gotta get what you want, kiddo. Life is short."

Is that what our divorce was about? Him going after what he wanted? A sexy young thing? And what is it that I want? Love. The all-encompassing, self-sacrificing, friends-and-lovers kind of love. When do I get that? *How* do I get it?

In many ways our marriage seemed like I was the only one sacrificing, but I'm sure Cliff feels like he missed out on things he wanted to do—golfing with the guys, drinking with his college buddies, and going out with younger women. So, obviously, we didn't share the 1 Corinthians 13 kind of love, rather we were more self-serving than self-sacrificing.

I've been trying so hard to do the right thing—fire up the grill of the blackened coals of my marriage, stir up a career from scratch, raise a daughter. Sixteen years have passed since I started college, and I'm still trying to find myself, figure out what I want out of life. But my choices seem increasingly limited, as if I'm rummaging in my refrigerator and finding only expired meat, overripe fruit, limp vegetables, and moldy bread. This is what I've been left with.

Cliff's decisions have determined my future. Or did God calculate all of that into His will for my life? It gives me a headache in my left temple.

"So how's that new client of yours? The one who was at dinner the other night?" Cliff snaps his fingers in quick succession. "Joe? Jake?"

"Jack. He's fine."

"You know who he is, right?"

"Yes, I believe we've met."

"I looked him up. Asked around."

His admission surprises me. What was he doing that for?

"He's got a multi-million dollar travel company. He creates these once-in-a-lifetime tours for the rich and shameless. Of course, his clientele can afford a once-in-a-lifetime event every six months. Wouldn't mind a little piece of that action. I'm sure I could put a deal together that would benefit us both."

Warning bells go off in my head.

"Would you mind hooking us up?"

I blink. Disappointment, as raw and distasteful as uncooked broccoli, lodges in my throat. "Is that what this is about? You want an inside track to one of my clients?"

"What is it to you, Kaye?" He leans forward, bracing his forearms on the edge of the table. "If I make a good deal, then Izzie benefits. Maybe you too."

More like Barbie, or someone like her, benefits with a trip to Bermuda or the Bahamas or wherever Cliff's latest whim takes him. But I refrain from speaking my mind.

He props an elbow on the table, dangling his fork over his plate and frowning at me. "You like this guy, don't you?"

I shake my head. Too quick to deny it. "He's a client. That's all."

"Then this is just an extension of that business. It's how things work in the real world, Kaye. You scratch my back, and I'll scratch yours." He gives me a broad wink. "You know, I saw him looking at you the other night. Is he putting the moves on you?"

This dinner suddenly comes into sharper focus. Dropping a shoulder and leaning forward, I press my advantage. "You're jealous."

He reaches out and snags my hand. "What if I am?" His thumb bumps over my knuckles. "Would you take pity on me?"

"You never stir pity in me."

"Maybe I should. You haven't mentioned the present I left for you on the porch."

Confused, I stare at him. "You left a present? For me?"

"Yeah. In a paper bag."

"Oh!" I jerk my hand away. A cold awareness rolls over me. "Oh no." *The bag.* I assumed it was *from* Sterling and *for* Marla.

"You got it then?"

I nod, not sure how to answer. But the truth is usually the best way. "I gave it to your mother."

"*What?*" His raised voice makes heads turn in our direction.

"I didn't know it was from you. There wasn't a note. And your mother has had these men visiting her. I just naturally assumed." Then I rest my head against my hand. "Great. Now she probably believes Harry . . . or Sterling gave her . . ." I meet Cliff's gaze. His jaw is tight. "What was in that bag?"

"*Things* that made me think of you."

From his heavy-lidded look, I imagine it wasn't anything a son should be giving his mother. Or that she should even see. It makes me start to laugh. And I cover my mouth, because Cliff is not smiling. His scowl is deep and dark.

"You're going to have to tell her, Kaye."

His tone kills my laughter. "Me? Why not you?"

"Because you're the one—"

The waitress interrupts at that moment with our food. The portions are small centerpieces in the middle of large white plates, special sauces dribbled around for effect and light dipping. Presentation, once again, is the key to palatable acquisitions. Silently we both concentrate on our meal.

"Want to try some?" I offer.

He wrinkles up his nose at my healthier choices. "Try this." He carves a bite of steak, forks it, and holds it out for me to eat off his utensil in a reminder of the intimacy we'd shared throughout the years. "A little fat won't hurt you."

I hesitate only a moment before taking the bite and chewing it thoughtfully. "Good choice. Very tasty." After clearing my palate with a sip of water, I toss out a delicate subject. "Barbara came over to the house the other day to see your mother."

He doesn't pause in carving into his steak. "Mom told me. Gave me an ear full. She's never liked Barb much."

Barb. His abbreviation of her name churns around in my head building up a good froth. "Seems to be a trend."

He chews and swallows, keeping his gaze on me. "You still think Mom never liked you either? That's bunk." He shrugs. "She may have given me grief before the wedding, but she didn't say anything afterward."

"She didn't have to."

"She likes you *now*. She wouldn't have gone to stay at your house if she didn't. Mother doesn't ever do anything she doesn't want to do."

I'm not so sure about that. I was convenient and an easy escape hatch from her real life. Besides, no one else was offering. "So"—I try to sound nonchalant and indifferent but am afraid my fangs might be showing—"are you still seeing Barbara?"

His gaze narrows and lines fan outward from the corners of his eyes. If he could only see the gray sneaking into his temple, then he'd know how ridiculous he looks with someone as young as Barbara. I bet when he takes her out, people assume he's with his daughter.

Feeling the weight of his stare, I try to explain. "It just seemed odd that she would visit your mom if things are truly over. The way you said. Especially since there was no love lost between them."

He clunks his steak knife on the edge of his plate. "Are you jealous?"

"Should I be?"

"Barbara is a determined lady." He grins, his chest expanding with a deep, self-important breath.

He's lapping up the fact that two women are after him! My hackles rise along my spine. Am I being played? Am I being pitted against someone like Barbara in a battle I'm sure I can't win?

Just when I'm about to throw in the proverbial towel, which at this time is a linen napkin, he adds, "But I'm not sure I see that working out. Besides, I have other interests."

A surreptitious glance in my direction tells me just which direction his interest is blowing these days. But how long will that last?

※※

"This isn't a good idea." I push against Cliff's chest, not hard, just enough to let him know I'm hesitant. But he doesn't seem to take note and kisses his way up my neckline. We're standing in my driveway. The cool fall air wafts over us. There's a romantic moon, but no real romance. Not yet anyway.

Cliff followed me home, saying he wanted to check in on his mother. But he's shown no signs of wanting to go inside. And he hasn't mentioned Marla once. This is right where I wanted all of this to lead. Isn't it? So now why do I want to tell Cliff to get lost?

That's not what I'm going to do, but giving in to his desires is a sure way to make him lose interest.

"Let's go to my place." His hands roam where they haven't roamed in a long time.

I hate to admit that my body yearns for this, for touching and kissing—but not from him. I squirm out of his embrace. "We didn't do this relationship right the first time." I'm more breathless than I realized. "I think we should do it right this time if we're going to try this again."

He rests his forehead against his fist. He's breathing equally hard, maybe more so. He takes a step toward me, hooking his arms around my waist again. "You're saying we should wait?"

"Yes." I place a firm, no-compromising hand against his chest.

"But we're married!"

"Shh. Your mother will hear."

"Let her. I don't care."

I stay focused without getting diverted. "The key word is *were*. We *were* married."

"That's a minor technicality."

"Minor technicalities is what got us into trouble when we were younger."

With a huffy sigh, he turns away and stares up at the sky, his mood darkening by the minute. Making him angry is not my intention. I want more than just a rendezvous with Cliff in bed. Because I know that is not the way to find permanence with him. I must resist. And it surprises me that telling him *no* is actually easier than I ever imagined. Maybe I'm not as desperate as I thought.

"We need to work out some things between us first." I take a step toward him, lay a hand against his back, feel his heat. "Obviously, we know how to make love. But it's the time out of bed that needs work. There's plenty of time for . . . well, you know . . . later."

He glances at me over his shoulder and shoves a hand through his thinning hair. "You're gonna drive me insane."

I laugh softly. "Try a new line."

"It always worked before."

My laughter fades. Did it work on Barbie? "I'm not eighteen anymore."

"You're right about that." He faces me again, runs his hands along my fuller curves, his gaze following. "So you've grown a conscience along with putting on a few pounds?"

My spine stiffens.

"Don't get me wrong, Kaye. I like a few curves. And you've got them all in the right places."

Remembering Barbie's enhanced curves all too well, I feel my spine stiffen. "I'm trying to learn from my mistakes."

He pulls me close again. "You think our marriage was a mistake?"

"I don't know yet." I push away, moving a few steps toward the house to give us space to talk. Which we were never particularly good at. "Besides, shouldn't we be setting a good example for Isabel?"

He comes up behind me, wraps his arms around my middle. "What do you mean?" He nuzzles my neck. "On how to drive a man to distraction?"

"How to handle a relationship in a godly way."

He snorts. "I'm godly."

I laugh at that. I can't help it. "Thinking you're god-like is not the same as being godly."

"I go to church."

I turn back to face him, keeping a couple of feet between us. "When?"

"I've been busy. But I will. When do you want to go? This Sunday?"

"You can lead a horse to water, but you can't make him drink."

"What does that mean?" He pulls me to him again. "You wouldn't lead me on, would you?"

"Never." I kiss him quickly, breezily, then back out of his embrace. "Good night, Cliff."

❦

After Cliff drives away, I remember I never picked up the mail, so I walk around the house to the mailbox out front. Harry Klum's station wagon is still parked in front of my house. Why didn't I notice it before? Maybe because my gaze was focused on my rearview mirror and Cliff's headlights. And my thoughts were on my heart. If Harry can work his way into Marla's heart, then maybe there's hope for me and Cliff. Patience is the key. It took us seventeen years to get in this predicament. It'll take time to set a new course.

I enter through the front door to avoid Cousin It who's barking in the backyard. Before I reach the front porch, the front door opens and Harry steps outside. I call out, "Hi, Harry."

"Have a good meeting?"

"Not what I expected. And you?"

He smiles. "Better than I expected."

"Good. I'm glad." We meet in the middle of the yard. "So how did it go?"

"She ignored me for a while but she hovered in the hallway. I kept trying to carry on a conversation, and she finally responded. But then I brought my rotor rooter." He grins and hikes up his sweat pants. "How can a lady say no to that?"

I laugh. "Is the drain working now?"

"Good as new. I also checked the disposal in the kitchen sink. Miss Marla said it wasn't working properly. Someone put a plastic spoon down it."

I wince. "You don't have to fix all my plumbing problems."

"It's my pleasure."

"Let me pay you for it." I open my purse and reach inside for my checkbook.

He shakes his head. "Wouldn't think of accepting your money." He scratches his head, and the thin strands of hair stand on end. "Marla said she liked the present I sent her. I guess she meant the candy I brought the other day."

My skin prickles. "She said that? She said, 'Thank you for the candy?'"

He rubs the back of his neck. "Not exactly. It was kind of baffling. She just said, 'Thanks,' then got all flustered and added, 'for the presents.'"

I start to laugh, then stifle it. I'm not sure what to do. Should I explain the situation to Marla? She wouldn't be happy that Cliff is interested in me again. Although maybe she'd prefer me as her daughter-in-law over Barbara.

"She's crying out for love," Harry says, "but she has a hard time accepting it."

I've never thought of Marla as crying out for anything. Maybe she is. Maybe that's why she thought she needed a facelift. Maybe she was simply lonely and scared. I know how that feels. In the past two years I've felt loneliness as I've never felt it before. But I also know Marla wants things on her terms. "Harry, have you ever been married?"

"Fifty-two years."

His answer surprises me. "Really?"

"We were high school sweethearts. I was seventeen and she was sixteen when we eloped. Folks said it wouldn't last. We'd still be married today if the cancer hadn't gotten her." He ducks his head.

Sympathy swells my heart. It's then I realize it . . . *that's* what I want. To be married for such a long time, where our love has only grown larger over the years, and when we can't imagine life without the other. Unfortunately Cliff can and has imagined life without *me*.

"I'm so sorry, Harry. How long has she been gone?" A tightness seizes my throat.

"Three years. It's why I retired. So I could take care of her." He remains quiet, like a moment of silence out of respect for his marriage, his wife.

"Tell me about her."

Harry's wrinkles deepen, lining his forehead and bracketing his mouth, aging him. He grips his hands as if they are too restless to be still.

My heart aches for him. What would Cliff say if I died? Would he mourn me in the same way? Would he get choked up at the mention of my name? Marla must have mourned in private but seems to have moved on. Or maybe she hasn't. Maybe she's simply running away from the pain, from the sadness.

"Mary," he finally says, "was sweet as cotton candy. Spunky too. Never met a stranger. Would talk to anybody. Didn't matter if they were famous or homeless." He scratches his head as if stirring up a memory. "She met Robert Redford once. We were in New Orleans on vacation. She walked right up to him and started talking like she'd known him her whole life."

Harry laughs, rubs his jaw. "She told him straight out what she thought of his last movie. She wasn't no pushover, but she was generous."

"She sounds wonderful."

He nods as if caught in his own memories then shrugs. "She was. To me anyway. And Marla . . ."

"What about her?"

"She has many of the same qualities."

"Marla?" Do I sound as astounded as I feel? "Marla," I repeat, trying to sound more resolute than quizzical as I run his adjectives through my head and compare them to the woman I know. Sweet? Generous? There's the set of encyclopedias she gave us for Izzie sitting on my bookshelf. And don't forget the picture she painted in an art class and gave to us for one of our anniversaries. Then there's all the advice she hands out so freely, which rarely helps but mostly makes me feel inadequate. Maybe it's just her way of trying to help.

Harry grins at me. "One of the first things I liked about Marla was when she showed a whole group of us pictures of her grand-kids. Pulled out a special folder from her purse and started telling us about each one. She was pleased as punch. She went on and on about Isabel, how beautiful she was, how smart, and bragged about her swim meets. I knew she had a soft heart."

Am I at fault for not seeing this side of my mother-in-law? Have I been so biased and judgmental that I couldn't see the good qualities? "Marla?"

"Yes, ma'am."

I shake off my surprise. "But don't you see that a lot where you live . . . in a retirement village?" I imagine all the elderly people in between Bingo, tap dancing, and trips to the mall show-ing off pictures of their grandkids. "Don't they brag about the grandkids every day?"

"Nope. Marla was the first I ever saw. It didn't seem like bragging or nothing, either. She just told story after story. One about how Isabel called the color brown chocolate when she was a toddler."

I smile at the memory. Marla always seemed disinterested in Isabel or she was always pointing out faults or ways I could bet-ter care for her—how to fix her hair, find cute, frilly dresses. I'm surprised, yet touched, by Harry's story. What else have I missed? Maybe the barricades in our relationship were as much my fault as hers. Am I too eager to pick out her flaws? Always sure I've been slighted?

A tiny crack opens inside my heart and tears rush to the sur-face. I try to stop them by changing the subject. "So, you were happy in your marriage, Harry?"

"Happy?" He tilts his head sideways as if it's an odd question. "Oh, sure." He rubs his thumb along his jaw. "We went through some hard times. Poor times. Struggled some, as most folks do,

I reckon. But I'd say we were happy. Happy as can be in this life. Life isn't always what you expect. It's tough. But I always knew Mary was there beside me."

His statement feels like a fork to my heart. Is that what happened to Cliff and me? Didn't he know I was there for him? Or did he take it for granted? My hesitation in jumping back into a relationship is that I no longer trust that he'll be there for me.

Which makes me question myself. Have I forgiven him? I've tried. I've prayed. When those angry feelings start to devour me from the inside out, I pray some more. The fact that he's never apologized lurks just beneath the surface like a bone spur, continuing to poke me with doubts and spikes of hostility.

"We were a team, Mary and me." Harry swipes his hands against the back of his pants. "I'm not sure I was always the best husband."

"Oh, I bet you were." After all, he's brought flowers and magazines for Marla. The candy brings another smile that I brush aside.

"I don't have many regrets in my life. But I wish I'd shown Mary, told her more often, how I felt. Taken more time."

"Didn't you?"

"Well, I went to work every day. For her. I came home every night. For her. Oh, I picked up my underwear, scrubbed the kitchen floor a time or two, mowed the lawn. It was *all* for her." He shifts his feet in the dying grass. "But I wish I'd brought her flowers more often. I wish I'd told her . . ." His voice cracks and he looks away.

I touch his arm, feel the strength of muscle under his flannel shirt, sense the tenderness of his passionate heart. "I'm sure she knew how much you loved her."

And I pray one day I'll know a love like that too.

❧

A yellow leaf rolls across the decking and skitters into the pool. Cousin It sits beside me, tongue lolling, as I slip off my robe. The coolness of the evening makes my skin pucker. Since we've moved into this house, I've only been in the pool twice. Both times when it was just Izzie and me. Even peering down at my black swimsuit, I can see how the lycra stretches more than it used to.

With the gentle night breeze, the water feels colder than I expect and I shiver as I slide into the dark water. Cousin It sits on the edge of the pool, my new lifeguard. At least she won't tell any secrets.

Stretching my body out, I begin long, lazy strokes and quick little kicks, the water churns into a froth behind me. My mind wanders back to my conversation with Harry. Did Cliff know I loved him by the way I stayed home and took care of his child, creating a home, a haven for him? Or am I as much to blame as he is for the way our marriage shattered? Do I need to apologize as much as he does?

I come spluttering up and tread water for a moment while that new and disturbing thought sinks into me like a heavy anchor. Maybe I'm maturing. Or maybe I'm delusional that simple words can solve complex problems. Maybe Cliff was showing me how much he loved me by going to work every day, supporting me and Izzy.

Actions do speak louder than words.

So what was he saying when he ran off with Barbie?

I dip my face in the water, because I don't like the answer. And yet I can't deny the truth. His actions over the past fifteen months (or longer) reveal how much he loves himself.

But there's another question nipping at the heels of that revelation: *Has he changed?*

The Bible says we all sin. So I know I've been selfish at times too. But I've tried to change. No, more than that. I've tried to let God change me. But what about Cliff? For that, I have no answer.

And that disturbs me most of all.

Chapter Sixteen

Tears fill Terry's eyes and spill over into my heart. My throat tightens as I watch her hug first Isabel then Gabe. We decided that once all the plans were in place and the swim-a-thon was a "go," we should inform Lily's family and get their blessing for the event.

Terry's house is the same—spacious, tastefully decorated—it gives the appearance that all is well. Driving past the front, no one would ever know or suspect the warm, inviting colors are shrouded by fear and grief.

Terry looks over at me sitting on the couch next to Jack. "You should be very proud of your kids."

Jack claps Gabe on the back. "We are."

"It was their idea." Through the glimmer of tears, I smile at the two teenagers, my heart expanding. I loop an arm through Izzie's as she sits beside me.

Terry grabs a tissue off the end table and dabs her face. "When we started on this journey, I resisted others bringing us dinner or anything, but I soon learned dinners were gifts of the heart. People needed to feel a part of something and help any way they could. By taking what they offered, I was giving them a gift back."

Guilt tugs at me. I should have been offering meals or help cleaning, something . . . but Terry and I drifted apart, our lives both struck by icebergs of different proportions.

Gabe's project is a gift of his heart to not only the community but also to his family. I glance over at him leaning against the door jamb. "Gabe is completing his Eagle Scout badge this coming weekend. Tell her what your project is."

Terry, despite her tears and more pressing concerns, leans forward interested. Gabe straightens, full of confidence and yet without pride. "We're revamping a park to make it accessible to children who, for whatever reason, can't utilize the equipment. You should bring Lily."

"Sounds like a wonderful idea. I hope she can come."

I touch Terry's arm. "How *is* she doing?"

With a weary stoop of her shoulders, Terry leans back in the recliner. "She hasn't been feeling well." Her voice drops to a hoarse whisper as if she doesn't want Lily to hear her from down the hall where she's resting. "I think the cancer is back." She gives a swift shrug. "But I don't know that for sure. We have an appointment next week. But I'm pretty sure it is. Her nails are growing."

My forehead creases.

"I know"—Terry gives a halfhearted, lackluster laugh—"that sounds crazy. But every time the cancer returns, her nails grow like weeds."

"What do the doctors say about that?"

"Everybody is different." She sounds like she's quoting a canned response. "What can they say? They've learned to trust a mother's instinct. They'll run some tests, and sure enough . . ."

"What will they do this time?" Jack's brows scrunch into a series of concerned lines. "More chemo?"

She gives a tiny, almost indiscernible shake of her head. Her gaze drifts away from us as if she's peering into a bleak future.

Izzie squeezes next to me, placing an arm around me, leaning into me for support and pushing me closer to Jack. "If we can just hurry and—"

I place a hand cautiously on her knee, trying to tell her to stop.

"What?" Izzie glares at me, shrugging off my touch. "What's wrong with that? We *can't* give up!"

"No one is giving up on Lily, Iz."

Terry reaches forward and clasps Izzie's hands within hers. "What she's trying to tell you is that this is an uphill battle. And the reality is that we're just trying to buy Lily time."

"What does that mean?" Izzie's tone borders on belligerent.

"Izzie."

"*No!* I want to know."

"Maybe it's not any of our business."

"It's okay," Terry's voice is calm, almost resigned, weary from a long battle I can't even begin to understand—a battle that makes my troubles seem miniscule in comparison. "It means, Isabel, that Lily can't win against this cancer. It is terminal. She will die. It's just a matter of when."

For a long moment Isabel is silent. Emotions flood her face, sweeping away any calm, polite exterior and churning up anger, fear, grief. The flush of her skin makes the pale fuzz on her scalp stand out starkly. Then she jumps up from the sofa. "*No!*" She bolts for the door. "I won't believe that."

The door remains open behind her. The soft night breeze floats through the den, bringing with it the smell of charcoal briquettes. Izzie's cries fill the stunned silence around me, her great gasping sobs push me to my feet. Gabe meets my gaze. "I'll go."

He closes the door quietly behind him. Silence fragrances the room like sprays of carnations, mums, and roses in a funeral home.

I turn my attention to Terry. "I'm so sorry. She—"

"It's okay. I was like that once." She leans back in her chair, crossing her arms over her chest as if trying to hold herself together. Or maybe she's already spent more tears than one body holds. "But I've come to believe there are worse things than death. Like when your child can't eat or can't stop throwing up. When she looks to you to stop the pain, and there is no medicine that works."

Silence thrums in the room, a silence of acceptance and deep anguish. Jack and I look at each other. He's seen this before when his best friend fought cancer. Recognition darkens his eyes. I don't want to go there. I don't want to believe . . . accept. But I have to think of Terry and sweet Lily.

"Does she know?"

Terry nods, her lips pressed together. "The last time she took chemo, there were some really bad days . . . weeks, and she told me she wasn't going to survive this. She didn't even ask. She just knew. When I broke down, she wrapped her little arms around me." Terry's voice cracks but she goes on. "She told me it was okay because heaven is a better place."

"The faith of the little children." Jack's voice resonates in my heart.

Terry's eyes fill again with tears but they don't spill over. "It seems simplistic to us, but I've come to understand it's profound and deep."

⁂

When we leave Terry and head to our car, Jack gets a cell phone call from Gabe. "They're walking home," he tells me. "Think they needed some fresh air. Some space."

"I hope Izzie won't give up and decide there's no point in doing the swim-a-thon."

"She needs a little time. But we'll encourage her to keep going. Gabe too."

"It's good for them . . . for *us* to do something."

Jack pulls his keys from his pocket and opens the passenger door for me. "Stay busy. Feel useful. Like we're doing something to help. Even when there really isn't anything we can do to fix the problem. That's why I bought so many of those games and machines for my house. When Gabe's dad was really sick, I'd bring the kids to my place. It kept them busy. Kept them from thinking about their dad. And worrying. I admit it was excessive, but their brief smiles took away any doubts. It felt like I was putting action to my prayers."

I squeeze his forearm, trying to communicate my feelings to him. "Was it like this for him?"

"Yeah. Too young to die. Or so I thought. But Lily—" He shakes his head. "It's even worse."

Our hands connect, only briefly, but enough to feel a bonding between us.

Then he pulls away and starts the engine. The daytime heat has started to relent, giving way to cool breaths, but there is no relief from this grief. A pressure builds in my chest. We drive down the street beneath the shade of oaks. Crepe myrtles are shedding their blooms, scattering pink, white, and burgundy petals over the lawns.

"Luke knew too."

His reference to Gabe's dad makes my heart quicken. "Did he talk about it?"

"Yeah. He had regrets. That he wouldn't see his kids graduate. That he wouldn't watch Gabe become an Eagle Scout or his other kids play softball or dance . . . everything. He worried about Pam and how she would manage."

"What do you say to someone about to die?" It's a rhetorical question, and I don't expect a response.

"I told him I'd be there for his kids. Anything they needed. Anything Pam needed."

I glance over at his determined profile. "You're a good friend."

"I don't know about that. Remember our bet that I won? For a long time I thought Luke was goofing off, not working hard enough. But the truth is, I was running from what was important in life. He had it right."

"Nothing matters more than family and friends."

He turns the corner. "You can't take money or anything else with you. And what you leave behind doesn't last long and doesn't mean as much."

"What's the old saying? 'No one has ever lain on their death bed and wished they worked harder.'"

"Exactly. But the reverse is true too. Do kids ever say about a dying parent, 'I wish they'd spent more time working, earning money'?" He shakes his head and turns on the blinker again. "Nope. Luke's death affected me, changed me. In a good way. Good can come out of tragedy. That's why I'm selling my house. What do I need that monstrosity for? A tax write-off? An investment?"

Has he given up on having a relationship or family? "So what are you going to do?"

"I'm turning part of my company into a mission organization. We'll not only offer great vacations to exotic locales, but we'll also offer clients opportunities to give something back."

The way he considers others and tries to offer solutions staggers me. "You may have more business than you can manage."

"I hope so. Giving is addictive."

"It's inspiring too." I want to reach out to him, touch his arm, his hand. I want to smile at him, lean into him. But I can't. No matter how much I want to love Jack, I can't. And I suspect he can't either.

His heart is with Pam and her children.

"I don't know if you've been keeping up or not," Marla says.

I glance up from my calendar where I've just booked two more meetings for potential clients. "With what?" I check my watch. "You're not due any meds for another two hours."

"With your teenage daughter." Condemnation saturates her voice.

"I try to, yes."

She's sitting on the couch, her ankles demurely crossed, and *Cosmo* sits on her lap. "So you've been paying attention to how much time she's been spending with that boyfriend of hers?"

My spine stretches taut. "Gabe isn't technically her boyfriend. And yes, they've been spending a lot of time together working on *two* projects."

"Well, *you* know what can happen in situations like that, don't you?"

I cross my arms over my chest. My skin feels hot and prickly. "What are you insinuating?"

She gives me her current cockeyed look. "What usually happens between teenagers?"

"You seem to be an expert," I challenge the woman who hasn't had a teen in almost twenty years. "Educate me."

She clasps her hands together and meets my gaze without reservation. All the kind thoughts Harry spurred in me go galloping out the window. "Teens today are not innocent."

My forehead furrows. "And you want her to be innocent?" I glance down at the article she's reading on *How to Please Your Man*. "Or wily to the ways of the world?"

"You act like she's innocent. She's not even on the pill."

That sets me aback. "Excuse me? There's a pill for staying innocent?"

"That *pill* you should have been on when you got pregnant, Kaye. Wake up and smell the coffee."

I draw a shallow breath and count to a quick ten. "Marla, I appreciate your concern for *my* daughter, but that is something that is between Izzie, her doctor, and myself."

"Don't tell me to butt out on this." She wags her finger at me. "And don't bury your head in the sand."

A quick prayer does little to smooth down my hackles, but I try anyway. I draw in a slow, deep breath. *Patience, God, I need some patience here. Right now. Real quick. Please!* "You know, Marla, my daughter isn't as innocent as you believe she is."

"See! Then you should be—"

"What I mean is that her innocence was shattered when her own father went off with another woman. I suppose the only good that came from that is that she and I have had many discussions about sex since Cliff left. She knows what causes what. And she knows how sex *outside* of marriage causes problems. She is well aware that Cliff and I *had* to get married. And she's very aware of what her father is off doing with someone other than his wife."

Two bright spots form on Marla's cheeks. "All I'm saying is that she should probably be better prepared. If you won't put her on the pill, then make sure she has condoms."

I take a long slow breath, count to ten, pray, then pray again. "Have you heard of abstinence?"

She laughs. "That is not a form of birth control."

"It's not simply a decision made in the security of the home," I explain and defend my stance. "It's a viable option, as long as strategies are discussed and implemented. Abstinence isn't a 'just-say-no' plan. You don't wait to make that decision in the backseat of a car. You strategize beforehand for how you stay out of situations that can lead to . . . well, you know."

Marla narrows her eyes at me. "I hope you know what you're doing. Or you could end up raising your grandchild while your daughter finishes school."

I have no answer. I simply want to walk away from this discussion. It's hard enough to discuss things openly with Izzie, which always makes me face my own failures in this area.

"Kaye," Marla's voice softens, "you always try to put an optimistic spin on everything, but you can't ignore reality here. Izzie is a healthy young woman. Gabe is a handsome young man. But they are hormonal. It's natural."

"We're not animals. We don't have to give into our base desires all the time. Do we? Teens can learn to say no."

"Are you willing to stake your daughter's future on that?"

On that? No. But on Izzy and her commitment to do what's right.

Absolutely.

ᔑᓀᔬ

If Marla thinks Gabe and Izzie have any time to be alone, then she hasn't stepped into my garage. Where my car no longer fits. My trunk and backseat are piled with cardboard signs. Half empty bottles of paint and containers of markers are scattered around the garage. Izzie and Gabe have done a wonderful job of recruiting teenage help. I try to keep the refrigerator stocked with Cokes and water, but they disappear as quickly as I can replace them. At night I stay busy popping popcorn and taking it out to the garage where several teen girls are sitting on the concrete floor making signs.

"That looks great," I say to Taylor, a cheerleader, who has become proficient at making bubble letters.

"Thanks," she chirps.

"Mom"—Izzie attaches a stake to the back of a sign—"we need some more of the donation sheets."

I place a bowl of popcorn on a plastic table holding rulers and markers. "I'll print some."

The driveway looks like a parking lot. Two boys with shaved heads get out of another car. Apparently Izzie started a trend. I say a quick prayer that all these teens will drive carefully and no accidents will occur. Gabe loads more signs into the back of his truck and takes off through the neighborhood. Some of the signs are promoting the park opening and others are advertising the swim-a-thon.

"Anybody need anything else?" I ask before heading back into the house. But the teens are busy discussing how many sponsors each have received.

"I've already gotten a hundred and fifty," Meredith, a member of the swim team who has even longer limbs than Izzie, brags.

While I'm sitting at my office computer printing more donation sheets, I can hear Marla moving around her room. I hope she's not annoyed at all the activity that seems to have descended upon the house. If I had known this was going to happen, it would have provided an excuse when Marla was looking for sanctuary. Her quiet retreat has become Grand Central Station. Then the doorbell rings, and I grab the warm papers off the printer.

Checking the peephole first, I smile and fluff my hair. "Hi, Jack."

"How are you?" He carries in rolls of butcher paper.

Together we take the rolls out to the garage where the girls stretch it out like white carpets as they begin mapping out signs for the school hallways. I give the extra donation sheets to Izzie. The laughter and craziness of the teens pushes the grown-ups back into the house. We shake our heads at each other and smile.

"They're good kids." I close the door firmly.

Jack follows me into the kitchen. "They are."

"Want something to drink?"

"Sure. I have some more Cokes and water bottles out in the truck."

"You didn't have to bring anything."

"I figure you're going to go broke keeping all these guys fed."

"I don't mind."

But he unloads flats of colas and water bottles while I pour a soda over ice for him. He gulps half the glass then grins at me. "I've got some news."

"Good or bad?"

He settles at the table, looking more comfortable than I feel. "I got a call today from the local affiliate of ABC. They want to do a spot."

"As in the news? That's terrific! That should stir up even more interest."

"Do you think Lily or her mom will mind?"

I lean against the counter, my excitement suddenly stymied. "I hadn't thought of that. I'll ask."

"Then let me know. The Southlake paper is doing a story on it too."

"The more publicity the better."

"I was thinking if we get the TV spot, then we could list the bank for donations."

"Perfect. The kids will be really excited. But maybe we should keep it to ourselves until I've spoken to Terry." The doorbell rings again, and I head in that direction. Over my shoulder I say, "I need to put a sign on the door so kids will just go around to the back."

When I open the door, I'm taken aback by the sight of my ex. "Cliff!"

He stalks inside. He's wearing a starched shirt, wrinkled from a day's work, sans tie. "Wanna tell me what's going on here?"

"Come on in."

He's already halfway through the entryway and marches on into the den. "I get a call from my mother telling me the phone is ringing constantly and visitors keep coming all night long."

"Cliff, you remember Jack, don't you?" I wave toward Jack who leans forward over the kitchen table and gives a nod to my ex from the other room.

His mouth flattens, then he smiles—that salesman smile. "Hey! Good to see you." He moves away from me and toward Jack, reaching forward with a hand. "How are you?"

Jack shakes his hand and stands as I enter the room. "I'll go on out to the garage so you guys can talk."

"Here's my card." Cliff pulls out his wallet and hands Jack his business card. "I've got an idea that might benefit both of us. Give me a call."

"Jack," I interrupt the business pitch. "You don't have to go."

He moves to the opening into the den, maybe to make a quick getaway, and taps Cliff's business card against his palm.

Crossing my arms over my stomach, I look to Cliff. "You were saying?"

"Oh, yeah. Uh . . . Mom is having a difficult time resting here. Apparently there have been lots of phone calls and the doorbell ringing."

"She didn't tell you what Gabe and Izzie are doing?"

"Who's Gabe?"

"A friend of Izzie's. Jack's nephew. You met him—"

"Of course. Sure, I remember. Nice kid." He's on full sales pitch.

"Do you remember Lily Martin?"

He shrugs, shakes his head as if he doesn't care and doesn't want to be bothered with trivial matters.

"Iz used to babysit for her. Anyway, we ran into her the other day at the wig shop. She's been fighting a brain tumor."

"That's too bad, but what does it have to do with all this chaos?"

"Izzie wanted to do something to help her, and Gabe joined in."

Jack leans against the door frame. "It's sort of a neighborhood Judy Garland and Mickey Rooney 'let's put on a show,' kind of thing."

Cliff nods enthusiastically in Jack's direction but his smile is set, his jaw clenched. "But I've got my mother calling and complaining."

"I'm sorry she's been disturbed. I've got a bunch of teens in my garage making signs for the swim-a-thon they're running. And donations are being dropped off day and night." I reach for the shoe box I've been using to collect the five-, ten-, twenty-dollar bills that have been left on my doorstep. "See?"

His eyes widen slightly. "They've raised all this?"

"So far."

"Kaye," Jack slides Cliff's card into his back pocket, "we could move the operation over to my house."

"Your house is going on the market. You can't have this kind of thing going on with Realtors and potential buyers coming and going."

"Don't worry." Cliff claps Jack on the back. "I'll talk to Mother."

"Maybe," I suggest, "Marla feels left out. She has a lot of friends at the retirement village. Maybe she'd want to round up some seniors who would donate."

"Good idea." Jack's smile is so wide that a dimple forms on one cheek. "You too, Cliff. I bet you've got a prominent circle of friends who—"

"Mother doesn't need to be running around corralling volunteers."

I match Jack's smile and feel a connection between us even across the room. "Then maybe she should go stay at your place for a while."

Cliff glares at me. "I said I'd talk to her."

"Thank you." Then I put a hand on his arm. "How do *you* want to help?"

"What do you mean?"

"We need a Web site set up."

"I don't know how to do *that*."

"Could you set up a bank account for all of the donations that are coming in? We'll need one for phone donations."

"Uh . . ." His gaze shifts toward Jack. "Sure. Call me about it later."

He pulls out his wallet and hands me a few bills, a fifty and twenty from what I can see. "When do you think all this will . . . stop?"

"The swim-a-thon is in a week and a half."

"I'll tell Mom things should calm down then."

Which tells me two things: Marla isn't looking to move out any time soon, and I won't be getting any help from Cliff.

Chapter Seventeen

It's a perfect fall day, bright and sunny with a cooling breeze that ruffles the trees surrounding the park, stirring up memories of crisp apples and pumpkin carvings. A fire truck sits in the nearby parking lot, the firefighters showing off their equipment to children and families who are flocking to the park for the official opening. I hope none of them recognize me from Marla's desperate call. Many of the parked vans have blue wheelchair stickers on the back windows.

The mayor of Southlake makes a quick speech, praising Gabe's efforts. "A fine young man with a bright future who will do much good throughout his lifetime."

Despite his tan, Gabe looks flushed as he endures the spotlight of approval. He's wearing a green baseball cap to cover his newly bald head. It matches Izzie's. The crowd of Boy Scouts and swim mates, along with a wide variety of families, clap and cheer as Gabe weaves his way through the crowd to the wooden bench and table. He climbs to the top where the mayor stands and shakes his hand.

The mayor slaps him on the back. "Say something."

Gabe dips his chin and looks over at Izzie. She beams up at him and clicks a picture with her cell phone.

The crowd encourages him with a smattering of clapping. A baby cries. Behind me, a mother whispers, "We'll play in a few minutes."

"Thanks for coming today," Gabe raises his voice so he can be heard. "I learned through my dad that someone's life doesn't have to be long to be effective and change things for the better. And I learned about perseverance through my little sister and all the obstacles she's had. I wanted to make a difference. Amy never could play with us on playgrounds. And so I wanted to make that possible." Then he steps down onto the wooden bench seat. "Thanks again." He gives an awkward wave. "Now let's go play."

"You heard him!" the mayor yells over more cheers.

Children run, limp, and roll along into the park discovering the equipment that accommodates metal limbs and wheels. The smiles from so many faces make my throat close and gratefulness surge up inside of me. It's one of those rare moments when I don't think the world is going to hell in a handbasket. Maybe there is hope in the next generation with kids like Gabe . . . and Izzie. My concerns for how the swim-a-thon will turn out soften into mushy hope.

I make my way through the small crowd gathered around Gabe and hug him. "I'm so proud of you."

"Thanks, Mrs. Redmond." He steps back from my embrace and gestures toward a woman with thoughtful brown eyes. "Have you met my mom?"

"It's an honor." I reach forward. "What a great son you've got here."

"Pam Thompson." She shakes my hand. "It's nice to meet you as well. I hear you have a pretty amazing daughter too."

"Thank you."

Together we watch from the edge of the park as healthy and disabled children play, wait in line for the slide, push each other on the swings, smile and laugh together.

"What a wonderful sight. You must be about to burst at what Gabe has accomplished."

"I am. And I'm grateful to Jack." She glances over at him as he helps latch a child into a swing, her eyes shining with unshed tears. "He helped make this dream of Gabe's come true. His dad couldn't."

"I am sorry about your loss."

"It's been a tough year. But Luke would be so proud of Gabe. I wish he were here to see this."

"Maybe he's smiling down from heaven."

"I'm sure he is." She clears her throat. "What a wonderful heart Isabel must have to want to reach out to her little friend and make the swim-a-thon happen."

"Gabe must have rubbed off on her. Before she met him, she was focused on her little world."

"Being a teen can be rough."

"Especially when you lose a parent."

Pam peers at me closer as if with an unvoiced question.

"Divorce."

"Sometimes that can be tougher than a death."

I shake my head. "Death is more permanent."

"You're right. But it doesn't have to mean the situation is hopeless. We have an eternal perspective."

I nod, understanding, and yet . . . even an eternal perspective clouds under tragedy. "Gabe is an amazing young man. I'm very glad he and Izzie are friends. His giving spirit is contagious. Just a few weeks ago she was an unhappy teen, focused on her own problems. Now she's focused and determined and living for something bigger and greater than herself."

"You can't teach that."

"You can inspire it though."

Pam smiles. "Jack has certainly done a lot of that with Gabe. He's become a really good father figure."

Something in her tone alerts me. Not that I should be alarmed if she's interested in Jack. It shouldn't bother me at all. "A lot of men," my gaze tracks a young boy running from one end of the park to the other, "wouldn't have bothered or taken the time."

"Jack isn't like most men."

So I've noticed. I purposefully steer my gaze away from him and look at Pam then. But she's watching Gabe and Jack, standing beside each other, smiling and talking to each other as they push two children in swings. My abdomen tightens. "How long have you known him?"

"Since college. I actually dated him before I met and fell in love with Luke." Her laughter rings out.

"Really?" With that kind of history, it's just a matter of time before she and Jack get back together. I ignore a twinge of jealousy. I should be happy for Jack. But why can one person find happiness twice when I seem to be having difficulty finding it the first time around?

A boy about the age of ten races up to us and hugs Pam around the middle. His face is red and splotched, shiny with sweat. "Mom, can we get ice cream?"

"Sure." She reaches for her purse.

"Let me." I hand the boy a five-dollar bill. He grins but his gaze shifts toward his mother for approval.

"Are you sure?" she asks.

"Absolutely."

When she nods, her son fists the money. "Thanks, lady."

"Mrs. Redmond," his mother corrects.

"You're welcome." I smile, softening his mother's formality.

He stuffs the five in his front jeans pocket then races off.

"That's Grant."

"He's cute."

"He's a mess. But he has a good heart too. One thing I'm learning is that you have to give it room to grow. Which is why I allowed Gabe to live with Jack temporarily. So you should be congratulated, Kaye, you're giving Isabel space so she can help others."

"I hope so." I stare down at my feet. The ties of my tennis shoes are as knotted as my insides. "It's not easy." Even though this woman would probably be my rival if I wanted to be involved with Jack, I feel a connection with her and so I confide, "I'm concerned how it will all turn out. Izzie is very caught up in wanting things to work out for Lily. She isn't ready to accept the possibility that Lily might not make it."

"We have to leave those worries in the Lord's hands." Her kind eyes look wise, as if they've been softened by her family's heartache. "The kids prayed for a long time that Luke would be healed. But he wasn't. I worried that would turn them against God. I worried about Gabe's grades through all of this. What didn't I worry about? But all my worry didn't make things better. Our kids are learning a lesson that can't be taught in school."

"I agree." I just wish Cliff would see the benefit too. He was moderate in his response with Jack in the room. But later he called and gave me an earful. "They're learning life lessons that could shape their future. But not worrying . . . well, it's easier said than done."

Pam gives a light laugh. "If everybody could do it, then we wouldn't call it faith."

"Oh, look!" I glance toward the parking lot and see Terry pushing a wheelchair where Lily is sitting and grinning. Lily's wearing her newly constructed wig that looks like a halo of ringlets. "You'll want to meet Terry."

A few minutes later we're sitting around picnic tables with Pam's children and passing out hand wipes for sticky ice cream smiles. The children slingshot in and out from among us, finally wheeling Lily and Amy over to the slides. With Lily out of earshot, I ask Terry, "How are *you*?"

She gives me a wide smile, which then wavers.

"What's happened?" I reach for her. "Did you talk to the doctor?"

She shakes her head. "I'm sorry."

"Don't be."

Pam's eyes soften. She sits quietly as we both wait for Terry to continue.

"Most people just want happy answers, so I've grown accustomed to that being my first response."

Pam nods as if she's experienced the same thing.

I lean forward and place a hand on Terry's arm. "You can just be you here. Happy or sad. Wild and crazy. Or mad as—"

"Probably closer to the latter." She shrugs a narrow shoulder.

Pam collects the trash her children left on the table and tosses it in a nearby can humming with bees. "Maybe I should go check on my kids."

"It's okay." Terry sniffs, wiping her nose with the back of her hand. "You can stay. I don't have any secrets."

"Is there something I can do?" I want to ask what the doctors said about Lily but I refrain, knowing Terry will tell me when she's ready.

She releases a shaky breath. "Miles doesn't want the swim-a-thon."

Her statement hits me squarely in the solar plexus. "Why?"

"He says we're not that desperate. But the fact is, we are. And it's really just his pride. But that's not the real problem."

I tilt my head, waiting for more.

"He wants a divorce."

"Terry!"

She crosses her arms over her stomach as if that can hold her together. "He says he didn't bargain for all of this. He can't handle it."

"I'm so sorry, Terry." Tears spring to my eyes. I want to hug my friend and punch her husband at the same time.

"We need to pray." Pam comes around the table, places a hand on both of our shoulders and completes the circle. And together, under the shade of a pecan tree, we pray for a miracle.

⁕

Sun-kissed from spending the day outdoors, my heart aches for my friend, but my face hurts from returning so many smiles. As the festivities tapered off, Gabe and Izzie insisted we go to Five Guys for cheeseburgers. Which meant Jack came too. When they finished, Gabe made excuses for them and said they needed to get to work on the swim-a-thon.

"Aren't you tired?"

"Mom, we're fine."

With that Jack and I were left alone in the restaurant. I watch Izzie race with Gabe across a street to his truck in the parking lot and am bombarded with Marla's insinuations.

"They're okay, Kaye." Jack's tone is teasing. "They have more energy than we do."

"Yeah, that's what I'm worried about." I sip my Coke and try to drown out Marla's voice in my head. When I'm ready to fall into the tub then crawl into bed, they look like they're ready to run a marathon. "They're good kids though."

He grins and dunks a fry in ketchup. Except he doesn't look wiped out either.

I bring my worries into the open. "Do you think . . . Gabe and Izzie are . . . you know?"

He watches me for a minute while he finishes chewing. "You mean, are they seeing each other in a more romantic way?"

My pulse kicks up a notch. I'm not sure if it's maternal concerns or the fact that I see Jack in a different light too.

"They *have* been spending a lot of time together." He reaches into the brown paper sack for more fries. "But would that be a problem?"

"Only if their interest becomes . . ." I shift in my chair, clasp my hands together in front of me, and wrestle with the best way to say this. "Gabe is older than Izzie."

"By only a few months."

"She's never really had a serious boyfriend."

"So?" Jack pops another fry in his mouth.

His lack of concern rankles me. "What about Gabe?"

He shrugs. "I don't really know."

"Have you ever talked to him about girls? You are"—how do I say this?—"stepping into a fatherly role with him." I cringe at my accusatory tone.

He leans forward, resting his forearm on the table. "Are we talking about sex here?"

I swallow hard. "Maybe."

"Maybe?" He laughs.

"Okay. Fine." I meet his gaze squarely. "Yes, let's talk about sex." My voice suddenly seems to carry through the small restaurant and several heads turn in our direction. Heat launches up my neck and burns my face. Laughter bubbles up inside me.

Jack rubs his jaw but laughs with me. A smile tugs the corner of his mouth to one side. "Look, I've talked to Gabe. He's not sexually active. And I don't think that he wants to be." He shakes his head. "I don't mean it that way. Every guy *wants* . . . well, you know. But he understands fantasy versus the reality of pregnancy, diseases . . . and he wants to wait for the right girl . . . woman."

"What if that girl is my daughter?"

"I meant, he wants to wait for marriage."

My lungs expand an inch. "Izzie too. Bu—"

"Gabe made a vow to God."

"That's powerful."

"Not easily broken. But temptation . . . that's not easy either."

"Exactly." I glance down at my hamburger, unable to eat the rest. "Izzie has seen a lot over the past few years with her father leaving us . . . me for another woman. She knows that Cliff and I *had* to get married. It's not something I'm proud of, and yet I don't regret it either because I have Izzie. But it's led to a lot of discussions. Even though I'm sorry that she's witnessed her dad and Barbara . . . not literally . . . I didn't mean that. But she's not stupid. She knows they've been living together." I'm rambling and I'm not sure how to get to my point without coming right out. "You're a single guy. And Gabe looks up to you."

His gaze narrows, making a deep crevice between his brows. "Are you asking what kind of an example I'm setting for him?"

I push back from the table. My heart is racing, and I wish I could jump up and leave. "I realize that's personal. It's your business what you do . . . or don't do. And I wouldn't say anything if Izzie wasn't spending a lot of time at your house and with Gabe."

His gaze is solid, penetrating. "I'm not a hypocrite, Kaye."

"Okay, well . . . good." I reach for my soda.

"Isn't this cozy?" a familiar voice interrupts us.

I look up to find Cliff standing beside our table. His collar is open, his shirtsleeves rolled up. "Cliff."

"Saw Isabel leaving with her boyfriend. I didn't realize it was a double date."

"Uh . . . hi, we were, uh . . ." I stop myself from making excuses. It's none of his business what I'm doing here with Jack.

Jack stands, shakes Cliff's hand, and pulls out a chair for him. "Join us."

"Can't. My order is to go." He thumbs over his shoulder toward the counter where a guy and gal are frying hamburgers. But Cliff doesn't turn away from us. "So, is *this* a date?"

Jack remains standing, meeting Cliff's gaze straight on. "That a problem?"

My heart skitters to a stop and my stomach plummets—not good with a hunk of burger inside. Did Jack say what I think he said? Is he insinuating . . . ?

Cliff's gaze shifts toward me then back to Jack. "Long as you know what you're getting yourself into."

"Long as you know what you've lost."

My mouth drops open. Before I can come up with a way to smooth things over, Cliff says, "I'll call you tomorrow, Kaye," walks away and grabs his order. It's then I notice he has two sodas. One for him. One for . . . Marla? I doubt he's taking his mom dinner. And that can only mean he's seeing Barbie again. Or someone else.

Jack steps around the table and sits beside me rather than across from me. But he doesn't put an arm around me. Still, his nearness is comforting and yet not. "You okay?"

"W-what did you tell him that for?"

"I thought it would be better for him to think we might be involved. Make him jealous." His mouth twists as if he's questioning himself. "You still want him back, don't you?"

I nod but the appropriate words jam in my throat. Cliff never stood up for me the way Jack just did. And now I'm sure.

I'm after the wrong man.

⤨ Chapter Eighteen ⤪

Gabe's truck is parked in front of the house when I arrive home. I fumble with the lock but finally push inside. No one greets me, not even Cousin It. The house is quiet. *Too* quiet. It's so peaceful. Did I enter the wrong one? Where's Marla? Where are Izzie and Gabe? We have a no-boys-in-the-bedroom rule, which I'm glad I implemented. Through the back windows, the pool appears empty. The crazy dog isn't nosing the glass or looking forlorn either. Is Marla hiding in her room or could she be with Cliff? Could the extra drink have really been for her?

The smell of scorched vanilla grabs my attention. I follow the odor toward the kitchen, check the stove, but then realize someone lit a candle and left it on the table. Careless. I lean over to blow it out.

A noise from down the hall makes the hair at the back of my neck rise. My heart thuds. Could it be Izzie and Gabe . . . doing something they shouldn't? My fist clenches and I march down the hall toward her bedroom. I give a smart rap on the door and jerk it open. The lights are out, and I grope for the switch. When the light pierces my eyes, I blink. The room is empty. No Izzie or Gabe.

The noise grows louder, and I grab the portable phone. It sounds like furniture moving in a back bedroom. And groaning.

Then I hear a moan from the other side of the hall. From my bedroom.

Marla! Could she be hurt? Could she have fallen? Had a stroke?

I dial 9-1-1 and race toward her door. My heart pounds. Didn't she have heart arrhythmia during surgery? Could she have had a heart attack? Without pause, I wrench open her door and stumble into the room.

Then I freeze like a big block of ice. I can't move. My heart manages a couple of feeble, uneven beats. Time seems to slow to a crawl as the next few moments feel like years.

My ex-mother-in-law lies on the bed in a position no one should ever see! She looks over the shoulder of some man, her lopsided face turning three shades of white.

I feel dizzy. But I'm unable to step forward or backward. I shade my eyes. At that second I recognize Mr. Klum's balding head, and Marla gives a half scream.

"Emergency, 9-1-1," a staticky voice comes from the phone. "What is your emergency? Hello? 9-1-1. Is anyone there?"

If the police show up, this is going to be difficult to explain.

I turn my back on Marla and Harry, step out of the room, and pray the image in my mind will fade with time. With the click of the door, I focus on the 9-1-1 operator. "No, uh, yes, I'm here. I'm sorry. Hello?"

"State your emergency, please."

"This isn't an emergency." I rub my forehead, lean against the wall in the hallway. "I thought someone was in the house. Maybe. But I was wrong. Well, there was someone in the house. I thought she was having a heart attack or something. It was my ex-mother-in-law. She's been staying here . . ." I shake my head. Focus. I amble down the hall, back to the den, and collapse onto the sofa, as if I've become disconnected from my own body. "At least it wasn't my daughter. I'm not making any sense. Am I?"

The door to my bedroom, now Marla's boudoir, opens.

"Thanks for calling." I click off the phone and sit up straight. Harry Klum steps out of the room.

I cover my face with a pillow like it's a floatation device and I'm on a plane and it's going down. Over water. I'll just sit here quietly, maybe Marla, Harry, my life will all float away.

After a moment of breathing in the dusty fabric, I hear a soft clearing of the throat. "Uh, Miss Kaye?"

I look over the edge of the pillow at Harry. He's a bit red in the face, but I'm not sure it's from embarrassment. Little tufts of his hair stand on end. His shirt buttons are mismatched. He rubs his jaw.

"Miss Kaye, I sure am sorry about all this. I just want to explain—"

"Oh, no. Please don't." I lean back into the sofa, clutching the pillow against my stomach, which seems to be experiencing a tidal wave. "Why don't you get yourself some water. Or a soda. Or whatever." He's obviously made himself at home. "Make it two."

He goes into the kitchen. When he returns a minute later, he hands me a can with the top already popped. Harry sits on the opposite end of the sofa. "I don't know what to say."

I'm not able to look him in the eye. "I don't think there is anything to say."

"It's not what you think." Harry pops the tab on his Coke and fizz bubbles up around the lip. We both watch it for a moment, then he slurps it up and I focus on my own drink. "I hurt my back last week working at the park. Miss Marla thought she could fix it."

"Uh-huh." I take a big gulp of my own drink but the bubbles resurface in me, and I belch in a very unladylike manner. "Sorry. Look, Harry—" I stop myself because I don't know what to say, where to begin. Finally I ask, "Is Marla okay?"

"She's a bit discombobulated . . . but she's fine."

"I know the feeling." Should I ask Harry's intentions? I suppose it's none of my business but maybe I already know the answer anyway.

He toys with the tab on the top of the can. "What were you asking me the other day?" He scratches the top of his head. "Have I ever done something stupid for love?"

I abruptly stand. I don't want to talk about love. About Harry and Marla. "Look, Harry, would it be all right if we—"

From down the hall I hear a thud. It doesn't sound like Marla hit the floor, more like a book hitting the wall.

"Should I go check on her?"

I shrug. I don't know the proper protocol for this situation.

⁂

When the doorbell rings, it gives me something to do rather than sit on the sofa and wait for Harry and Marla to emerge from her . . . my bedroom. Maybe I should have had the Valentine bed delivered here.

I jerk open the door, and a police officer greets me with an all-too-serious expression. I resist the urge to hold up my hands in self-defense. *I'm not guilty, officer. Really, I'm not!*

"Hello?" I manage instead.

"There was a 9-1-1 call registered from this address." His voice is steady, calm, official.

My heart jolts like I'm guilty. "Oh? Oh!" I always expected this would happen when Isabel was little. But I thought she would have made the call as a prank. "Oh, Officer, it was a mistake. I thought someone was in the house when I came home . . . but it was my mother-in-law . . . *ex*-mother-in-law. Believe me, you don't want to know the whole story." I hope he doesn't ask any more questions. "I told the lady on the phone . . . the operator—"

"These things always have to be checked out."

"I see." Does he?

A car door slams out front. I look beyond the police officer's shoulder to Anderson Sterling rounding his black, shiny BMW. It's nose-to-nose with Gabe's truck, and on the back side, which is why I didn't see it when I arrived home, is Harry's station wagon, now snugly sandwiched between the BMW and police cruiser. It looks like we're having quite a party.

As Anderson heads up the walk, his footsteps quicken. "Is Marla all right? What's happened, Officer?"

"Do you live here?" the officer asks.

"I was coming to see Marla Redmond."

"Is that you, ma'am?"

"No. I'm Kaye Redmond." I prop a hand on my hip. "You're a little late." When Anderson's eyes widen, I realize belatedly how dire that sounded. "She's all right."

"Excuse me." Harry brushes past me carrying Marla's large suitcase. He pauses when he sees Mr. Sterling. "Andy."

"Harry?"

The officer crosses his arms. "What's going on here?"

"More than you know," I mutter. "Harry! Where are you going? What are you doing?"

"I'm sorry, Miss Kaye. Marla insisted. She's packing the rest of her things now."

"Packing?" But how will I explain this to Cliff? I lean heavily against the door.

"You sure everything is okay, ma'am?" The officer stares at me as if expecting an honest answer.

I'm not sure I have one for him, but I meet his inquiring gaze. "Have you ever had one of those days?"

"If it's not an emergency, then I'll be going."

"Not *your* kind of emergency." I follow Harry out the door. But I'm guessing fireworks are about to erupt.

Just as the police cruiser squawks its siren before pulling out and leaving us behind, Izzie and Gabe round the corner with

Cousin It loping alongside, tethered by her leash. When they see the cruiser, they pick up their pace. With Harry burdened by the suitcases and carrying them toward his station wagon, and Anderson walking into my house, I stand in the yard alone and greet my daughter and Gabe.

"Mom! What is going on?"

I smile and shake my head. "Hard to explain. It's all a misunderstanding."

"What's Mr. Klum doing with Marla's suitcases?"

"Apparently she's decided to leave."

"That's good, right?"

"Let's not talk about it right now. Okay?"

Then Marla walks out of the house. She's wearing dark glasses and a scarf over her hair. With head down, she pulls the wrap tightly around her and doesn't bother to pause and talk to Mr. Sterling who follows behind her like a lost puppy.

"Marla!" Anderson chases after her. "What are you doing? Have you lost your—?" He grabs her arm, turns her to face him. "What happened to your face? Did Harry do that?" He clenches his fist at the sight of the last remaining bruises. Didn't she tell him about her surgery? "I'm gonna kill him!"

Marla stops Anderson with a firm hand on his arm. "You will do no such thing."

"But he's hurt you!"

"He has *not* hurt me. Good grief. Don't be so dramatic." She touches the side of her face where the final bruises are receding into her hairline.

"Then . . . what?"

She purses her lips. "Stop this, Anderson. We're not seeing each other anymore."

"You're leaving with Harry? Harry Klum!"

Her lips purse. "Yes."

"But why?"

"Because he sees me in a way no one else has."

"And how's that?"

"Like a real woman."

"What does that mean?"

Should I hide behind the mailbox and allow them a private moment? It's all too fascinating, appalling in some warped way, yet definitely eye-opening.

Anderson shakes his head as if Marla is making the worst mistake of her life and turns back toward his car. As he jerks it into gear and pulls away from the curb, a vase of red roses tips over in the passenger seat.

Marla passes me, not meeting my gaze, and I rush forward. "Marla! Let's talk about this. You don't have to leave." I can't believe what I hear myself saying! But this isn't how I want our time together to end. "Not like this anyway."

She holds up her hand but doesn't look in my direction. Her scarf flaps in the breeze. She lifts her chin high, and her spine stiffens.

"Let's talk about this."

"Do *not* say a word." She waits at the curb for Harry to drive the car forward ten feet. "I do not want to discuss this situation. Ever."

Of course, she's embarrassed. I am too. But not talking isn't going to solve our problem. "Look, Marla, I'm sorry. I didn't mean to intrude. Honest. I thought you were hurt. I thought—"

She jerks open the car door, slides into her seat, and slams the door shut. She stares straight ahead, not looking in my direction.

"What happened, Mom?" Isabel stands beside me.

I want to tell her this isn't the worst thing that could happen. There are a lot worse things out there that I don't even want to mention or think about, things that my friend Terry is having to face. And I realize that Marla has been running her entire life. Running from fear or to get something that will make her happy. But none of that will work. "You can't keep running."

Still, she won't look in my direction.

I tap the window. But there's no response. I sigh, look to Harry for help. His hands rest on the steering wheel. He shifts the car into Park and opens his door. Slowly he gets out and looks at me across the hood. "Don't worry, Miss Kaye. I'll take good care of her."

"But where are you taking her? Back to her apartment?"

"To my place in the village."

As they drive off, I watch Harry's dull red taillights, then his blinker flashes momentarily before he turns the corner.

"Mom, what happened?"

I shake my head. "I came home, heard a strange noise . . . thought it was Marla in pain." I lower my voice. "She and Harry were"—I tilt my head to the side—"you know."

Izzie stares at me for a full minute before I see the spark of understanding in her blue eyes. "Eew!"

"Yeah, well, there you go."

⤙ Chapter Nineteen ⤛

Sometimes I feel as if I'm standing on the brink, teetering, tipping over. Gravity can have its way or I can lean into the force to make it a semblance of a dive. Would that make me feel better, make me feel as if I'm still in control?

Tonight I literally stand with my toes on the edge of the pool and imagine standing on the blocks at the swim-a-thon, leaning over, sticking my backside out for the world to see, and then . . . belly flopping into the water. *Chin down. Keep chin tucked under.* Since I won't have to wait for a "whistle" or "gun," then I can go like lightning. Before anyone has a chance to really notice my . . . shortcomings. The water will cover a multitude of sins. Or so I hope. Because my Lycra bathing suit will not.

With Marla gone and Izzie doing homework with Gabe, I back away from my pool and pretend to walk up to the blocks. With one swift move, I pull my cover-up over my head, toss it onto my towel, step on the "blocks," which tonight is only the tile-rimmed edge of the pool and dive for the water. It's chilled and I come up gasping. My thighs hit the top of the water hard, and my skin stings. At least I'm fully immersed in the water. From here, I can swim. Kick a lot. Splashing—lots of splashing—covers my poor form. Or so I hope.

In the meantime I need practice. Not only to build up my stamina but to whittle down my deficiencies. Of which there are many.

I swim laps with Cousin It sitting on the side of the pool, her tongue lolling, brown eyes watchful. I hope she makes a good lifeguard if I suddenly need her. But a scream or holler would bring Izzie and Gabe if I get a sudden cramp.

As I reach forward in stroke after stroke, my mind drifts, lapping over the most recent events. Tomorrow I'll call Marla. That is, if she'll take my call. Until then, there's nothing I can do about the situation.

Besides Izzie's *eew!*, she hasn't said much about her grandmother's behavior. Lack of decorum has become all too common in this family. It's not the example I want set for Izzie on how to conduct a relationship. She's bombarded from the news and movies to magazines and books, with the belief that normalcy is relative. Marla's actions may be what society calls the norm, but aren't Christians called to a higher standard? Shouldn't we at least make an attempt to do things God's way?

It solidifies my reasons for, and hardens my determination to get Cliff back. If Izzie sees how her mother handles herself in relationships, and that a marriage *can* work out, even after a betrayal, then maybe it will encourage and help her understand the power of prayer.

❧

It should be no surprise when Cliff arrives at the house. But I'm not at all prepared. Instead of dressed and ready with a quick line about his mother's leaving, I'm bobbing in the deep end, treading water, huffing and puffing from all my exercise when Cousin It's warning barks resound off the rooftop.

"It! Stop!"

She stops barking and starts wagging her tail, rounding the end of the pool to greet Cliff.

He frowns and puts out a hand. "Get back. Stay put."

She hesitates, wavering, as if unsure what to do.

I eye my towel. How ladylike can I manage to get out of the pool and retrieve my towel and cover-up? With it dark except for the pool light, I hope my flab won't be too apparent to my ex and make him long for Barbie again. So, gathering my courage as my arms are beginning to feel like limp spaghetti, I make it to the side of the pool and climb the short ladder. The cool, night air hits my body, and I shiver. I dash past Cousin It and scoop up my towel. She grabs my cover-up and takes off with it. But at least she's out of the way. Wrapped like a hasty, last-minute present, I face Cliff. "Hi." I pray Marla hasn't made me into the villain in our latest confrontation. "How are you?"

"Good." He looks good in a dark suit. His crisp white shirt hugs his neck. He walks forward and leans in for a brief kiss on my cheek. His face is cool from the blast of air conditioning in his car, but his lips are warm. A surprise. And I take it as a good sign. "We need to talk."

I nod but don't offer to go into the house. This is our best chance at privacy. "I thought so."

He turns away from me, and I brace myself for a serious discussion about his mother. He tilts his head back and peers up at the night sky where gossamer clouds whisper past. "It's nice back here."

"Thanks." Pride blossoms inside me. Accomplishing this much as a single mother was important to me. I've never owned anything on my own, and this step of independence from Cliff was scary and difficult. For him to acknowledge my little achievement warms me.

His silence, however, worries me. I give him a minute, but he doesn't say anything else. "So what did *she* tell you?"

He turns back to face me, his right eyebrow arched. "Who?"

"Your mother?"

His left matches his right. "I haven't talked to her." Then his brows scrunch into a frown I recognize from experience. "Why? What's wrong?"

I roll my lips inward, wishing now I hadn't said anything. Patience has not always been one of my virtues. "That's not why you came over?"

"No." He crosses his arms over his chest.

I swallow hard. Is it about Jack then? I don't want to get into that either. Marla seems like a safer topic. "So you don't know that she moved out?"

His gaze shifts toward the house then back. "She's not here?"

I shake my head. "Not anymore."

"Where is she? What happened?"

"It was a misunderstanding. Really. And she overreacted a little." An understatement to be sure.

"Mother will get over it." His statement surprises me. The way he relaxes his arms and frown, he seems suddenly relieved, almost glad. Which makes me frown. What is going on? What *did* he come to talk to me about? Us? Remembering the jealousy he displayed when we were at the burger joint, hope begins to rise inside me. I take a step toward him, wrapping my arms around myself, suspecting his arms will soon be warming me. "So what did you want to discuss?"

"I need a favor."

I hesitate but only briefly. A favor of a kiss? A favor of forgiveness? "Okay."

He glances at his watch. "Two favors."

I smile, knowing where this is headed. I've known Cliff for eighteen years. He's not one to come out and say what he wants. He's a salesman, making whatever he wants sound beneficial to others. I suspect he's going to ask to get back together. Why else would he be so dressed up? Why else would he not know or care where his mother is? I decide I will toy with him, drag this out only slightly before giving in. I give him a half-lidded glance. "What is it?"

"I thought maybe you could tell Isabel, but it wouldn't hurt if you were the one to tell Mother too."

It's definitely a backhanded way to get around to our reconciliation, but I will be happy to be the one to spread the news. "About?"

He meets my gaze then glances down, scuffs his dress shoe against the decking. He blows out a rush of air at the pale half-pie moon. "This is harder than I thought it would be."

"You don't have to be worried, Cliff." I place a hand on his arm. Saying he's sorry has never been easy for him. "You know I—"

He pulls his hand away, plants it on his hip. "Here's the deal. I'm getting married."

My smile widens. "Yes, I know."

"Tonight."

"Tonight?" It's not exactly a down-on-the-knee proposal, but I know how Cliff works. I touch my wet hair. How will I have time to pack? To dry my hair? Use my Velcro rollers? But none of it matters. I can be ready in a flash. "What time is the flight?"

His stares down his aquiline nose. "Two hours. You sure are understanding about this."

I carefully wipe my hand against my towel then place it against his chest. "I knew this would happen."

"You did? And you're not mad?"

"Mad?" I raise up on tiptoes, leaning toward him. But something isn't right. Cliff takes a step backward. A cold sensation washes over me, replaced by a flush of heat. I drop my hand to my side. "Wait a minute . . . who are you marrying?"

"Barbar—"

"Barbie?"

My world tilts. A roaring noise fills my ears. Is it my blood? Or myself screaming? I blink, trying to absorb what has happened, what he's saying. Words from my past assault me.

"I don't love you anymore," Cliff said when he left.

"I don't want to get married! It's my life too! Just get rid of it!" Cliff yelled at me when I tracked him down at the fraternity house and told him I was pregnant.

"I'm busy, Kaye. You're in college. You have your own life to live now," my father said after he and my mother divorced. But I knew what he was saying: he had his own life to live and didn't want to be bothered with me.

I feel the weight of all of those painful words pressing into my heart, piercing me, crushing me.

"Barbara told me I should have just called from the airport."

I'm not sure if Cliff is talking to me or himself, but then he looks straight at me.

"I thought I should tell you myself." As if now he's going to do the right thing! The right thing would be to stay with his wife!

"No!" I shake my head. I will not accept this. Not again. Not ever!

"You thought . . . you and I?" He chuckles, ducks, and shakes his head. "Kaye, really, I told you—"

"What was all of that about the other night?" I take a step toward him, this time my hands fisting in tight, angry knots. "You wanting to get back together? What were you? Bored? Getting back at her? What?"

He shrugs. "I was confused."

I stare at him for a long moment, my gaze sweeping over him. "Confused? You were confused? About which woman you loved? What you wanted? I don't think so!" My lungs tighten and I can barely draw a breath but I press forward. "You were being selfish! That's how you've always been. I've tried to see you as something else. But it always comes back to *this*. You don't think about others, about Izzie, or me! Not even your own mother! And you're not thinking about Barbara. You're thinking about yourself."

"Now, wait a minute, Kaye! I came here because I thought you should know. I thought it would be easier for Isabel if you told her. I'm trying to do the right thing."

"No, what you thought is that Kaye could clean up your mess once again. That I could make it all right, that I could smooth things over so you wouldn't have to deal with your daughter's hurt feelings or your mother's wrath. Well, you know what? Forget it. *You* handle it. *You* tell them yourself."

"I can't believe you're acting like this, Kaye. What's got into you?"

I clench my fists. And without thinking, without stopping the anger from taking over, I shove Cliff hard in the chest. The shock registering on his face is reward enough.

But then he teeters on the edge of the pool for a second, his arms flailing, one leg kicking out, and then he topples into the water with a huge double-decker cheeseburger kind of splash. When he comes up spluttering and cursing, slapping his hand against the water, his suit jacket soaked through and through, I leave him with Cousin It barking and go into the house.

When I reach my bathroom, my limbs trembling and shaking with the aftershocks of my anger, I anticipate tears. But they don't come. I stare at my flushed image in the mirror. I blink fast and hard. But still no tears emerge. Turning away from the mirror, I sit on the counter and draw slow, deep breaths. There was a time when I thought something like this would kill me. I thought I'd curl into a miserable ball and shrivel up. But the emotions I'd always thought might overtake me, don't materialize. Anger pulses through my veins hot and fast. But sorrow? No. Depression? Not that either.

Shouldn't I be crying? If I loved my husband? But I'm not. I'm angry. I'm boiling mad. So mad I could punch something or someone. Cliff's face comes to mind, the shock of when I pushed him draws a smile from me. And then I know.

I don't love Cliff.

I tried to do so. I tried for eighteen years. I tried to make it work. And I would have given the rest of my life to make it work, to try again to love him.

It almost feels as if a burden has been lifted, as if I'm feeling a righteous anger. How *dare* he lead me on! How dare he treat our daughter in such a careless, heartless way! How dare he treat his mother without the respect she deserves! My assessment of Cliff was right. And I almost feel pity for Barbie and what she'll have to put up with in the coming years. Almost, but not quite.

A light rap on the door makes my breath catch in my throat. "Who is it?"

"Mom? You okay?"

I turn the knob and allow her entrance. The sound of teens laughing and goofing around follow her into the closed space.

"What's going on? Who's here?"

"Some of the swim team. We're working on the swim-a-thon."

I rub my forehead, remembering as I raced through the den so quickly, not even noticing who was there. Or maybe I didn't care. But now looking back, there were several faces I recognized besides Gabe. And if I remember right and wasn't hallucinating, there were a couple of shaved heads—besides Izzie's and Gabe's.

"Did some of your friends shave their heads?"

She closes the door behind her, shutting out the noise but then laughing. "They think I've been trying to show the coach I'm more determined to win. So they wanted to prove they were competitive too."

Laughing, I shake my head. "Soon the whole school will be bald."

"By then my hair will have grown back." She hugs me close. "Are you okay?"

"Yes. I'm fine. Is *he* gone?"

"Who?"

"Your father."

"Oh, yeah." Her mouth pulls to the side in a half-smothered smile. "You sure you're okay?"

I smooth my hands over her back, thankful that we have each other, as we hug. The irony that she put me in a lifelong relationship with Cliff hits me, because if it wasn't for her I'd be falling apart now. "Yes, Izzie. I'm good."

"Really?"

I look her in the eye and feel a peace come over me. "Yes." Then I hold her in my arms, feel her soft hair against my face. "I love you."

"I love you too, Mom." Her embrace is solid and comforting.

After a moment, I pull away. "Is the pizza here yet?"

"Yeah." She studies me, searching my face for something that might tell her I'm coming unglued. "Mom?"

"Yeah?"

"You pushed Dad in the pool?"

I nod and then a giggle bubbles up inside me. I cover my mouth.

"Mom! What did he do this time?"

"Same ol' same ol'."

And she begins to laugh, then hugs me close again. "I'm proud of you, Mom."

"You are?"

"Yeah, I wish you'd done that a hundred times before now."

I rake my fingers through my wet hair. "Oh, I shouldn't have done that. It wasn't the most mature thing to do."

"Mom"—she braces my shoulders with her hands—"it's okay to be angry. Especially at him."

I feel my lip start to tremble and snag it between my teeth, but the tremulous feelings expand, making my whole body shake.

"You know what? I think God is really angry at him too."

I start to shake my head, but Izzie brackets my face with her hands.

"No, Mom. He is! What Dad did was wrong! Anger isn't a bad thing. You can't sugarcoat it. You can't hide it. It will eat you from the inside out."

"So you're saying shaving your head is far healthier?"

She grins and rubs her fuzzy head. "Maybe. Wanna try it?"

"Not tonight." My throat burns with unshed tears. I don't want to tell her the latest. I want to protect her. And I don't want to give Cliff the satisfaction of smoothing out all the wrinkles he's caused. My first priority is Isabel, and she has the right to know what her father is doing. It will be better if it comes from me. At least for her. Not Cliff. "He's getting married again, Izzie."

She wraps her arms around me. "Good. Then maybe you can let him go."

Her calm response is a balm to my injured soul. I hug her close, grateful for her. She's an amazing person, this daughter of mine.

⤙ Chapter Twenty ⤚

Most of the kids have headed home. Gabe and Izzie are studying for a calculus test at the kitchen table. Looking up at the dark sky and twinkling of stars, I'm back on the diving board, the tips of my toes dangling in the water. But I've changed my swimsuit for comfy jeans and T-shirt. Overhead there's the occasional blinking lights of a plane. Could it be Cliff's plane? I imagine him—all dry and redressed—snuggling with Barb in first class as he tells her how I thought he was proposing to me. My jaw clenches tight. A fall breeze ruffles my hair and tosses a handful of white crepe myrtle petals carelessly into the pool.

"Well, God," I shift my gaze toward the moon, "I guess I read this one wrong, didn't I?" I rub my hands down my jean clad thighs and stretch out my bare feet. "How did I *not* see this coming?"

"Are you entertaining?" Jack's voice startles me. "Or can I join you?"

My pulse thrums. He stands at the back door, which I didn't hear open. He's wearing worn jeans and a faded red T-shirt. I offer him a smile that doesn't feel very self-assured. "Sure, come on out."

He settles on a slatted chair next to me. Close but not too close. He props up the back from when Izzie had it in flat lay-out-get-a-tan position while I go back to staring up at the sickle-shaped moon. My heart should feel as if it's been carved right out of my chest, but it doesn't. Maybe I'm simply in shock and don't know I'm emotionally bleeding to death. Or maybe there's nothing left of me to lose. I sense Jack watching me, but then he clasps his hands over his flat belly and watches the stars with me.

I suspect he knows what happened. Probably all of Southlake knows. There were teens here when it all went down. "You don't have to watch me. I'm not suicidal or anything."

"I didn't think you were. I enjoy being with you."

I give him a dubious glance. I'm not about to get hopeful over a man again. Barbie outclassed me; Jack is playing an entirely different sport. It's better not to hope than to be crushed.

"It's true." His smile is fifty percent its usual wattage. "But yeah, I did want to make sure you're okay."

"So you heard?"

"Isabel told me but I won't say anything—"

I wave a hand as if it's all unimportant. But I know better and I suspect Jack does too. "It doesn't matter. I'm ten degrees beyond humiliation."

"Nothing *you* should be humiliated about."

I snort out a laugh. "Oh, yeah. Nothing. I just broadcasted an announcement that I was hoping my ex would come back. So I take his mother into my house to care for her. And what does he do?" My voice spikes and I turn down the volume. "Elopes with Barbie."

"That's a reflection on him, not you."

I allow his comforting words to soak into my withered emotions then shrug. If what Jack says is true, then am I only upset because of what I suspect others are saying or thinking? Or am I truly distraught that Cliff has rejected me once again?

Jack touches my arm, drawing my gaze to him. "A *poor* reflection."

"Lots of guys probably think he's cool for dumping the old bag and getting a trophy."

Jack rubs the back of his neck. "Have you met the woman he married?"

I can't conjure up a smile.

"And any man who has would know Cliff got the bad end of that bargain."

"Or Barbie did."

"Exactly."

I shake my head but a smile tugs at the corner of my mouth. But it's quickly erased by morose thoughts. "Have you ever felt like you couldn't measure up?"

He slants a glance my way. "Then I became a Christian. The fact is I couldn't measure up. Ever. But God doesn't ask us to measure up. He gave us the stopgap."

"Jesus," I whisper the name reverently.

He nods. "It's all too easy to look at ourselves the way the world does." He tilts his head toward the house. "As if we need a facelift. A wig. A husband." He thumbs his chest. "A wife. Whatever. In the world's eyes, we *don't* measure up. Look how the world raises someone to celebrity status—the ultimate in measuring up, and then the world works hard to bring them back down to size. The world celebrates adultery or at the least excuses it. We need to see ourselves the way God does—in an eternal sense."

The force of his words knocks into me and makes me breathless. Words I've heard in church come back to me—*You are deserving. Because of the blood of Christ. You are a child of the King of kings and Lord of lords.* If only I could remember that when I feel everyone's gaze on me, sizing me up, critiquing me from head to toe. It's the defense I need against Marla's critical words. It's what I need when I simply ache for normalcy. For being like everyone else in the world. Through a tight throat, I manage to say, "You're right. I know you're right."

"Have you ever said, 'Mirror, mirror—who's the fairest of them all?'"

A rueful laugh escapes me. "As a little girl."

"Of course. Every little girl, I would imagine, wants to be the prettiest in the kingdom."

I shrug, not wanting to admit anything. "What do guys want? To be Lancelot?"

"They have a different measuring stick."

The corner of my mouth curls upward. "Which brings us back to the trophy wife."

"Instead of asking a mirror, shouldn't women be asking God? He'd have a different answer than they might expect."

I rub one foot over the other, feeling fully exposed. "I used to tell Isabel when she was little that she was God's princess. When did I stop that? Probably not long after she stopped wearing crowns and when preteen-itis started."

"And the attitude wasn't that of a princess?"

"Not a storybook princess anyway."

He laughs.

"You have a lot of insights into the female psyche for a single guy."

He shrugs. "I had three older sisters."

"Oh, boy. Now I know why you've stayed single."

He laughs louder this time. "Nah. They're all great. And I got to date all their friends." He clasps his hands together and props them behind his head. "Seriously, growing up with them taught me a lot. And I can guarantee all my clients' wives love me. Because if they're going on some safari to Africa or hunting guinea in Scotland, I know what women need and want on a trip like that."

"That's good to know if I can ever afford a vacation."

He winks. "I'll give you a good discount."

I lean my face into my hands, massage my scalp, and brush back my hair in a huffy motion. "I really thought God wanted us back together. Was that crazy?"

"I can't tell you what God wants for you, Kaye. But I can tell you He wants what is *best* for *you*. Is that a wishy-washy husband who can't be true to his wedding vows?" His candor and the bite in his tone surprise me. A warmth floods me. "God lets the foolish make their own decisions. Which takes Cliff out of the picture and out of your life." He takes my hand and cups his around it. My skin tingles and my stomach completely flips over. "I think you deserve better."

Is he makin' a move on you? Cliff's words—complete with sneer and disdain—taunt me. I pull back from Jack, uncomfortable with the intensity of his gaze and his uncanny ability to see into my desires.

"You're a child of God. Don't you think God believes you deserve the best? Or do you think He wants to give you leftovers and table scraps?"

I stand suddenly, jolted by his words and the strengthening truth they ignite in me. But the distance from Jack settles my nerves. The cool decking is solid under my feet. I stare down at the still water as if staring into my own soul. My spine straightens. He's right. I've been acting like a beggar.

I imagine myself in rags, holding out a tin cup, waiting for a compliment or kind word from Cliff. Suddenly I feel dirty and in need of a bath. I lean outward toward the pool and let gravity pull me down into the water. At the last second I tuck my chin, kick my feet up, and make a clean slice into the water.

Cold splashes over me, taking me down into a curtain of bubbles. I come up, laughing and sputtering and brushing my wet hair off my face. Mascara runs down my cheeks. But I'm smiling up at Jack. For a moment I tread water, feeling the weight of my jeans pulling me downward in an undertow. Then Jack stretches out a hand toward me. I lunge forward grab his hand and feel myself hauled up out of the water. Water sluices off me, forming a puddle at my feet. My T-shirt hugs me tight and I pull the material away from my skin. My jeans cling to my legs, the weight of the water tugging in a downward pull. I yank at the belt loops in the opposite direction.

I laugh again, the chill of the night settling into my bones. "I can't believe I did that. You must think I've lost my mind."

"I'm glad you didn't shave your head. I think you're going to be saying that a lot more in the coming months and years."

Tilting my head, I study him, searching for underlying motives. "Why is that?"

"Because I think God has a different plan for you than you ever imagined or thought possible."

With only a foot separating us, I imagine leaning up and kissing his mouth. But it's a crazy thought that I bat away. No. No more men. Not now anyway. "Are you a turn-lemons-into-lemonade kind of guy?"

"Not really. I've seen plenty of folks get lemons and nothing sweet or satisfying ever comes from it."

"So how do you know I won't just wither into a bitter old woman?"

"Because"—he closes the gap between us—"you're practical enough to know there are a lot worse things that could happen than losing ol' Cliff. Right?" Then he cups the side of my neck, letting his thumb slide down the column of my throat. A chill passes through me that has nothing to do with the cold weather and in its wake heat takes its place. "And because you're too beautiful for that to happen."

Staring up at Jack, his shirt splotched from pool water, his cheeks tan and taut with a confident smile, I can't seem to contain my exuberance. Without thinking, contemplating, or planning anything, I reach up and kiss him full on the mouth. His lips are warm and pliant. It's that touch of flesh against flesh that stuns me, makes me question what I am doing. Confused by my own behavior, I panic. Before his arms can push me away or close around me, I pull back.

"Right," I whisper breathless. Heat rises up inside me. "Thank you."

❧ Chapter Twenty-one ❧

What was I thinking?
I'm not sure I *was*. Bubbles come up to my chin as I'm submerged in my own tub, my fingers and toes pruning, while my thoughts flounder in a sea of uncertainty. Was it some sort of desperation that had me reaching out to Jack . . . kissing him? Or is my heart's desire Jack?

And what of him? Did he kiss me back out of want, need, desire? Or was it some sort of a pity kiss?

I sink deeper in the tub, grateful at least that I have this last refuge of my own now that Marla has moved out of my house. Which only reminds me that I need to call her and let her know her son is a royal jerk. In this, I believe, she and I will fully agree.

Like a cork bobbing in the water, my thoughts wobble and dip in a new direction. Izzie seems to be the only adult in our home these days. She figured out long ago that her father wasn't coming back. She knew what I couldn't see. What I didn't *want* to see. What I *refused* to see. She knew I needed to let go. And boy did I! Of my sanity.

There I was, plunging into the deep end of the pool like a total idiot. What was I thinking? I wasn't. I was reacting. Crazily. Just like Izzie shaving her head. I needed space from Jack. Something about him unsettles me. Is it because I care about him too much? Is it because I'm afraid of being rejected again? Is it that I know if *he* rejects me it will hurt *much* more, much deeper than anything else?

But he didn't push me away. When I think back to our conversation, he actually seemed to encourage something between us. More than that, he defended me. Me! When did Cliff ever defend me? When did my father?

Is Jack simply waiting for me to be ready? Am I? I'm not sure. And I have to be sure. While blowing air bubbles out my nose, I let my body slide down in the water until I'm covered from head to toe.

⁂

It's the final walk-through of Jack's house before the For Sale sign goes in the yard and the information lists on MLS. After working all morning on finalizing curtains and rugs plus adding the perfect pillows to the leather sofa in the den, I meet him at the front door when he arrives. It's a bit of a reversal, me welcoming him to his own home, and I feel as awkward as a teen at her first dance.

"Welcome." I focus on the additions to his house rather than the way the sun lights up bits of gold in his dark hair. And then, of course, there's that bright smile of his. I try to ignore the jitteriness in my belly and the memory of that insane kiss. "Come on in."

His gaze remains on me rather than glancing at all the accessories and details I've added to his house. "How are you, Kaye?"

"Good. I'm good." I walk ahead of him, turning sideways, and bump into the doorway.

"You okay?"

"I'm fine." I rub my arm but keep two steps ahead of him. Throwing my arm out wide, I step back for him to get a good look at his new décor. "So what do you think?"

His brow dips inward briefly before he dutifully walks through the house, noticing each detail, each new change from the framed photos I used from my own house to the hand towels in the guest bath. After trailing him through the den, kitchen, dining room, office, guest bedrooms and master suite, I can't wait any longer for a response.

"Well?"

He looks at me then. "It feels . . . wrong."

My lungs compress. "What do you mean?"

"It's nice. But . . ."

Nice. How I hate that word. I brace myself for what he doesn't like and feel the prickle of disappointment in not having pleased him. This man holds my heart in his hands and with even the slightest criticism I sense he could crush me. "But?"

He makes a slow turn in his den. "It's not *me.*"

"It's not supposed to be. It's not your house anymore. It's a house on the market."

"Yeah, but . . ." He shakes his head, his gaze landing on a black and white photo of Izzie and me in a wrought iron frame.

A hot flush bursts outward from some core place within. Does he think I'm trying to move in on him? Take over his life? I used the pictures to give the office a homey feel, and it seemed the easiest to pull them straight out of my own house. Or was it some psychological fantasy I was having?

"Jack . . ." I step toward him. Maybe we should deal with the kiss and get it over with. It's best to state this straight out. "About the other night. I should have . . . well, I shouldn't have kissed you like that. It was irresponsible. And I didn't mean . . ." I can't quite bring myself to say "anything." Because that isn't true. I pick up the framed picture and hold it against my middle. "I'm not trying to . . ." I'm at a loss for words.

"Make a move on me?" He pauses a moment, leaves me hanging, as if running my words through his mind again. Is he relieved about the kiss? Disappointed? Reading him is about as easy as reading a doctor's handwriting. "It's not *that* at all. The house doesn't feel exactly like *you* either. I mean, I see the pictures of you and Isabel, but—"

"It's not supposed to be a reflection of me either. If it was, then I didn't do my job. I went with the architectural details of the house, accented and emphasized the beamed ceilings, the archways, the shapes of the rooms." I smooth a hand over the frame. "This just seemed to fit here. But it's not . . . well, you know."

"You're right." He takes the frame from me, his hand brushing mine and sending tiny tingles along my spine. "It does belong here." He sets it back on the shelf, tilting it just the way I had it. Izzie and I smile out at him from our framed home.

When he faces me again, he looks confused like a little boy who's had a scarf suddenly whisked off his face after being turned around and around. "What do I do now?"

My insides jump at the implication. Does he mean—do I kiss you again? That would be all right. Definitely better for him to make a move this time. Or does he mean—how do we handle this new development? Is he having regrets, doubts, misgivings? "What do you mean?"

"Do I stay here? Get a hotel room? What?"

My stomach drops. He wasn't thinking of *me* at all. "You can stay. Just keep things tidy. Which I don't think will be a problem. You don't seem the messy sort."

His mouth compresses and forms grooves in the brackets surrounding those lips I've only just begun to appreciate. "Okay. I can do that."

I should stop looking at his mouth. "When you move," I stare into his eyes, which have some sort of hypnotic effect on me, then clear my throat, "you can make *that* place your own."

He nods his head as if convincing himself. "All right then. Good."

"You really don't like it?" *Shut up, Kaye! You don't need a pat on the back. Or a congratulatory kiss.*

"The house looks beautiful. Like it's out of *Architectural Digest*. It just doesn't feel like it's mine anymore."

I place a hand on his shoulder then realize my mistake and pull my hand away. "That's the general idea."

"It just feels false. You know, like I'm lying."

Is that what I'm doing by denying these feelings for him? "You're not. You're showing someone what their life *could* be like if they bought the house and moved in. You're showing off the house's potential. It's marketing."

The memory of us discussing dating and marketing together comes back to me. So, how can I show off my best assets to him?

"You did a great job. Really. The house is a showplace. I never imagined what could be done here." He turns around in a tight circle, looking over the den and up at the ceiling again. "Amazing."

"Good." I laugh with a combination of relief and nervousness. "I'm glad you like it."

"It's not the only thing I like." He steps toward me and slips a hand around my waist. "And don't ever apologize for kissing me."

"Oh, Jack, I . . . uh . . ." My gaze shifts to his mouth again.

"I know. I understand."

Good because I don't. I swallow a sudden lump in my throat.

He gives a slight shake of his head, as if he's battling something inside himself. Then he leans forward and places a firm yet gentle kiss on my mouth. Before I can respond, he pulls back. "Thank you."

My days are filled to overflowing with helping Isabel and Gabe with the swim-a-thon by running errands, depositing checks, checking the Facebook page and providing pizza and popcorn for teens who come in and out of my house. In spare moments, when I'm sitting at a traffic light or lying in bed at night in the moment before I fall asleep, I try not to imagine my ex romping around Vegas with Barbie who's probably wearing a gargantuan diamond on her left hand, and instead conjure up an Elvis impersonator (complete with toupee, potbelly, and polyester blue-suede jumpsuit) marrying them, which gives me a momentary sense of satisfaction.

Then my thoughts drift toward Marla. Guilt is a common companion for me but not in this instance. I simply wish we could part company as friends. Apparently that might be too much to ask from Marla, but still I attempt to reach out to her. She doesn't answer her phone or return calls. I'm not sure if she went back to her apartment or stayed with Harry. Part of me wishes she would move in with Barbie and Cliff. Which gives me another chuckle.

Mostly though, I want to apologize to her (for what, I'm not sure), but I want her to know that everything is okay. I wish her happiness, which seems elusive to those who are inclined to stay knee-deep in drama. It's a concern I have about my own daughter who is easily caught up and carried away by chaos. Her reaction to her father's elopement was my first glimpse at a new, hopeful attitude in her.

And surprisingly, a glimpse into my own craziness. Which might be attributed to Jack.

I attempt to shake off my reactions to him. It's foolish. Some desperate part of me wishing for something far better than my ex. Jack and Pam should get together. It makes sense as they've known each other for years. The kids are comfortable with Jack. He's already a father to Gabe. Yes, that is definitely how it should go. Maybe that's why he hesitated before kissing me the other night. Maybe he is torn between what is right and what he desires.

But a tiny fantasy starts in my head, and I convince myself my attraction to Jack is a way to seek revenge on Cliff. My ex would be stunned into silence and one-upped for sure. So I am content with the fantasy and not about to act on it. I've already made a fool of myself with Jack. Once . . . okay, twice is too much.

The Tuesday before the swim-a-thon, a simple phone call puts every absurd thought out of my head and places the event in jeopardy.

"Lily's back in the hospital." Fear saturates Terry's voice.

"Oh, no. I'm so sorry, Terry. What can I do to help?"

"Nothing. I just thought you should know. She probably won't be at the swim-a-thon on Saturday."

"We understand. What are the doctors saying?"

"She has a blood infection."

"Oh." I'm not sure what that means and I waffle about what to say. "There are good antibiotics that can fight that, right?"

"They're trying."

I wish I had a medical degree so I'd know how to interpret the information. "What can I do?"

"Pray."

So with that disturbing news, I call Isabel out of the den where she's sorting through the pledges that have been made by teachers, businesses, parents, and citizens of Southlake. The numbers have grown astronomically. A good thing about living in a wealthy community is that money abounds, and in this community with churches on almost every corner, giving hearts abound as well.

"Hey, Mrs. Redmond." Gabe grins up at me from the schedule he's been concocting on who will swim at what time at the natatorium. "Aren't you going to swim?" He hands me my own pledge sheet.

"Me?"

"Yeah, Izzie said you were. Jack's swimming too."

Remembering my late night swims, thinking about donning a swimsuit in public, which would not showcase my best assets, I waffle yet again. "I'm not a good swimmer."

"You don't have to be." He nudges me with his broad shoulder. "Don't worry, there'll be lots of lifeguards around who can save you if you start to drown."

"Terrific."

Isabel plops down beside Gabe on the sofa. "I bet you could get some of your clients and friends from church to make pledges, Mom."

"I'll think about it." I tip my head in the direction of her bedroom. "Can I have a word with you, Iz?"

"Sure." She follows me. "What's up?" Her gaze is innocent and oblivious to the pounding of my heart that pumps fear through my veins.

I clear my throat. "Terry called. Lily won't be able to make it Saturday."

Her face collapses. "Why? What's wrong?"

"She's back in the hospital." I hesitate, then decide I should reveal my concerns. Better to prepare rather than delude ourselves that all will be well. When it might not. "It sounded pretty serious."

Her face blanches. "Which hospital?"

After I answer, she grabs Gabe and they head out to visit Lily.

I stay at the house, keeping the other volunteers working and finalizing the schedule with Jack's help when he arrives with burgers and fries for everyone. After a while, all the kids drift back to their own homes, leaving Jack and me alone.

He catches me glancing at the clock on the mantel again. "They're fine."

I rub my hands along my thighs and push up from the floor where I copied the schedule onto poster board. "Oh, sure. I know."

"You trust them, don't you?"

"As much as any parent trusts a teen. Or teens. And driving."

"Gabe's a safe driver."

"It's everyone else on the road that worries me."

He studies me for a moment. "That's not what you're worried about."

"You're right. It's Lily . . . and Izzie." I pace across the room. A shiver ripples through me and I decide to distract myself with another subject. "How's the house sale going?"

"We had a Realtors' tour come through today. You'll be glad to know they all deemed the house beautifully decorated. A real showstopper."

I'm not sure if it's his words or that warm gaze that makes my skin tingle.

"And I forgot to tell you, a friend of mine needs to sell his house and will be calling you for your services."

My gaze slips sideways toward the clock.

"It's almost eleven o'clock. Does Isabel turn into a pumpkin then?"

"It's her curfew. And hospitals close up for visitors after . . . what? Eight or nine o'clock?"

"They may have stopped somewhere for dinner. Or to talk. Does Gabe know Izzie's curfew?"

"Yes."

"Then he'll have her back here."

"I hope so." The words aren't completely out of my mouth when my cell phone rings. I recognize the cell number. "Hi, Gabe."

"We're on our way home, Mrs. Redmond."

"It's kind of late for you to be at the hospital."

"We went by Lily's house and picked up some things for her mother."

"That was nice of you. Is there anything I can do?"

"I don't think so."

"You both have school tomorrow."

"Yes, ma'am."

My worry has nowhere to go, not even to push into anger. "How's Lily?"

"She seemed okay. She was sitting up in bed, talking and joking around."

"Good. Then it's probably just a bump in her road. Hopefully she'll be out of the hospital soon."

"Yes, ma'am."

"Thanks for calling and letting me know you're on your way." I close my phone, caress the facing as relief washes through me.

Jack waits for me to fill him in.

"Gabe said Lily was doing okay. They're on their way."

Jack rolls up the poster-sized schedule of the swimmers and snaps a rubber band around it. "They're good kids."

"They are. I was worried what would happen if . . . well . . . I don't want to think about it. Izzie is so caught up in helping Lily. She's determined to help Lily get well."

Jack cups a hand along my jaw and neckline. My stomach does a slow roll. "I'd tell you not to worry but I suspect that won't help."

All I can do is stare up at him, until my gaze drifts downward toward his mouth. The memory of his kiss lingers. "I know something that might take my mind off it."

"Oh, yeah?" He moves closer.

I can only nod.

He takes my hand and pulls me toward the sofa. "This is what I do when I'm worried." He sits me down, settling next to me, his arm snug around my shoulders. My heart is pounding in my chest. Maybe this isn't the time for making out. But I also don't want to say anything.

Then he looks me straight in the eye, his gaze serious and calm. "I dump *my* stuff at the foot of the cross."

My chaotic heartbeat slows as guilt flows through my veins. Why didn't I think of that? Because I was thinking of myself and my own needs. Then, instead of kissing me, he tucks my hand in his and bows his head. At first I'm not sure how to take this abrupt change. But as he begins to pray for Lily, her mother, and Izzie, my heart tumbles head over heels. There was a time when I felt *I* was the only one praying. I'd lie in bed at night, Cliff snoring beside me, and I'd pray for our marriage, our family. But no miracle happened. And now . . . how can I believe?

When Jack gives my hand a gentle squeeze and looks up, I ask, "So you believe in miracles?"

He rubs a thumb over my knuckles, dipping thoughtfully into each groove. "Yeah. They don't always happen. If Gabe's dad had lived, that would certainly have been a medical miracle. But I know they happen. I've read about them, witnessed them." His hand cups mine as he studies me for a long, uncomfortable moment. "You don't?"

I tug my hand back, erase the feel of his skin against mine. Miracles seem as far-fetched as a fairy tale ending of Happily Ever After. "I don't know."

⤙ Chapter Twenty-two ⤚

The next day I stop by the hospital to visit Lily and see if Terry needs anything. Besides the usual flowers, I take some magazines, a stuffed animal, and cookies. Lily sleeps through my entire visit. When her mother slips out of the room briefly to see me off, she hugs me close.

"If you need me, don't hesitate to call. Okay?"

She nods, tears brimming her eyes but not overflowing. I start to walk away, but then Jack's prayer comes back to me. Turning back, I place a hand around my friend. The right words elude me. Doubts bombard me. I clutch at the only solid foundation we have and His words, greater than my own, flow of their own accord, "*Our Father, which art in heaven, Hallowed be Thy name. Thy kingdom come. Thy will be done in earth, as it is in heaven. Give us this day our daily bread. And forgive us our debts, as we forgive our debtors. And lead us not into temptation, but deliver us from evil: For Thine is the kingdom, and the power, and the glory, forever. Amen.*"

Terry joins me in saying the last couple of lines and then we hug. It feels as if she is putting all the words she can't say into her embrace, and I try to convey my feelings to her as well.

❊

Not far from the hospital is the retirement village where Marla lives. It's where Harry lives too. It's a quiet and peaceful gathering of apartments and houses. There are no children running, yelling, or riding bikes, only a crew of maintenance men sawing branches off a giant pecan tree. All that's missing is the neon sign—circle with slash through it over pictures of young children. After I check Marla's apartment and find no one home . . . or at least no one answering the door, I locate Harry's residence two streets over.

History is filled with the demise of bearers of bad news. I don't kid myself that the news I'm supposed to drop like a nuclear bomb on Marla will not be well-received. But decapitation isn't Marla's style. I imagine she will inflict pain of a different kind. Before I change my mind, I knock on Harry's door. A heavy, thick wreath decorated with pumpkins and apples, golden and burnt orange leaves along with a gigantic bow overwhelms the small door. I recognize Marla's handiwork. It reminds me of how close we're getting to Thanksgiving. Jack would say there is much to give thanks for. In the chaos of my life, I suppose it could all be worse. But I'm not able to go there.

After a moment's pause, Harry opens the door. He's wearing his usual mismatched clothes, but I notice his shirt has been ironed. It's a sure sign Marla's taken over his life. "Come on in!" He grins and opens the door wide. "I've been expecting you."

"You have?" I step inside the darkened apartment where the shades are drawn, blocking out the bright sunshine. After I blink a moment, allowing my eyes to adjust, I notice the apartment is smaller than Marla's. It's quaint, decorated with antiquated furniture that appears to be in pristine condition. The Victorian sofa doesn't seem to match Harry and I'm guessing reflected his deceased wife's tastes. The light from the television gives the room a ghostly cast of shadows. Although the sound is muted,

I recognize the women on *The View* arguing about something, their mouths stretched tight as they gesticulate wildly.

Harry punches a button on the television and the picture fades into black. He then turns on a table lamp that offers a rosy hue over the room. "How've you been, Kaye?"

"Good. And you?"

"Never better."

"Is Marla here?"

He gestures toward a door along a hallway leading away from us. "She saw you coming up the sidewalk and ran to the bathroom."

Irritation pulses through me, and I start toward the bathroom. This is getting ridiculous.

"I saw you on television." That's stops me cold.

I freeze. "You did?"

"We were watching the news the other night." He clears his throat. "There was a spot about Gabe's park reopening and Marla pointed you out in the crowd."

"Yes, it was a big event. I have some more news for her today. Some news I'm not sure she's going to be very happy about."

"Uh-oh." Harry's brow collapses into furrows of worry. "Are you sure you have to tell her then?"

"Afraid so." I feel a little like the cowardly lion having to march into the wizard's chamber. With trepidation balanced out by a healthy dose of irritation, I head toward the bathroom where she's hiding. I lean against the door facing, mustering strength I don't have. Then I knock.

No answer.

I look toward Harry. He gives me an encouraging nod, reminding me of when I urged him to speak to Marla when she hid in my bedroom. I smile back at him, take a deep breath, and try again, more forcefully.

When she continues to ignore me, I begin as if I'm with Izzie when she was twelve years old. "Marla, I know you're in there."

"I'm *in* seclusion."

"Seclusion is when someone goes to a monastery, not one's boyfriend's."

"He is not my—"

"Come on, open up." I feel as weary as Dorian Gray at the end of his life, tired of the pretenses and charades. "I need to talk to you."

The door opens a crack. "What's wrong?"

Her face surprises me. She's wearing no makeup, but her features aren't as lopsided as they were right after surgery. Her skin, however, has a red cast, like she's experienced a very bad sunburn. Around her eyebrows bits of skin flake off like she's molting.

"Marla, your face! It looks . . ." I can't say she looks like an insect. "Like you're, uh . . . healing."

She purses her lips. A twitch at the corner of one eye reveals her doubt. "What's wrong?" Perfectionism and selfishness fall by the wayside when Marla's focus turns to a crisis. "Is it about Isabel? Has she done something else to herself now? She hasn't gotten a tattoo, has she? Or pregnant?"

The concerns I had about telling Marla shrink under the force of her judgment. "It's not about Izzie. It's about Cliff."

She opens the door wider. "Is he all right?"

"I imagine he's doing just fine." Actually I don't want to imagine anything of the kind. "Or not. I don't know." I cross my arms over my stomach as if that will suppress the wobbly feeling inside. "He came to see me before he left."

"Left? Where'd he go?"

"To Vegas. To elope."

Shock widens her eyes. "He didn't!" Her brow crinkles, and she smooths the spot with her forefinger. "Well, if he was going to marry anyone, then I guess I'm glad he chose you."

How far have we come? When I was nowhere close to her motherly dream for Cliff to now I'm ideal compared to Barbie.

"At least we know each other, Kaye, and—"

"I didn't go to Vegas, Marla. He took Barbara." I bite out the name, forcing myself not to call her Barbie or any other name that comes to mind.

"What? NO!" She slams the door back against the wall and barrels into the hallway, shouldering me out of the way. "Where's my phone?"

"It's too late." I follow after her. "They left over a week ago."

She comes to a sudden halt in the den. She lifts her shoulders in an awkward movement, squaring them. Harry stands frozen in place as if unsure what to do or how to respond. She tilts her head toward the door, and Harry slips out the entrance, the bolt sliding into place. And I'm left alone with Marla.

I feel bad for him, like he's been dismissed by the queen. "Harry could have stayed."

"This is about *family*."

"But this is *his* apartment."

"He doesn't mind."

How does she know? "He has a nice place."

"It needs some updating. Maybe we'll hire you to do that."

I sigh. "Don't rearrange this man's life."

She wheels around on me. "It's my business, isn't it?"

"I care about Harry. And you." The latter isn't as hard to say as I thought it might be. It's as if the years of difficulties have become fuzzy with distance. "Why are you denying he's your boyfriend? Usually when a woman sleeps with a man—" It's out of my mouth before I can stop it. Marla doesn't move a muscle. Not even a twitch. "Are you two . . . married?"

"Heavens no. And we are not"—she lowers her voice—"sleeping together."

"Could have fooled me."

She lifts her chin a notch.

"It's none of my business. Just please, try not to hurt him. I mean, he's a nice guy. Be kind to him."

She stares at me as if I've accused her of torturing the man. "So when did Cliff and . . . *that* woman . . ." Her mouth twists.

I am starting to feel sorry for Cliff's new bride. She doesn't have any idea what's in store for her. "Over a week ago. They're married by now and enjoying their honeymoon."

Surprisingly that last word doesn't bring a bitter taste to my mouth. But Marla wobbles. Her hand juts out to balance herself against the sofa, then she sits on the coffee table. Even her slight weight is too much for the delicate legs and the table tips. I grab her before she falls. She clutches my arms, and I help her stand. Her hands begin to tremble. When I get her situated on the sofa, she tips her head into her hand. "What was he thinking?"

I have no answer.

"Doesn't he know how ridiculous he looks? Going around with a woman who's . . . barely that! It's one thing to destroy his marriage and go out with the woman. But I thought she was just a midlife crisis and he'd realize—" She stops her tirade and looks up at me.

"I thought so too." I shrug. "He made his choice."

"And he told *you?* But not *me.*"

A sticky point. But I suspect Cliff cares more about what his mother might say, even Izzie, than facing my wrath. Where once that would be painful to admit, now I don't much care. "He had to tell someone. Maybe it was easier to face me."

Marla flexes her hand as if in a conscious opposition to what she might otherwise do. "The next time I see him—"

"It's too late now." Silently I hope she won't treat Barbara the way she treated me—as an interloper. My magnanimous attitude surprises even me. There was a time when I would have gladly helped with Barb's water torture. But not anymore. She and Cliff aren't worth the energy it takes to ratchet up my emotions. "I'm sorry, Marla." And I am. About the news. About Barbie. About everything. "Maybe Cliff sees something in Barbara that we haven't." Maybe she sees something in him that I'm blind to.

Marla snorts. "I suppose marriage to Cliff isn't easy."

"That's an understatement." I sit next to Marla on the sofa. "They're both going to have their work cut out for themselves." There will always be someone younger, someone in better shape. Not to mention how easily Cliff gets bored.

"So you actually want their marriage to work out?"

I cross my legs and give her question a moment of contemplation. I never thought I'd wish for Cliff's marriage to another woman to be successful. Maybe my heavy hope is buoyed by the salt of doubt. But then again, who needs more upheaval? Izzie certainly doesn't. It would be nice if her parents were steady and unwavering at last in their relationships. "At first, I thought a plane crash would be a good answered prayer."

Marla nods her agreement.

"But that would only hurt Izzie more. And another divorce? I don't want that. Not for Cliff or Barbara or Izzie. Like it or not, she'll have to see her dad occasionally."

"And her stepmother."

"Yes." That's a bit harder to swallow. "But it'll be okay."

"Are you sure about that?"

I shrug. "I'm not sure of anything. We'll have to make it as right as possible."

"How can you do that?"

"It's what we women do, isn't it? We spruce up bad situations to make them as nice as possible."

Her eyes narrow and yet amazingly appear the same size. "You're a stronger woman than I ever could be."

I laugh. "Oh, I don't know, Marla. I think you give me a run for my money."

She shakes her head. "I've been a coward for years." She waves her hand as if shooing away an irritating thought. "How are you doing with this new turn of events?"

Her question stuns me. Has she *ever* asked me how I'm doing? Even when Izzie was born? "I'm okay."

She looks dubious at best. "And Isabel?"

"She says she doesn't care. She's glad Cliff's not moving back in. I think maybe she could see her father's true character better than the rest of us."

"I bet"—Marla wags her finger—"he gets her pregnant and they end up having kids."

There's a happy thought. The corners of my mouth feel weighted. "Maybe he'll learn to be responsible this time around."

"Do you know who you're talking about?"

"We can only hope for the best." A miracle, as Jack would say. And the thought of him makes me smile.

She releases a long, slow sigh. "What are you going to do, Kaye?"

I clasp my hands in my lap, my fingers encircling my bare, left ring finger. This time there isn't a tightening in my chest. "Get on with my life. Which is what I should have done a long time ago."

She gives a tiny snort. "Do you regret trying to get him back?"

I shake my head. "Not at all." I tilt my head. "Well, I did at first. But now . . . no. I have no regrets."

Marla taps her fingers along the arm of the sofa. "How is that possible?"

Her question startles me. "What do you mean?"

"I have regrets. So many regrets. How can you not regret marrying so early?"

"I regret getting pregnant before I was married. But not having Izzie. I'm sad at Cliff's choice, but I know I gave my marriage the best I could. We all make mistakes, Marla, but I guess the best we can do is to learn from them and try to do better the next time."

She leans back into the sofa, which seems so stiff and unrelenting. Marla's shoulders sag. "But I've made so many. I feel like there's a big scoreboard up there somewhere showing how many times I've made poor choices."

LEANNA ELLIS

Her admission stuns me, and for a moment I flounder. Does she think I've been judging her? "No one is keeping score."

"God is."

"He wants to wipe away all those mistakes and regrets and turn them into something wonderful."

"How is that possible?"

"Well, I made a mistake by getting pregnant, and I did my best to make things right."

"And you ended up with a husband who, I can say this because he's my son, is pretty worthless."

"But I also have a wonderful daughter."

"What if she ends up like her father?"

"That will be her choice. But I don't think she will. She's observed things I never wanted her to see or know about, but now maybe she'll consider them before she acts. She'll know the other side—the side full of pain."

Marla takes several slow breaths. With her chin tilted downward, the skin along her neck gathers like crumpled cloth. "Maybe that's another mistake I made."

"What?"

"Not letting Bradford's sins rip apart our family." Her hand tightens on the armrest, her knuckles whitening. "Maybe if Cliff had seen how devastating his father's behavior was, then maybe he would have chosen a different path. But I tried so hard to make things as perfect as I could. So no one would have to suffer."

I swallow hard. How I've wanted to protect Izzie from pain! But there is no hiding from pain. It's better to accept it and move through it together, rather than suffer in silence. Suddenly the perfect picture Marla always tried to paint of her family is washed away and the gritty reality remains. "Did Bradford cheat on you?"

She gives a sharp nod. "Many times."

An invisible hand fists my heart in a painful grip. Now all she has said through the years falls into place. Disappointment slams into me. It could be another reason Marla disliked me as I aligned myself with Bradford. But I had no idea he was unfaithful. Did Cliff know? "Like father like son." I cover her hand with my own. Words pile up in my throat in a rush. "I'm so sorry, Marla. So sorry."

She gives a lopsided shrug. "I was wrong. In so many ways."

"I think that's what God wants us to see. How our imperfections give us a need for Him."

"I don't know about that. I just know that I can't do it anymore." She slides her fingers into her hairline and tugs her hair back. I can see the red lines from her facelift.

"Do what?"

"Be perfect." She gives a bitter laugh and frames her face with her hands. "Have you seen me lately?"

I place a gentle hand on her arm. "No one wants you to be perfect, Marla."

She sniffs and looks away, tears filling the corners of her eyes.

I slide my arm around her narrow shoulders. "God doesn't expect perfection either."

"I always thought He did."

I shake my head. "Nope. Not at all." I give her shoulder a squeeze. "He's like the makeup that covers our imperfections."

She turns to look me in the eye. "Apparently I need to take out stock in that kind of foundation."

·⟨ Chapter Twenty-three ⟩·

Teenagers spill out of my house like water overflowing a dam. They are doing last-minute preparations for the swim-a-thon, moving like schools of fish swishing to and fro, racing against the current. Jack arrives with an assortment of pizzas—cheese, pepperoni, sausage and hamburger—which fills my kitchen with a yeasty, tangy, greasy smell. Cousin It trembles with anticipation. Her pink tongue drips slobber on the kitchen floor. She stares at the table as if it's a smorgasbord laid out just for her. The raucous noise, at times, reaches deafening levels.

While the kids jockey for slices of pizza, Jack settles at the kitchen table, tilting back the chair. He asks a cute, perky blonde named Joanne how she did on her history test.

"Ninety-two."

"Nice." Jack then slides a foot out and trips a gangly teenage boy, who bumps into Joanne. "Watch it there, Max." He laughs as the boy's face turns scarlet. He's well aware of which boys like which girls and vice versa and has enjoyed trying to set them up. "These swimmers"—he grins at me—"have better moves in the water than on land."

He seems at home here. *At home.* The thought wallops me.

A loud chorus flares out by the pool and we turn simultaneously. Some boys toss one of their own into the pool. Jack and

I make eye contact and shake our heads. That's when I realize Jack and I have begun communicating through glances. Then I locate an old beach towel. I head to the back yard and toss it over my shoulder, "You're not going to abandon me here alone, are you?"

He grins. "I'm not that cruel." When the doorbell rings, he jumps to his feet. "I'll get it."

"I wouldn't blame you if you ran out the door and didn't come back."

"Not a chance." His words light my insides with a heady warmth.

It's becoming comfortable with him here. So comfortable I don't feel like I have to dress up but am dressed in my relaxed jeans and oversized T-shirt. The realization makes me trip over my own feet as I stumble out the back door. I lean back against the brick wall, slow my sudden rapid breathing. What are we becoming? A family? As much as I like having Jack around and relying on him, even leaning on him in times of difficulty, I recognize the staccato beat of fear in my heart. Will all this end when the swim-a-thon is over? Will I once again lose a family?

After handing the towel to the soaking boy, his clothes dripping all over the patio, he shakes his head, flinging water worse than Cousin It. Izzie squeals and turns away. I stare down at my now spotted outfit.

"Sorry, Mrs. Redmond." I consider telling him I'd rather not be "Mrs." anymore but decide it's not worth the bother.

Then I notice that three, no four, other boys have shaved their heads.

"What's up with the new do?" I point to my own head.

He ducks his head and rubs his bare top. "Iz started a trend."

I glance at my daughter who is sitting on the diving board eating a slice of pizza. Fuzz covers her scalp and gives her a concentration camp survivor look. It always gives me a double take. "So you're all shaving your heads?"

Jason shoves the soaked boy in the shoulder. "Only those of us who are competitive swimmers."

My gaze meets Izzie's and I wink. Trying to contain a smile, I return to the house. Jack is standing in the middle of the den.

His smile has been wiped clean, his eyes have darkened like a storm. "Guess who's here?"

"We didn't get the invitation!" Cliff steps around Jack. "Didn't know there was a party going on. Is it BYOB?"

We. His phrasing makes me freeze. Following in his wake is Barbara. Barbie to those of us who know her well. Of course, she looks radiant. And I look spotted with pool water.

"Cliff! What are you—"

"Wanted to come say hello to Isabel." He dares to cup my shoulders and press a kiss to my cheek. "Where is she?"

I nod toward the pool. As he moves past me, I'm face-to-face with my ex's new wife. If I were to look in the mirror, I suspect I'd see Barbara in ten years' time. "Hello, Barbara. Congratulations. How was your trip?"

"Lovely."

She slips an arm through her new husband's—and I catch site of the rock on her manicured finger (a good carat and a half, but not as large as I'd imagined in my worst nightmares). She smiles a purr-fect I-caught-the-canary grin. *Good, she can have him.*

"Perfectly lovely."

My gaze slips toward my only friend in the room. "Jack. You've met Cliff . . . and his new bride."

Jack shakes both their hands, but I sense a tightness in Jack's features, and a wariness in Cliff. "So, you took the jump."

"A total free fall." Cliff kisses the top of Barbie's head like she's a prized possession.

Her gaze skims over Jack as if checking out what is now off-limits.

The back door opens and Joanne comes inside. She eyes the four of us. "They want more pizza."

"Why don't you take the boxes out there?" I help her stack the boxes and hold the door for her.

Cliff's gaze follows the teenage swimmer. She has long lean legs, firm muscles, and perfect tan. I want to punch my ex. "So you have parties every Friday night with the whole high school?"

"They've been working on the swim-a-thon for Lily."

"Oh, yeah, I remember you telling me about that. Of course. Right. So when is that?"

"Tomorrow."

"Right." He looks from me to Jack, and I can almost see the wheels in his head turning as if making little adjustments. "For a minute there I thought maybe you and Jack here were seeing each other."

Barbara's hand tightens on her husband's arm, and he laughs.

An awkward pause has us all looking at our feet, out the windows toward the kids having fun at the pool, anywhere but at each other. I don't dare look at Jack. I don't know what he's think-ing, what excuses he might be struggling with. The love lives of teens seem so much simpler than at my stage. I need something to say or do rather than run screaming from the room. "Would you care for some pizza?"

"We've eaten—"

"—not hungry."

"Oh, well, then." My mind is a blank. I have nothing to say to either one of them. I'm not sure there is proper etiquette in the ex-wives' handbook (if there is such a thing) for how to handle situations such as this. Am I required to entertain the new Mrs.? Am I supposed to smile? How many times do I have to turn the other cheek before they crack?

After a long, awkward pause, Cliff claps his hands, the sound making me flinch. "Maybe we'll just go out and say hello to Isabel."

"All right." I slide my hand sideways indicating they're free to go by themselves. I'm not providing escort.

Cliff takes a large step forward then stops. "So, uh, Kaye, you did tell Isabel, didn't you?"

I open my eyes wide. "About?"

"Our marriage."

I'm not inclined to make this easy for him. It's not necessarily out of spite, more out of a sense of outrage that he would think Jack and I wouldn't be seeing each other in any way other than playing chaperone to a bunch of teens. Not to mention that Jack didn't jump in and correct him. Through a gritty I'm-not-going-to-let-you-faze-me smile, I say, "I told her."

"And?"

"What?" What does he want? A parade?

"How'd she take it?"

"She wasn't bothered in the least." I don't bother telling him her reason being that he wouldn't be moving back home.

With total ignorance, he grins. "Good." Then his smile falters as if he's wondering why or if there's a punch line that he missed. "Okay then." He opens the door for his bride and they walk out to the pool together. "We'll be back."

Oh, goodie. "Be careful around the edge of the pool, Barbara. It can get slippery when wet. I wouldn't want you to fall in."

Cliff shoots me a dark, warning look.

Cousin It spies new victims . . . visitors and launches an attack . . . welcome. Barbara squeals and huddles behind Cliff, forcing him to protect her.

When the door closes, I draw a slow breath. Jack is watching me. Assessing the damage. It's not Cliff though who has made me feel suddenly weepy. "Sorry about that."

Jack shrugs. "You handled that well."

"Yeah, well . . . and about that . . . you know?"

He takes a step toward me, sliding an arm around my waist. His sudden nearness throws me off balance. But his chest is solid and firm. "Wanna be making out when they come back in?"

I laugh, nervous, anxious, eager. Hopeful. "That would certainly shock him."

He winks. Does that mean he's kidding or serious? I'm tempted to say "yes" and wrap my arms around his neck and go for it. But instead I step away.

"You let me know. I'm available." His words confuse me. I search his gaze for a deeper meaning but can't decipher his motives. His gaze shifts toward the bank of windows looking out over the pool. "How will Isabel react to her guests?"

"I don't know. She was okay about the marriage."

"But to have the woman pranced in front of her friends."

Tilting my head to the side, I study my daughter as she climbs out of the pool. "I know."

Isabel isn't smiling. But she's not pushing Barbara into the pool either. She has more restraint than I do. My gaze shifts across the backyard where Gabe is holding Cousin It by the collar. *Let her go!* I want to yell but resist. I'm thankful my bad behavior and attitude haven't rubbed off on Izzie. She locks one arm behind her, and pinches her fingers together, one toe rolling inward. Her nervous stance makes it an easy decision when I hear her cell phone go off. I move away from Jack and toward my sanity, scoop up her cell off the coffee table. Opening the back door, I call, "Iz, your phone."

She grabs her towel, wrapping it around her lithe body, and jogs toward me. She gives me a quick I-can't-believe-this look, her gaze boring into me, and takes the phone. She walks toward her bedroom. "Hello?"

Cliff and Bridezilla enter my house again. "Isabel said we could sponsor her per lap."

"Of course." I hand him a page from the stack of forms on the kitchen counter.

With a flourish, he signs his name. "What's the recommended amount?"

"Oh, I don't know. Jack, how much did you sponsor Gabe for?"

"A hundred."

"Total?"

"Per lap."

I recognize the tightening around the corners of Cliff's eyes. But I also know it's become a competition to him. He never wants to be seen as cheap. "Sure. Great idea." He finishes filling out his information. "So what time is this swim-a-thon tomorrow? Maybe we'll just swing by and check it—"

His words are cut off by the slamming of Izzie's door. She races down the hall toward us. I only catch a flash of her as she turns toward the front door, but I realize she's dressed in shirt and shorts. Her face is red and tear-streaked.

"Isabel?" I follow her to the door. But by the time I reopen it, she's out of sight. "Izzie!" My voice echoes in the stillness.

"I told you she hates me." Barbara's voice is low and tight.

"Kaye," Cliff's eyebrows slant downward, "you've really got to get the kid some help. She needs therapy or something."

I ignore them and seek out Jack's gaze. "Where could she have gone?"

"And why?" Jack nods as if answering his own question or reading my thoughts. "I'll talk to Gabe."

He goes to the pool, and I can see him kneeling down at the water's edge and talking to the teen. They don't look at all alike and yet they seem to go together nicely as a father/son pair. In a swift motion, Gabe pushes up and out of the pool, water sluicing off his lean torso. Jack hands him a towel from a lounge chair.

"What's Isabel going to do this time?" Barbara tilts her nose upward—did she have a nose job at some point in her life? I imagine her as a teen with a big nose and geeky glasses. "She already shaved her head."

"She's really out of control, Kaye." Cliff chimes in, and his two cents aren't worth that much.

I meet Gabe at the back door. "Who was on the phone?"

"I don't know. She was okay before that?"

"Yes, ma'am. Seemed to be." He towels off before stepping in the house. "I'll change and go look for her."

But then my phone starts ringing. "Maybe that's her." I grab the receiver. "Hello?"

"Is this Kaye Redmond?"

I swallow a sudden lump in my throat. "Yes."

"This is Terry's sister. She wanted me to call." She pauses long enough for my heart to stutter forward. "Lily"—her voice breaks on the last syllable—"she passed away this evening."

I sink against the doorframe of my kitchen. "Oh, no." My throat clogs with tears. I rub a hand over my face and try to think, try to right my world. Pressure pushes on my chest and I manage a breath. "I am so sorry. What can I do to help Terry?"

"Nothing. She just wanted you to know and asked you to continue on with the swim-a-thon."

"Did you call my daughter, Isabel . . . Izzie, earlier?"

"Uh, yes, I did. Just a few minutes ago. I didn't know you were related. I just have a list of names and numbers."

"That explains . . ." My hand clamps around the phone. "Please, tell Terry we're all thinking of her, praying for her. If there's anything I can do, please don't hesitate to call."

"Thank you. We'll let you know what the funeral arrangements are."

After I click off the receiver, I stand in the kitchen a moment. My heart pounds and tears threaten again. I let them fall but then try to push them back. I can't fall apart right now. I have things to do. I must find Izzie.

"Kaye?" Jack's voice is close but I can't turn toward him. I can't face him. If I do, I'll fall apart.

I grip the arm of a chair, squeezing the wood for support. "Lily passed away this evening."

Jack swears under his breath. "So that's why Isabel raced out."

My throat works against the assault of hot tears. "I need to go look for her."

He puts a hand on my shoulder. I want to lean into him but I resist.

"I'll help." His keys jingle.

"I guess I'll have to go too," Cliff adds with a heavy sigh. "Why does Isabel have to be so dramatic?"

I whirl around and glare at him, as if Lily's death is his fault. "Because she's a sensitive young woman who cared about someone besides herself. Because she has a heart."

Which, of course, he doesn't.

⤐ Chapter Twenty-four ⤏

It's dark out, but darker within. My heart feels like it's weighted with water, bloated and sinking with the knowledge that Lily is gone. I ache for my friend, for my daughter, for all of us. The world is a sadder place without Lily's smile, without the hope of her recovery. And I know my faith should be a comfort. She is, after all, in heaven, but it was too soon for her to go. Sometimes it just feels like God isn't listening.

My anxiety climbs at the thought of another child missing from my life. *Izzie.* Where is she? I need to see her, wrap my arms around her, reassure her and myself that we have each other. No matter what.

My cell phone rings. It's not Darth Vader. It's not "If I Loved You"—Cliff's theme song, which should be—"I Never Loved You." It's simply my regular ring tone, but I recognize the number in the tiny window. Gabe. We skip the formalities.

"She's not at the high school." His tone is direct, calm, and beyond his years.

"She hasn't come back to the house." I sound more alarmed, but then I'm the mom. "Where are you going next?"

"I don't know. I've been to the hospital. Terry's. What do you think?"

I don't know either. Panic wedges somewhere between my ribcage and diaphragm like a block of wood. "I've driven around our neighborhood and haven't seen her anywhere."

I refrain from telling him my latest desperate move was to put Cousin It on a leash and let her sniff Izzie's clothes. "Find her," I told the dog, and now we're taking a circuitous route through the neighborhood.

"She didn't take a car." If she had, I would be even more nervous since she doesn't have a license. "She couldn't have gone too far." But I know she was devastated by the news and I'm not sure how responsibly she'll act. Barbara's words haunt me: *What will she do now?* I wish I knew the answer to that. Which gives me an idea.

"Why don't you try the natatorium? Maybe she went there."

As soon as I disconnect, a pair of headlights flash in front of me. I recognize Jack's truck as it pulls to the sidewalk. I slow down, tugging on the leash. The dog barks and lunges.

The side window rolls downward. Jack leans his elbow on the truck's door. "Any luck?"

I shake my head, feel that block of fear swell like wood in the rain. "What should I do?"

"Keep looking."

My mind races, going in circles like Cousin It zipping around the pool and barking at evil birds flying overhead and at dangerously invading lawn mowers. "Should I call the police?"

"Not yet. Let's give her another hour. If she doesn't show up then, we'll call in the National Guard if we have to."

His in-charge demeanor has a calming effect on me. "Any ideas?"

"Does Cousin It have any leads?"

"I'm not sure if she's chasing Izzie's scent or a squirrel's."

His mouth starts to pull into a smile but stops short. "Have you checked the park?"

"The one two streets over."

"What about the one over by Lily's house?"

"No, that's a good idea."

"I'll swing back by the house again then sweep through the neighborhood."

It takes me five interminable minutes to drive to the playground, the dog in the navigational seat, her nose pressed to the glass. This is where Isabel sometimes took Lily when she babysat. A blanket of darkness has settled over the swings and teeter-totters. This is not a safe place for a teenage girl to hang out alone at night. My gaze scans the shadowy edges along the trees that border the park. Then I notice one of the swings twirling around in a slow rotation.

Izzie.

Cousin It barks and lunges forward, scratching the dash and glass inside the car. Of course, Izzie can't hear her. I'm not sure if she heard the car engine, doesn't care or is oblivious to everything around her. I pull my cell phone out of my back pocket and call Jack. "She's here."

"Want me to come?"

"Not yet."

"I'll stick close if you need help."

"Thanks. Will you call Gabe?"

"Absolutely."

I pocket my cell phone in my hip pocket and turn off the ignition. Slowly, carefully, I emerge from my car, keeping an eye on Izzie. She's at least a hundred yards away. I don't want to startle her or cause her to take off again. At an even pace, I approach. She just keeps twirling the swing around until the metal chains twist too tight, then she reverses herself. My tennis shoes crunch the gravel while the dog scrambles trying to gain footing in a mad effort to reach Izzie first. But she doesn't look up.

I should have left the dog at home, but I didn't want to take the time to put her in the crate. Leaving her in the car makes me worry about what part she might eat. I stop at one edge of the swings and hook Cousin Its leash around a pole. When I reach Izzie, I sit on the swing next to hers. The plastic seat hugs my thighs in a tight, unflattering vice, knocking my knees together.

We sit quietly beneath the sliver of a moon and the twinkling stars. I think of the childhood ditty, *"Star light, star bright, wish I may, wish I might, have the wish I wish tonight."* But my thoughts turn into a fervent prayer for the right words to say to my heart-broken daughter. Explaining why something like this happens seems impossible, especially when I don't understand it myself.

I reach toward her and brush a finger along her arm. "Are you okay?"

"I guess you heard." Her voice sounds jagged.

"Terry's sister called."

"Me too." She leans her head against the metal chain and her swing stills, the toes of her flip-flops sink into the soft dirt. "It's so unfair."

"It is."

For a long moment, silence pulses between us. From far away a fire truck's siren wails the way I wish I could.

"Why Lily?"

I don't know. I'm wondering the same thing. This difficulty is so much worse than when Izzie came to me for help with algebraic problems in seventh grade or when the boy she liked in eighth grade rejected her or even when her father left. Kids shouldn't have to deal with death at any age. "Why *any* body? Why Gabe's dad?"

Her eyes flash defiance. "That's not an answer."

"I wish I had one, Iz. But I don't."

She kicks at the dirt and bits fly outward, the gravel pit beneath her swing dug long ago by thousands of tiny tennis shoes. "Why did God take her? Or did He? Does He care? Does He exist?"

Oh, man. The tough questions demand more than pat, easy answers. "Should He have left her here in pain? Maybe *that* would have been cruel."

"If He's God, then He could have healed her, right? Why didn't He do that?"

I sigh, allowing my heart the space to calm. "I don't have the answers to all your good questions, Iz. No one does. Life is dirty and messy and painful. We live in a fallen world. It's not a popular thing to say today, but it's true."

She chews the inside of her mouth. "Tell me about it."

"You've had a rough year."

"Not as rough as some."

Her answer surprises me and I'm encouraged at the growth in her maturity. "That's true." I lean left taking tiny tippy-toe steps in the dirt, turning my swing around and around. "Maybe it's to make us think what comes after this life *is* better."

She snorts.

"Maybe it's all just a product of sin?"

"Oh, so you're saying Lily did something to make her deserve this?" The anger in her voice is palpable and it resonates in my chest.

"No. But whether her cancer was caused environmentally or through some genetic flaw, maybe it goes back to somebody's sin. Maybe. I simply don't know. But sin has consequences, not always for the one committing the sin. Just like you getting hurt is a consequence of your dad's and my divorce. I hate that. For me, that's been the worst part of your dad leaving." My hand fists around the swing's metal chain. "But I couldn't prevent it. You're the reason I wanted him to come back."

Izzie is silent for a moment while she pushes that thought around. "It stinks."

"Yeah."

"I'm not doing the swim-a-thon."

I remain silent. *Breathe. Count to ten. Say a little prayer—Not my words but Yours.*

"What's the point anyway?" Her tone is demanding, petulant.

"Her parents still have medical expenses."

"Lily won't—" Her voice splinters, crushed under the reality.

"No, she won't benefit. But she wouldn't want her parents to suffer any more either."

"Her dad left."

"Yes."

Isabel sighs heavily, her shoulders rounding. "And her mom really needs the money."

"I'm sure she does."

"What if there's money left over?"

"I don't know. What would happen to it?"

She scuffs the bottom of her flip-flop through the trenches in the dirt. "Give it to a charity?"

"That sounds plausible. Maybe a charity that does research to prevent and stop that kind of cancer, which would help others."

"Good one, Mom." She glances over toward me and a hint of a smile plays about her mouth. "How do you do that?"

"What?"

"Change my mind."

"You did. All by yourself. Because you're a compassionate young woman." I stand, feel the back of my thighs branded by the pressure of the swing, and walk toward her. I finger her tiny pierced earring. "You have a good heart."

Then she's suddenly leaning into me, her arms around my waist, her hot tears burning my stomach. It's at that moment I know she's going to be all right. It's not going to be easy. But she won't be dragged down by this. She'll find purpose and a way to do something constructive with her grief.

Holding my daughter, I realize I've never been more proud of the person she's becoming.

✘✘

The next day cars line up outside the natatorium as swimmers, parents, and teens crowd the sidewalk. Isabel walks beside me, fuzzy, bare head tipped downward, sunglasses securely in place. She is quiet and reserved, not even acknowledging friends' greetings. I give a few nods and tight smiles in an effort to keep everything normal. Most here don't know about Lily yet.

The smell of chlorine hits me strong, as the chemical pungency stings my nasal passages. My thoughts and feelings for Terry fire through me this morning. What must she be going through in the wake of her baby's passing? My thoughts are a big jumble clunking around in my exhausted brain. But the water is clear and blue, the green tile sparkling, and the ropes in place as they should be. The familiarity in an uncommon moment is calming to my frazzled nerves.

"Mrs. Redmond." A tall man in warm-ups greets me with an extended hand. "Coach Derrick."

"Yes. Thank you for letting us use the natatorium."

Izzie moves off leaving us alone.

"No problem. Glad to help. I've been really impressed with Isabel and Gabe's determination for this."

I nod feeling suddenly weepy. "Well, I better help with . . . uh . . ."

"Sure." He steps out of my way. "I'll be around all day, so if you need anything, just let me know."

"Thanks. We appreciate all you're doing." I offer him a smile that doesn't quite hold. My usual smile-no-matter-what mentality was washed away in last night's events.

When I turn away, I see Jack sitting in the booth with the sound equipment. He cranks the sound system. He made a CD of some of Lily's favorite songs, and Miley Cyrus's "Girls Just Wanna Have Fun" gets the natatorium humming. His gaze settles on me, and he gives a nod in my direction.

He and Gabe stayed away last night, giving Izzie and me time alone. Thankfully once Cliff knew Izzie was safe, he and Barbara left before we returned from the park. He seemed content that we'd found her and didn't want any more drama. But I wasn't alone. Jack was available if I needed him, hovering nearby but not intruding.

A splash makes me turn. Gabe emerges from the depths of the pool and waves. He's one of the first scheduled swimmers. He pulls out of the pool and stretches his shoulders, pulling his long arms backward in a slow backstroke and giving his long, lean muscles a shake.

"Five minutes 'til start time." Jack's deep voice blasts through the speakers. He adjusts a knob. "The schedule is posted on the front wall. Swimmers check your times and report to the blocks five minutes before your allotted time."

I walk toward him and lean on the railing between us. "Should we announce about Lily?"

"It's up to you and Isabel." He searches the crowd until he spots her. "How is Izzy today?"

"Hanging in there. We spoke to Terry on the phone last night. I think that helped her. Terry too. She needed to know others cared so much and were feeling such sorrow." I show him my video camera. "Brought this to take some pictures. I thought I could give Terry a copy later so she could see how many people were here for her, for Lily."

"Good idea. Pam said she wants to go by and see Terry today. Said she wanted to go with you if that's all right."

Pam. It's a casual statement that somehow unsettles me. Because it means Jack spoke with Pam sometime between last night and this morning. It shouldn't matter to me. But it does. "Sure."

He looks out at the scattered crowd climbing into the stands and swimmers rallying together, many of them bald. "It's pretty amazing, isn't it? Our kids did this."

My throat tightens. *Our kids.* My heart stutters. "I just wish Lily could have seen all of this."

He cups a hand over my arm. "Maybe she is."

Then he silences the pounding musical beat and lifts the microphone to his lips. The resounding silence ricochets inside my chest. "Morning all. We have an announcement to make." He shakes his head as if finding the words difficult to say. "It's not easy." His voice reverberates off the rafters. "Lily passed away last night."

An audible gasp echoes through the building.

"We feel Lily would want us to continue on with the swim-a-thon. She wasn't a quitter. She fought hard as I know each of you will swim hard today. The money we raise today will go toward paying off her parents' enormous medical bills and the rest will go to charity to help find a cure so other kids like Lily won't have to die."

Jack's throat works up and down, the muscles contracting, and I cover his hand with my own. He meets my gaze and for a long moment I feel connected to him.

Then he clicks the microphone again. "Let's have a moment of silence in memory of Lily."

I glance at Isabel. She's sitting on her block, head in her hands, back hunched. Then I close my own eyes and offer my feeble attempts at a prayer for Lily's family to find peace and for the rest of us to find meaning in all of this. At the end of what seems like a very long, very quiet minute, Jack clicks a key on the sound board and piano notes float through the arena from Steven Curtis Chapman's "Cinderella."

When Isabel stands, Gabe is standing right beside her. He opens his arms and she steps into his embrace, laying her head against his shoulder. The growth of their relationship doesn't surprise me or frighten me anymore. After a moment Izzie looks up and their lips brush. A tiny pinch in my belly makes me feel intrusive and I glance away.

"Don't worry." Jack watches me, and my cheeks warm. "They're good kids."

I press my lips together to keep them from trembling. "I know."

I can't explain my strange emotions, happy for my daughter to find someone as nice and caring as Gabe, and yet . . . I feel suddenly very alone.

"It's gonna be a good day." Jack places a hand on my shoulder. I want to dip my head and lay my cheek against the back of his hand. But he said, *Our kids*. Gabe is becoming his son. And Pam should be his wife.

I sniff away more tears and offer a watery smile. "What time are you swimming?"

"Same time as you."

My stomach drops.

He grins. "Wanna race?"

I give a nervous laugh. "I don't stand a chance."

·⁕{ Chapter Twenty-five }⁕·

The day is half gone, and the dollar amount posted on the white board continues to climb. Each time a swimmer finishes their laps, they add up how much they earned and the amount is posted. Swimmers' legs are wobbly as they've given everything they have in honor of Lily's memory.

At first it felt wrong somehow for kids to be laughing and enjoying themselves, cheering for their friends in the pool, eating fast food. Carrie Underwood's "Ever Ever After" blares out from the speakers, her voice ricocheting off the rafters and soaring out over the pool. But we can only be sorrowful for so long. I'm not sure Lily would want us to mope around. It wouldn't reflect her spirit. Those that leave for the arms of Jesus want celebrations. The concentration on the swimmers' faces as they start their laps, then the slack exhaustion as they emerge from the pool, turn into smiles of accomplishment and satisfaction as they see their contribution posted on the white board.

"Hey, Mrs. Redmond." Jeanne, one of the swimmers, takes my offered bottle of water.

"Good job." I close the lid to the giant cooler filled with iced water bottles.

"Thanks. I'm wiped out." She unscrews the top and takes a long pull. "Where's Izzie?"

"In the stands." I wave toward where I saw her last. Then I see Gabe talking to his mom, Pam, when Jack approaches them. He gives Gabe a clap on the back and Pam a hug. A long hug. Not that I notice. Why shouldn't he? They're friends. Good friends. Probably more than friends. I ignore the way my stomach clamps in on itself.

"I'm good." Jeanne sips her water.

Glancing down, I realize I was offering her another. "Oh, yeah. Good. Good job today."

She gives me a side glance and walks away. I busy myself dunking more bottles into the icy bath.

"Kaye?"

I freeze, look at Pam. "Hello."

We toss back chitchat, my smile forcefully bright when she asks, "Have you been to see Terry yet?"

"Not yet."

"I was thinking maybe we could sneak away from here together."

"Oh, well, uh . . ." I'd actually thought of going just before my scheduled swim in hopes of missing my race with Jack. Chicken that I am. "I guess that would be okay."

Two minutes later at Pam's insistence, Jack assures me he can handle everything until we get back. With his usual smile, he adds, "Just be sure you're back in time for our race."

"Ooh," Pam coos as we head toward my car. "Sounds serious between you and Jack."

Startled, I study her expression but don't find any spite or prying as I might if Marla had said this. "Not at all. Just a joke. I don't stand a chance."

In so many ways.

We're silent in the car until we're almost to Terry's house. A nervousness seizes me. "I'm not sure what to say."

"No words are necessary. Trust me, I've been there." She has. "We're just offering hugs, a shoulder to cry on, and our support."

With a trembling feeling inside, I park in front of Terry's home. Already there's a pink mourning wreath on the door. "We should have brought something."

Pam touches my arm. She has a calm, reassuring way about her. "*Something* won't make her feel better."

But *something* would give us something to talk about, something to say, something to focus on. Or that's what Marla would do. That's how she would respond. So maybe Pam's way is best.

Surprisingly Terry is more pulled together than I ever would have imagined. She shows us inside and we meet her sister, Beth, before she hurries off to the kitchen and gives us a few minutes together.

Terry gives me another fierce hug. "Thanks for coming."

When tears threaten, I blink hard. "We didn't want to intrude."

Pam waves us toward the sofa and sits down with us. "I could use a distraction or two."

Pam sits on one side of Terry. "Can we get you anything? Or do anything for you?"

"I can't think of anything. Of course," she gives an odd laugh, "I can't put two thoughts together."

Pam nods and I follow suit, sitting next to my friend, my heart as heavy. Then silence invades. I glance at Pam, try to take cues from her. She seems content in the emptiness where I want to fill it up. But with what?

"This wasn't supposed to happen." Terry leans back into the sofa and rubs her brow. "When Lily was born, I never imagined something like this could happen. When I married . . . I never thought anything could break us up. But Miles can't cope. He's a basket case. He says he may not even go to the funeral. Can you imagine?"

Pam scoots closer to Terry and places an arm around her shoulder. "Men struggle with grief, with expressing themselves."

"Maybe I should have been there more for him. Maybe I ignored him too much while I tended Lily."

I touch my shoulder to Terry's. "You did what you had to do."

"Even when Luke was dying," Pam's voice is feather-soft, "I felt guilty for taking care of the kids, thinking he needed me. And when I took care of him, I felt guilty for not being there for the kids. I felt fractured."

Terry nods, her mouth compressed into a tight line. "Exactly. It was a no-win situation." She stares down at her clasped hands, her knuckles white. Then her shoulders begin to shake. "I'm all alone."

As quickly as the tears appear, she jumps up from the sofa, sniffing, wiping her nose with a tissue she pulls from her pocket. "I'm okay." She holds out a hand to keep us from approaching. "Really."

Pam crosses her legs. "Have you ever read Proverbs 31?"

"Who hasn't?" Terry searches her pocket.

I spot a box of tissues on the table and hand her a fresh one. "It's the overachieving woman of the Bible."

"With servant girls," Terry adds.

Our laughter diffuses the tension in the room.

"That's what I used to think." Pam rubs the palm of her hand. "But then someone explained to me what it actually says. It says a woman of noble character—"

"That makes me feel like a failure right there." Where is Pam taking this conversation? I thought we were supposed to help lift Terry's mood?

"Yeah." Terry paces. "All I can think of doing at the moment is anything but noble. Like smacking my husband. Or punching the wall."

I nod.

But Pam claps her hands. Just one solid clap. "Exactly. But in reality, in the original language, that word isn't noble. It's valor."

I blink. "Really?"

Terry stills then blows her nose.

"Gives a whole different picture to that passage, doesn't it?"

Terry nods and I stand, move toward her and place my arms around her. "You definitely qualify for a medal of valor."

≫⋖≶

Back at the natatorium, I'm sitting on one of the boards, my bare feet in a puddle of water, dreading my turn in the lane, next to Jack. He hasn't emerged from the dressing area yet. I do a little stretching, not that it will help much. Mostly I cinch the terry-cloth belt at my waist and pull my cover-up tighter around me. The swimmer in the lane where I'll soon be plunged does a flip at the end and strokes back across the pool. Something red to my left catches my eye. Harry walks in my direction and carries red roses in his arms.

"Kaye!" He grins as he approaches. "How's the event going?"

"Fine, thanks."

"When we first got here, we heard Lily had passed away, so we went and got flowers for Isabel."

"That's very sweet of you. She's up in the stands somewhere." I glance upward until I locate her fuzzy head.

He nods, his gaze following mine. "Are you getting ready to swim?"

"Unfortunately, yes. It'll probably be half a lap."

He laughs. "Then I won't bother sponsoring you per lap. How about if I just leave a check?"

"That's very thoughtful of you, Harry. Thank you. How's Marla?"

"She's around." He leans toward me, and I smell some light aftershave on his skin. "She was feeling . . . well, you know. She's

. . . around here somewhere. Didn't want to make a show of being here."

I'm actually surprised she came. Maybe it's a step in the right direction. "That was kind of her to come too. Please thank her for us, in case I don't see her."

"I will. I will." He lifts the roses and lets them fall back to his other hand, making tiny bits of water pop outward.

"You really love Marla, don't you?"

His lips flatten. "Have for a long time."

"Did you meet in the village?"

"Oh, no. I unstopped many a toilet at her house. Twenty-five years worth."

"Really!"

He nods. "Knew her husband too. He was a good man. Attentive to his home. And I try to be as well. I don't want you to think I'm some stranger stalking Marla."

I laugh. "Not at all. I can tell."

"You can?"

I lean back, resting my weight on my hands, the board scratching my palms. "That other man . . . Anderson. He was peculiar. He didn't care about Marla. Not the way you do. Or I didn't think so. Not the peripheral things in her life anyway. But you . . . you're just different, Harry. In a very good way." I imagine what a good husband he was and what a good husband he'll be to Marla if she ever gives him the chance. "Do you have children, Harry?"

"No, we never did. We weren't able and there weren't test tubes for that then. But we had each other. And that was enough. But now, now that my wife is gone . . . I wish we'd had children . . . grandchildren."

I cup my hand around his and give a little squeeze. If anyone can teach Marla about love and what it means, I believe Harry can. "I think you'll be good for her."

"I'll try. But what about you, Kaye?"

"Me?" I stand and give my arms a shake, doubtful they'll be able to pull me very far in the water.

He looks down for a moment. "Cliff married someone else."

"That was for the best." It's a glib line that comes straight from my heart. There was a time when I might have said those exact words but not meant them. They would have rung false. But not now. "Really, I'm all right."

"You gotta look at the bright side."

"You're right. And I think, maybe . . ." My gaze swerves toward Jack, who is walking toward us, his torso bare, his tan skin gleaming with water droplets, his smile bright. "If I'm lucky enough to win the heart of a man someday"—my smile wavers but my heartfelt words steady it—"then I hope he'll be as kind as you."

⋇⋇

The swimmer ahead of me is still going strong. He pauses at the edge of the pool and holds up a hand, signaling he's going to attempt another five laps. "No problem."

Jack steps beside me and I'm embarrassed to confess my heart kicks up a notch. "Giving me a head start?"

"Of course. By the time I hit the water, you'll be exhausted." I smile. "And my chances increase."

"Only if we swim one lap."

"I'll be lucky to do one."

He puts an arm over my shoulder and I seek out Pam in the crowd. Do Jack's actions upset her? She seems oblivious, talking to Gabe and Izzie. Maybe she's not the jealous type. She's a lot closer to the Proverbs 31 woman than I am.

"I've got my money on you."

His statement stuns me. "You do?"

"Absolutely." He steps away and onto the block. Before I can come up with a clever response, he makes a clean dive. Inwardly

I groan imagining the belly flop I'll do in a few minutes. But hopefully he'll be too busy to notice.

Keeping my robe over my swimsuit, I watch Jack a few minutes as he overtakes the swimmer in my lane. Heat works its way up the back of my neck. It feels as if everyone is watching me watch Jack, so I wander off toward the bleachers in hopes of catching Marla. It's not hard to spot her. She's lurking around a corner, keeping to herself. She wears a scarf over her head and around her neck, resembling a burka.

"Marla!"

She hesitates, looks as if she might make a run for it but then stands still while I walk toward her.

"Thanks for coming today to support Izzie. I know she really appreciates that."

"Sad thing about that little girl." Her lips press together as she shakes her head. "Hard to understand something like that."

Nodding, I thumb over my shoulder. "I saw Harry. He gave a very generous donation."

"We went in together."

She always wants the credit. But I suppose it doesn't matter today. So I force a smile. "That's very nice of both of you. Thank you. It's for a good cause."

"Isabel has her swim cap on. Is she still hiding her bald head?"

"Actually her hair is starting to grow. But it creates drag. For faster score times she keeps a cap on in the pool. It won't be long before she'll be sporting a short do."

"Well, she's young. It'll grow."

I manage not to roll my eyes the way Izzie would. There's not much else to say. "What are you going to do about Harry?"

"Harry?" Marla waves a hand as if he's an afterthought. "Oh, he is congenial."

"You mean he does what you want?"

Her lips purse, and she gives me a hard glare. "I don't appreciate that remark."

"He really loves you."

"I know." Her voice is quiet, not triumphant the way I imagined.

"Do you love . . . care for him?"

"In a way. Not like Bradford. Not like Anderson. But now I'm beginning to see that was superficial. Fun and freeing, but shallow. Since my surgery . . . well, it's over with Anderson. But Harry . . . is different. He sees me . . ."

"As you want to be?"

"In ways I never imagined. I don't even think my husband did that. Bradford only saw what he wanted to see."

My heart expands toward her. It's the deepest nonconfrontational conversation we've ever had. "He loved you too, Marla."

"For a long time after his death, I doubted that. But I suppose he loved me as much as he could love anyone."

"Isn't that all there is for any of us?" I look up in the stands and see Isabel sitting with friends. She learned the hard way that parents disappoint. As I did. "We're all flawed. And we just do the best we can. We have to rely on God's grace."

Marla slants a gaze in my direction. "Does that mean you've forgiven Cliff?"

I take a slow breath and release it, surprised that I don't feel that old tightness in my diaphragm. "I suppose I have. Honestly, I haven't thought about him much. I've been too busy. And I'm not sure I felt like I needed to forgive him. He's acted the way he usually does. I shouldn't have expected more from him. Unrealistic expectations were my fault. So maybe I simply needed to forgive myself."

The corners of her mouth remain tense. "For trying to change him?"

"For choosing him in the first place."

Her eyes widen, one more than the other. But then she nods. "I chose poorly too. But there's always a second chance." Her gaze drifts toward Harry, who's talking with a couple of swimmers. My gaze veers like the pull of a strong magnet toward Jack. His strokes are strong and smooth, sure and confident. It feels as if my blinders have been removed. A bit of an old hymn comes back to me, "I was blind but now I see."

I do indeed, just as Dorian Gray finally saw the sin in his own life rather than projecting onto others. And amazingly, it's okay. More than that . . .

It's freeing.

❧❀

It's not much of a race when I make my pseudodive off the boards and into the cool water. Jack's several laps ahead of me. I had a chance to appreciate his long, smooth strokes, his strong kick—good form. Not that I'm an expert, but I have watched my share of swim meets and practices. My form is lacking, casual at best, and I find myself angling to the left and end up bumping into the ropes. Jack pauses, treading water.

"Keep your eye on the wall." His coaching style is natural. Then he kicks out and moves a few feet away. "Or were you trying to distract me?"

I splash water at him and try to kick off something . . . but there is nothing, and I go under the water and come up spluttering. Thankfully Jack is further down the lane and spares me any more embarrassment.

After I've managed another lap, Jack passes me, makes his flip at the wall, and gives me a thumbs-up.

Already I'm gasping for air but I push off the tiled wall and switch to a backstroke. This time I bounce from the right rope to the left and end up treading water for a minute in the middle of the pool. I switch to a lazy sidestroke and watch Jack move past me several times.

By the time I reach my goal, my legs wobble and my shoulders ache as I pull myself out of the pool. I swam more laps than ever before, probably in my whole life put together. Jack is still going strong, but I turn my lane over to the next swimmer, a younger, leaner candidate, who makes a splash as she hits the water.

Someone has moved my cover-up, so I wrap my towel around me, wishing it covered a bit more of me. I log my laps and contribution to Lily's Cause. It'll be up to me to contact all who sponsored me and collect their payments. Turning, I see Pam sitting on the front row of bleachers and talking to another mom, but her gaze follows Jack as he continues swimming. A tightness seizes my stomach. Her eyes shine, her smile full. It's not a muscle cramp, but suddenly I can't draw a deep breath. Raw, unfettered emotion bubbles to the surface. Feeling disjointed, like I've got a light case of the bends, I need some fresh air and a minute alone.

When I reach the warmth of the outdoors, I sit on the sidewalk, pull my knees to my chest and rest my cheek against my knee. Fall in Texas is full of extremes with temperatures ranging from low forties to the nineties, much like my emotions these days. But oak leaves have changed to yellows and browns and have begun fluttering to the ground.

Closing my eyes, I feel a slight breeze stir the hair at my nape as it begins to dry. And suddenly tears spring forth. I'm not sure where they are coming from or why they continue but they are from a deep place of loneliness. I feel as if all my dreams come pouring out. Some dreams, like Jack, I was never even aware of until recently. I let the disappointment and sorrow wash over me. I suppose it's a day for tears.

I don't understand. Why after all this time, after trying hard to make things work, am I left alone?

But you're not.

The still, small voice is not so much in my head as in my heart.

In that moment I realize the truth: that's been my fear all these years. But I'm not alone. I look up at the sun-bleached sky until the sun's rays make my eyes burn and water even more. As I squeeze them closed, I feel a smile emerge and spread across my face. I'm not alone. I never have been. And I'm okay with that.

"I'm okay with that, God," the words whisper out of me. "If it's just You and me, God, from here on out, all right. I don't need a man to make me feel complete. I can't depend on Izzie to always be here with me. I don't understand all that has happened, but You've changed me. I can't see the road ahead, but I trust You. I trust You."

I'm not sure how long I sit there before I sense I'm not alone anymore. A hand presses on my shoulder, and I open my eyes to Jack's concerned face.

"You okay?"

I rub the corner of the towel over my face, and still my cheeks feel stretched in some goofy grin. "Exhausted, but . . . yeah, okay."

The words are not fake as they might once have been, but authentic.

Jack sits down beside me, a towel draped over his shoulders. His skin is cool but dry. His hair sticks out in all directions. "You sure?"

"Never better, actually." I stare out at the blue sky that seems endless and unfathomable. "How'd your swim go?"

"I exceeded expectations."

I turn my smile on him.

His brow crinkles. "Okay, what's up? You win the lottery?"

I laugh and shake my head, feel a water droplet roll down the side of my face. "I can't really explain it. I just feel . . . good."

He rubs his flat belly. "I'm starving."

"You sound like Gabe."

"Just a growing boy."

"There's pizza and sandwiches inside."

He shakes his head. "After all this I need a real sit-down dinner."

"Okay."

"So you'll join me, then?"

I glance back over my shoulder at the natatorium's brick wall. "What about the swim-a-thon?"

"It'll keep going until we get back."

"Do you want to see if Gabe and Izzie want to go?"

His gaze electrifies me. "Not really."

"What about Pam? I saw her . . . inside."

He tucks his chin down and studies me beneath heavy lids. "Gabe's mom? Why Pam?"

"I thought . . . well, it seemed to me . . ."

"What?"

"That you two were . . . that y'all were maybe seeing each other."

"You're full of funny ideas, Kaye."

"It makes sense."

"Because I was her husband's best friend? And she's a lonely widow?"

I try to read his expression but can't. "I guess, yeah. But . . . you know . . . the kids too?"

"Oh, yeah, right. Of course. It makes sense." He shakes his head. "We dated before she and Luke started seeing each other."

"Yes." And duh!

"We weren't right for each other."

He's quiet for a long minute while a couple of teens pass us and head toward a car across the lot. "You didn't think I could be interested in you?"

"N-no." My voice stutters.

"We're going to have to work on that."

Suddenly I understand what he's asking me, and my heartbeat quickens. The corner of my towel slides off my knee and I place it back, my hand trembling ever so slightly. "So you're asking me to dinner . . . as a date?"

He nods, his eyes wide as if I'm mentally slow. Which I guess I am. "Yes, Kaye. I want to take you out on a date. Remember that kiss?"

My face flames. "Which one?"

"Exactly. I wasn't kidding when I told you I was willing to suffer through another one any time you wanted." He's watching me as if my emotions are playing across my face—shock, denial, shock, understanding, shock, exuberance. "*Now* what are you grinning about?"

"Just an inside joke." I glance up at the sky again and wink. *Thanks, God.*

"I *do* stand a chance."

⤙ Epilogue ⤚

The house is quiet, almost too quiet. Izzie has taken Gabe driving, showing off her new license. I've got my cell phone in my robe's pocket. Just in case. I pour a fragrant cup of coffee and carry it outside. A mild spring breeze ruffles bits of hair that have fallen out of my Velcro rollers.

The cough and whir of a neighbor's lawn mower erupts nearby. It sputters and the clean scent of freshly mown grass wafts toward me. A twig sticking up in the flower bed snags my attention. Frowning, I notice several twigs sticking up out of the ground where once my rose bushes bloomed copiously. But Cousin It saw to it they never bloomed again.

I set my coffee cup on the patio table and walk over to the bed with new mounds of dirt piled up around several twigs. A breeze makes the gate swing open. What is going on?

Before I can close the gate, Jack backs his way through the opening. Behind him rolls a squeaky red wagon. Inside it are good-sized twigs sticking out of green gallon cartons. He sees me and his hazel eyes brighten. "Morning."

I should have known. A smile emerges even as I touch a roller on top of my head. "What are you doing here? I thought you said last night you had work to do."

"Believe me, this is work." He waves toward the plants. "I've been waiting a good six months to take care of this."

While he situates the red wagon where he wants it, I yank out my curlers, toss them beside the coffee cup then fluff my hair, trying to finger comb it into some semblance of order. "And what's that?"

"Roses. I'm replacing the ones that Cousin It dug up last year."

I walk toward him again. "What makes you think she won't dig these up?"

"She wouldn't dare." He grins, then touches one of my curls, causing a ripple in my belly. "What happened to your rollers?"

"I thought I'd hold off on the Halloween look till October."

"I kind of liked it."

I shake my head, then glance behind him. "Where's your buddy?"

Occasionally, in the six months that Jack and I have been seeing each other, he brings Cousin It over to say hello. I have to admit she's calmed down a little. Only a little. She's still rambunctious, counter-surfs, and takes running leaps into the pool, but if she dares to dig up a rose bush then I suppose I'll forgive her. Maybe she's also torn down my barriers. The way God demolished the ones around my heart.

"She's with Pam and the kids." Jack pulls a shovel off the wagon and starts digging in the flower bed Cousin It destroyed. I watch him for a few minutes as he shapes the hole to his liking, then carefully tips a gallon-sized carton on its side and pries out the dormant rose bush.

"So, what color did you get?"

"My favorite."

His answer makes me laugh. Sure enough, the label strapped to a branch flaps in the breeze: Lincoln Red.

"Don't worry. I got something for you too."

It's then that something on the branch catches the light. Peering closer, I see it's a ring. Not just a ring, but a diamond ring. A good-sized diamond, so large it makes my eyes widen. It sparkles in the morning light. When I look at Jack, he's quit packing dirt around the base and is watching me. Careful of the thorns, he slides the ring off the branch. "I remembered what you said."

I can't manage a word, not even a stutter. But I arch an eyebrow.

"You know . . . about a husband bringing flowers. Not just on Valentine's or anniversaries. And not ordered by a secretary."

A husband? I swallow hard, trying to suppress a blooming smile as I remember that long-ago conversation so peppered with my anger toward Cliff. It all seems silly now. Those desires have so often been met over the past few months each time Jack has brought me bunches of daisies and sprigs of handpicked pansies.

"These will take a while to grow. But we can enjoy them together." He slips an arm about my waist.

"It's not Valentine's."

"Or our anniversary yet. It's not even a president's birthday. So, how about"—Jack steps toward me—"just because I love you?"

I loop my arms around his neck. "It's not exactly what I imagined."

He cocks an eyebrow at me and pulls back only slightly. "Not romantic enough?"

Tears form in my eyes, clog my throat.

"Would it be better if I rode up on a white steed?"

I shake my head, rest my hand over his heart. "No, this is . . . perfect."

And I thank him with a kiss that I hope shows my full appreciation.

Before I finish, he pulls away. Raising his hand, he waggles his pinky at me. The diamond catches the light in a rainbow of colors. "You didn't answer my question."

"Oh?" I let the smile take over. "And what question was that?"

He tips his head sideways, a nervous gesture, pulls back a step, and drops down to one knee. Looking up at me and squinting against the morning sunlight, he begins. "Kaye," his voice cracks, "I love you. I have ever since Cousin It knocked all your books out of your arms. I can't imagine you not being a part of my life. When you were trying to get Cliff back, noble as it was, I thought it might kill me. You deserve so much more. Better than me too. But this is all I have to give. My life . . . my love. Will you be my wife?"

God's will is amazing. It so often takes turns that are curiously surprising and more generous than I deserve. I drop down to my knees and into Jack's arms.

"Absolutely," I whisper against his mouth.

Then we seal the deal with a kiss that not only takes my breath, but gives me life.

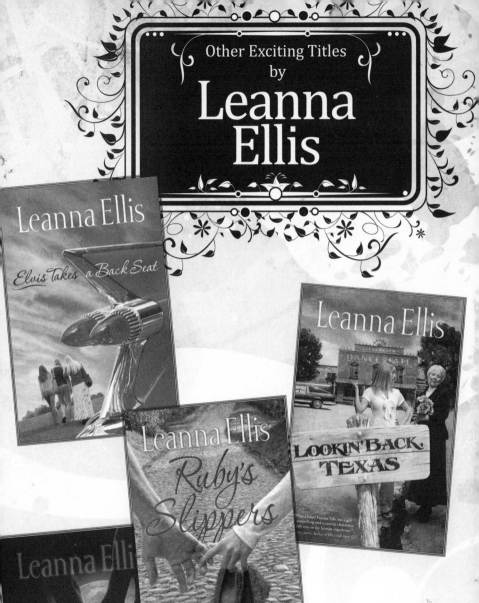

Other Exciting Titles
by
Leanna Ellis

Leanna Ellis
Elvis Takes a Back Seat

Leanna Ellis
Ruby's Slippers

Leanna Ellis
LOOKIN' BACK, TEXAS

Leanna Ellis
Once in a Blue Moon
a novel

B&H
FICTION

www.PureEnjoyment.com